Gorecki raised a hand. "I'm sure you've seen a lot, Mr. James, underage drinking, monitoring in-school detention duty and such, but this here's serious."

"You're a cop, you said?" Vargas said. "Not in Evanston PD. What precinct?"

"I'm a special agent, actually."

Both detectives raised their eyebrows.

"DEA?" Gorecki guessed.

Now he did produce his badge. "FBI, Chicago field office."

Gorecki inspected it. "Special Agent James," he said mostly to himself. Then a glimmer of understanding came over his face. "I—" he started to say but stopped abruptly.

This happened sometimes. Ezra would be having a perfectly normal conversation with somebody, but then a headline would flash through their mind, and their whole demeanor changed. For an entire year, Ezra's name appeared in the *Chicago Tribune*, sometimes making the front page.

Eventually people remembered seeing one of those headlines.

His jaw clenched as he waited for Gorecki to continue.

"You've helped a lot," the detective said, biting his lip. "You can rejoin your friends inside."

How Everything Turns Away

by

Steven J. Kolbe

How Everything Turns Away

Cover Art by *Diana Carlile*

The Wild Rose Press, Inc.
PO Box 708
Adams Basin, NY 14410-0708
Visit us at www.thewildrosepress.com

Publishing History
First Edition, 2021
Trade Paperback ISBN 978-1-5092-3813-2
Digital ISBN 978-1-5092-3814-9

Published in the United States of America

Dedication

To Susu, sine qua non.

Chapter One

Thursday

The only noteworthy thing to happen during Ezra James' short tenure as head of security at Saint Joseph and Mary School happened while he wasn't paying attention.

Minutes before the incident, Ezra stood looking out at the bell tower through the floor-to-ceiling windows of the auditorium lobby. The St. Peter bell tower, he remembered from his own time at SJM, was one of the oldest structures in Evanston, almost as old as the Chicago suburb itself. Partially obscured by darkness and snow, it rose triumphantly from the highest point of elevation on the school grounds, red brick and wrought-iron windows three stories up. Conversely, the new multi-million-dollar auditorium, where he now stood, hadn't existed when he graduated.

In a sense, he was looking back into the past, which is perhaps why his thoughts then turned to the recollection of a warm April afternoon, twenty-some years earlier, to a day after school when he took his high school sweetheart up to the top of the tower to write their initials on one of the wood beams. Arms around each other, they looked out on the grassy field where this auditorium now stood, wondering what their futures held. He recalled, too, her blue plaid skirt, knee-high socks, and wry smile.

Wind buffeted the glass, and white swirling snow replaced the spring greenery in his mind. Ezra's gaze shifted from the bell tower to the reflection of himself in the glass, namely his plastic security badge. The white rectangle alone distinguished him from the other middle-aged men in suits attending tonight's Christmas concert. At eighteen, he would have worn this name tag proudly, but now it merely indicated how far he'd fallen. Six months ago, a special agent of the FBI, he toted a gun and a badge. Now he wore a plastic ID and a yellow-handled taser.

Sure, he could produce his badge if needed, and his gun sat snugly in its case in the trunk of his car, but the current name tag said it all. Ezra had become a glorified security guard. His ASAC, Jeremy Cromley, placed him at the school back in August as a probationary assignment. At least he received probation and not a suspension. Suspended agents rarely came back from it.

"It's supposed to turn into a blizzard," a woman behind him said.

"I heard it's going to be a thunder snow," the other woman with her offered.

"What's thunder snow?"

Ezra vaguely knew these women—and the men with them—but not well enough to join their conversation, so he remained silent and listening.

"It's a thunderstorm during a blizzard," one of the husbands clarified. "It's supposed to be worse than the blizzard of 2011. Warm air is coming off Lake Michigan."

"No, no, the storm's shifting," the other husband interjected. "Didn't you hear the report on the radio?"

"That's exactly where I heard about it."

"We had twenty-one inches of snow in '11. All of Chicago did. They had to dig our car out of Lake Shore Drive. You're telling me this is going to be worse?"

As if to silence the two men, a lightning bolt divided the night sky into five jagged sections. In the flash of light, Ezra saw a woman in a red swing coat and black evening dress walking from the parking lot toward the bell tower. He strained his eyes to make out her face through the blowing snow outside and the glare on the window. Then the woman disappeared into the darkness and haze.

Fr. Remy Mbombo came up to stand beside Ezra. "Are we reminiscing?"

The priest was ten years older but a good three decades wiser. Unlike the security director's mostly black hair, Remy's was a salt-and-pepper blend, giving him a distinguished "Morgan Freeman in the 90s" look. As head chaplain of SJM, Remy often accompanied Ezra to events like the Christmas concert. In fact, they were both required to attend most extracurricular events.

"What do you mean?" Ezra asked.

The priest pointed in the direction of the bell tower, which flashed in and out of view due to the heavy fall of snow. "Memories of your days here must never be far from your thoughts."

At Ezra's nod, Remy added, "I have something for you: Bishop to F2."

"Leave it to the school priest to checkmate with a bishop."

"Are you so certain it's a checkmate?"

The ghost of a smirk on the elder man's face told

Ezra the game was over. Nevertheless, he reviewed his mental chessboard, located Remy's rook on the D-file, his own king on E1, and then he knew for sure the holy man's bishop undoubtedly had him pinned.

"I would've seen the attack if the board were in front of me."

"Ah," Remy said, "but rarely is everything right in front of us."

Ezra spotted English teacher Heather Jarno, too late, descending upon them like a raven, small but dreadful. Ms. Jarno wore her black hair in a bob, everything pulled back but her bangs, giving her an artistic, Audrey Hepburn flair. This, coupled with her slim pear-shaped physique, made him stand a little taller the first time they'd met. Then, after she'd unleashed a torrent of invectives directed at Jeb, the octogenarian janitor, all interest for Heather Jarno evaporated.

Now she stood before them with that same look of fiery disappointment on her face. "The penises," she blurted, one hand on her hip, the other pointed menacingly at Remy. "Have you made any headway on the *penises*?" She said the word like a distasteful slur rather than a body part belonging to half the population.

"We have the suspect out back, tied to a whipping post," Ezra said. "We assumed you'd provide the flair."

Ignoring him, she bore her gaze into Remy with still greater intensity.

"We explored it—" he began.

Ezra cut him off. "The Case of the Phallic Graffitist was a hard nut to crack." He smiled at his own pun. "The phalli in question have a girth of ordinary proportion, but a length closer to a giraffe's neck. Numerous sizes and locations."

"Such as those on my car," she sneered.

"The very instance that gave the perpetrator away."

"I already told you he was one of my students. The boy's ruined five copies of *To Kill a Mockingbird* already."

"Your car didn't give him away, but rather the quality of the painting. The dorsal veins...of that specific organ are difficult to represent at such a large scale."

One side of Jarno's mouth rose, perhaps in contempt, perhaps in ridicule. Ezra didn't care.

"At least he used washable paint," Remy offered.

The teacher scowled at both men. Fr. Remy's collar granted him no clemency today.

"What I mean," Ezra continued, "is this student clearly has both artistic talent and anatomical knowledge."

"So who did it?" she asked.

Ezra withdrew from his breast pocket a myrtle green Moleskine with dotted pages, some of them filled in to become bullet points. He read each bullet consecutively. "Gifted, male, freshman, allowed the freedom to take his time without your constant supervision. These factors led us to one person."

Recognition dawned on her face. "Trevor Matthews?" She looked like a woman staring at the ghost of a loved one, half disbelief, half heartbreak. "How can you be sure?"

He fanned the notebook open and handed it to her. As she read the dotted pages, he continued, "Trevor is the only boy in your honors class, the only class you can leave unattended to grade papers in your office or run off photocopies in the teacher's lounge."

"But—"

"He's likely being egged on by those other boys you're having so many difficulties with."

Her brows crinkled in disbelief. "I've never as much as said an unkind word to Trevor."

"What about his friends?"

Remy chimed in, "Boys can be like wolves. Especially at this age. Teenagers in general are pack animals."

"Then there is the washable black paint we found in Trevor's locker this morning," Ezra added. "And the identical drawings in his notebooks. Practice most likely. Although, some boys his age have compulsions or other reasons to draw…" He stopped short before saying "penises" again. Ms. Jarno's nose was already wrinkled in disgust.

"I'll have to reprimand him, I suppose," she said weakly.

"Or enroll him in an art class." Ezra smiled. "Do they still bring nude models to the school?"

She stared at him.

"Joking, of course," Ezra said.

"Sure," she said and wandered off, looking dazed.

Whenever he demolished the teacher's newest theory and in the process her self-confidence, Ezra sometimes felt a pang of guilt. He felt this most as she walked away and he contemplated her retreating pear-shaped backside.

If his soon-to-be ex-wife, Julia, hadn't rendered his heart unusable, he may have asked the English teacher out on a date. But then, after the pangs of guilt faded like the lights of a fireworks display, he was left with the smoky reality of Heather Jarno's abrasive pettiness, plus the fact that she took the gold medal for spreading school gossip. Then both attraction and guilt subsided—in that order.

Remy leaned close. "We feel less empathy for the suffering of those we are not actively trying to sleep with," he said so only Ezra could hear. "It is why those singing competition reality shows always give the sad backstory of every beautiful young woman with only half a voice."

Ezra considered this for a moment, wondering if Remy meant to encourage compassion for Jarno or if he merely noticed Ezra's waning desire for her.

"Ready, *mon ami?*" Remy asked then.

They walked back into the seating area.

Tonight's itinerary featured performances by each grade of SJM. So far, the program included "Jingle Bells" by preschoolers who kept wandering off stage; "The First Noel" by third graders who kept wandering off key; and "Adeste Fideles" by fifth graders who had clearly wandered as far from Rome as humanly possible.

Next up was a nativity play by the middle schoolers and, capping off the concert, the high school choir would sing "Silent Night" in English, German, French, and Spanish.

"These nights out with you may be the worst part of my impending divorce," Ezra griped.

Remy patted him on the back. "Come now. How else would you spend this fine Thursday evening?"

They returned to their seats in the front row of the auditorium. Four hundred seats seemed too large for the small, K-12 school, yet it filled to capacity for every event. At the Halloween concert, Ezra had even spotted a certain film celebrity, an uncle to an elementary schooler.

Standing this close to the stage, he had a better sight of backstage than most patrons did. For this reason, his attention zeroed in on stage left to where senior Mason Scout sat in a hard plastic chair. Once a week, give or take, Ezra confronted the cocky quarterback about some issue. Mason stole all the chocolate bars from the concession stand; he cursed out teachers; he sold marijuana gummies to freshmen. Every time he weaseled out of it. The chocolate reappeared, the teachers recanted, and the gummies turned out to be candy, not THC. And all of that happened in September.

During his time as a special agent, Ezra James had known plenty of people like Mason Scout. Usually, their time came. They became sloppy or their crimes escalated from misdemeanors to felonies. Then again, he thought of some of the powerful men he'd known, men who were seemingly immune to consequences. Mason's father struck Ezra as one such man. Henry Scout gave generous endowments to the school each year thanks to a dozen profitable car dealerships. The state-of-the-art auditorium they currently sat in was mostly thanks to the Scout family's generosity, and everyone at SJM knew it.

This set Mason apart. Then you added his success at bringing the school's football team to a state title as quarterback, and the little twerp was practically untouchable. Principal Catherine Weeks absorbed every complaint with a serious demeanor, yet Mason never served so much as a detention. In fact, his transgressions were never spoken of again. At least the criminal-in-training was a senior. In six months, he'd be someone else's problem. And in the real world the same amount of family money covered far less ground.

Tonight's nativity play featured the entirety of the fifth grade class. Front-and-center, though, in a crisp blue and white shawl was Mason's little sister playing Mary. Mikayla Scout being cast in this crucial role would've told Ezra everything he needed to know about the family's standing in the community—if he hadn't known already.

Stage-right, he saw Cynthia Scout step just into view. She was stunning for a middle-aged woman. Her rich brunette hair, dark as a chocolate mousse, fell to chin level, and her thin yet strong arm held a cell phone to her ear, which she talked into energetically. She could've been the heroine of a sixties movie negotiating with some off-screen antagonist. Was she animated with excitement or anger? Ezra couldn't tell.

"Do you see Cynthia Scout?" he asked Remy.

"Where?"

Ezra pointed with his chin, not wanting to draw too much attention. "How good are you at reading lips?"

"Not." Remy watched her now as well. "Does someone have a *crushing?* This is the term, no?"

"No. I mean, yes, but it's a *crush.*" Ezra felt his face getting hot. "I'm just curious."

"There's a French saying. *Trop enquérir n'est pas bon.* Too much inquiring—"

"Isn't good," Ezra said and finished the quote. "We say, *Curiosity killed the cat, but satisfaction brought it back.*"

Remy chuckled. "How vulgar."

Cynthia Scout came back into view, pressing buttons on the phone now. Texting maybe?

Remy leaned close to Ezra and lowered his voice. "So what sort of satisfaction are you hoping to get from Mrs. Scout?"

Before Ezra could respond, a clap of thunder shook the auditorium, and the lights cut out.

****

Had Detective Lucia Vargas not already rescheduled twice, the snowstorm would've made an easy excuse. But her friends kept telling her thirty-two was the new twenty-five, and no self-respecting twenty-five-year-old canceled a date over a little snow.

Trish, her best friend, set up this particular blind date after Lucia refused to join one of the current rages in online dating apps. Then Trish insisted on picking her outfit, an emerald V-neck blouse with black slacks and heels. She chose this only after Lucia refused to wear a dress.

"It's snowing!" Lucia had protested.

Her sister Areli was also curious. "Why won't you join a dating app?" she asked now. They were sitting on Areli's bedspread, a kitschy Aztec print in orange, purple, and teal pictographs of warriors and geometric shapes.

"Because I'm a detective, *hermanita*," she replied. As she'd only passed the detective's exam two weeks before, Lucia still relished every opportunity to call herself a detective.

"Okay," Areli replied, "then what was your excuse last month?"

"Police officers in general don't do dating apps," Lucia explained in a dignified tone. "Tinder, Facebook,

Instagram—all that stuff's for civilians."

"Instagram *isn't* a dating app."

She gave her little sister an incredulous look. "Detectives do things the old-fashioned way. You meet someone, have drinks—"

"Run a background check."

Lucia pointed at her sister's Chem II textbook. "Finish your homework."

Areli threw up her hands and returned her attention to a chapter entitled *Properties of Gases and Solutions*. In turn, Lucia opened her message app, curious, if not hopeful, to see if her date had canceled. No such luck. She didn't have anything against meeting new people or finding love, but she did have some doubts about Trish's judgment in men.

Trish's last pick took Lucia to a Tex-Mex chain restaurant in a mall. Then he asked if she found being called "Mexican" offensive. When the check finally came, after what felt like a decade of awkward silences and even more uncomfortable questions, he just stared at her. It became clear that he wanted her to pick up the check. This was an actual improvement over Trish's previous set up. That gem, even though he well-knew she was a police officer, showed up stoned.

"Knock, knock," a voice said from the doorway.

Lucia looked up from her phone and saw her mother, still in a janitorial uniform.

"Mija, ¿por qué eres tan elegante?"

Before she could respond, Areli exclaimed, "Lucia has a date!"

"I hate that you're learning Spanish now," Lucia added.

Areli didn't remember Mexico, not like Lucia and

their mother, and she never showed much interest. Not until sophomore year, that is. The entire sophomore class at Evanston Township High School spent spring break in Cancún, visiting museums, churches, and the Mayan pyramids at Chichén Itzá and Tulum. The trip was purely educational, Areli claimed. However, Lucia suspected her little sister spent just as much time meeting boys on the beach and sneaking into nightclubs as she did absorbing the rich Mayan history. At any rate, when Areli returned, she had a new interest in her Mexican heritage, including a desire to "learn Spanish for real."

"I think it's nice your sister is learning Espanish," their mother said.

*"Sp*anish," Lucia corrected her.

"It's my language. I say it how I want."

"Are you coming or going?" Lucia asked her mother.

"I have to change. Then it's the restaurant."

"If you still lived here, you'd know," Areli said.

Lucia playfully pushed her sister's head away. "But then I'd have to put up with you."

The apartment was a two-bedroom near the Northwestern campus where their mother worked in the facilities department. Areli, a high school senior now, was certain to be accepted to the university, and Señora Vargas' employee tuition reduction would make it almost affordable. This was a huge step up from the junior college Lucia matriculated to after high school. And even though she finished her degree at the University of Illinois, she couldn't help feeling both proud and unaccomplished at the thought of her sister attending the prestigious Northwestern University.

"Okay, *hijas.* I go now. You girls have fun," their mother said. Then she added in a conspiratorial tone, "Especially you, Luciana."

Her mother alone called her Luciana—never Lucia or Luce as many of her friends did. Although, more and more, people called her Officer Vargas, and now Detective Vargas.

"I'm going too," she said.

Areli sat up on the bed. "Already?"

Lucia kissed her forehead. "If I don't go now, I might never."

Areli pointed at Lucia's hair. "Better fix that first."

Her hair was still pulled back into a severe bun. Lucia didn't have to wear it like this on the job anymore, but it had become her routine. In the bathroom, she undid the hair pins and ties and raked her fingers through the chestnut curls, pulling them in turns over and behind her shoulders. She had just settled on wearing it over only her left shoulder when her phone rang. The screen read "Sac," short for Satchel, her new partner.

"What do you want?" Lucia asked.

"Whoa, whoa, does the lady have evening plans?"

"I do have a life outside of work."

"You're a detective now, *chica.* You have no life."

"Do not call me *chica.* What's up?"

"There's been an incident at that ritzy private school."

"Roycemore?"

"No, the Catholic one."

"St. Athanasius?" she asked next.

The phone filled with the sound of Sac's notepad as he riffled through the pages. "St. Joseph and Mary.

The boys and girls school."

"What happened?"

"A girl's dead. Or almost dead."

"Well," Lucia said, "which is it?"

More riffling of paper. "I guess we'll have to go see for ourselves." He paused. "Unless you have somewhere better to be."

"See you there in five."

" *I* won't even be there in five."

Lucia hung up with the press of a button. She missed the days when you could slam the handset of your phone onto the base with a bang.

Chapter Two

Ezra stood and surveyed the darkened auditorium. Like fireflies, phone screens flicked on all over the room, illuminating the faces in the crowd. Then flashlights came on, searching up and down the rows and aisles like two dozen spelunkers. Well-meaning fathers began their amateur investigations of the situation. They needed answers to why the lights were out. Little did they realize the commotion they caused only crowded the aisles for the security director.

Instinctively, he pressed his watch. The face lit up and showed eight-fifteen. "I need to find Principal Weeks," he told Remy.

"Perhaps lightning or wind has knocked down a tree and hit a power line," the priest replied. "I'll go check on it."

"Be careful."

The pair split up, Ezra pushing through their row in the direction of Principal Weeks' seat and Remy weaving his way up the aisle toward the lobby. As Ezra moved, he instructed concert patrons to return to their seats, sometimes flashing his nametag, but it was an uphill battle. The principal's usual seat was empty by the time he reached it.

Emergency lights clicked on, offering a dim light. Ezra noted the time was still eight-fifteen. He scanned the auditorium again, searching for Principal Weeks but also, almost subconsciously, for the woman in a red swing coat. The woman he'd seen outside during intermission still lingered in his mind. He hadn't seen her enter the building, but that didn't mean she hadn't come in after intermission ended.

He then spotted Weeks and navigated toward her through the disorganized throng of bodies. She stood talking with a family Ezra recognized from church. "Catherine!" he yelled and waved.

The principal turned, nodded, and strode down the aisle to meet him.

"What happened?" he asked.

"Lightning must've knocked out the power," she said. "Where's your partner in crime? Aren't you and Father Remy usually yoked together at these events?"

"He's investigating outside."

The stage lights clicked on in earnest. Ezra checked his watch again. Eight-sixteen. As he watched, the minute ticked over to seventeen. The power had been out for less than two minutes, but the scene was anarchy.

Almost nobody remained in their seats. A middle school girl sat in the aisle with one shoe off, a small halo of concerned adults examining her ankle. On stage, fifth graders huddled around their teacher. One by one, as the stage lights remained on, curiosity replaced fear, and the children wandered away from their teacher until only one boy hung close, clutching the corner of her cardigan.

A low rumbling noise came from every corner of the auditorium as families debated what to do. Then the overhead lights came on, illuminating every corner of the auditorium. Even the scared child gave an embarrassed laugh and stepped away from his teacher. Stage left, still in a metal folding chair, an unfazed Mason Scout scrolled through his smartphone.

"Mr. James," Remy shouted over the noise. Ezra turned and hustled toward the priest. Usually the picture of tranquility, Remy frowned, his brow furrowed.

"What is it?" Ezra asked.

"Jeb has found something."

Eighty-year-old Jeb Stanton was one of two part-time groundskeepers at St. Joseph and Mary. The other was a few years out of high school. Remy hurried Ezra through the double doors that led to the lobby. Concert patrons lined the floor-to-ceiling windows, absorbed in watching the raging snow just beyond the glass. Ezra pulled on the exterior door. It burst open like the top off a jack-in-the-box and bounced off the wall.

"Thank God!" Jeb shouted over the wind. "There's something you need to see. Well, someone. Come, come!"

The groundskeeper began walking faster than Ezra thought the old man could move. Jeb's hands shook at his sides, though Ezra didn't know if this was from shock or the cold. As they moved in the direction of the St. Peter bell tower, visibility diminished to just a few feet. A soft layer of snow rolled across their path and, in the distance, Ezra saw the fuzzy glow of a streetlamp but not much beyond that. He turned on his flashlight, and a thousand snowflakes lit up like bullet tracers. He shut it back off. A burst of lightning briefly revealed what lay ahead. Ezra saw on the ground downhill from the bell tower a bright red garment. Like a red swing coat. Another flash of light, and he saw black leggings and two bare white feet. *Where are her shoes?*

"I was in the lobby when the power cut," Jeb said. "But the streetlamps stayed on, so I come out here and seen her lying like this."

Once they were upon the young woman, theories washed over Ezra like baptismal water—one, two, three: jealousy, lust, murder. There in the snow lay Brooklyn Hannigan, student-teacher for the music department. Red-headed, vivacious, and twenty-two, she was possibly the most beautiful woman he'd ever set eyes on. Apart from Julia, of course. "Has someone called the police?" he asked.

Jeb nodded.

The three men—a special agent, a priest, and a groundskeeper—crouched down beside her.

"What do you see?" Remy asked.

"A lot," Ezra replied.

Brooklyn's labored breathing suggested she'd been seriously injured. He glanced up the hill at the three-story bell tower. Had she fallen? Beneath the coat, she wore a formal black evening dress, and her perfume smelled fresh. Additionally, she wore dark eyeliner and bright red lipstick, both of which contrasted markedly with her almost white skin, a combination of the cold and her natural skin tone. She clearly meant to meet someone tonight.

He moved the collar of her coat to check her pulse, and the frayed end of a short length of one-quarter-inch black rope rolled out. The rest, which resembled a hoodie drawstring, encircled her neck. *Seems like a puny noose,* Ezra thought. He pushed the rope aside and pressed two fingers to her carotid artery.

"Go to the parking lot," he told Jeb. "When the EMTs get here, tell them her pulse is weak and that I didn't want to move her."

The groundskeeper rose from his crouched position, every bone in his body releasing a tiny pop or creak, and he retreated toward the parking lot. Ezra removed his black pea coat and wrapped it around Brooklyn's bare legs. He returned to her neck, checking for rope burns. There were none but, at the nape of her neck, he felt a round blister as from a burn. This could explain her unconsciousness.

"Ezra," Remy said. "They're here."

Two EMTs, one stout, one rangy, pushed past and knelt beside Brooklyn, laying their stretcher beside her.

"Her breathing is labored. Pulse is forty beats per minute," Ezra told them.

They nodded.

"There's also a blister at the back of her neck."

They nodded again and rechecked her vitals nonetheless.

I'm FBI, he wanted to tell them. *I know things.* Then he would have to explain the name tag and possibly his probationary status. Instead, he stood by as they loaded her onto the stretcher and began moving in the direction of their ambulance, which Ezra could hear but not see through the snow.

He and Remy followed behind them until the parking lot came into view. Most of the cars were still there, no doubt thanks to Principal Weeks keeping everyone inside. Behind the ambulance were two unmarked police units, the flashing lights on their dashes being their only give away. Two plainclothes detectives—a man and a woman—waited beside the ambulance.

The male could've been in his forties or a rough

thirties, balding with a paunch. His shoulder holster flapped unsecured from the lapel of his rumpled suit. The woman was younger, probably early thirties. Her caramel-colored skin, dotted with freckles, caught Ezra's attention. As did her breasts.

He never cheated on Julia, not even these past six months after she left, but he wasn't blind either. Her chest was narrower than her waist but still full, and her outfit—a V-neck blouse she clearly picked out for an occasion other than this emergency call—only accentuated her physique.

Remy nudged him and nodded toward the auditorium. He would check in with Principal Weeks. Ezra nodded, and the priest trudged down the hill.

"What's her condition?" the driver asked from inside the ambulance.

"Stable," the stout EMT replied.

The male detective stepped up to the driver's window. "Where are you taking her?"

"NorthShore."

"We'll be by."

Once the ambulance drove off, the detectives finally acknowledged Ezra's presence. "Who found the girl?" the man asked him. "You?"

Ezra gestured toward Jeb who was slowly making his way back to the auditorium with Remy. "The groundskeeper found her. I just secured the scene."

The male detective laughed and turned to his partner. "Secured the scene, huh? With all the forensics shows they have out now, I'm surprised we don't meet a specialist every crime scene."

"Actually, I'm in law enforcement. This security assignment is temporary."

"Law enforcement?" the female partner asked, slightly less suspicious.

He noted a ghost of an accent in her voice, something Latin, Spanish or Portuguese or even Italian. It was too faint to distinguish. He slipped a hand into his jacket and touched his badge, but then thought better of it. He flashed his name tag instead. "Director of Security, Ezra James."

"I'm *Detective* Gorecki," the male officer replied. "This is *Detective* Vargas."

"Do you remember where you found her?" Vargas asked.

The wind died down, and with it the visibility improved just enough for Ezra to make out the shape of the nearby bell tower. "Over by the tower."

He led them back and told them what he knew as they walked. "She's a student-teacher, but I don't know her well." He pointed his thumb back at the lit auditorium lobby, which had also come more clearly into view as the snowstorm ebbed. "There are a number of teachers and students here for the Christmas concert. They could tell you more."

"What does she teach?" Vargas asked.

"She's been shadowing our choir teacher, Sister Dewberry. She sees every grade in the school."

"The school is K-12?" she asked.

"That's right."

The impression left by Brooklyn's body in the snow resembled a crude snow angel.

"Here it is," Ezra said.

He summarized her state when he found her. Then, noticing a furrow in the snow farther up the hill, he speculated aloud that Brooklyn might have fallen from the tower and rolled to this spot.

"Okay," Gorecki said. "Girl goes up to hang herself. Waits around for the right moment, maybe loses motivation or realizes her rope isn't fit for the job, and then—Bang!—death by lightning." He seemed proud in his estimation.

"Girl's still alive, Gorecki," Vargas pointed out.

"I don't think it was lightning," Ezra said. "The bell tower has a lightning rod."

"Maybe she slipped," Gorecki continued. "Got struck as she fell."

Vargas interrupted their speculation. "We'll be able to make more determinations at the hospital."

"I think she was meeting someone," Ezra stated.

"A lot of people dress up to commit suicide," Vargas replied.

Gorecki smirked. "Die young and leave a good-looking corpse."

"What about the perfume?" Ezra asked her.

"Habit," she replied. "Most of what we do is rote."

"Her dress was a synthetic blend yet showed no damage from the lightning, and there was no exit wound. I think a taser or a live wire made that burn."

Gorecki raised a hand. "I'm sure you've seen a lot, Mr. James, underage drinking, monitoring in-school detention and such, but this here's serious."

"You're a cop, you said?" Vargas asked. "Not in Evanston PD. What precinct?"

"I'm a special agent, actually."

Both detectives raised their eyebrows.

"DEA?" Gorecki guessed.

Now he did produce his badge. "FBI, Chicago field office."

Gorecki inspected it. "Special Agent James," he said mostly to himself. Then a glimmer of understanding came over his face. "I—" he started to say but stopped abruptly.

This happened sometimes. Ezra would be having a perfectly normal conversation with somebody, but then a headline would flash through their mind, and their whole demeanor changed. For an entire year, Ezra's name appeared in the *Chicago Tribune*, sometimes making the front page.

Eventually people remembered seeing one of those headlines.

His jaw clenched as he waited for Gorecki to continue.

"You've helped a lot," the detective said, biting his lip. "You can rejoin your friend inside."

Ezra didn't move. As an FBI agent, he technically outranked them both, but that didn't mean they wanted or needed his help.

"Perhaps he could—" Vargas began, but her partner gave a dismissive shake of his head.

The two detectives stepped a few yards away and conferred in furtive tones. Ezra wondered what the older detective was saying about him. After a few exchanges, Gorecki stomped through the snow toward the tower, and Vargas returned to Ezra.

"Sorry about that," she said. She seemed confused. "Could I speak with your principal?"

Ezra pointed to the auditorium. "She's gathered everyone in the lobby."

Principal Weeks met them at the door, ushering them into the dry warmth. The two women shook hands. "Catherine Weeks," she said. "SJM principal."

"Detective Lucia Vargas."

So the detective has a first name, Ezra thought. *Lucia, from the Latin for "light."*

"The concert is just concluding." Weeks gestured toward a group of about twenty adults in the lobby. "I've gathered some folks who were in the lobby when the power went out or who knew Brooklyn well."

"We'll speak with each of them," Vargas said.

"The last person to see Brooklyn before this evening is our third grade teacher, Ms. Pierce."

Weeks pointed out a blonde woman in her late twenties. Ezra recognized her, as he'd had the occasion to speak to her about a number of student issues, typical elementary school hijinks mainly.

"First name?" Vargas asked.

"Sarah. Sarah Pierce."

After Detective Vargas thanked Weeks and went to Ms. Pierce, Fr. Remy joined Ezra and Catherine. "The cavalry has come."

She nodded. "Indeed." Then to both of them she said, "I know you two must have better places to be. Why don't you head home early tonight?"

Ezra usually stayed at events until all students and families had left. "That's all right," he said. "I may be of assistance to the detectives."

Weeks shook her head. "I think they can handle it from here."

"I know these people. They might speak more candidly to someone—"

"Mr. James," she cut in. "The last thing we need is too much—attention. I'll see you in the morning. You can do your weekly review of the CCTV footage and see if there's anything useful."

With that, she turned and left.

He stood back and observed Detective Lucia Vargas at work. She spoke easily with Ms. Pierce, professional but friendly. In the well-lit lobby, he could see Vargas' dark eyeliner and ruby red lipstick. The makeup complemented her full cheeks and animated eyes far better than Brooklyn's makeup had. For one, Vargas was smiling and chatting away while Brooklyn had been lying still as death in the snow. For two—

"What now, *mon ami?*" Remy asked.

"You heard the boss. I'm no longer needed."

Remy patted him on the back. *"C'est la vie."*

"Although that's a common sentiment these days."

"No, no, don't go down that road."

"Is there any other road?"

"Better is the end of a thing than its beginning." The priest's reply seemed like a non sequitur.

"Proverbs?"

"Ecclesiastes," Remy replied.

Ezra hated Ecclesiastes almost as much as he hated Job, the story of a man who did everything right yet kept getting shit on. Remy assigned all seven wisdom books after Ezra's first confession. Ezra doubted anyone got such a stiff penance.

"So what's it mean?" Ezra asked.

"It means in the end they will need you. Mark my words."

"Well, they don't need me now," he said. "Goodnight, Father."

"Have you forgotten?" Remy raised his keys in the air. "I drove."

Chapter Three

Lucia's first partner, Patty Sturgeon, once gave her this sound piece of advice. "Whenever you take a statement from someone, assign them a word. That way when you're writing your reports, you'll have a way to describe them quickly." Since that day, Lucia did this with everyone she met, on *and off* the job.

In the early years, the words were things like *shaky, angry,* and *drunk.* However, as her powers of observations developed, so did her word choice. Soon this suspect was *restive* or that victim *indignant.* For Director of Security Ezra James, Lucia chose *nonchalant.*

Yes, he stood there cool, calm, and collected as the EMTs loaded the young woman, Brooklyn Hannigan, into the ambulance and as the thunder snow blew their coats and hair as if they were standing beside a tornado. Then he waited patiently for them to approach before sharing his theory that Brooklyn had been attacked. He believed this was an attempted murder, yet he stood there like a statue until they were ready for him. He was FBI, yet he let them run the show.

Patient was the wrong word. Patience suggested humility, and once Ezra James did open his mouth, Lucia ruled humility out immediately. He paraded his observations before them as if he were teaching a class on crime scene analysis. When he begrudgingly told them he was a special agent of the FBI, Lucia was neither surprised nor impressed. She wrote down what he said, taking it with a grain of salt. She doubted this would fall under his federal purview or that his ASAC would want him involved. They would make their own determinations once they had a chance to speak with Brooklyn's physician. For all they knew, Brooklyn fainted and had a skin condition that caused blisters. Ezra James' theory about a taser and a fall from the tower seemed premature, even eager.

Perhaps Lucia chose *nonchalant* because of its connotation, at least in her mind, of dissimulation, of pretending to be something you're not, like seventeen-year-old Holden Caulfield roaming the streets of New York City, pretending to be an adult all the while acting like a child.

Often when she thought of a word, especially an English word, she also recalled where she first came across it. For *nonchalant,* that was in college. In those days, she wrote down and looked up every word she didn't know. She still did this, in fact. When her English instructor had them read *The Catcher in the Rye,* she filled up several pages of the spiral-bound notebook she had dedicated to vocabulary words.

As she escorted Ezra James back to the auditorium, her mind ruminated on memories of that novel. She'd struggled with *Catcher*, not just the words but the purpose. Why follow this sad, foul-mouthed boy around New York City? When she first read the scene in the hotel room, she decided to give herself a break and read a Spanish translation. Her instructor would never know the difference. To her dismay, the translator had rendered Salinger's novel using several Spanish words she didn't know, including the Spanish word for nonchalant. *What is "impassible"?* she had wondered.

Crestfallen, Lucia returned to the novel in English and added the word *nonchalant* to her notebook. She had reached a tipping point, a crossing over into dangerous territory. Just six years in America, and already she was becoming more literate in English than in her native tongue.

She let the memory and the complex emotions it evoked subside as she and Ezra approached the glass doors of the auditorium. Before she could grasp the handle, a well-dressed woman pressed the door open and greeted her.

Principal Catherine Weeks struck her as a no-nonsense sort of woman, the kind you meet in upper management positions. Here Weeks organized student schedules and presented at board meetings, but she could've just as easily organized spreadsheets and presented at shareholder meetings. Weeks indicated a group of about twenty concertgoers she felt Lucia and her partner should speak with. Lucia checked her watch. It was already past nine.

"We'll speak with each of them," she assured the principal.

She approached Sarah Pierce first. The third-grade teacher and supposed last contact of Brooklyn Hannigan reminded Lucia of a sorority girl all grown up. Fit and blonde, Sarah Pierce wore a red floral print dress and heels.

"I hear you knew Brooklyn."

"How is she?" Pierce asked.

"She's stable. They're taking her to NorthShore."

"I just saw her. I was telling Catherine that we had

lunch today. This is so surreal."

"Did Brooklyn have any medical conditions?"

"I don't think so." She touched the fingers of one hand to her temples. "To be honest, I don't really know her all that well. We have lunch in the lounge and talk at sporting events, and we've had lunch a few times outside of school, but I don't know her well enough to know her medical history or whatnot."

"Where did you go today?"

"El Caribe."

"Fancy."

"They have a lunch menu," she said defensively.

"Why'd Brooklyn want to leave school?"

"She's been having boy-problems."

Yes, *sorority-sister* would be a good pick for Sarah Pierce. "What sort of problems? Who's the guy?"

"She wouldn't say."

"Someone here at the school?" Lucia asked.

She patted her hands on her floral dress. Wiping away sweat? "She…she didn't go into the details."

"But you suspect he was connected to the school?"

She nodded. "Don't quote me, but the way she talked about their interactions made me think some of those *interactions* took place here."

Lucia tried to think of a nuanced way to ask the next question, but then decided on bluntness. "Did they have sex at the school?"

"Oh no, nothing like that," she replied. "Okay, so a few weeks ago Brooklyn said she saw him on Friday night, but she was at the football game Friday night."

"Maybe she saw him after the game?"

"I don't think so. She helps the band teacher, Ms. Hugo. They set up an hour before the game, and it takes them time to pack up afterward. *I* usually don't get home until ten, so I can only imagine when she does."

Sarah Pierce said this with utter conviction. The third-grade teacher honestly believed Brooklyn couldn't have seen her mystery man after ten o'clock. Unfortunately, Lucia knew better than anyone that Friday nights were long. Only the happily coupled or hopelessly single went home before ten.

Lucia pointed at Pierce's left hand, the ostentatious wedding ring with rows of diamonds set in white gold. "Where's the mister?"

"Working," she said flatly. "He's a first-year associate, so there are a lot of late nights."

For the first time, she lost her sorority-sister pep. *Working late* was a favorite cover of wayward husbands. Then again, most lawyers worked constantly their first year.

"Associate meaning he's an attorney?"

She nodded. "Sheffield and Sheffield. It's on Monroe."

"I know it." Lucia jotted down the name. It seemed unlikely that Brooklyn would sleep with a man and then confide in his wife, but it was worth a follow up. After all, the two women left school together for lunch, and then the next time anyone saw Brooklyn she was lying unconscious in the snow.

"Is that all?" she asked.

"For now," Lucia replied.

Lucia asked for Sarah Pierce's contact information *nonchalantly* so as to not arouse suspicion and jotted it next to her husband's law firm. She then looked up and scanned the room for Ezra James. He was gone. She tried momentarily to recall the hotel scene and to remember if Holden Caulfield had slept with the prostitute or not. It wouldn't change her mind about Ezra, but she wanted to know and kicked herself for not remembering. Then she moved onto the other nineteen bystanders. Several of them mentioned a French teacher, Martin Durand, whose wife left him that summer for another woman. How this related to the incident at hand they didn't know, but they wanted to pass on the information. Lucia filed this under "biggest school gossip." Others informed her of a shifty refugee student from Haiti. This she filed under "xenophobes aplenty." Almost everyone informed her that, at the time of the incident, it had been snowing.

****

Nearly two hours had passed since the 9-1-1 call. While Lucia interviewed witnesses, Gorecki photographed the scene and checked inside the bell tower. Then he joined Lucia and took statements from concert-goers. When they were done, Lucia and Gorecki retreated to his silver muscle car to compare notes. Snowflakes came in slowly now, settling on the windshield and either melting or blowing away.

"I cannot believe this is your car," she said.

"Stick around long enough, honey, and this too can be yours."

"Don't call me *honey*."

"Affirmative-affirmative," Gorecki replied. It was his subtle way of reminding Lucia that he thought her recent promotion was a double quota filler.

She ignored him. "What I'm saying is I can't believe a plain-clothes detective is driving around in a sports car. Isn't the whole idea to blend in?"

He patted the black dashboard. "Sure, but if I'm

chasing a perp, you know I'm getting him in this baby."

"If speed is your deal, you should've gone with the 5.2-liter."

"Sure, I'll just drop an extra thirty-grand for a car that's not even that much faster."

"Not that much faster?" she asked, incredulous. "The 5.2-liter has a supercharged V8, double the horsepower, and twice the torque. It's so fast that its transmission needs an extra gear."

"Fine, so you know cars," he said.

"My uncle's a mechanic," she said. "Plus, in high school, I dated a guy who raced."

"Oh, was this back in ye Old Mexico?" he asked, pronouncing the word *ME-hi-co.*

Lucia glared at him. "Lower Wacker," she said. "South Chicago."

"I know where Lower Wacker is."

It was past time for Lucia to change the subject. "What did Catherine Weeks have to say?"

"They might offer Brooklyn Hannigan a full-time position in the spring."

"What's keeping them on the fence?"

"She said a parent submitted a letter of support but then withdrew it."

"Did Catherine say why they withdrew support?"

"Nope. She didn't ask."

"Who's the parent?" she asked.

"A woman named Cynthia Scout. She has two kids in the school." He flipped open his notes. "Mason is the star quarterback, and Mikayla is a fifth grader who played Mary in the nativity play tonight. The whole family, including husband Henry, came to watch."

"Mary? That's a big role at a Catholic school."

"Are you speaking from experience?" he asked.

She laughed. "Catholic school, no. Catholic, yes." She considered her next statement a moment. "Although, I haven't been to mass since leaving *Old ME-hi-co.*"

Gorecki ignored her. "Sister Dewberry, that's who Brooklyn is shadowing. She said Brooklyn has seemed down the last couple weeks. Then Brooklyn came in this morning 'her old bouncing self.' Those are the nun's words."

"I figured."

"Brooklyn left the school for lunch today and didn't come back."

"Until tonight."

"True," he said.

Now it was Lucia's turn. "Her teacher-friend, Sarah Pierce, said Brooklyn's been having relationship issues. She thought it might be with someone at the school."

Gorecki recapped, "College girl has a breakup. Gets depressed. Suddenly snaps out of it. Takes a half day, maybe to visit some friends and family. Walks up three flights of stairs and removes her shoes."

"Shit," Lucia agreed. "Senseless."

Both detectives knew well that suicide attempts were sometimes preceded by hours or days of euphoric acceptance as the individual felt released from their earthly troubles. Also, removing one's shoes before jumping off a bridge or building was a common ritual.

Gorecki asked, "You said the friend was named Pierce?"

Lucia nodded.

"I spoke to another teacher. Named Jarno," he said.

"I think she's English."

"What did she say about Sarah Pierce?"

"Nothing. It was about her husband. Jarno called him *handsy.*"

"What's the context?" Lucia asked.

"The teachers had a Christmas party last week. Mark Pierce came up behind Jarno in the kitchen and slapped her behind."

"Did he mistake her for his wife?"

"Beneath the clothes."

"How did he—"

"He slid a hand down her dress. He claimed it was an accident. I would've asked him about it, but he wasn't there tonight."

Lucia nodded. "Pierce said he works late a lot."

Gorecki laughed. "I've heard that one before." He laughed again, though Lucia could tell it was about something else. "Did they tell you about the French teacher's wife?"

"The lesbian?" Lucia asked and nodded her head. "You'd think they'd never met a gay person."

"Many of them probably don't even know if they have." Gorecki laughed a final time.

She opened the passenger-side door. "So, I'll meet you there?"

He raised an eyebrow. "Meet me where?"

"The hospital."

"Oh that?" he replied, staring straight ahead. "You can handle it."

Lucia looked around the black leather and chrome interior. "Hope you let Ash drive this from time to time." Ash, short for Ashley, was Gorecki's wife. "I hear this model's great for grocery shopping."

Before he could fire off a pompous retort, she closed the door behind her.

****

North of St. Joseph and Mary, Evanston Hospital, commonly referred to as NorthShore, was nearly as old as the suburb itself. Although you could hardly tell this from the outside. After dozens of renovations and expansions, the red-brick edifice blended in perfectly with its up-to-date surroundings.

The ICU was located on the fourth floor, but the ER was on the ground floor. Lucia checked with the ER first. It was uncharacteristically busy for a Thursday evening.

"Snowstorm," explained the charge nurse, a round man with a salt-and-pepper crew cut. Splattered blood and melted snow gave his green scrubs a tie-dye look. "We have several MVAs at the moment. Which one are you here for?"

"None of them," Lucia explained. "EMTs brought a girl in from St. Joseph and Mary School."

The nurse wrinkled his brow. "A girl?"

"Sorry, a young woman. She's in her twenties."

"Oh," he said and started toward a row of beds. He stopped at one, perplexed, and then turned to an orderly. "Tomas. Where'd they put the unconscious woman?"

"Upstairs."

"Who moved her?"

Tomas shrugged. "I just work here."

"All right." The nurse huffed. "I've been pulled a hundred directions tonight, and two ambulances are on their way right now." He led Lucia to the elevators.

"Upstairs" was quiet in comparison. The only

35

noises were the steady beep of cardiac monitors and the hums of ventilators, IV pumps, and various other equipment.

When they came to Brooklyn's room, a female doctor was just leaving. The charge nurse held out a hand by way of introduction. "Dr. Khin," he said, "this detective would like a moment."

"Of course." After dismissing the nurse, the doctor turned to Lucia. "What do you need?"

Lucia pointed into the hospital room. "EMTs brought Brooklyn Hannigan in earlier. Can you tell me how severe her injuries are?"

"Very." The doctor frowned. "Three broken ribs, a broken ulna. That's an arm bone. Bruising down the left side of her body. There's some cranial bruising as well."

"Hematoma?"

"No…"

"But?"

"Brooklyn's in a coma," Dr. Khin said.

"Would all of this be consistent with a three-story fall?" Lucia asked.

Dr. Khin studied the patient through the glass window and then nodded. "Yes, I could see that. If that's the case, she's lucky to be alive.

"What about her neck?"

The physician plucked the chart from its rack and looked through the papers. "Blistering with significant subdermal damage." She looked up from the chart. "Possible electrical burn."

"Lightning?"

She shook her head. "No, that would be far worse. There's no Lichtenberg scarring, no exit wound."

"What kind of scarring?" Lucia asked.

The doctor seemed exasperated but answered, "It looks like a tree or branching lightning. It shows how electricity branches out through the skin. With serious voltage as from a lightning bolt, we would likely see that pattern."

"Would lightning have killed her?"

"Possibly."

Lucia couldn't help but notice how much the medical expert's diagnosis echoed the observations made earlier that evening by Ezra James. "What do you think caused the injury then?"

"Could be lots of things. A live wire, a car battery…"

"A taser?"

"Sure, if held on long enough."

It seemed Ezra wasn't as overeager as Lucia initially supposed. Although this lent a certain level of suspicion in its own right. When a magician guesses your card, it's because they put it in your hand in the first place. Was Ezra himself somehow mixed up with this girl?

"Did they find any defensive wounds or signs of sexual assault?" Lucia asked. "Did they do a rape kit?"

"They did. There were no signs of rape."

"And how did her blood come back?"

Dr. Khin flipped through the papers again. "No drugs, illicit or otherwise. Blood count is good. Thyroid and enzymes are all good."

"So you don't think she fainted?"

"You said she fell three stories?"

Lucia nodded. "We believe she fell from the belfry of a three-story tower."

"I'm no detective," the doctor said, "but it sounds like she jumped. Or was pushed."

"Does Brooklyn have a history of mental illness?" Lucia asked.

"Nothing came up, but that doesn't mean her records are all up-to-date," Dr. Khin said, waving her hands back and forth. "Our hospital doesn't have every record, and she wasn't awake to fill anything out."

From down the hall, someone called for the doctor.

"I must go," she told Lucia. "I'll send over a copy of everything we have."

Lucia thanked her. "It's a shame if she jumped. She's a beautiful woman."

"Young people do strange things," Dr. Khin replied. "And the pregnancy doesn't help."

"Of course," Lucia replied automatically, then stopped. "Wait, what?"

"You didn't know?" She pointed at the unconscious patient on the other side of the glass. "That girl is two months pregnant."

Chapter Four

Friday

Every Friday, Ezra did his all-school check. He walked the halls—entered classrooms, scanned through security footage, and gave Principal Catherine Weeks a verbal report of his observations—all before the first bell.

This Friday, however, his calendar read, "Ψ eight a.m." He readied himself leisurely and then headed downtown to Northwestern Memorial to meet with his psychiatrist. Over the last six months, the sense of embarrassment he felt at entering an outpatient psychiatric clinic had subsided—but not disappeared. A small part of him still felt judged by unseen eyes.

On television, psychiatrists' offices are always ornate, calming environments that contrast with the internal turmoil and past trauma of their patients. The doctor, old, wise, and dressed in clean white linen, steers the conversation so expertly that one moment the patient muses on the minutiae of his daily life, then seconds later ascends into a life-altering epiphany.

For Ezra, the psych wing of Northwestern Memorial was just as busy and chaotic as everywhere else in his life. Furthermore, Dr. Henry Palacios didn't care one bit if Ezra experienced an epiphanic breakthrough, just so long as he stayed on his prescribed drug regimen.

Dr. Palacios' office consisted of a room roughly the size of a closet into which an office chair, a ratty loveseat, and a small computer desk were stuffed. During their appointments, his gaze rarely left his computer screen. Small but muscular and compact, he reminded Ezra of an MMA fighter.

Ezra caught a number of Mixed Martial Arts bouts as his ASAC—Assistant Special Agent in Charge— Jeremy Cromley followed both traditional boxers and the mixed martial arts fighters. In MMA, punching, kicking, grappling, and just about everything short of biting and eye-gouging was allowed. As a result of this passion, Cromley filled his office with photographs of famous bouts. Ezra could almost always pick out the boxers from the MMA fighters, the prior standing tall with overblown biceps and pectoral muscles, while the latter crouched into themselves, their shoulders disappearing into their necks.

In contrast to Cromley's office, only two photographs hung on Dr. Palacios' wall. One featured a palm tree on the sandy shore of a lake, a white and gray cloud looming in the distance. The other showed a young man in front of a narrow, cascading waterfall, a distant look in his eyes. Other than these two photographs and the standard college degrees and medical licenses, the office was sparse.

Dr. Palacios typed away at his computer.

"Did you take that photo?" Ezra asked.

Palacios looked up. "Which one?"

"The waterfall."

"Yes. That's Angel Falls."

"You're from Venezuela, right?"

Palacios nodded. "My brother and I took a trip to Canaima one summer."

"Did he emigrate as well?"

"This was a long time ago." The psychiatrist shifted in his chair, facing Ezra now. "How is your mood today?"

"Normal."

"What is that?" the psychiatrist asked.

The question confused Ezra. "What is normal?"

"To you."

"Not overly excited, not overly down. Just…" He waved one hand horizontally through the air.

Palacios rocked his hand in a back and forth motion. "You feel so-so?"

Ezra nodded.

"Any drug or alcohol use?"

"None."

"Not even alcohol?"

"I don't like feeling out of control. In law enforcement, you need to be alert at all times."

"You've returned to your regular duties then?"

He looked away. "No."

"Okay, now for the three questions I ask every appointment," Dr. Palacios said and smiled. "Are you thinking of harming yourself?"

"No."

"Harming others?"

"No."

"Do you see anything in this room that isn't here?"

"I suppose I wouldn't know, would I?"

The doctor smiled.

Ezra continued, "There's nothing out of the ordinary."

"Good, very good." Palacios turned back to the screen and reviewed the four medications Ezra was taking. "These are going well?"

"Fine," Ezra said. "Some dizzy spells. First thing in the morning."

"How dizzy?"

"When I first stand up, I have to catch my balance."

"That's fairly normal."

There was that word again. Normal.

"Although," Palacios continued, "this is a lot of medication. You've been stable since your incident at the café. That was, what, six months ago?"

Ezra nodded.

He kept reading. "Bipolar I. One hospital stay. No incidents before that?"

"No," Ezra lied.

"Late onset like this is rare but not unheard of. Most people with your condition exhibit signs in their teens or twenties—not forty."

"What can I say? I've always been a late bloomer." He smiled stiffly and waited for Palacios to accept his explanation.

"Look, I'm just your doctor. I can't force feed you these medications."

Ezra examined his brown leather shoes. The tan laces were beginning to fray at the ends.

The doctor sighed. "I can take you off these two." He pointed to the screen. "They're small dosages and were meant to be short term. But it will have to be gradual." He pointed at the screen. "What do you have left of these?"

"A few weeks' worth, maybe two."

"Go home and cut them in half. That will get you through the month. Then you can discontinue after that. If your symptoms return, though, I want to hear from you. Do you know the three symptoms?"

Ezra counted them off on his fingers. "Suicidal thoughts, homicidal—"

"No, no, symptoms of mania." He wrote them down on a yellow legal pad as he spoke. "One, you start sleeping fewer than three hours a night. Two, you feel euphoric like nothing could go wrong. Three, you start having high-pressure talking when no one can get a word in edgewise." He handed the yellow sheet of paper to Ezra.

"Got it."

"And Ezra, when you're manic is when you need to come in, but it's the last time you're going to want to. You're going to feel indestructible, but if it turns on you, and it will, there's no telling what you might do."

Palacios didn't have to tell Ezra this. He'd experienced it firsthand again and again. However, he hated feeling like a walking pharmacy. "I've got it."

"Emergency contact still Julia James?"

"Can you leave it blank?"

"No parents or siblings?"

"I'd prefer a blank."

"I'll leave it as is."

Ezra said nothing.

"Pharmacy still on Dodge?"

Ezra nodded.

Outside, Ezra found the sidewalk blocked by a man carrying two giant crates of oranges. The man's hat nearly covered his eyes, and his teeth held a manila envelope.

As Ezra moved closer, the orange man mumbled something.

"Are you talking to me?" Ezra asked.

The man continued to talk through the manila envelope in his mouth and gestured with his head toward the clinic doors. Ezra took the envelope out of the man's mouth.

"You've just been served," he said over his crates of oranges.

"It's wet," Ezra complained.

"Not my problem."

****

The young woman at the pharmacy counter couldn't have been more bored if she'd been an actress playing the role of Bored Teenager on a TV sit-com. Actually, the actress would've been alert if for no other reason than her one line was coming. This young woman didn't know her line was coming, however, because it took Ezra several seconds of talking and then waving to get her attention.

She placed her phone face down on the counter. "What?"

He repeated his name for the third time. "I have two prescriptions."

She sighed and disappeared into the stacks of shelves, then resurfaced, a cautious expression on her face. "These them?"

Even the least experienced pharmacy tech knew what lithium treated and that his other prescription must also be for the loons. Ezra never enjoyed telling people about his condition. A teacher at SJM, unaware of his diagnosis, once told him that you simply couldn't trust manic depressives. "Drug users and thieves," she characterized them. "They lie also, of course."

Ezra simply nodded and repeated, "Of course," and then hated himself for doing so.

The tech behind the counter, with her silver crucifix and grunge-band T-shirt, eyed him with continual suspicion as he punched his pin into the credit card machine. Then she handed him the bottles of pills with a disappointed frown, as if he were a fifteen-year-old trying to purchase condoms. How much of this judgment was real and how much perceived? He'd never know.

Ever since his hospitalization, Ezra lived in constant fear of raising his voice, of missing an appointment, of taking a spontaneous trip, of doing anything human that someone—his mother mostly but also Dr. Palacios—could misconstrue as "insane" and use as a reason to commit him.

He took his contraband and left the counter, burying his face in his phone in order to avoid further eye contact with anyone else in the pharmacy. On the way out, he stopped at the front counter. "Can I get a carton of slims?" He pointed to the brand he wanted.

The clerk raised an eyebrow. "Are they for you?"

Purchasing cigarettes for another person seemed suspicious, so he replied, "You bet."

****

Ezra's mother lived in a four-story apartment building in south Evanston. She lived close enough for Ezra to visit and help with weekly chores but also far enough away to maintain his sanity. The instant he opened her front door, the hallway filled with the angry voices of news reporters.

"I don't know who all these people are," his

mother said over the blare of the TV.

The TV commentators were discussing a pride rally taking place somewhere warm—San Diego maybe or Miami. The marchers smiled and danced, rainbow flags and banners held aloft.

"What do you mean?" he asked her.

"Who are they?"

"They're gay people," he said, bemused.

"No one is gay, Ezra."

"Um, those people are," he replied. "Look, they have signs."

"But who is talking them all into it?"

He looked at his mother with a mixture of confusion and concern. "I don't think it works like that, Mother."

"I have an article you need to read," she said. "It explains all this."

"An article? Or a social media fan page?"

"Why are you being like this? All I've ever done is *love* you." She emphasized the word as if it were a slur.

He pulled the carton of slims from the bag and handed them to her. "Love you."

She tore into the cardboard ravenously. "What else do you have there?" She pointed to his bag.

He shook the bag, and his medications rattled in their orange bottles.

She packed a single cigarette box now, tapping it against her palm ritualistically. "I hate that you put that poison into your body." She withdrew a single cigarette and lit it.

"I know, I know."

Chapter Five

Lucia didn't leave the hospital until close to midnight. Nevertheless, visiting the school early the next morning still fell to her. The horizon was a warm red and the sky above a soft lilac as she approached the school's chapel. The bell tower loomed menacingly against the fiery sky, but the brick church attached to it seemed almost inviting.

She marched up the hill, her feet crunching through four inches of uncleared, frozen-topped snow to meet the priest. As she neared it, her gaze climbed the edifice of the chapel and tower. The chapel's two green spires stabbed heavenward, and then the tower rose up between them, piercing the sky with a thin arrow-tipped cross. As a shiver ran through her system, she lowered her gaze to the front doors. The door swung inward.

"Detective!" Fr. Mbombo said in alarm. He wore plain clothes but, being the only ebony face at a very ivory private school, he wasn't hard to recognize.

"I'm a little early."

The priest stepped back, holding the door open. "Come in, come in."

The chapel opened into a narrow, ill-lit atrium. Fr. Mbombo shoved open the interior door while still guiding the exterior door closed with his other hand. He ushered her into the long nave of the chapel, a room filled with stained glass and two rows of walnut pews.

Sunlight poured in through the east windows, sending a spectrum of colorful beams into the pews along the opposite wall. Beyond the streaming lights stood a white marble altar. An almost life-sized wooden crucifix hung on the wall behind the altar. Lucia's church in Chihuahua had been beautiful and filled with ornate statuary, but it was small, its windows merely functional, and its altar little more than a wooden table.

"How is Brooklyn?" the priest asked as they walked down the center aisle toward the altar.

"Stable but unresponsive."

He sucked his teeth. "A coma then?"

Lucia nodded.

Fr. Mbombo stopped at the massive altar and bowed. As a matter of decorum, Lucia mimicked the gesture and then followed the priest to a small room left of the crucifix.

"This is the sacristy," he replied. "It is where we store our patens and cloths and where we wash out our communion cups and chalice." He indicated a small sink, which drained into the exterior wall. "The water goes directly outside so the body and blood will not end up in the sewer but will instead feed a holly bush," he explained. "In the Catholic Church, we believe—"

"I grew up Catholic," she said.

"But no longer?" he asked. "I am sure there is a story there."

Lucia's heartbeat quickened. The discomfort she felt upon initially entering the church now increased exponentially. She formulated a round-about explanation, not sure if she would use it. She didn't want to lay her religious baggage at this man's feet.

Before she could decide what to say, the priest

continued, "I didn't mean to imply you needed to tell me your situation."

"No," is all she managed to reply. "We're primarily interested to know if you've noticed anything out of the ordinary."

"Such as?"

"Has anything gone missing recently or been tampered with?"

He contemplated this question for some time, staring at the carpet just outside the sacristy. What event or detail was he now recalling? Finally, he shook his head.

"Have you ever seen our chalice?" he asked. "It is the prize possession of our parish."

He drew a key from his pocket and unlocked a small cabinet. As he did this, he described the item. Handcrafted in brass and gold-plated at a 16th-century, Polish monastery, the chalice was a gift from the Pontiff himself, John Paul II. He bestowed the chalice upon SJM during his first visit to America.

"I was not here in the '70s," Fr. Mbombo explained, "but I have always felt its significance during the masses I offer here."

As he swung the cabinet door open, Lucia peered inside. The cabinet was empty.

The priest slapped his forehead humorously. *"Mais bien sûr,* I placed it in my office only yesterday."

Is the chalice missing? Lucia wondered. *Is this his way of telling me something without incriminating one of his flock?*

"You must see it," he insisted.

They left the sacristy, and he led her to a hallway on the opposite side of the altar. At the end of this stood two doors, one marked simply "Office" and the other "Stairwell." He unlocked the office door. The chalice he described sat atop his desk. In the light pouring in from his clear window, the sacred vessel sparkled and shone.

Well, there goes that theory, she thought.

"How do you access the bell tower?" she asked.

"I'll take you there."

The stairwell next door was narrow and, at several points, Fr. Mbombo had to simultaneously duck and pivot to progress upward. Lucia, six inches shorter than he, ascended easily in comparison.

Outside, Lucia examined the belfry, the giant brass bell, and the wrought iron guardrails. Brooklyn Hannigan's footprints were still partially visible, though fresh snow half-filled them now. Gorecki had taken her shoes into evidence, but the impression they left in the snow remained.

What had gone through Brooklyn's mind as she stood here moments before the groundskeeper discovered her unconscious body three stories below? Did she come alone or was this meant to be a rendezvous? And what caused the electrical burn at the nape of her neck? Perhaps only Brooklyn herself knew the answers to these questions. Unfortunately, she lay in a coma across town.

She surveyed the belfry, walking along the snowless edges, but found no footprints aside from Brooklyn's. Gorecki had been surprisingly careful. It didn't add up. If Brooklyn jumped, then what burned her neck? If someone attacked her, then where was the evidence? Every touch left a trace, but here the only traces were Brooklyn's.

Across from the chapel, she could just make out a black surveillance camera above the main doors to the auditorium. "Can I see the footage from that camera?"

"You will have to wait for Mr. James. He reviews all the CCTV footage on Friday mornings."

"All of it?"

"There are four cameras in total, I believe. He will know more."

"Mr. James is FBI."

The priest nodded.

"Do you have any idea why he's running security at a school?"

"I will let Ezra himself tell you that story. You are speaking with the students today?"

"That's right."

He gestured toward the line of cars arriving. "Then we had better get you down there."

"Before we go, can you also tell me about Ms. Jarno?"

"What do you want to know?"

"Is she trustworthy?" Lucia asked.

"Define *trustworthy.*"

That was all he needed to say. Nevertheless, Lucia continued, "She told my partner a story about one of the other teachers. The teacher's husband, actually."

"Who is the teacher?"

"Sarah Pierce. Her husband's a lawyer."

"Yes, they are parishioners. He is a bit…awkward."

"The word Jarno used was *handsy.*"

"Heather Jarno is not a very trusting person," Fr. Mbombo said. "She has brought many suspicions to me that have turned out to be, let us say, unfruitful.

However, that doesn't mean she is dishonest." He opened the door to the stairwell and turned to her. "You will investigate her claims, I assume?"

"Of course."

****

Principal Catherine Weeks struck Lucia as a no-nonsense woman in complete control. This impression only grew as Fr. Remy Mbombo and she stepped into the principal's office. Not a paper was out of place, nor a chair askew. Lucia noticed a dark wood bookcase. The titles on its shelf ranged from leadership and educational monographs to literary classics and best-sellers from the last dozen years. The shelves contained no bookends, no framed inspirational sayings, nor any other items meant to fill out the bookcase.

Before sitting, Lucia leaned toward the shelf and read a title at random. "*The Beggar's Maid.* What's that about?"

Weeks turned to regard the book. Her gaze went directly to it. "Have you read any Alice Munro?"

Lucia shook her head. "Would I like her?"

The principal bobbed her head side to side, considering. "Munro won the Nobel Prize a few years back. She writes short stories primarily. They're about growing up poor in Canada."

"Well," she said, "I grew up poor in Mexico. I'll have to look her up."

Weeks jotted down the author and title on a post-it and handed it to Lucia.

Bona Fide, Lucia decided then. That would be her term for Catherine Weeks. It perfectly characterized her. Weeks was a *bona fide* principal, equal parts leader and academic.

"My partner told me you were considering Brooklyn for an open position."

"That's half right," the principal replied. "We want to expand the music department, and Brooklyn expressed an interest."

"But you need board approval first?" Lucia guessed.

"Yes, but it's diocese approval." Weeks looked to Fr. Mbombo, who nodded.

"The bishop will likely approve it," he said.

Weeks opened her desk drawer and removed a typed letter.

"Is that Cynthia Scout's reference letter?" Lucia asked.

The principal's eyebrows shot up in surprise. "How did you know?"

Lucia smiled. "You told my partner about it last night."

"Oh, of course." She smirked. "I thought for a second you were one of those Sherlock Holmes detectives."

"Far from it. You should hear me on the violin."

Weeks laughed. Then said, "As you can see, it's glowing." She handed the letter to Lucia.

After reading it over, Lucia asked, "Why did Ms. Scout rescind the letter?"

"She wouldn't say, and I haven't heard anything that would make sense of it."

Lucia frowned.

"As for the students," Weeks continued, "we have a few places we can start."

Like any principal worth her salt, Catherine Weeks had a list of suspects ready before the crime even occurred. Fiona Fleming, a sophomore mean-girl, had been on her radar ever since she threw a cup of urine at Brooklyn from the second story balcony in the science wing. It turned out to be lemonade but was still wildly inappropriate.

Mason Scout, in addition to being an all-around troublemaker, visited Brooklyn at her apartment Halloween night, along with two football teammates, Royce Ainsley, a fellow senior, and Daniel Toussaint, a sophomore. Armed with a guitar and a healthy buzz, the teenagers hurled landscaping pebbles at Brooklyn's window until she finally opened it. Then Mason serenaded her while Royce strummed away. The student-teacher, terrified of rumors getting back to the school, reported the incident the following Monday morning. Mason, Royce, and Daniel each received an after-school detention and a thousand fist bumps from their male classmates.

"Do you suspect anything untoward was happening between Brooklyn and one of the students?"

Weeks sighed. "Honestly? I have no idea."

"I would be surprised," Fr. Mbombo replied. Then he chuckled to himself. "Although, I am often surprised."

For the second time that morning, Lucia wished she had a microscope that could peer into the priest's ear and view his secret thoughts. She returned her attention to the list of names. "These four students sound like a good start. Do you want to call them in?"

The principal sighed again. "Yes, but there's a problem. I know it is your legal right to speak with them without parental permission, but this is a private school, and we always have to consider blow back."

"You think their parents will pull them from the school because of an interview?"

"I've had parents do more over less."

Fr. Mbombo spoke now. "We hoped you would allow Ezra to do the questioning while you…" He seemed to search for the right wording.

"Did the listening?" she asked.

Weeks nodded. "Our parents sign a contract, which includes our security policies, but it states we will contact them prior to outside police involvement. If you're an observer, then there's really no reason to contact them."

"And no reason for them to contact a lawyer," Lucia said. This was their best shot then to find out what happened without unnecessary obstacles. "So where is Ezra?"

The principal and the priest shared a look.

"An appointment," Fr. Mbombo said.

"That's vague enough," she replied.

A long silence ensued before something crossed Lucia's mind. "Tell me, Catherine, what sort of equipment does Ezra carry? A sidearm, handcuffs?"

"No, no firearms. Many of our parents expressed concern over an armed officer stalking the school grounds. They feared it would unsettle students."

"All he carries is a whistle and flashlight," Fr. Mbombo said. He thought for a moment. "Plus there is his little green notebook. That is where Ezra keeps his mind."

"He always has that notebook," Weeks agreed. "Well, that and his taser."

Lucia removed her own notepad and jotted down the word *taser*. Although she doubted she'd forget it.

Chapter Six

When Ezra arrived, an unmarked police car occupied his usual spot in front of the school office. He drove around the faculty section of the parking lot for a few minutes before parking on the street.

"Where have you been?" the secretary asked when he finally opened the front door. Denise was thin and brunette, not long out of school herself, and rather easy on the eyes.

He fanned out the lapel of his jacket. "I lost another button. If you see one lying around, please save it for me."

"She's going to fire you." With a smile Denise used her pencil to point at a row of students in seats. "There's actual work for you today."

Three students sat in every other seat—Fiona Fleming, Royce Ainsley and, to Ezra's surprise, Daniel Toussaint. Daniel was a new student from Haiti and, with one or two minor exceptions, a model student. The other two he could pitch out a window. He wondered if Mason Scout would also be joining them.

Catherine Weeks appeared then from the inner door of her office. Ezra saw Remy and Detective Lucia Vargas sitting at Catherine's desk. In contrast to her outfit the previous night, Vargas wore a bland gray pants suit and a simple yellow blouse. Catherine motioned for Ezra to enter.

"What's the move here?" Ezra asked.

She indicated the detective. "Detective Vargas is going to observe while you question some students."

Ezra shook his head. "I hate this parent contract business."

"This is how it's got to be," she said.

"Fine, but it looks like you're missing a student."

"Denise called Mason Scout down. He just hasn't arrived yet."

"That's the shock of the century," Ezra replied. "Maybe you can send a search party."

"Ms. Jarno has a planning period now. I told her to make a sweep."

Ezra nodded. "Let's get this started then."

Catherine opened her office door again and explained the situation to the students. She then led each one to a different room and shut the door.

"We'll start with the girl," he said.

Fiona Fleming, pale and freckled, barely cleared five feet tall. Usually brash and animated, she cautiously rose from her chair, tugging on one of her loose blonde curls. Her shoulders slumped forward, and she didn't make eye contact with anyone as she entered the office.

Ezra and Detective Vargas took one side of Catherine's large mahogany desk with Remy on Fiona's side as a show of support. Catherine stepped into the hall and shut the door, though not all the way. Ezra recalled the school's motto, *Veritas Liberabit Vos*, The Truth Shall Set You Free, and it made him wonder if Fiona would be honest. Would she show Detective Vargas her true self or try to blind her with a polished veneer?

"Students seem to like Ms. Hannigan," Ezra began.

"It's easy to be well-liked when you're a whore," Fiona replied.

Catherine burst into the office. "Fiona!"

"What? God! Just because she jumped from some tower, I'm not going to sit here and act like I didn't hate that woman."

"So you know about the attempted suicide?" Ezra asked.

"Everybody knows," Fiona said. "And you know what? I'm happy she jumped."

"Fi-on-a," Catherine said through gritted teeth. "Do you have any idea how angry your mother would be if she could hear you?"

Fiona rolled her eyes.

"Or your father?"

Fiona slouched down in her seat. Norman Fleming, Fiona's stepfather, coached football at SJM and often came to the office to upbraid Fiona worse than Catherine had.

"Where were you last night?" Ezra asked.

"Are you a real cop? Because if you're not a cop, then I don't have to tell you anything."

Catherine buried her face in her hands.

"You can sit there and pretend I don't exist," Ezra said, "but I'm sure Principal Weeks would be happy to let you spend the rest of the day in the ISS room."

"Sounds good to me. It beats spending all day in this stupid school."

They sat in silence.

"Fiona," Remy said, "we are on your side. No one here thinks you were doing anything illegal last night, other than perhaps a little underage drinking." He smiled at Catherine knowingly. While a genius at *sans voir* chess, Remy was even better at setting his parishioners at ease. Like any good priest, he knew when to wait and when to press. Ezra's years of FBI interrogations paled in comparison to Remy's decades in confessional booths. "Tell Mr. James what you told me last week."

"Why don't you, Fr. Remy?"

"You know I cannot share anything from a confession."

Fiona looked at her hands. "About Ms. Hannigan?" she asked.

The priest nodded.

"About why I hate her?"

He nodded again.

She groaned. "Brooklyn just acts so self-righteous. Like okay, she's not even a real teacher, but she barks all these orders at us. Or she talks to us like she's our buddy and then talks crap behind our backs."

"Like with Lizbeth," Remy said.

"Exactly. I told Brooklyn in confidence that Lizbeth slept with Nick and then Brooklyn went and told—" Fiona gestured toward Catherine. "And then Principal Weeks called all the parents, and now nobody is even talking to me." She pulled at the seam of her jean skirt. "That's why I threw the pee."

Teenage mean girls were definitely not Ezra's forte.

"Fr. Remy is going to sit with you for a little while and Mr. James and I will be right next door," Vargas said.

"One more question," Ezra said. "Do you have any classes with the new French teacher?"

Fiona brightened. "French III. And I'm in the French club."

"He's a pretty good teacher, huh?"

"He's the only reason I'm still at this school."

"And handsome. I mean, handsome compared to a dork like me."

"What? What do you mean?"

"Never mind," Ezra said. He didn't need her to answer. Her bright red ears said everything.

Catherine ushered them out of the office and led them to the ISS room, where Daniel Toussaint awaited. "I'm going to have a word with Fiona," she said and returned to her office.

Vargas opened the door to the ISS room but then closed it. "What was that all about?" she asked Ezra.

"About the French teacher, you mean?"

She nodded.

He shrugged. "I know Fiona's been spending a lot of time with Mr. Durand, and I've also noticed Brooklyn and him sitting together at games, drinking punch at dances, that sort of thing. I thought she might also be jealous of Brooklyn."

"Is he the one whose—"

"Wife left him, yes. Martin Durand. Recently divorced, two kids, he used to teach at a college."

"So, you think Brooklyn started up with Durand and Fiona found out about it, and that's why she threw the urine?" Vargas asked.

"I don't know a lot about teenagers," Ezra said, "but marking one's territory with urine seems pretty universal."

"The principal said it was lemonade."

"And thank God for that."

The In School Suspension room carried a different atmosphere than the principal's office. With its bare walls and bright overhead lighting, it seemed more institutional. Most of the other rooms in the school were softened by off-white plastic filters over the lights, but there were none here. The ISS room felt more like a real interrogation. Daniel Toussaint sat at a long white table.

"Daniel, thanks for meeting with us," Ezra said. They sat down across from him.

The teen didn't acknowledge them.

"I'm director of security here. I'm sure you've seen me around. I was hoping you could answer a few questions for me."

Still nothing.

"I heard you were a tough guy," Ezra said. "Hell, I know you're tough. I saw the beating you gave St. Ignatius. What did you get, a hundred yards rushing and two touchdowns?"

This disarmed Daniel momentarily. He looked up but, just as he made eye contact with Ezra, he broke it again, looking down to somewhere beneath the table.

Haitian refugee, Ezra thought. An older brother or uncle, maybe, taught him not to say anything to authorities unless absolutely necessary. Saying the wrong thing to a police officer in somewhere like Haiti could get you more than arrested. Ezra folded his hands. This was no use.

He and Vargas stepped out of the room together.

"Want to take another run at him later?" she asked.

Ezra shook his head. "That kid's not talking unless he has to."

They moved to the nurse's station where Daniel's

teammate, Royce Ainsley, waited. He was as athletic as Daniel but bulkier. Royce had aimed for that He-Man body but overshot the mark. He looked fine during football season but cartoonish when basketball season came around.

Royce pointed at Detective Vargas. "Is she the new trainer?" Not the sharpest cleat on the field, Royce thought he'd been called to the office to see the physical therapist. "It's my right shoulder."

"She knows," Ezra lied and nodded at Vargas.

Vargas took his lead and sat down beside Royce. She stretched his arm out to the side and then made little circles with it. "So you hurt this at last night's game?" she asked.

Royce looked at her strangely. "We didn't play last night."

"No? What did you do instead? It looks like there's some tightness." Vargas nodded to herself. "Definitely some tightness. You may have re-injured it."

"I was working at a soup kitchen."

"Trouble with the law?" Ezra asked and smiled.

Vargas pushed the arm forward and back in a butterfly stroke.

"Community service looks good on college applications. A bunch of us from the football team went."

"Did Coach Fleming go?" Ezra asked.

"Yeah. And Coach Larson."

"Isn't he the basketball coach?"

"The teams volunteer together. It's a lot of the same guys anyway."

"Who all went?"

"A bunch of us."

"Mason Scout? He's on the team, right?"

"Naw, not Mace. He went to the pageant."

"What about Daniel Toussaint?"

"Hmm," Royce said, hesitating.

"You know, tall Haitian kid? Likes to trick-or-treat?"

"No, not Daniel either."

Vargas folded Royce's arm and started flapping it like a chicken wing.

"What are you doing?" he asked her.

"I'm, um, assessing the cuffs."

"That's not how the last trainer did it."

"Well, that's why we fired her," Vargas said.

"The last trainer was a dude."

"You can go back to class now, Royce," Ezra said.

Royce picked up his bag and walked out.

Ezra heard voices out by the front desk. He craned his head and saw Cynthia Scout chatting with Denise at the front desk. Denise produced a clipboard, and Cynthia began writing on it. Then her son Mason appeared beside her. He joined the conversation and soon Denise was chuckling. Cynthia and Mason turned to leave but, as she grasped the handle of the door, Catherine emerged from her office and intercepted them. She placed a hand on the glass door and glared at Denise.

"Is Mason here for our meeting?" she asked the secretary.

Cynthia Scout answered instead, "Actually, I'm taking Mason to an appointment."

Denise looked between the two women and then told Catherine, "I told Ms. Scout that she could sign Mason out. Was that okay?"

"Of course," Catherine replied and removed her hand from the door.

Cynthia led her son out the front doors, putting a pair of Jackie O. sunglasses on as she went.

Remy emerged from Catherine's office. "There's something else Fiona would like to say."

The girl stood with Remy in the doorway, looking mopey. "You can't tell anyone I told you."

Ezra agreed.

"We've been doing experiments in Coach Larson's class. Electricity experiments with these big batteries."

"9-volt batteries?" Ezra asked.

"No. Bigger. Like car batteries."

Ezra thanked her. She picked up her bag and left.

"What do we do next?" Remy asked Vargas.

"We are interviewing the roommate across town later today," she said and checked the clock on her phone. "Then we'll speak with the aunt. She lives in Champagne but has been sitting with Brooklyn."

"Does she have no parents?" Remy asked.

Vargas shook her head. Then to Catherine, she added, "I'd like to speak with the faculty as well."

"I am pulling each of them during their planning periods. I should be able to speak with everyone by the end of the day and give you some ideas of who might know more." Catherine pulled an extra-large calendar off the front desk. "It looks like everyone's here."

"Not everyone," Denise said. "Coach Larson called in sick."

Catherine pointed at the calendar. "But there's no sub written down."

As they debated the correct procedures for substitute record-keeping, Vargas and Ezra continued their discussion. "I saw you speaking with Sarah Pierce last night," he said.

"She didn't have much to say, but Heather Jarno made up for it."

"Oh boy," Ezra replied. "What did the school gossip have to contribute?"

"She said that Sarah's husband made a pass at her."

"When?" Ezra asked, though he really meant "Why?"

Ms. Jarno may have been physically attractive, but she more than made up for this with a personality so grating the Army could have weaponized it. He imagined a thousand Jarnos wandering across enemy lines, bringing down the morale of the entire opposing nation.

"Some of the faculty had a Halloween party at the Pierce's house," she said. "After a few bottles of wine, Mr. Pierce slid a hand down the back of Jarno's dress. He claimed it was an accident."

"I often accidentally slide my arm into strangers' clothing," Ezra said. "Just this morning, I inexplicably found my hand in Fr. Remy's sock."

"Ha," Vargas replied.

Ezra added more seriously, "The husband angle is worth following up."

Vargas cleared her throat. "There's another thing."

Ezra waited.

"Sarah Pierce had lunch with Brooklyn at El Caribe yesterday. Then Brooklyn didn't come back."

"So Sarah is the last person to see Brooklyn before the attack?"

Vargas shrugged. "We're still working on the timeline." She slid her notepad into the pocket of her gray suit jacket. "I would like to come back and review the CCTV footage when you're ready."

"How does one o'clock sound?"

"That sounds great," she replied.

"So is that it?" Remy asked.

"One more thing," she said. "We need the contact information for your students and staff. Phone numbers, addresses, email, anything you have."

"Denise," Remy said. "Would you please print a contact sheet for Detective Vargas?"

The detective thanked him, took her stapled packet, and left. As she went, Vargas held the door for an entering mother, Annette Fleming, who walked meekly to the desk. "I'm here to check out Fiona."

Catherine nodded. "Ms. Fleming. How are you today?"

She gave Ezra a sidelong glance. "Did he interrogate her while wearing that?" She nodded at the yellow taser in its belt holster.

"There was no interrogation," Catherine said.

"I assure you," Ezra said, "at all the posh schools, their security folks carry these."

"Those cause ventricular arrhythmias," Annette said, "sudden cardiac arrest—even excited delirium."

Catherine nodded enthusiastically. "We all remember your report at the PTA meeting, but if you remember our report, Mr. James is a federal agent. He will only use the taser if there's a life-and-death situation. That," she said, pointing to the holstered weapon, "is the compromise. We wanted him to carry his service weapon, but we met you halfway."

Annette Fleming shuddered in disgust. "I wish he didn't carry anything."

Ezra took this opportunity to make his exit, as did Remy. Ten minutes later they sat in the teacher's lounge drinking lattes. As a special gift to the parish, the owner of several local coffee shops provided SJM with a home espresso machine and an assortment of syrups. The steamer attachment made a terrible mess the first week, so Catherine made them remove it. Microwaved milk, however, tasted nearly as good.

Ezra took a long sip from his pumpkin spice latte and thought about Coach Larson's electrical experiments. "How'd you get the girl to tell you about Larson?" he asked Remy.

"I just told her what her name means: Gift from God."

"That's nice. Is it true?"

"All children are a gift from God."

"So, no?"

"Do you know what your name means, Ezra?"

"A gift receipt?" He laughed at his own joke.

"Helper."

"That seems ironic," Ezra said.

"Only to you." Remy sipped his own latte, a caramel brulée. "This is very nice. We do not have this coffee in Africa."

"Which part of Africa are you from again?"

Remy smiled. "Oh, you know. The hot part."

Ezra returned to their previous topic. "So you told her about her name and she fessed up about Larson?"

"I also may have mentioned Brooklyn had an electrical burn."

"I wish you hadn't done that."

Remy nodded in understanding.

"What did you think of Daniel?" Remy asked.

"Stoic."

"How so?"

"He didn't say a word."

"They can be like that around authority figures."

"Who, refugees?"

The priest set his coffee down. "Slaves."

****

For the next hour, the priest told Ezra about the year he spent in Haiti preaching, distributing medical supplies, and doing everything he could to gently oppose slavery in the tiny Caribbean Island.

The *restavek* system, a still-intact form of child servitude imposed by the richest families of Haiti on the children of the poorest families, was integral to the social class system in the struggling country. The fact that Daniel had been a child slave until only recently was a big mark against him in Ezra's book. Violence always begets more violence, not only in his professional experience but in the collective experience of the whole world. As much as Remy liked this student, as much as he wanted to protect him, Ezra would have to pass this information along to Vargas and her partner.

"Do you have time for a quick confession?" Ezra asked.

"Always," Remy said.

Right there in the empty lounge, Ezra confessed the normal things: thoughts of the girl at the coffee shop, resentment toward the Bureau, and fresh anger toward Julia.

"Has something happened?" Remy asked.

He produced the divorce papers from his briefcase.

"This was always going to happen," Remy said.

"But it wasn't always going to happen this morning. The guy caught me on the way out of my psychiatrist's office. He knew my schedule."

"How?"

"My Google schedule is still shared with Julia."

Remy shook his head. "Ezra."

"I know what you're going to say, but I have a plan. A new plan."

"Other than finding the real Coast-to-Coast Killer?"

"I have to find the real killer. I owe it to John Lewis Straugh."

"You did not put him in prison on purpose."

"He doesn't know that," Ezra said. "He still thinks I planted evidence against him, like everybody else."

"Not everybody believes that, Ezra."

He ignored this kindness. "Finding the real killer is my only hope of being exonerated and getting back to normal, but there's something else I need to do."

"What is that?"

"No meds."

"You have to take your medication, Ezra."

"Only if my doctor says I do, right? I just met with Dr. Palacios, and he took me off two meds. I was on four; he took me off two, so now I'm down to two. That's halfway there."

"What will getting off your medications prove?"

"That I'm not crazy!"

"You were most unbalanced when you were not medicated. Or have you forgotten? Do you need me to play the tape?"

Once, after his incident at the café, Ezra called Julia at home. She didn't answer, so he left a message.

They still had a landline with an answering machine then. He left a three-minute message filled with a rambling, breathless rant, clocking in at two hundred and fifty words per minute. He sounded like a drunken auctioneer. Ezra passed on the miniature tape to Remy to play for him if need be.

"No, no."

"If you get your old job back," Remy continued, "you think Julia will come back?"

"She didn't want to have children who are, you know, disturbed. If I can show her I'm sane, it will change everything."

"There is nothing you can do about your DNA. Even if these genes were not expressed in you, you could still pass them down. She knew about your past, she met your mother, and she still married you. There is something else there."

"But can't you see how this would solve everything?"

Remy shook his head. "If she is not coming back, then she is not coming back. You cannot force her. All you can do is make sure you are healthy and happy in case she does return."

"Happy?" Ezra sighed. "I can't be happy without my wife."

"Then at least healthy. For now, that is enough."

Remy blessed Ezra, forgave him his sins, and continued.

"Slow down, *mon ami*. Assist the detective with this one. You could do some real good." Remy tapped the scar running down his face. The priest had never explained how he'd received it. Whenever he tapped it, though, Ezra knew it must have been a situation far worse than the one Ezra currently faced. "Do you know your mistake last night?" Remy asked.

"I should've stayed."

"No, in our chess game."

Ezra thought about this. "The bishop. I could've taken it when you first advanced."

"With impunity."

"How'd you know I wouldn't?"

"This business with John Lewis Straugh, with Julia leaving, has made you...oh, I do not know how to say it in English... In French, we say, *chat échaudé craint l'eau froide,* a burned cat is afraid of cold water."

"Once bitten, twice shy, maybe," Ezra said.

"I did not bother protecting my bishop because I knew you would be suspicious of such an obvious play and would second guess your instincts." Remy rose. "The Little Sisters of Teresa are hosting their banquet tomorrow night. Come."

"For one, I don't drink."

"Then come to socialize and meet more of the parish."

"And for two, I don't gossip."

Remy smiled. "One can be social without gossiping."

"Maybe on normal occasions, but these banquets are for drunken socialites to gossip about other drunken socialites."

"Then come and save me from gossiping."

"Why do you want me to come, really?" Ezra asked.

"Maybe that gossip you so disparage will turn up something. I think there is more to this than you see."

"Like what?"

"I think God isn't done with you yet. Otherwise, why put a murder right at your feet?"

"Attempted murder," Ezra said. "And we still don't know what happened."

"I see it all, right there behind your eyes. You are putting it together: motive, method, and madness. Promise me you will come to this tonight. Consider it penance."

Chapter Seven

Even though Lucia phoned ahead and Gorecki knocked loud enough to wake the whole apartment building, Brooklyn's roommate, Autumn Elkhart, answered the door in her pajamas. Her hair hung loosely in a sleep-frazzled bun, and she yawned theatrically. Her loud red and pink pajama pants reminded Lucia of a Jackson Pollock painting, and her ratty gray T-shirt announced in large red letters, "No Human Is Illegal."

Autumn Elkhart scowled at Gorecki through the cracked door but then saw Lucia and smiled apologetically. Unlike her svelte roommate, Autumn was easily a size twenty-two. There was no judgment involved on Lucia's part, only anxiety over the comments Gorecki would make, either in the roommate's presence or immediately after they left. Autumn's entire appearance, however, made Lucia reassess her initial impression of Brooklyn.

Gorecki introduced himself and Lucia. Autumn welcomed them inside.

Other people's homes always fascinated Lucia. Some mirror their inhabitants, with each aspect of the owner's life represented in some way. Others were like photography negatives. She remembered visiting a prominent lawyer's downtown loft. At trial, he was well-groomed, organized, and sharp, but his loft was such a pigsty she could barely find the kitchen.

Brooklyn and Autumn's apartment fell into the prior category. Every detail told a story about the two young women, as if the entryway and living room had been decorated by the director of a film. The dining table set consisted of a rustic square table plus four wrought iron chairs. Polka dot curtains complemented the baby blue walls from which hung vintage Parisian posters, black-and-white photographs, and oil paintings.

As the three of them sat at the rustic dining room table, Lucia asked, "Are you an artist?"

"That's right," Autumn said.

Gorecki pointed at a two-foot painting, which consisted of triangles of different colors, shapes, and textures. Crooked, flaming arrows pierced each triangle. "What's that one about?"

"I call it *Toxic Masculinity,*" she said. "Have you found the guy who hurt Brooklyn?"

Gorecki placed a small, black recorder on the table and hit record. "What makes you so sure it's a guy?"

She laughed derisively. "I thought you two were detectives."

Lucia ignored the comment. "When did you last see your roommate?"

"Yesterday morning. She went to school, and I went to the studio."

"So, for all you know, she didn't come home during the day?"

"She must have come home. At the hospital, she had on a black dress, but she went to school in pants."

Gorecki smiled. "You certainly watch her legs closely. See something you like there?"

Lucia's partner sure knew how to make a woman queasy.

"Your studio is at the Art Institute?" she asked, reading from her notes.

"School of the Art Institute of Chicago, yes. I'm there eight to four every weekday."

"This is your first year there?"

Autumn nodded. "Brooklyn and I met at Champagne. Then I was accepted at SAIC for my MFA, and Brooklyn found the student-teaching position at SJM."

It was a lot of initials to absorb.

"Can anyone confirm you were in your studio that entire time?" Lucia asked.

"People come and go, but yes. When I'm working on a project, I don't even break for lunch."

Gorecki asked the next question. "Was Brooklyn seeing anyone?"

Autumn told them about the affair, or at least as much as she knew. As with Sarah Pierce, Autumn knew the basics but not the details.

Brooklyn's relationship with the mystery man began in early October. He took her out most Thursday and Friday nights, but Autumn never met him, nor had she seen any pictures. Brooklyn wouldn't even describe him other than commenting on his physical strength and keen intelligence.

"Why wouldn't she tell you his name?"

Autumn's lips went thin. "I think either it violated school policy…"

"Or he's married," Lucia said, supplying the other logical reason.

"Did you know she was pregnant?" Gorecki asked.

Autumn nodded. "At the beginning of the semester, Brook came home one day enamored."

"With the school?" Gorecki asked.

"With the French teacher." Autumn gestured at the Parisian posters and then to a woodcut over the bookshelf. The white cursive letters read *Je t'aime*. "She's taken French since high school. She even sings it. She sang an entire French opera for her recital last semester."

"What are you saying?" Lucia asked. "Did Brooklyn say she slept with Martin Durand?"

"She didn't *not* say it."

"What *did* she say?"

"Last week, I found her on the bathroom floor bawling her eyes out." Autumn spat the words. "Then she shows me this positive pregnancy test. 'At least tell me who the guy is,' I say. She shakes her head. 'Is it that French teacher?' I ask. She doesn't say a word."

Gorecki turned off the recorder. "We'll be in touch."

"She was having dinner with someone last night," Autumn said urgently.

"Who with?" Gorecki asked.

"I don't know. But I have her phone on my 'find my phone' app, and it said she was at Blue Basil."

"Did she know you were tracking her?" Lucia asked.

"I was protecting her," Autumn said.

The company that handled Brooklyn's phone service, Finlox, was a social media/cell provider/video production company out of Finland. Lucia had been unable to access any of Brooklyn's phone data using the usual channels, and when she called the company's home office in Helsinki, she was forwarded to a prerecorded message detailing their privacy policy. "They'll sell the data to profit off a customer, but they won't give it to us to save that same customer?" Lucia had asked her partner.

Gorecki went the court route and discovered they couldn't even make a request for Brooklyn's information as long as she was alive and, theoretically, capable of objecting. Therefore, Autumn's app could prove extremely useful.

Lucia held out her hand. "We're going to need your phone."

She removed a yellow phone from her kitchen counter, a bar with three stools. "Okay, but I just need to do something real quick." She unlocked the phone, but before she could do anything, Gorecki jumped from his chair and snatched it. He was surprisingly spry for a man with more gray hairs than black.

"We'll be in touch," Gorecki said.

The detectives turned to leave.

"It's Martin Durand," Autumn said to their backs. "He did this to her. I know it!"

Gorecki opened his mouth to respond, but Lucia placed a hand on his arm. Autumn would accept it better coming from a woman. "What happened to your friend is inexcusable. All of it," she said. "But until we know more, jumping to conclusions won't benefit anyone."

Autumn averted her eyes and stared at *Toxic Masculinity* on the wall beside them.

Lucia hoped she wouldn't do anything foolish like seek vengeance.

As the detectives moved through the doorway,

Autumn stopped them. "Did I mention the break-in?"

Lucia turned. "There was a break-in?"

She nodded.

"Did you file a report?"

"No. Nothing was stolen. Or rather, nothing was stolen for good."

Gorecki removed his notepad but then held it closed against his thigh. "How did you even know someone broke in?"

"I came home one afternoon, and the front door was wide open."

"Maybe Brooklyn left it that way," Gorecki said.

"No. I left after her."

"Maybe you—"

"Brooklyn got this black pearl necklace, a gift from her secret guy. It's real pearl, white gold, not tacky at all. When I came in, I looked around and saw the opened case on her dresser."

Lucia stepped back into the apartment. "So why didn't Brooklyn report it missing?"

"She was going to, but then a few days later, the same thing happened, and the necklace had been returned. I remember her saying something about it." Autumn searched her memory. "She asked me, 'Do you think he wanted me to know he returned it?' So I asked her, 'Who? Who wanted you to know?' But she still wouldn't say."

"Where's the necklace now?" Lucia asked.

The three marched into Brooklyn's room.

"We should really have forensics—" Lucia started, but Gorecki began rummaging through her dresser.

He removed a black necklace case and placed it on top of the dresser. Lucia held her breath as he opened it.

The case was empty.

****

Ezra put off reviewing the CCTV footage until his meeting with Detective Lucia Vargas that afternoon. When he made his way down to the small monitor room in the south quadrant of the school, he found Remy already deep in conversation with Vargas.

"At mass on Wednesday Brooklyn seemed reserved," Remy said, "but I wouldn't say sad."

"The roommate said she knew about the pregnancy since last week," Vargas replied.

"Sorry, I'm late," Ezra said.

As its name implied, the monitor room contained five monitors fed from various surveillance cameras. Two cameras were located in the halls, one in the auditorium, and two outside, showing most of the school grounds.

"We'll make Evanston Police a copy of these recordings," Ezra said.

Vargas thanked him.

He took hold of a round controller and reversed all five screens in fifteen minute increments, moving from daylight to night time, until the timer read 8:00:00. "Here's Thursday night, eight p.m.," he said.

They watched at four times speed for several minutes. One exterior camera soon showed Brooklyn Hannigan in a black dress and bright red coat as she walked toward the chapel and then disappeared behind the building. She reappeared alone moments later in the belfry of the tower. Then, uncoerced, she removed her shoes, swung one leg over the railing and then the next.

She stood there motionless as if waiting for something. A gust of wind kicked up a cloud of snow thirty feet below, which filled the entire campus like a snow globe. Ezra lost sight of her entirely. Then all five monitors went black.

When the feed returned nearly two minutes later, he could just make out Brooklyn lying motionless in the snow at the foot of the tower. Then the cloud of snow obscured the camera's view again.

"Roll it back to eight again," Vargas said. She scanned the other monitors as the tape began. She pointed to the auditorium feed. "There."

Mason Scout sat to the left edge of the stage, scrolling through his phone. He scrolled idly for several moments. Then he looked up with a jolt just before the camera shut off.

"That's when the lightning struck," Remy recalled.

Ezra rolled it back again and, on an interior camera, they watched Jeb, the eighty-year-old, leave the main school building. At the door he stopped, adjusted his coke-bottle glasses, and buttoned his coat. As he pressed the door open, the camera cut to black.

"Is Jeb nearsighted or farsighted?" Ezra asked Remy.

"Neither," Remy replied with a smile.

"And he's the weekend groundskeeper only?" Vargas asked.

"Thursday through Sunday."

"Every week?"

"Every week."

The detective shifted in her seat. "Is that common knowledge?" she asked Remy.

"It's no secret that Jeb has poor eyesight or that he works on the weekends generally. Any interested party could have found out his schedule."

"How long were the cameras down?" she asked.

"Two minutes," Ezra replied. "When the power cuts out, they have to reboot."

"Has that ever happened before?"

Remy pointed in the direction of the auditorium. "They put in new stage lights at the start of the year and tripped a breaker. The whole school was in there for an assembly. Anyone could have timed it."

Ezra shrugged. "Anyone with access to the Internet could have looked up the owner's manual for these cameras."

"But the power outage," Vargas said, "could have given them the idea. Where's the main breaker?"

"The auditorium," both men said in unison.

"How does that not surprise me?" Vargas asked.

Minutes later, they stood inside the auditorium's utility room, examining the circuit breaker. "Who turned the power back on last night?" Lucia asked Ezra.

"Nobody. It was automatic. Power went out a few seconds at most. Then the systems started rebooting."

"Look," Vargas said and pointed out two indentions in the main cable.

"Do you think someone rigged a shut-off switch?" Ezra asked.

"Maybe," Vargas replied. "Were these markings here last week?"

The three looked at the tiny indentations in the black cables. Who would even notice something so minute unless they were looking for it?

"Okay," Ezra said to no one in particular, "Mason Scout connects a switch to the main power line and cuts the power right when Brooklyn falls."

Remy raised his hand.

"I know, I know, you're going to ask, 'How?' We just saw him on the video when the power went out," he said. "Maybe Mason used some sort of wireless device from his phone."

Remy kept his hand raised.

"I know, I know, you're going to ask, 'How did he know Brooklyn was about to fall? How did he know when to cut the cameras?' This was planned, set up in advance, and timed to the second."

Still, Remy's hand hung in the air. Vargas interjected, "You'd better let your priest speak."

"The *how* doesn't matter if we don't know the *why*." Remy said. "Why would an eighteen-year-old with money and every prospect kill a student-teacher?"

"A pregnant student-teacher." Ezra let the words hang in the air.

"I have a mass to prepare," Remy said. He thanked Detective Vargas and left.

Vargas opened her notepad, found a page, and handed it to Ezra. "Here's our interview with the roommate."

He read over her notes, which detailed everything from the interior decoration of the apartment to the roommate's outfit and posture. Autumn described a lover, whom she claimed was Martin Durand, the new French teacher, and spoke about Brooklyn being distraught over her pregnancy. At the bottom of the page, written in small caps, was the word "Obsessive."

"Obsessive?" he asked.

Vargas sighed. "It's a long story."

"So you want me to speak with Martin Durand?" he asked next.

"If you could. We're still working on Brooklyn's

timeline, which is slow-going."

"Have you spoken with Sarah Pierce's husband?"

"Believe me. It is on my to-do list." She frowned. Her eyes had brown bags under them as if she'd stayed up all night working on this case. "Speak to the French teacher today if you could and let me know. I'll call you later today."

"If I don't call you first," he said and smiled.

"Cute." She returned the smile, but then added, "You know, in a goofy dad way."

That one hurt.

Chapter Eight

Thirty minutes after leaving SJM, Lucia sat at her desk in the Evanston Police Department. Gorecki held Autumn's phone and periodically read off time stamps and GPS coordinates from the phone tracking app. Meanwhile, Lucia charted Brooklyn's day on a map of Evanston. The bullpen contained a half dozen metal desks with office chairs. Each desk perfectly represented the detective who occupied it. Gorecki's overflowed with files, food wrappers, and half-finished sodas. Lucia's looked like the desk in the catalogue, a place for everything and everything in its place, which is why they sat at her pristine desk and not Gorecki's haphazard one.

Brooklyn left her apartment and drove to work Thursday morning. There she stayed until lunch time, when she traveled across town to El Caribe. She stayed there until one o'clock. From there, she drove to Centennial Park and wandered up and down the beach for several hours.

"Who goes to the beach in winter?" Gorecki asked.

"Someone who has a lot to think about," Lucia replied.

At two thirty-six, Brooklyn left the park and returned to her apartment. She remained there just twenty minutes before driving to Evanston Township High School.

"Didn't you go there?" Gorecki asked.

"My sister Areli goes there now. You?"

"Cairo High, class of '98." He pronounced it "Care-o."

"Really?" she asked.

"What? You didn't know I was a country boy."

"No." She smiled. "But it does put some things in context." Lucia looked at the time difference again. "So Brooklyn returns to her home long enough to change and then heads to ETHS."

"Do you think she had a job interview?" he asked.

"She wore a black evening dress to a school interview?" Lucia asked.

"Maybe that's the only dressy thing she had," he said more to himself.

"Or she knew she'd be having dinner right afterward." She pulled up the high school's phone number. Their website listed the time of operation as seven a.m. to four p.m. Her clock read four-ten. She called anyway and got an answering machine. "I guess we'll have to go in the morning," she told Gorecki.

"Tomorrow's Saturday, Luce."

She almost told him not to call her Luce, but then for some reason it didn't bother her. Normal people were wrapping up their workday, but Lucia and Gorecki were still just getting started. Every question they answered opened another lead they'd need to follow up before Brooklyn's trail went cold.

They returned to the GPS. From ETHS, Brooklyn drove twenty minutes south to nearby Rogers Park, stopping at an apartment complex called Withering Manor. An hour later, she left Withering Manor, drove to Blue Basil, where she stayed an hour. At seven forty-seven, she left the restaurant and drove to the school, where her data stopped.

Lucia studied the address of the apartment complex. "Why does that look familiar?" She reached into her bag and removed the SJM contact sheet. Ten single-spaced pages, it contained every contact method for the students, teachers, paraeducators, and even janitors of SJM. She riffled through the pages until she came across the faculty section and pointed to a name.

Gorecki leaned over and read aloud, "Martin Durand, French."

"Security director James should be meeting with him as we speak," she said.

Lucia texted Ezra. Hopefully, he would see it before finishing up with the French teacher. Brooklyn spent nearly an hour at Durand's place, which would certainly qualify as probable cause to bring him in for questioning, but until they knew more, she wanted to wait. They could only hold a suspect for seventy-two hours, and Martin Durand didn't seem like a flight risk. If anything, he would stick around as long as possible to assert his innocence. They had plenty of time.

"I'm going to Blue Basin," she announced to Gorecki.

"Your car or mine?"

"You're coming?" she asked, surprised.

"Wouldn't miss it for the world."

She smiled a real smile. "In that case, your car."

Every type of cuisine has its own palate, its own music, its own ambiance, and its own decor. The first step into a Mexican restaurant is met with trumpets and cilantro and sizzling *carne asada*, families laughing and wait staff code-switching between English and Spanish, often merging into Spanglish. On the walls of a Greek restaurant invariably hang a blue and white striped flag, an ancient map of the Aegean Sea, and a picture of a crisp white Orthodox church against deep blue waters, while a wave of fried phyllo dough wafts through the air. For Japanese restaurants, there are flowing landscapes, calligraphy, ginger, wasabi, rice wine vinegar, and metal knives and spatulas clanking like off-beat drumsticks. Fusion restaurants, on the other hand, all look, sound, and taste the same. At least they did to Lucia. She could never tell the difference between a Korean Taco and a Peruvian Egg Roll, and she wondered if anyone could. Fusion restaurants like Blue Basil, with their clear, solid glass and angular tables, modern bars, atmospheric instrumental music, and experimental food combinations, felt homogeneous and cultureless. The more you mixed elements, the less unique they became. Red and blue made purple, but so did navy blue and pink.

Lucia stopped at the top stair in front of the glass building.

Gorecki stopped too. "What's the matter?"

"Nothing."

A thought shimmered at the edge of her consciousness. *Is this how white supremacists consider other races? Is the modern world like a fusion restaurant free-for-all to them?* The thought made her want to immediately buy a *kimchi quesadilla.*

Most of the tables inside were empty. The hostess, dressed in all black, examined her wine-colored nails. Lucia extended a photograph to her. In the photo, Brooklyn stood with her roommate Autumn next to the stainless steel Cloud Gate sculpture, affectionately nicknamed "The Bean."

"Did you work last night?" Lucia asked her.

The hostess looked up. "Every night."

"Did this woman come in?"

"Which one?"

"Either one."

She studied the photograph and shrugged. A reservation ledger sat on top of her station. She spun it around to face Lucia. "Here's the list of reservations."

In the six-thirty p.m. slot, lining up perfectly with the GPS data from Brooklyn Hannigan's phone, someone had written *Hannigan (2)* in purple ink. The name and number were crossed through; a check mark appeared to the right.

"What's that mean?" she asked, pointing to the check mark.

"That both parties arrived," the hostess replied.

Lucia showed Gorecki, who leaned over her shoulder and snapped a picture on his phone.

"Brian!" the hostess called into the restaurant.

A ruddy young man in a waiter's apron and black pants appeared beside them. "What's up?" He wiped his hands on his apron.

Lucia showed him the photograph. "Did this woman come in last night?"

He cocked his head to the side.

"You're telling me you don't remember a girl this beautiful?" Gorecki asked.

As if answering an accusation against his masculinity, the waiter took the photograph in hand. "Oh yeah, I remember her."

Lucia wished Gorecki didn't do things like this, convince people of what they knew.

"There's a two by her name," Gorecki continued. "So who met her for dinner?"

The waiter shook his head. "A guy maybe?"

Lucia tried now. "Can you describe him?"

"Um, I don't really take that much notice of guys." He puffed his chest out in the universal sign of unassailable heterosexuality.

Lucia rolled her eyes. "Tall? In a wheelchair? Had eight octopus arms? There's a woman's life at stake here, so please try to remember."

His already ruddy complexion reddened more brightly. "Sorry. I really don't know. We have a lot of people come through. It's college students and young professionals. There's a lot of beautiful women in Chicago." He frowned and handed the photo back. Then he looked instinctively at the hostess as if she might have an answer.

Lucia returned her attention to the hostess. "Do you have security cameras here?"

"We don't really cater to the surveillance crowd," she said obliquely.

People who frequented high-end establishments didn't relish the idea of having their every encounter on camera.

Then the hostess added, "The stop lights have cameras, but I think they just get license plate numbers and that sort of thing."

Gorecki took down the waiter and hostess' information. He then assured Lucia that he'd pull license plates from anyone who drove through the four intersections around Blue Basil from an hour before the reservation until the time Ezra found Brooklyn. That would hopefully cast a large enough net. If anyone even remotely connected to the school met Brooklyn for dinner, they would find out.

Chapter Nine

Ezra's visit to Martin Durand's locked classroom at the end of the day told him nothing. He looked around the hall and then crouched down onto the floor to see if he could make out anything through the crack under the door. Nada.

"He's not here," a female voice said behind Ezra.

The bell had rung several minutes before, but students and teachers still filtered through the halls. He turned and saw Fiona Fleming. "I'm embarrassed," he said from the ground. "Why isn't Monsieur Durand here?"

"Because of his fucking bitch of an ex-wife."

Ezra waited for her to elaborate.

"I'm sorry I called her a bitch, but that's just how I talk." She paused. "You know what? I'm not sorry, because she is a fucking bitch." She took a deep breath. "I mean, she only lets him see his kids every other weekend which is why he leaves early. Otherwise, he'd have to wait until eight to pick them up."

"Does Principal Weeks know he leaves early?"

Fiona paled. "Are you going to tell her?"

Ezra assured her that he wouldn't. "Tell me more."

"I would, but I'm late for wrestling practice."

"You're the manager or something?" he asked.

"Why would you think that? Because I'm a girl? Typical white male—"

He began to apologize.

"I'm fucking with you!"

"Oh good, because I thought maybe a cute girl like you—" he started to say.

"I mean about the misogyny thing. I totally am a wrestler—and I blow these wimps out of the water." She threw her backpack over her shoulder and strolled off down the stairs. "I'm sorry for all the swearing," she said, stopping halfway down the stairwell. "If you tell Mr. Durand about what I said, could you leave that part out? He doesn't like it when I swear." She looked far away for a moment and then smiled. "He says I'm too lovely a girl to say such unlovely things." With that, Fiona Fleming tossed her curly blonde hair over her shoulder and skipped off to wrestling practice.

Were male teachers supposed to call their female students "lovely"? What if Brooklyn's pregnancy wasn't the reason for her attack? What if Brooklyn found out something she shouldn't have?

Ezra's phone vibrated with a text from Vargas.

—*Brooklyn spent an hour at Martin Durand's place last night*—

—*When?*— he texted back.

—*Five to six*—

—*How do you know?*—

—*Roommate was tracking her phone with an app. Brooklyn didn't know*—

He took a beat to absorb the information. Clearly, Brooklyn had a close relationship with Martin, which he hadn't volunteered to Catherine Weeks during their informal meeting. She spent all of Friday visiting with each faculty member during their planning periods. Well, each faculty member beside the basketball coach,

Benjamin Larson, who had called in sick that morning.

Then there was Brooklyn's roommate. How long had Autumn Elkhart been stalking Brooklyn, and to what end?

Ezra crafted his next response carefully. *—Durand left school early today. I'm heading to his apartment now. Will pursue the student angle—*

—Fiona Fleming?—

—What if Brooklyn found out something she wasn't supposed to?—

Vargas started to reply but stopped.

—Do I bring up that Martin is the last person to see Brooklyn before the attack or should I wait?— he texted.

The response came back fast and sure. *—Do it—*

****

If you walk off the grounds of St. Joseph and Mary and look south, you'll encounter a sea of intricate and beautiful roofs, two and three stories high, poking through lush green trees. This is not where Martin Durand or most of his colleagues lived. In fact, if SJM were a public school, Durand would've lived miles outside the school boundary. Twenty minutes away, in nearby Rogers Park, sat Durand's apartment complex, Withering Manor.

Though the building itself didn't inspire awe, his front door at least was state-of-the-art. Rather than a rusty metal lock, a plastic fob sensor jutted out from the doorknob. Ezra knocked on the door and a few seconds later stood face-to-face with the French teacher. He now noticed what every woman at SJM long ago noticed, Martin's athletic build, strong chin, and soft blue eyes. Ezra assessed the man's outfit—checkered

Oxford shirt, a blue bow tie, and thin-framed silver glasses—and wondered if Martin had stolen it off the mannequin of a Humanities Professor.

From the drabness of Withering Manor's exterior, Ezra expected a sparse bachelor's pad, but the living room was decorated with antiques, oil paintings, and solid oak bookcases filled with leather-bound and hardcover books. Family photographs covered one wall. His ex-wife, Gemma, appeared in all of them. Her blonde curly hair caught Ezra's attention. She looked like a grown-up version of Fiona. He decided to use this as his opening.

"I spoke with Fiona Fleming this morning," he said. "I can't help but notice her resemblance to—"

"My daughter, I know." Martin gestured to his little girl. She sat cross-legged in front of an oversized plastic castle. "That's the running joke at the school, anyway."

The little girl did, in fact, resemble Fiona. Showing preference for students who resembled your family— wife or daughter—was only natural, mammalian behavior 101, but that didn't rule out something more sinister.

"So why all the pictures of your wife?" Ezra asked next. "Sorry, your *ex-wife*. Don't people usually try to build a little distance between their ex and themselves after a divorce?"

"I don't have any idea what people do. I believe it's good for the kids to continue to see us as a family. No hard feelings. And who knows, Gemma may still come back one day. I don't want to rule out that possibility either."

"I don't think women come back from something

like this," Ezra said.

"I hear you are in the same boat," Martin replied.

Ezra gritted his teeth. He thought carefully and decided to keep his focus on the students. "What can you tell me about Daniel Toussaint?"

"He's a new student, very bright, gifted athlete. His conversational French is about as good as mine, though his grammar needs work."

"Do you have any reason to believe he might have violent tendencies?"

The French teacher furrowed his brows. "Is this a race thing, Mr. James?"

"Nothing of the sort. He and a few buddies went by Brooklyn's house Halloween night. They pelted the window with rocks and then serenaded her."

"I heard about that," Martin replied, frowning.

"Also Daniel was supposed to help out at the soup kitchen last night but didn't show. Any idea why he skipped it?"

Martin shrugged. "Kids do stupid things."

Ezra decided to close in on the subject at hand.

"How well do you know the student-teacher? The one who jumped from the bell tower."

Martin shook his head. "You and I both know Brooklyn didn't jump or try to hang herself or whatever ridiculous story the kids are saying. This was an attack," he said. "I wish I could help. I really do."

There were two reasons to say this out loud. Either he deduced the situation and was being honest because he had nothing to hide, or he knew his involvement with Brooklyn would come to light and wanted to get ahead of it.

"Would you say students liked Brooklyn?"

"Generally, yes. She's butted heads with a few of the students, as do we all."

"Students like Fiona?"

"Fiona comes to mind. However, I can't imagine anyone having this much of a grudge against Brooklyn. Not for everyday classroom conflicts."

"How would you describe her?"

"Friendly. A bit talkative. Nosey. The kids say good things about her, so I'm sure she'll make a good teacher someday. There's some talk about her starting full-time in the spring."

"How would you describe her physically?"

"Red hair, average height, blue eyes," he said as if describing a perp.

"Would *sexy* be a fair description?"

He scratched his neck. "Sexy?"

"To you, I mean."

"To me?" he said. "Objectively? Sure, she's attractive."

"How about subjectively? Did you and Brooklyn ever hook up?"

Here was Martin's opening to come clean.

"Oh no, never."

"You're a single man now."

"I'm sorry, but in my eyes and in the Church's eyes, Gemma and I are still very much married. That may seem old fashioned to you."

"It doesn't," Ezra said. "Do you know anyone she may have been having a relationship with?"

"As I said, I wish I could help, but that's all I know."

Interrogations, interviews, taking statements, whatever you wanted to call it, were different every time. Every beat cop, state trooper, detective, and special agent Ezra had ever worked with approached these conversations a little differently, as did every person being interviewed. What Ezra learned during his brief military career in the Air Force's Office of Special Investigations was that no matter what your style, you eventually had to be the asshole. Not with every person or every conversation, but eventually there you were, poking the bear. Or perhaps he just preferred the style.

"What drew you to study French literature," he asked, "rather than something more useful?"

"What do you mean by useful?"

"Spanish, Chinese, Klingon, hell, I bet pretty much any other language comes in handy more often than French."

"Not necessarily. French is the second most learned—"

"But don't all those Parisians speak English? My friend in the Bureau studied French all through high school and college. Then his junior year at Yale, he did a year abroad in Paris. They wouldn't even let him speak it, just replied in English."

"That may be the case in Paris, but I assure you the native speakers in Africa—"

"You spent some time abroad?"

"I did some work with the Church after college. I even considered joining the priesthood when I returned to the states, but then I met Gemma."

"And the rest is history, as they say," Ezra said. "Or should I say it was history? I think I read a piece of French literature in college, a novel about an older man who had an affair with a teenage girl, a student of his if I remember correctly. Do you know that one?"

"I'm afraid not."

"Oh, don't trouble yourself. I'll find out."

Martin opened his mouth to speak, but Ezra cut him off. "Yesterday after school, where'd you go?"

"Home."

"Alone?"

Martin averted his eyes and then pretended to hear something in the kitchen. "I should check on—"

"Alone? You came home alone yesterday and remained here alone all evening?"

Tapping one foot, he looked back through the doorway at his daughter. "No. Brooklyn stopped by."

"Because from what I hear, she did more than stop by. She stayed. What reason could she have to stay here for over an hour?"

"An hour? No," he said. His eyes met Ezra's. "She wanted a letter of recommendation." He pointed out the front window. "I invited her in while I typed it up. She couldn't have stayed more than fifteen, twenty minutes."

"Then you printed it off?"

"Emailed it."

"Where?"

"Evanston Township High School."

That's all Martin knew, or all he was willing to share. Ezra didn't force him to share more.

Martin knelt beside his little girl and her castle. The figurines were standard castle fare: a princess in a pink conical hat with a long train, a knight in shining armor, a prince charming, a queen, a king, and a jester.

"I bought this castle thinking she'd create her own King Arthur and the Knights of the Round Table, her own Beowulf and Grendel. Instead, she just recreates everyday scenes from our lives."

"Princess!" the miniature knight said now. "Your mommies are here. Time to get off the toilet!"

"I'm pooping!" the princess shouted back through the wall. "Tell my mommies to wait a minute. Sheesh."

"She's cute. Is she in the preschool?"

He nodded. "The four-year-old class. Our son's a second-grader this year."

"Can you think of anything else?" Ezra asked.

"Nothing." Martin bit his lip. "Brooklyn has a roommate. That may be worth following up on."

"Evanston PD already interviewed her."

"Daddy, can I have more apple juice?" the little girl asked.

"*Demandez en français, s'il vous plaît.*"

"*Je voudrais des jus, Papa.*"

"*S'il...*"

"*S'il vous plaît.*"

"Bye, bye, little princess," Ezra told her.

She ignored him.

"She gets very absorbed," Martin said. "Don't worry."

"Oh, I'm not worried," Ezra said, but he had a feeling that Martin Durand was worried. Very worried. "Before I forget, can anyone account for your whereabouts after Brooklyn left?"

"No. The kids were with Gemma this week, so I got ahead on my grading."

"You did that here, not at the school?"

He nodded.

"Did you put any grades in the computer, by chance? Those might be time-stamped."

He shook his head. "Just graded essays by hand. Is

that going to be a problem?"

Not for me, Ezra thought. "Just try to think of anyone you may have spoken to or places you may have gone, food you ordered, things like that. Jot down the approximate times if you can. It may prove important if there is a more extensive investigation." There would certainly be one.

"Honestly, I stay in the house when the kids are gone." He seemed to consider this for a moment and then nodded. He walked unevenly to the door and opened it for Ezra. "Oh, and detective, before I forget, it's Heloise and Abelard. What you read in college. It's like the French equivalent of Romeo and Juliet."

Ezra knew this, of course. He wrapped his scarf around his neck, thanked Martin Durand, and left. The French teacher didn't seem violent, but everyone was capable of violence.

****

Ezra drove back to the school to update Remy, but then he went to the crime scene instead. Maybe Vargas and her partner missed something.

He crunched his way through the snow up to the bell tower and climbed the stairs. From the belfry, he could see the whole school, but several inches of snow still covered every surface besides the shoveled streets and sidewalks.

He examined the belfry. Along the edges were signs of wind and toe prints from two different sets of shoes. He surmised these were left by Vargas and Gorecki but texted Vargas a photo nonetheless.

—*These yours?*—

She responded moments later. —*Gorecki's and mine, yes.*—

—I assume the wedge-toes are yours?—

—You clearly don't know my partner very well— she replied. Then a second later, she added, *—Sorry, yes.—*

One set of prints, which he took to be Brooklyn's, led through the belfry and straight to the railing. Whatever happened occurred while she stood on the ledge. Did she jump and then get tased on the ground? That seemed unlikely, but so did much of this.

Then again, there stood the bronze bell. Depending on its chemical composition, it could make an efficient conductor. What if someone wired it with car batteries like the ones Coach Benjamin Larson supposedly had. If Brooklyn stuck her head into the space between the bell and the belfry platform, the wired bell would've shocked her unconscious.

Then again, wouldn't there be more than this single set of crisp, confident footprints leading straight to the ledge? There would be prints in the snow from where she knelt and where she fell.

In the failing evening light, he barely caught a tiny glint of metal by the railing. He turned a plastic sandwich bag inside out, then picked the metal up. On closer inspection, it resembled the eye of a necklace, silver or white gold from the looks of it.

For some reason, Ezra recalled a piece of writing from college about lovers who fit together like a hook into an eye. Not a necklace clasp and an eyelet. A fishhook and an open eye. He knew that kind of relationship, even as a college student.

He bet Brooklyn knew it too.

Chapter Ten

Lucia left Blue Basil and headed to the law office of Mark Pierce, alleged lusty husband of primary school teacher Sarah Pierce. Gorecki did not offer to accompany her, but she couldn't exactly blame him. Gorecki had a wife and a dog at home. Lucia had a frozen dinner and a stack of library books. Most evenings she finished up reports or visited her mom's place to bother her little sister. So Friday evening, she visited Mark Pierce alone.

The law firm of Sheffield and Sheffield took up the third floor of a glass high-rise on Monroe in downtown Chicago. As Lucia stepped into Pierce's cramped cubicle, she lost all faith in the affair theory. Pierce was a far-sighted, pudgy man in a worn-out suit and a ten-dollar haircut. Brooklyn wasn't just out of his league; they played different sports, in different countries, at different points in history. All Mark Pierce needed to complete his ensemble was a thick layer of tape around the bridge of his glasses.

After Lucia showed him her badge, Pierce offered her his seat, the only chair available.

"It's fine. I'll stand," she replied. "How well do you know Brooklyn Hannigan?"

"Who?" he asked.

"Did your wife not tell you about last night?"

"About what?"

She shifted her weight to her back foot, acquiring a stance of incredulity. "About what happened at the Christmas concert."

"The *school* concert? What could've possibly happened at a school concert?"

Lucia pinched the bridge of her nose. "Let's start over. Where were you last night?"

"Here," he said.

"Until when?"

"Time is conceptual at this point," he said, laughing at his own wit.

Lucia thought about slapping the man. Instead, she asked, "Where did you go after work?"

"The gym."

"Straight from here to the gym?"

Pierce nodded.

"Extreme Energy?" she asked. It was just down the street from the firm.

"The place with the smoothie bar?" He laughed again. "That place is like two hundred bucks a month. No, I go to Run Fast Gym."

Run Fast Gym consisted of a single room packed gill to gill with treadmills.

"Let me get this straight, you're a lawyer and your wife teaches at an upscale private school, but you go to the sketchiest gym in Evanston?"

"St. Joseph and Mary doesn't pay any better than Orrington Elementary did. It just means our kids, when they're in school, will get to attend for free." Pierce paused to take a long sip of coffee from a bright yellow thermos with *World's 2nd Best Lawyer* scrawled across one side. "As for me, I'm a first-year associate; I'm practically paying the Sheffields to work here."

Maybe, Lucia decided, if she bonded with him, he would be more helpful. "I love *Better Call Saul.*"

"Who?"

She indicated his thermos.

He picked it up. "I found this in the break room."

She guessed bonding wasn't going to happen. "Look, there was an incident at the school involving a student-teacher named Brooklyn Hannigan. If you think of anything relevant, give me a call." She gave him her card. "Or you can tell Ezra James. He's the security director."

Mark Pierce laughed a third time.

"What? What could possibly be funny about that?"

"I still can't believe that guy's in charge of security. You know his story, right?"

"I know he works for the FBI."

"Have you ever seen a federal agent working in school security?"

Lucia didn't reply.

"You really don't know about him, do you?" He looked her dead in the eyes. "Special Agent James planted evidence in a federal case. The Straugh Case. That was him. He put a guy in prison for two years, some tech genius. Then the courts overturned it. I can't believe you didn't read about it. You're in law enforcement, for Pete's sake."

He pushed files around on his desk until he located a copy of today's *Chicago Tribune.* Above the fold were two headlines. The main one concerned a recent social-justice protest held downtown. Underneath that was a smaller headline: *Disgraced Federal Agent First to Find Victim.*

The lead paragraph focused not on the victim,

Brooklyn Hannigan, but instead on Ezra, reminding every *Tribune* reader of the agent's scandalous past.

Lucia had heard about the Straugh Case and knew the Chicago Field Office assisted with it, but the fine details escaped her. None of the murders took place in Chicago or even Illinois. CTC was the name given to the serial killer because he'd bounced from coast-to-coast. Someone fingered this Straugh guy for it, and the local FBI assisted. Then it went to trial. She couldn't recall the rest.

"I was in Springfield when that all happened," she said. "This is only my second year at Evanston PD." *And my first month as a detective,* she wanted to say. "What else do you know about Ezra James?"

"Rumors mainly. Lots of them." He shifted his attention back to his computer. "Google him. The *Tribune* sold ads for a year thanks to all the stories they wrote about him."

She held up the paper. "Can I keep this?"

He nodded.

On her way out, she stopped by the front desk. "Is this the only way into these offices?"

The secretary nodded.

"Do you know Mark Pierce?"

"What's this about?" the secretary asked.

"I just need to confirm something." Lucia showed her badge. "Did Mark work late last night?"

"He works late every night," she said, "but yes, last night, too."

"Until when?"

"I left around nine. He was still here. You can check his computer, though. The firm's intranet monitors when everyone logs in and logs out and whether or not they are actually doing work or just have their computers on."

"Sounds like a fun place to work," Lucia said sarcastically.

The woman rolled her eyes and then let her gaze rest on the counter between them.

The groundskeeper found Brooklyn's unconscious body around eight-fifteen p.m. If Mark Pierce worked until nine, he would've needed some help. Although Lucia supposed he would've needed far more help convincing Brooklyn to sleep with him.

Her next stop was to Run Fast Gym where she spoke to a college student manning the reception desk. She confirmed that Mark checked in at nine-forty-five the previous night and stayed until eleven.

"Little guy," the student said. "He comes in after most people have left so he can get the machine right in front of the TV."

Lucia made a quick visual check of the room. There were three dozen treadmills but only one TV, and it wasn't large.

She wanted to cross out Mark Pierce's name in her notebook. Earlier, she'd written "affair" beside his name, but now crossed that out and added the closest word she could think of to characterize Mark Pierce: *Drudge*.

****

Saturday

First thing Saturday morning, Gorecki sent Lucia a text.

—*Just left a file on your desk.*—
—*What about?*— she replied.
—*Daniel Toussaint.*—

—It's my day off.—
—Suit yourself.—

Lucia groaned. There was no way she was going in today. Everything would still be there waiting for her Monday morning.

She stared at her keys, then picked them up anyway and headed to the door.

The Toussaint file lay on top of her desk, a list of license plate numbers on the top. She looked around the bullpen for any sign of Gorecki but didn't see him.

The timestamps began at five-thirty p.m. and stopped at eight p.m., representing the time frame from when Brooklyn left the French teacher's apartment in Rogers Park to when she appeared on the CCTV cameras at SJM. Gorecki had highlighted four plate numbers in green. They were, in chronological order, Rebecca Dugan, Brooklyn Hannigan, Cynthia Scout, and Autumn Elkhart.

So the roommate *had* followed Brooklyn to the restaurant. She forgot to mention that little bit of information in her interview.

In the right margin, Gorecki added notes in blue ink. Beside Rebecca Dugan's name, he wrote, "Adoptive mother of Daniel Toussaint, international student at SJM." Beside Cynthia Scout's name, he wrote, "Mother to Mikayla, a fifth grader, and Mason, a senior, both at SJM."

So Gorecki had done his homework. This surprised Lucia, though it shouldn't have. He was in fact a city detective in Chicago, not a Cairo bumpkin.

She then read through the Daniel Toussaint file. The Dugans, Rebecca and Patrick, owned a restaurant in North Chicago but were long residents of Evanston.

They never had children of their own but frequently fostered or adopted teenagers from difficult situations.

She read on. The adoption forms contained limited information about Daniel's biological parents. The father, a police officer, died during a riot in Cap Haïtien when Daniel was seven. The mother found work in the Dominican Republic and left her son with an aunt. When the mother never returned, the aunt sent Daniel to live with a wealthy family in Port-au-Prince to be educated and to serve as their *restavek,* or child servant. This is why Daniel came to the attention of a Catholic adoption agency, and through this agency he came to the attention of the Dugans.

Lucia had never known a slave personally. She knew of them but hadn't interacted with one before. As a girl, she'd seen people treated just as poorly as slaves, though. Chihuahua teemed with men desperate for work and with child laborers. One boy from her neighborhood sold tamales out of a blue cooler, the top held on with duct tape. If he didn't sell enough tamales, his father would beat him. If he sold everything but it took too long, his father would beat him. Lucia eventually concluded the father just wanted to beat his son. Lucia's own home life, not much better than his, didn't afford her the freedom to pity the tamale boy, but her heart certainly went out to Daniel now. The things some people went through in life…

Lucia debated swinging by the restaurant but decided instead to call first. Rebecca Dugan told her Daniel had volunteered at a soup kitchen Thursday night. Lucia knew from her conversation with Royce Ainsley that Daniel had never shown up. After she related this fact to Ms. Dugan, the line went silent for a moment, then the sounds of muffled whispers told her Ms. Dugan was conferring with someone away from the phone.

"Can I call you back?" Ms. Dugan asked finally.

"This is very important, ma'am."

A new voice came on the phone, deeper, less sure. "Hello?"

"Is this Daniel Toussaint?" Lucia asked.

"This he."

"We know you were not at the soup kitchen Thursday night."

Again the line went silent.

"We need to know where you were."

Lucia waited for the line to go dead, but instead Ms. Dugan returned. "He says he drove around with friends and ate hamburgers."

What a strangely worded alibi. Then again, English was a second or possibly third language for the teenager.

"What friends?"

"Paul Baptiste," she said. "He works at M Burger. It's in Water Tower Plaza."

"Who else?"

"He says he only knew Paul."

Lucia jotted all of this down and thanked Ms. Dugan.

Paul Baptiste's information came up immediately on the website Finlox, a popular new social media site. A Haitian refugee, Paul Baptiste left Haiti after the 2010 earthquake. That single disaster killed a quarter of a million people, displaced millions more, and sent the country into anarchy. As well as being in the country longer than Daniel, Paul was four years older. Not old enough to buy Daniel beer but certainly old enough to offer him a little more freedom.

Next, she called Water Tower Plaza. M Burger opened at eleven.

"And Saturday is supposed to be my day off," she said aloud to the empty bullpen.

Chapter Eleven

Late that morning, Ezra received a lunch invitation from Detective Lucia Vargas. The invitation was both confusing and conducted entirely via text messages. When he suggested they get Vietnamese around noon, she said no.

—*Where?*— he texted.

—*The M Burger at Water Tower Plaza*— she replied.

This couldn't be just lunch. —*On my way.*—

He arrived at Water Tower Plaza at a quarter to eleven. Detective Vargas was already there, dressed for a day on the job: black pants, plum blouse, and a three-quarter sleeve black blazer. Just as he expected, this was not a social lunch. In fact, he doubted they had come to eat at all. Vargas sat in a plastic chair, pushing the chair onto the back legs like a high schooler waiting for class to start.

"Is this the cool kids' table?" Ezra asked.

She looked around the empty food court and gestured into the distance. "I think there are some empty seats over there."

He nodded toward the burger joint. "I should remind you I'm not officially assigned to this investigation beyond the grounds of St. Joseph and Mary's."

"Want me to run it by your ASAC?"

"Quite the contrary," he said.

Before going up to the counter, she brought Ezra up to speed about Paul Baptiste, the friend Daniel Toussaint supposedly spent Thursday evening with.

"So you spoke with him?"

"Yes. I spoke with Daniel and his adoptive mother."

She told him how little she'd learned from the conversation. At first he'd lied about his whereabouts, claiming to have attended the volunteer night at the soup kitchen. Once caught in the lie, he offered a vague account about driving around with his friend Paul, eating hamburgers.

"Why did he lie about it?" Ezra asked.

"I suspect something illegal, underage drinking or illicit drug use, maybe."

"Before I forget." Ezra pulled the plastic bag containing the necklace eye from his pocket. "I found this in the belfry."

She examined it closely and then pocketed it. "We'll see if a busted necklace or bracelet surfaces."

"I don't remember Brooklyn wearing any jewelry when we found her."

Lucia shook her head. "Shall we?"

M Burger was nearly deserted at eleven a.m. Paul Baptiste's supervisor, a nineteen-year-old with bad acne and wavy red hair, allowed Paul to visit with Ezra and Vargas.

"Daniel Toussaint claims he spent last Thursday night with you and some of your friends," Vargas said.

Paul looked from Vargas to Ezra.

Ezra nodded encouragingly. "It's important for Daniel that we verify this."

"Yes, we spent Thursday night together."

Paul's English was better than Daniel's. His enunciation was more precise, and his accent was merely ornamental.

"How many people in total were in your car?"

Paul hesitated, then said, "Four." Paul gave them the names, which Vargas jotted down.

"Two in the front, two in the back?"

"Yeah."

"Daniel said you got food. Where from?"

"It was just fast food."

"Around here?" Vargas asked, naming a few local favorites.

"We went to Big Benny's."

"What did everyone order?"

He gave a detailed account of their meals.

"That was the Benny's on Chicago Avenue?"

"I don't know the streets," he said.

She gestured beyond the building. "It's around the corner, a few minutes' walk from here."

"Yes. That's the one."

"All four of you, even Daniel?"

"Yes, even him."

"Right near that college." She snapped her fingers. "What's it called?"

"Loyola Law Center," Ezra said.

"Yes," Paul said with more confidence. "That's the one."

A young couple filed past, their arms interlocked. The pop song playing overhead seemed to be there just for them. Paul's eyes followed them to the counter. His boss manned the register now.

Lucia cleared her throat. "Okay, Thursday night.

You went to the Big Benny's on East Chicago Avenue. And ordered hamburgers."

Paul nodded emphatically.

"Did you get fries? Have to get fries with a burger."

"Yes," Paul replied, still nodding.

She smiled. "There's your first mistake, Pauley."

He stopped nodding.

"They're remodeling. Putting in a bigger..." she snapped her fingers again.

"Fryer," Ezra said.

Paul seemed to be considering his options. "Okay, Daniel was with me, but it was just the two of us, and we didn't go to Benny's. He lied to the Dugans about that."

"Did you tell him to lie?" Vargas asked.

More people joined the line now. The sizzle of beef and smell of fry oil wafted past them.

"Lots of people panic when they're being interrogated," Ezra tried.

Paul spoke up, haltingly, "It wasn't Daniel's idea. Someone at his school told him not to say anything."

Ezra asked, "A teammate?"

"A coach. He asked Daniel what he was doing when the teacher was attacked."

"Which coach? His football coach?"

"I don't think so."

"Coach Larson?" Ezra asked.

"That sounds right."

Vargas jotted down something in her notebook. "What did the coach say exactly?" she asked.

"He told Daniel to come up with a better alibi." Paul swallowed hard. "I think Coach didn't want Daniel

114

getting into trouble."

"What were you two doing?"

Paul looked down at his hands.

"You need to tell us. If you're involved in drugs or were out drinking, that's not good, but it will help establish Daniel's alibi."

"Nothing illegal. He said he needed a ride to a pawnshop."

"Was he buying or selling?" Vargas asked.

"He didn't say. I think he wanted to find something, though. We drove around for a couple hours."

"Did you go into the shop with him?" Vargas asked.

Paul shook his head. "He wouldn't let me."

For the next five minutes, Vargas wrote down the name and approximate location of each of the pawnshops the boys visited. Paul remembered a surprising number of their names. For others, he gave physical descriptions or where they were in relation to other landmarks. Ezra pulled them up on his phone, one by one, until Paul confirmed Daniel and he had visited them. The list contained seven stores, most of them in Chicago proper. He couldn't remember what order they visited them.

"Is the order important?" Paul asked.

Vargas sighed. "Considering he probably stopped once he found what he was looking for, yes. Do you remember if you stopped in Chicago or back in Evanston?"

Paul put his face in his hands. "No." Then he added, "You're not going to deport him, are you?"

Vargas closed her notebook. "If what you've told

us is true, we'd have no reason to."

Ezra stood. "And you're sure you don't know what he was looking for?"

Paul shook his head. He had the hollow look of someone who'd just given blood.

Vargas gave him her card and told him to call if he remembered anything else.

As they left the food court, Ezra asked Vargas, "Are they really remodeling the Benny's on East Chicago?"

"How should I know?"

"Think we can trust Paul Baptiste?"

"For now," she said.

"Today feels like a good day for shopping," he said.

"You want to hit some pawn shops?"

"Bingo."

Then Vargas stopped dead in her tracks. Her fingers wrapped around Ezra's arm like a vise.

"What?" he asked.

She pointed straight ahead.

"Jane's Pretzels."

"You're a pretzel girl, huh? I never would've guessed."

"Buy me a cinnamon-sugar," she said. "You owe me."

He didn't ask what he owed her for. His gaze was on a sweet almond pretzel for himself.

Chapter Twelve

Ezra and Vargas decided to visit the pawnshops Paul Baptiste mentioned. "Cool car," Vargas said as she climbed into Ezra's purple sedan.

"Thanks," he said.

"I was being sarcastic."

"It's a sleeper," he replied.

"As in, what, just fit for sleeping in?"

"It means it looks ordinary but is a good street racer," he explained.

"I know what a *sleeper* is," Vargas replied. "Sarcasm again. So are you some kind of car guy?"

"No, I just asked around the office about fast cars that blended in."

Vargas laughed. "*The office,* he says, like it isn't the FBI field office. I love that you brag about a car you know nothing about and then undersell your job."

He loved this car. With its hardwood dash, brown leather seats, and analogue clock, it transported Ezra to a different era. Add in the six-speed manual transmission and the car fit Ezra perfectly.

He started it up and headed instinctively toward Chicago Avenue. They drove in silence awhile before he asked, "Is the FBI an aspiration of yours? Were you one of those little girls who watched *Silence of the Lambs* until the tape broke in the VCR?"

She ignored the question, dripping as it was with

condescension. "Why would you need a sleeper as your personal car? Did you do a lot of stakeouts on your own time?"

He went quiet again.

"Keeping an eye on the missus?" she asked and laughed.

Ezra didn't. Laugh that is.

"My mistake." She produced the list of pawnshops. "Before we check these out, I want to stop by Benjamin Larson's place. Do you know the address?"

Ezra nodded.

Coach Larson called in sick Friday, possibly even skipped town. He lived in an apartment complex called Prairie Palace, but there was nothing pastoral or palatial about it. The three-story, indistinct building was nestled between a strip mall and an overpass, a short drive from Evanston. The blinds, off-white and broken in places, were the first thing Ezra noticed.

While the outer walls of the building were free of graffiti, the dumpsters were covered in it. As they drove by, the pungent smell of soupy garbage billowed in through the windows. Ice and snow had melted and mixed with whatever was inside the dumpsters. Clearly, this place was not a top priority for the Department of Waste, not with the inches of packed snow and ice covering the roads in every corner of Chicago. He parked along a side street that was well-concealed by houses and boxwood shrubs. The spot gave them a clear sight of Larson's apartment.

"So where does Larson fall on your list of suspects?" he asked Vargas.

"Everyone's a suspect," she replied. "I'm sure you know how that goes."

"And the French teacher, Martin Durand?"

"Oh, you know," she said again.

Not knowing more about their process bothered him for some reason. Did she suspect him of being involved somehow? He was peering at the front of the apartment building through a boxwood bush when a knock came at his window. There stood a giant panda, or rather an adult dressed in a panda suit.

"Good concealment," Vargas scoffed. "Are you going to get rid of him?"

"No, I thought I'd let him alert everyone in the neighborhood to our presence."

"That seems like a poor plan."

Ezra rolled down the window. "What can we do for you?"

Panda-man said nothing. Likely he couldn't hear through the ridiculous panda mask. When he did speak, the words were muffled.

"What's that?" Vargas asked.

"Leave or die," the panda-man said louder.

Ezra unclipped his holster. He inched his yellow taser out slowly, but Vargas clasped his arm. She raised an outstretched hand toward the panda-man and took a flyer from him.

"Beef Stir Fry" it read in large, mock-Chinese letters. The panda-man padded off down the street in the direction of the strip mall.

"He doesn't walk like a panda," Ezra said.

"You thought he was a real panda." She chuckled and shook her head. "After we're done with the pawn shops—"

"Yeah?"

"We should come back for some egg rolls."

"Think they have that spicy mustard?" he asked.

"They must. It's a rule."

Moments later, Ezra spotted Larson's car. He recognized it from the faculty parking lot. A UNLV sticker, red letters over top a cowboy hatted and generously mustachioed mascot, took up most of the back window of his silver pickup truck.

"He's home."

"Let us go and make our visit," Vargas said.

"Why do I know that line?" he asked himself.

She gave him an enigmatic look and stepped out of the vehicle. "You take the lead," she said as they mounted the stairs.

Coach Benjamin Larson taught chemistry I & II, physics, and all of the AP science courses at SJM. In Ezra's own time in school, he never saw a boy's head coach teach such challenging courses. Most career coaches, in his experience, taught PE, health, or social studies. Rarer still was a basketball coach working over the weekend as Larson seemed to be when he answered his door. His laptop sat on a simple glass-topped coffee table. Beside it lay a stack of lab reports.

"Mr. James?" he asked. It was half a greeting and half an attempt at remembering Ezra's name. He wore the stubble of a blond beard, perhaps to compensate for his receding hairline.

"Sorry to bother you, Coach, but we have a few questions."

Ezra introduced Detective Vargas and explained the purpose of their visit. Larson invited them in.

The coach, middle-aged and balding, still looked solid and virile. He had the "coach look" some carry even off the field, casual but commanding. His short, blond stubble helped. "Hope I haven't done anything wrong."

Ezra smiled. "So do I. We have a few questions about one of your students." He pretended to consult his notes. "Fiona Fleming."

They discussed the sophomore for a few minutes, her mood, her behavior, things Ezra already knew before asking. He then explained that they were investigating the attempted suicide of the student-teacher.

"Do you know her?" he asked Larson.

"Everyone knows Brooklyn. It's a small school." Larson explained that he'd only spoken to her a few times, though. He turned to Vargas. "Is there a formal investigation, then?"

There was something in his voice. Hopefulness? Nervousness? Or maybe he was just nosey, as teachers tended to be. Instead of answering, Vargas found a seat in a brown recliner beside the coffee table. She rocked a few times, her gaze scanning the room, settling on the stack of lab reports and Larson's open laptop.

Ezra decided to also ignore the question. "What did you think of Brooklyn? As a woman, I mean."

Larson looked warily over at Vargas, then met Ezra's gaze. "There's something about her. A glow. Something…" he searched for the word.

"Something electric?" Ezra asked.

The basketball coach laughed. "I heard you FBI guys had a dark sense of humor."

So Larson knew Ezra's background, and he knew Brooklyn had been shocked. A lot of folks around the school knew more than they were willing to let on.

Larson patted his slight paunch with both hands as

if he were a cartoon bear. "I'm a bit past my prime, though. Ten years ago, heck, five years ago, I would've jumped into the Brooklyn Hannigan pool with both feet."

Vargas cleared her throat, and Larson shifted from foot to foot. "Not really. A student-teacher and all," he said, closing the laptop and tidying the lab reports. "But if she decided to stay on as a teacher, I might've asked her out. Back in the day, I mean. The women I see these days are divorcees or middle-aged women who, like me, never got the marriage thing figured out."

As he spoke, he gesticulated like a man doing charades. His hands seemed to convey that marriage was something like a new Internet router lying there between them. Ezra imagined Larson complaining, *I can get the sex part to work, but the damn cohabitation keeps coming in and out. Do you think it's my Ethernet cable?*

Ezra wished marriage were that easy. He wished marriage were an external object to be tinkered with rather than two internal forces to be reconciled.

"Who are you seeing now?" Vargas asked.

"No one…at the moment." Larson held his breath in between phrases. "Sorry, but I've got a bit of that…Christmas stomach bug…that's going around." Then he asked, "Do you have a card or some way I could follow up?" He looked over at Vargas, but she made no sign of leaving his recliner.

"Fiona did mention one other thing," Ezra said. "Car batteries. She said you were doing an electrical experiment last week."

The absence of footprints in the belfry still bothered Ezra. Wiring the bell could explain it. At the time of Brooklyn's attack, Coach Larson was across town at a soup kitchen, a fact confirmed by multiple sources, but if he rigged the bell ahead of time, his location at the time wouldn't matter. The bell would require some serious amperage, though.

Larson moved to his coat closet and removed two modest batteries. Vargas stood from the recliner to inspect them with Ezra. They weren't even car batteries but small and worn out 6-volts. These wouldn't have worked. Ezra wasn't even sure car batteries would conduct enough wattage through the one-ton bell.

"Is this all you have?" Ezra asked, disappointed.

"All we need. A friend who works at the country club gave me these when they transitioned their golf carts."

As the men spoke, Vargas moved around the perimeter of the living room and kitchen, which were separated by a short bar with wooden stools. She ran her hand along the wall, almost touching but not quite, and Larson's gaze followed her steadily.

"All I remember from high school circuits was the potato battery," Ezra said.

"Our experiment is a little more involved than that. We're testing the conductivity of different metals. We run a current through various wires and test the brightness of these lights." He pulled up a picture of the floodlights on his phone. "The size of the batteries and the lights allow us to see the physical principles on a big-ass scale."

"Is that the scientific term?"

"Actually, I think our textbooks say *huge-ass*, but I'm paraphrasing." He burped involuntarily and grimaced. "Fr. Remy and some of the families from the parish have even lent us some gold and silver items to include in our experiments. With a simple electrical current, we can tell the purity of the metals."

"Eureka," Ezra said.

Larson laughed. "Exactly!"

He was even smarter than most of the teachers Ezra interacted with at SJM, which was saying something. "Couldn't you just use D-batteries and a flashlight?" Ezra asked.

"These kids vacation in the Swiss Alps. They aren't going to remember a flashlight."

"Are you saying they're spoiled? It must be hard to come in every day and teach kids whose parents make ten times your salary."

"I don't mean any disrespect. I'm just saying teaching is only half content. The rest is presenting it in a way these kids will remember a year from now."

"I don't know," Ezra said. "I still remember my potato battery."

"Sure, but it didn't make you run out and become a scientist, now did it?"

Ezra switched gears and asked about Martin Durand's character and involvement with Brooklyn. In typical male fashion, Larson had little reaction to the French teacher. "The girls seem to like him, though," he said. Then after a moment's reflection, he added, "He reminds me of myself when I started."

"What? Tall and handsome?"

"Naïve," he said.

"How so?"

"The students take advantage of him a lot. It happens with first-year teachers."

"Take advantage how?"

"They lie, pretend not to understand simple things, push boundaries."

"Didn't he teach college before this?"

"College isn't high school," Larson said. "Plus, I think he was a Ph.D. candidate or something. They teach a specialized subject to a bunch of college students who actually want to learn French. Here it's teenagers who have a language requirement to fill, parents who need their kid to have a 4.0 if they want to have any chance of getting into the Ivy League, and an administrator who could lose her job at any moment."

Vargas finished her survey of this area and moved quietly into the rest of the apartment, the hallway first, then the bathroom. Larson shifted his feet and craned his head to keep an eye on her.

"I thought Principal Weeks was renewed for another three years," Ezra said.

"What?" he asked.

"Catherine Weeks. I thought she was renewed."

"She's supposed to be."

"When?"

"A week from Monday. But with this hanging over the school, who knows what will happen."

Getting back to Durand, Ezra asked, "If teaching high school is so much worse than college, why make the switch?"

For a second Larson looked as though he was going to hurl. "Something about the ex-wife. I'd talk to Ms. Jarno. She knows everything about everything around here."

"Even the stuff that hasn't happened?" Ezra asked with a smile.

"Especially that."

Vargas emerged from the bathroom and then headed down the hall and into what looked like Larson's bedroom. The coach turned instinctively toward the hallway, but Ezra pulled him back by the shoulder.

"Do you text with any of your students?"

"Text?"

"Text, call, Finlox?"

"Finlox, that's the new social media app?"

Ezra nodded.

"No, I don't use any of those with students. It's against school policy for teachers to contact students directly. If I need someone, I call home or pull them out of class."

"But with coaching that must be difficult. Especially if you have a student running a few minutes late to the bus or who doesn't show up to the soup kitchen, for instance."

"Daniel?" Larson guessed.

Now Vargas rejoined them. "Daniel Toussaint lacked a solid alibi for the night of the attack, so he made one up."

Larson bit his lip.

"He said he got that advice from a teacher at SJM," she said and paused to let it sink in. "He said that teacher was you."

Instead of answering, Coach Larson rushed into the bathroom where they heard him empty the contents of his stomach.

Larson returned, wiping his lips with a dish rag. "I'm sorry. As I said, the Christmas bug."

"Why did you advise Daniel to lie?" Vargas asked.

"I knew it would make him look guilty," he said.

"Plus he's already got two strikes against him."

"What are those?"

"He's black," Larson said.

"And an immigrant," Vargas guessed.

Larson nodded.

"How late did the soup kitchen run?"

"Until eight-thirty, but we stayed to clean up till about nine. When was Brooklyn found?"

"Groundskeeper found her just after the power outage at eight-fifteen."

"There you have it," he said as if this absolved him. He seemed to have forgotten they were discussing Daniel's alibi, not his. Larson wiped the last bit of vomit from his mouth but not his chin. A bit of orange still hung from his beard.

Ezra thanked him for his time and opened the door for Vargas.

Before she walked through it, however, she turned to Larson for one more question. "Have you been traveling?"

"No."

"But you're planning a trip?"

What could her angle be for this line of questioning, Ezra wondered.

"Oh, the luggage." Larson looked behind him toward the bedroom. "I'll probably take a short trip as soon as school gets out."

"Where to?" she asked.

He shrugged. "Sometimes I just get packed up and light out for the territory, see where the road takes me."

She didn't seem convinced, but she left it at that. They returned to Ezra's sedan.

"People certainly have some vague alibis around

this school," she said before getting in.

"White male of good standing, he probably doesn't think he owes you a better one," Ezra said. "I can say that."

"Why? Because you're a white male of good standing?"

"Undoubtedly."

Did Larson in fact have the Christmas bug or were nerves running the coach ragged? Even if he was sick, Ezra supposed the questions could cause him to vomit. He'd follow up again on Monday. A forty-eight-hour bug would be gone by then. It wouldn't be conclusive, but it might tell him something. Furthermore, having an alibi didn't rule Larson out. There were plenty of two-man jobs or work hired out.

They climbed into the car.

"What if no one attacked Brooklyn?" Vargas asked.

"What are you thinking?"

She shook her head. She was cutting him out again.

"Mind if I smoke?" Ezra asked.

Vargas shook her head, but as she did so she wrinkled up her nose.

He put the cigarette back in the pack and pocketed it. "What's the first pawnshop?"

Vargas read off the name.

Ten minutes later, they sat outside Chicago's #1 Grade-A Pawn Store. Iron bars covered the windows and graffiti coated the brick walls. The proprietor was a fat man in his fifties with slick-backed hair. His name badge was yellowed and grimy as if from a combination of tobacco smoke and fryer oil. It read simply "Dick."

They showed him a photograph of Daniel. "Have you seen this person?" Vargas asked.

"Maybe," Dick said and turned around to sort a tray of rings.

"Could you take a closer look?" she asked.

"I know my rights," he said without turning. Then he muttered, "Chicago PD bossing me around like I don't know what's what."

"Guess this guy's not going to talk, Special Agent James. Better go get that federal warrant."

This got the man's attention. "Now, now. Let's not get ahead of ourselves." He looked at James and must've recognized him at least vaguely and took the photo. "I saw him."

"When?"

"He came in last week."

"What was he looking for?"

"How should I know? He walked around a couple times and left."

"If all he did was walk around, how do you remember him?" Ezra asked.

"He had this backpack. I figured he wanted to steal something. These black kids come in all the time and try to steal stuff, but I've got it all behind glass. See? Also, he had on that school uniform in the picture." He pointed to the white shirt and blue plaid tie. "Don't get many Joseph & Mary kids in here."

"If you have everything behind glass, how do you know these kids are trying to rob you?" he asked.

"They come in and look, but they never buy."

Then Vargas, a bite in her voice, asked, "Did you ever hear of window shopping?"

"Not these kids. They're different."

"Different than what?" she asked.

"Forget him," Ezra said, taking her shoulder. "This was a waste of time."

They spent the rest of the afternoon questioning pawnshop owners to see if any of them recognized Daniel Toussaint. As they drove, they talked.

"So, what made you decide to tag along?" Vargas asked. "I'm sure the school's not paying for weekend duty, are they?"

"Oh, justice, crime and punishment, protecting the innocent, all that."

"In other words, security is boring you to tears?" she asked.

He laughed. "I suppose there's more."

"What?"

"The kid."

"Little miss beauty queen?"

"Not her, the…" He held his hands out like he was cupping a pregnant belly.

"Oh, God. You're one of those?"

"Catholic?" he asked.

"A white man with strong opinions about the unborn. When it's the life of a young woman, you're on the fence. Throw in a fetus, and *voila*, we have a worthy cause."

"It's not like that," he said, defensive now. "Julia, my wife, she was pregnant. Before she left, I mean. We lost the baby."

Lost felt like the wrong word, as if they'd misplaced the baby somewhere, as if they could still find it again if they looked hard enough.

"Sorry. I didn't know."

"So when I heard Brooklyn was pregnant…"

"I didn't mean to pry."

"It's fine. This all happened after the Straugh trial. The retrial, I mean. Julia learned she was pregnant on a Sunday, and I found out about my probation that Monday. The stress was hard on us both."

He did light a cigarette now and drew hard on it.

"Damn," Vargas said.

"I don't know if Brooklyn wants the baby or is going to get rid of it with the father out of the picture. It's vulnerable, and if I can protect it, then I ought to try, right?"

"So why the FBI?" Vargas asked.

"What do you mean?"

"Did you always want to be a cop?"

He thought about this. A year ago, he would've given a pat answer. He would have summarized his career trajectory as if he'd planned every step. Now something different came to mind.

"There was a week in high school when I thought I'd make a hell of a novelist. I even wrote the first chapter of a sci-fi book."

"What was it about?"

"An alternate reality. In it everyone wore hats all the time."

Vargas waited a moment. "Is that the whole book?"

"I didn't explain it properly. Everyone wore hats who normally wouldn't wear hats. Hat-wearing types, on the other hand, your cowboys, baseball players, firemen, they never wore hats."

"Firemen don't wear hats."

"What do you mean? They wear those bright red hats."

"Those are helmets."

Ezra, realizing the flaw in his teenage understanding of the fire department, segued. "Ever since fifth grade, with the exception of that one week, I've wanted to be a detective."

"What happened in fifth grade?"

"I read *Silence of the Lambs*."

"In fifth grade?"

"What can I say? I was advanced for my age."

"And unsupervised, apparently."

Ezra just nodded. He never knew how much to share with new people. Even otherwise kind people could be surprisingly judgmental—not overtly perhaps, but their attitudes often changed. Their smiles became fixed, their laughter polite, their conversations short.

"My father died when I was young," he said, "and my mother, she didn't handle it well. Manic episodes, men, some of them not so great."

"Absent dad and a crazy mom? You can join the club I'm forming."

"Oh yeah? What club is that?"

"It's called Interesting People." She laughed. "I can't believe you waited this long to tell me something about yourself that makes you half-likable."

"I guess I'm just used to…"

"Bragging about yourself?"

"Most of my life I've been trying to impress teachers, professors, employers, trying to convince people I was good enough."

"And you never stopped to ask if *they* were good enough," she said, not looking at him.

****

A half-dozen pawn shops later, they began to doubt themselves. Then they reached the end of the list Paul

Baptiste had given them. If this one didn't work, they'd have to start choosing pawn shops at random.

"Last stop," she said, adjusting her plum blouse. "Heinz Pawn and Loan."

Ezra looked over at the detective beside him in the car, the afternoon light fading behind her. In the distance stood a couple-colored sky, light blue, purple, and pink dappled with clouds of white. Right beside him sat a sight far lovelier in sable, gold, and plum.

The proprietor, Gerard Heinz, was a pale man with white hair and a jeweler's squint. Neither Ezra nor Vargas wore badges or uniforms, yet he greeted them with "Good afternoon, officers" as they entered.

Ezra held up the photo. Just like every other pawn shop they'd gone to, Heinz recognized Daniel. "Did he buy anything?" Ezra asked.

Heinz shook his head.

Great, Ezra thought, *another swing and a miss.* It seemed Daniel really had just driven around.

Heinz continued, "He sold something, though."

Vargas gave her leg an excited tap. "What?"

"I was counting the register late Thursday night when a young African American male I'd never seen before entered what should've been the locked front door of my pawn shop. I instinctively touched the revolver I kept beneath the counter."

"Because he was black?" she asked.

"What? No, sorry, that's not what I meant." Heinz blushed. "I've been robbed twice this year, and both times it was because I forgot to lock *that.*" He pointed an accusing finger at the entry door. "When I saw it was just some kid, I took my hand off the revolver. Then I noticed his attire."

"How was he dressed?" Lucia asked.

"He wore nice clothing—a button up shirt and pressed khakis, the kind they wear at the private schools, and a plaid tie. Even though he towered over me, height-wise, his shirt was still a size too large. The outfit suggested that either the shirt was not his, which seemed unlikely, or that he was still young enough that his parents expected another growth spurt or two. 'You is open?' he asked me in an accent I couldn't quite place."

As Heinz narrated the event, Vargas explored the shop, stopping at a display case filled with firearms. She examined it intently, finally stopping to take a few pictures with her phone. Heinz didn't seem to notice.

"What kind of accent? Ball park?" Ezra asked.

"I honestly don't know. I see a lot of Haitian refugees, but I also see East and West Africans, people from all over the Caribbean, Central and South America. I don't want to assume."

Vargas took a final photo, then joined them at the counter. "What did you tell him?"

"I said I was closing up. Then he asks me if I could buy something. The kid takes something metal and heavy from his backpack and places it on the counter. I flick on my jeweler's lamp, and the cup shines, I kid you not, as bright as the sun. Gold plated at the very least, and quite old." He rubbed his left hand with a rag. The wrist showed a smudge of grease, but Ezra guessed nervousness more than anything drove the wrist rubbing.

"Why didn't you alert the authorities? You must've known it was stolen," Vargas said.

"Look, I get a lot of stuff, some stolen, some legit."

"That's hardly an excuse."

"So, when I get something suspicious, I call around and see if anyone's missing anything. I try to track down the owner and go from there. In this case, the owner didn't want to press charges. He just gave me a price to pay the kid whenever he comes back." He stopped rubbing his wrist. The grease was gone.

"Has Daniel come back?" Ezra asked.

"Not yet. And he didn't leave a name or number either. Strange kid."

"Do you have the name of the owner?" Vargas asked.

"I'm afraid I can't give that out."

"But it has been returned to the owner?" she asked.

"That's correct."

Ezra gave her a surprised look. "How did you know?"

"Your priest friend showed it to me when I first visited the chapel," she told him. "I thought he was trying to tell me something, but I didn't know what it was." She turned back to Heinz. "How were you able to track down the chalice?"

"Let's just say the kid wasn't exactly hiding his affiliations well."

"Right, the school uniform," Ezra said.

Heinz nodded. Then he laughed.

"What's so funny?" Ezra asked.

"Just coincidental is all. That school has been giving me some very strange business as of late."

"What kind of business?"

"Look, I answered your questions about this kid because he seemed a bit mixed up and because you asked some very specific questions about him." He started turning off the lights in the display cases and locking the jewelry up in a large metal box. "But don't go thinking I make it a habit of airing all my customers' business with the police."

"You've been very helpful," Ezra said.

Heinz walked over to the firearms display case, and Vargas moseyed over with him. "Did you see something you like?" he asked.

She pointed out a black revolver with a wooden handle. "How much for the .38 special?"

"You've got a good eye," Heinz said. He side-eyed her, perhaps sizing up what she could afford. "With my law enforcement discount, I could probably let it go for two bills."

She turned to leave.

"One-seventy-five," he said. "Final offer."

"Let me sleep on it." She smiled. "Something tells me we'll be back."

They thanked the pawnbroker and left.

Outside, the sky had become the color of a child's watercolor, a blend of reds, purples, oranges, and yellows in random layers.

Ezra drove Vargas back to the mall parking lot where she'd left her car, and then he took himself to evening mass. Spending that much time with Detective Vargas had stirred up feelings he hadn't had to worry about in quite some time.

Chapter Thirteen

Every Saturday evening, Ezra attended mass at the chapel on the SJM campus. He enjoyed evening mass because he was usually awake enough to understand it and never overslept. After mass, he usually hung around to speak with Fr. Remy, who was still in his Roman collar and stole. Tonight was no different.

"Has anything gone missing recently, Father?"

Remy wrinkled his nose at the word "father," perhaps because Ezra rarely called him this. Without answering the question, he waved at an elderly couple as they exited in the distance.

"Father," Ezra repeated.

"My secretary, Denise, asked me that very question last Saturday. She stood in the doorway of my office, looking just as concerned as you are now. I knew it could only mean bad news."

"So what went missing?"

"I thought at first someone was sick. I asked if Cheryl, one of our extraordinary ministers, had the flu. Maggie said, 'Not this week.' Since she said 'not this week' rather than 'not Cheryl,' I knew no one was sick. Then I thought of our new shipment of sacramental wine, which had just arrived. I asked if anyone had gotten into it. When she shook her head, I knew something was missing. I asked if it was a purificator or a paten or, worse, the ciborium. When she pointed her thumb to the ceiling to indicate a more expensive item, I knew what I had feared the moment Maggie leaned sadly against the door frame. The chalice was missing."

"That's what I'm here about," Ezra replied. "The chalice disappeared from the church and turned up at a local pawn shop."

"The electrical experiments."

"Excuse me?" Ezra didn't know what to make of the non sequitur.

"Coach Larson, his class has been running conductivity experiments in Chemistry. That's Daniel's class," Remy said. "He borrowed several gold, silver, and brass items from the church."

"Do you know why Daniel might've pawned it?"

Remy didn't. The chalice should have been in a museum, he explained, and then the sacred vessel disappeared. He had considered calling the pawnshops, but he had a mass to prepare, and the matter slipped his mind. Thankfully, the parish had several backup chalices, which were just as beautiful, just as sacred, and just as capable of transforming sacramental wine into the blood of Christ.

Ezra was confused. "The man I spoke to earlier today said you tracked it down."

"Mr. Heinz, yes. He came to see me the following day. We spoke for no more than five minutes. He produced the chalice for me to inspect and asked if I wanted to involve Chicago PD. I told him that it was not stolen. When he pressed me, I explained that we exist to serve the needs of the parish. 'Freely we have received, so freely we must give,' I said. Heinz accepted this and asked me what it was worth."

Out of curiosity, Ezra asked, "What is it worth?"

"Far less than the soul who took it."

"Monetarily."

The priest laughed. "You don't want to know. I told the pawnbroker to offer the seller five thousand dollars. The parish would give him whatever he needed to make it worth his time. Then, after Heinz set the chalice on my desk, he replaced his hat and left. He still hasn't sent me a bill."

"Heinz says Daniel Toussaint hasn't returned to the pawnshop."

"No?" Remy asked. "I cannot say I am surprised. I am sure that he feels a tremendous amount of shame."

"You think?"

Remy nodded.

"Do you think his theft has anything to do with the attack on Brooklyn?"

"I doubt it." The priest ran his hand over his short salt-and-pepper hair. "His seems a crime of necessity."

"So does Brooklyn's attack."

"These are two different needs. One is for sex, the other is for money. I would be surprised if there is any connection."

"One can have multiple motivations."

"*C'est vrai*," the priest agreed weakly. "This feels more like opportunity. What else are you working on?"

"Too much."

Remy tapped the scar running down the left side of his face. "What is the *opportunité facile?* The low hanging fruit, as it were?"

"We spoke with Ben Larson today."

"I don't mean with the case. With your life. What has been clouding your judgment these many months?"

"Not this again. I'm not visiting John Lewis Straugh. He has nothing to do with this case."

"Yet he has everything to do with your confidence as an investigator. Straugh was an honest mistake. I am sure he will tell you so himself—if you allow him the chance."

Remy placed a hand on Ezra's shoulder and looked him in the eye in a way that always cleared Ezra's addled thoughts.

"I will see you tonight, *mon ami.*"

"The Little Sister's banquet," Ezra replied.

"I worried you had forgotten."

"Forget my penance?" Ezra asked humorously, but Remy was already moving away, chatting pleasantly to a minuscule old woman with a walker.

****

Traffic cameras caught Cynthia Scout's car passing by Blue Basil around the time of Brooklyn Hannigan's reservation. Ms. Scout worked at a boutique nearby, and Lucia intended to confirm that her job was the reason for her driving through that intersection.

Rows of boutiques, bookstores, and niche restaurants filled the streets and avenues of downtown Evanston. The shop where Cynthia worked was located a few blocks from Centennial Park and specialized in objects fashioned from repurposed bicycle parts. Here hung a rope ladder composed of pedals welded to chains; there stood a collection of handlebar lamps. From every corner of ReCycle Trifles sprung decorative pots, rocking chairs, picture frames, and every knickknack imaginable, all of it fashioned from repurposed wheels, seat posts, brake pads, and derailleurs. The place smelled of leather and chrome.

A college student stood behind the glass counter when Lucia entered. She wore cognac boots, black leggings, a formless, baby blue sweater, and blonde dreadlocks. On Lucia, this disparate assemblage of fashion choices would've looked dowdy, at best, and insane, at worst. However, on this angelic-but-apathetic-faced student, the getup worked.

Fashion always seemed like a game of manhunt to Lucia. The popular girls with their perfect hair and daddy's cars passed secrets to one another like children hiding behind bushes and tree trunks. By the time Lucia found the last clue, the girls were hiding in new places and everything had changed. Too only the most beautiful girls could keep up with the absurd style shifts while still appearing attractive rather than ridiculous. At a certain point, she gave up on fashion and turned her focus to more worthwhile pursuits.

"Is Cynthia Scout working today?" Lucia asked the would-be sweater model who gave her a blank stare. "Hello?" That got her attention.

"Sorry, what?"

"Ms. Scout. Is she here?"

"Cynthia only works during the week."

"Did she work on Thursday?"

"I don't know. Is that during the week?" she asked, her voice all sarcasm now.

Once Lucia flashed her badge the clerk became rapidly more helpful. She explained that Cynthia's shifts ran from noon to six, Monday through Thursday. Apparently, she considered Friday the weekend. Most likely, Cynthia left ReCycle Trifles and drove past Blue Basil on her way to the school concert. No one had mentioned when she arrived for the concert, but Ezra

James said he saw her backstage just before the power outage.

"Did she mention any plans for this weekend?" Lucia asked.

"The Little Sisters' Banquet."

St. Joseph and Mary held an annual banquet to raise funds for various women's groups, the clerk explained. This year they chose homeless mothers. It mirrored the previous year's theme of drug-addicted mothers.

"Who are the Little Sisters?"

"Little Sisters of Teresa. It's, bar none, the most exclusive women's group in town." Her voice dripped with envy. "Cynthia is the president."

"Does the whole parish get to vote? Or is it more of an oligarchy situation?"

She gave another blank stare.

Lucia turned to leave but pointed at a bike saddle on the wall. "What's that?"

"A sconce."

Lucia thanked her and stepped outside.

She could see Blue Basil from where she now stood. Three people associated with the school drove by the restaurant the night of the attack. Daniel Toussaint had been driving around with his friend Paul Baptiste, trying to hock a golden chalice. They knew that now, though why he needed the money was still a mystery.

Brooklyn came here to meet someone for dinner, though the identity of the dinner companion still eluded them. Cynthia left her part-time job near the restaurant to drive to the school concert. Although, she could've easily made a pit stop on the way.

This left one person not associated with the school

directly but certainly with Brooklyn: the roommate, Autumn Elkhart. Clearly, Autumn followed her to the restaurant, perhaps to learn the identity of Brooklyn's paramour or perhaps for a more sinister reason. Before they grilled Autumn again, Lucia wanted to speak with Cynthia. Attending the Little Sisters banquet was a perfect excuse.

****

The two-story parish center of SJM would've been less conspicuous in Grant Park with its modernist constructions, museums, and proximity to Chicago's high-rises and skyscrapers. Here, among the turn-of-the-century understated brick buildings, the glass center clashed terribly. How this glass-paneled, black-steel monstrosity was an improvement upon the dignified brick campus, Lucia didn't know.

At the entrance of the parish center, two women in their fifties with matching bobs assailed Lucia. Their hair colors were a motley assortment of blondes, browns, and whites. Their matching hairdos reminded Lucia of two brindled Labrador retrievers her uncle once owned.

"Ticket?" brindled bob one asked.

Lucia flashed her badge.

"That's a funny-looking ticket," brindled bob two remarked.

"Evanston PD," she said. "I need to speak with Cynthia Scout."

Bob-two smiled at her friend. "This may be the most inventive way I've ever seen someone crash our little shindig."

"I'm not—" Lucia started.

"Don't you remember the firemen?" bob one

replied, ignoring Lucia. "They insisted our sprinkler system needed an inspection."

"I would've let them inspect *my* sprinkler system," bob two whispered, just loud enough for Lucia to hear.

"This is ridiculous," Lucia said finally. "How much are tickets?"

"Last minute tickets—"

"—are twelve hundred," the two brindled bobs said in tandem.

Lucia gaped at them. "*Dollars*? How much were they in advance! You know what, never mind. Is Ezra James here?"

The bobs nodded in practiced unison.

"Can you tell him that Detective Lucia Vargas needs him?"

"Get in line, honey," bob two replied with a suggestive laugh.

"Detective Vargas needs *to speak to him*," she rephrased, "about an ongoing case."

Lucia stepped back outside into the cold night. Upon her arrival at the center, deep crimsons and violets splashed the sky. Now, those colors were fading to dull blues and charcoals. In the distance, a crescent moon sliced through the night sky, edging ever closer to the St. Joseph bell tower like a set of fangs. Less than two full days had passed since the attack on Brooklyn Hannigan, yet Lucia had easily put twenty hours into this case. If she didn't come up with something solid soon, the next few days could be just as busy and fruitless.

Her breast pocket vibrated. She checked her phone and found a text from her best friend, Trish.

—*Are you excited for tonight?*—

—*Why?*— Lucia texted in reply.

—*Your date! Adrian rescheduled. Remember?*—

That's tonight? She could've sworn Trish said *next* Saturday.

Trish texted the time and the restaurant and a brief description of Adrian as "tall, dark, and spicy." Lucia just shook her head. Adrian had chosen, of all places in Chicago, Blue Basil. At least she still had a few hours, enough time for a power nap.

"Detective?"

Ezra James, in a navy suit, red-and-white snowflake tie, and black pea coat, stood beside her now. The bobbed church lady wasn't wrong about him. With his dark crew cut, steely blue eyes, constant five o'clock shadow, and well-defined shoulders, Ezra James could've been the lead from a film noir.

"Vargas," Ezra said, this time louder.

"Sorry."

"You needed me?"

She nodded hesitantly. "I want you"—she cleared her throat—"to speak with Cynthia Scout." Suddenly very warm, she pulled her jacket and blouse away from her neck. "Cynthia's car passed by Blue Basil during Brooklyn's dinner date."

"Be on the lookout, wealthy Caucasian woman in suburb," he said in a mock-dispatcher tone. "Last seen carrying a designer handbag while exiting a specialty foods store."

"Funny," she said sarcastically, though it did make her smile.

"Who spotted her?"

Lucia pointed to the camera on a nearby stop light.

"Got it. I'll find out how well she knew Brooklyn,"

he said. "Do you need anything else?"

Lucia shook her head.

Ezra James disappeared inside, and Lucia felt his absence, felt the warmth subsiding beside her. Then a gelid gust of wind drove even that ghost of warmth away, and she was all alone.

Chapter Fourteen

The Sisters of Teresa Charity banquet was the most important non-liturgical event of the year. The banquet involved the most money, the most high-profile guests, and the most drunken incidents. Because he did not work for the parish, just the school, Ezra didn't have to attend—the chief of police and his wife, as well as the deputy chief and her husband, would be there if anything went awry—but Ezra received a free ticket. Then there was the matter of his penance.

The "sisters" entirely transformed the parish center for the banquet. For weeks, women came to set up, adding lace tablecloths, white rose bouquets, and even a crystal chandelier suspended from the ceiling. By the time they were finished, the main hall looked more like a wedding reception at the country club than an annual fundraiser hosted by a five-woman committee.

Jeanne, and her near-twin Evelyn Ainsley, guarded the entrance to the banquet, taking tickets and lightly ribbing the attendees. Both women were in their fifties, had teenage children, and wore their hair bobbed with streaks of various blondes and brunettes that complemented and hid their naturally graying hair.

Ezra found a seat at one of the round tables. An usher approached him and asked to double-check his ticket. He stared at the man blankly.

"It's okay," said a voice from behind him.

An elegant Vietnamese woman laid her hand across his forearm. "You're a guest of Fr. Mbombo's, are you not?" she asked. She had small but alluring features, and the sleek teal fabric of her evening dress complemented her soft, golden skin.

"That's right. I'm Ezra James. You are Mrs. Tien?" he asked, unsure.

"Missus makes me sound so old! Call me Ellie."

She proffered her hand, palm down, to be kissed. He shook her fingers instead. She frowned but then laughed at the blunder. Ellie led him to the head table, long and elevated with a blue satin cover that flowed to the floor in deliberate folds. The Little Sisters of Teresa spared no expense.

"Where are your *sisters*?" he asked.

"My much older sisters, you mean?"

She wore her jet-black hair pulled into an ornate bun. Ezra believed she was born, though not raised, in Vietnam. Ellie had the poise of a woman much older than herself but the youthful beauty of one several years younger. The time she spent with her four "sisters" only accentuated these polarizing qualities.

At twenty-nine, Ellie explained, she was the youngest woman on the committee by fifteen years, but her husband was the same age as theirs. "A silver fox," she said woodenly. While the children of the other sisters were in the upper school or off to college, Ellie's children were in the lower school. One was in first grade and the other in third.

"They must keep you busy," Ezra said.

She just laughed, then continued. "But you asked where the rest of the committee is, not who I am. Evelyn Ainsley and Jeanne Sowers are greeting people in the foyer. I'm surprised you didn't see them on your way in."

"Are Evelyn and Jeanne the leaders of your club?"

"Technically, but they leave all the minor details to the rest of us."

"Minor details like planning, decorating, finding speakers, and acquiring auction items?" he asked.

Ellie touched the side of her nose.

He smiled. "I have to confess, I always have difficulty telling those two apart, Evelyn and Jeanne."

"New parishioners often do, and waitresses ask if they're sisters," Ellie said. "Which they both love." She gestured to two empty seats at the head table. "Here you are."

"Which one?"

She turned her head left and right. "Fr. Remy should be around here somewhere."

Ezra grabbed the backs of the chairs, pulling one out for Ellie and sitting in the other himself. A waiter swooped in and offered them glasses from a full tray. Ezra took a water glass, and his companion took what appeared to be white wine.

"Did either Jeanne or Evelyn know the student-teacher?" he asked once the waiter had gone.

"Are you asking," she said, then lowering her voice, "in an official capacity?"

"Oh no, Evanston PD is handling the case."

He nodded toward the table occupied by the chief, deputy chief, and their spouses. The couples chatted happily.

"But there is a case?" she asked, eyes wide.

"I shouldn't say." Now that he'd piqued her interest, he delved deeper. "Everyone around here seems to know the girl who was attacked."

She shook her head and drained her wine glass. "You could say that."

"Doesn't Jeanne have a son at the school?"

"No, that's Evelyn. Jeanne's son is in college. Evelyn's oldest is as well, but her middle boy, Royce, is a senior at SJM."

More tables filled up around them. Ezra recognized several prominent families from the school. Others he knew from church. He knew their faces but not their names. Still more were strangers to him.

He returned his attention to Ellie. "Royce Ainsley. Tall, bulky, athletic type? Always wearing an Ohio State sweater?"

Ellie beamed. "That's the one."

"Going there in the fall, I assume?"

"I doubt it." She smiled mischievously. "He wants to play football."

Many of the boosters at SJM believed Royce was NFL material. However, no division one schools had recruited him. If he wanted to play at Ohio State, his only option was to apply as a regular student and try out for a walk-on position. This meant he'd have no athletic scholarship and no certainty of playing time.

Ezra took all this in, but only said in reply, "Stranger things have happened."

"Not this time."

Ellie said she heard from another parent that a division two school in Arkansas offered Royce a full-ride scholarship for the fall, and the family expected him to take it.

"Evelyn and Jeanne are collecting tickets.

Ezra gestured toward the empty seats beside them.

"And the rest?"

She frowned. "Cynthia Scout is with the caterers. I don't know where Annette Fleming wandered off to."

"Annette Fleming," he said as if the name were unfamiliar to him. "She also has children at the school."

"She has a girl in the upper school, who's a bit of a troublemaker if you ask me, and a little boy, who's three or four."

"That would be Fiona Fleming."

Ellie nodded. "She was nearly expelled a few months ago."

Ezra, of course, remembered the details. Fiona flung a glass of lemonade from the balcony in the two-story wing of the school. Ezra sat with Principal Weeks, Fr. Remy, Fiona, and her parents to discuss the matter at length when it first happened. They sat for over an hour while Fiona said nothing.

Ellie laughed now. "Good thing Brooklyn has quick reflexes."

"Do you know why Fiona threw it?" Ezra asked. He knew, but he wanted to see if Ellie did.

Ellie made a crude gesture, banging a fist into her open palm. "She told the principal about Lizbeth and Mason Scout…"

This was new. Fiona told them the boy was Nick. He filed this new information under the growing file of things he didn't know and might never know.

"Why did Fiona care?"

Again, Ellie gestured, this time implying Fiona and Mason had done the deed before Lizbeth came along.

Ezra didn't know what to think now. Fiona lying about a troublesome situation was not new, nor Ezra having to untangle the web of lies. Fiona did throw lemonade, which she led her target to believe was urine. This fact he knew. He also knew the target was Brooklyn, the student-teacher, and it concerned a boy, either Mason or Nick. Nick seemed innocuous, so he wanted to believe it concerned Mason. Almost always drama returned to Mason Scout.

Fiona's mother, Annette Fleming, arrived at that moment, and their conversation had to switch gears. "Ellie!" Annette extended her arms wide for a hug.

Though her hair shone like gold and her skin was peach-perfect, Annette looked terribly uncomfortable. The longer Ellie didn't hug her, the more uncomfortable she looked, until finally Ellie rose from her chair and embraced her "sister."

Annette acknowledged Ezra with a nod and a stiff, "Mr. James."

He glared at his table setting. "I have three knives."

Annette craned her head over his dishes. "Yep."

"Why?"

"Well..." she began, tugging at a lock of her blonde hair. Fiona had the same nervous mannerism.

"Butter, salad, fish," Ellie answered for her.

"I need a knife for salad?"

Ellie patted him on the shoulder. "I thought you attended SJM?"

"Just my junior and senior years. And even then, I was one of those scholarship kids you always hear rumors about."

Annette smiled, something Ezra had never seen her do before.

A familiar face walked into the parish hall, catching Ezra's attention. He nudged Annette and asked, "They invited the basketball coach?"

"Benjamin Larson?" Ellie asked and looked in the direction of Ezra's gaze. "He's taken the boys to the state finals twice since he's been here. Parents love a winner."

Benjamin Larson's suit may have come from a department store, but he wore it like an Armani. Apparently, he had recovered from his stomach flu just in time.

The tables filled up, including the head table, and waiters arrived with appetizer plates, seared scallops with garlic butter and fresh basil leaves.

Ezra took the transition as an opportunity to arrive at his point. "How well does Cynthia Scout know Brooklyn?"

"Well…" Annette started and stopped.

"We all know Brooklyn," Ellie said, proud to be connected to the tragedy. "The Little Sisters have taken her under our collective wing, so to speak."

"What all does that entail?"

"We sit with her at games, include her in our event planning—"

"Do you invite her to dinner?"

"Sure," Ellie said.

Annette gave her a very obvious—even to Ezra's out of the loop mentality—"shut up" glare.

"Did anyone have dinner with her the night she was attacked?"

Neither Ellie nor Annette had, nor had any of their "sisters" mentioned any dinner plans.

"Was Brooklyn seeing anyone?"

They shook their heads. If Brooklyn's beau was connected to the school, she kept it under wraps.

"Did either of you know about the pregnancy?" he

asked just to see their reactions.

Complete and authentic shock was their reply.

Waiters arrived at each table in turn, beginning with the head table. They took appetizer plates away, some still containing remnants of seared scallops, and replaced them with salad plates.

When the waitstaff retreated, Ezra added, "I know you will want to share this with the others, but please keep this a secret for the time being."

From the unspoken glee on Ellie's face, he knew she would share it at the earliest opportunity. While he still had their attention, he asked, "What do you know about the new French teacher?"

Ellie smirked. "What don't I know?"

"Did I hear his wife left him?" Ezra asked.

"Left him for another woman," she whispered. "Mr. Durand stayed home with the kids while she worked at a law firm."

Annette sat quietly listening, her face bright red. Either the reference to the French teacher's predicament embarrassed her or it angered her. Or, Ezra suspected, Annette wanted desperately to say something she shouldn't.

"And you, Ms. Fleming," he asked Annette, "what's your impression of *Monsieur* Durand?"

She took a quick breath. "He's very intelligent. My Fiona loves him," she said, then blushed again. "Enjoys his class. He taught college, you know."

"Part-time in the evenings," Ellie added. "While his wife tried cases during the day, he stayed home. Then one day, she ran off with the secretary. It's something right out of one of those period shows. Only, you know, with the roles reversed."

"*Mad Woman*," he suggested.

Ellie erupted in laughter. The joke wasn't that funny. He snuck a glance at Annette. She seemed preoccupied by a table across the room. The chief and deputy chief of EPD and their spouses sat chatting away. He looked down the long hard table. At the other end sat Evelyn Ainsley and Jeanne Sowers. Cynthia Scout should have been beside them, but her seat was empty. Fr. Remy's seat beside Ezra was also empty.

He returned his attention to Ellie. "So Martin Durand's wife left. Then what happened?"

"This woman—"

"Gemma," Ezra provided the name.

"Yes, Gemma and her lesbian—"

"Partner."

"Yes. She and her partner filed for custody. And won!"

"That makes sense," he said.

Ellie's mouth hung open. Even Annette turned to Ezra for an explanation.

"The mother always wins custody."

"Oh. I suppose that's right."

"So why did Mr. Durand come to SJM?"

"All the name partners at Gemma's firm send their kids here, so she followed suit. Durand couldn't afford the tuition. Luckily, we needed a French teacher."

"How is he with the students? Teenagers must be a bit different from college students."

"They seem to like him," she said. "The girls that is. They can't stop talking about him."

"He's a very good teacher," Annette added in his defense. "Fiona's French has improved tremendously."

"Did he work with Brooklyn?" Ezra asked.

Annette's eyes narrowed. "Why would he work with Brooklyn?"

Perhaps Annette's reticence about the rumors wasn't about protecting her friends but about protecting Brooklyn's reputation. Certainly much had been said about the student-teacher these past few days, and not all of it came from students.

Ezra considered his next question for a moment. "How is Brooklyn with the students?"

Annette went silent again.

Ellie took over again. "Brooklyn's great! She's a perfect fit for SJM. That is, she was. Can't teach much if you're in a coma. She's in a mild coma—if you haven't heard. Although, I'm not sure how a coma can be mild."

Ezra shrugged. "It probably means they think she'll come out of it."

Waiters emerged again to exchange salad plates for the main course, lobster. Cynthia Scout followed alongside them, her dark-chocolate hair swishing back and forth as she walked. Evelyn Ainsley and Jeanne Sowers might have run the meetings, but it was clear that Cynthia was the reason everyone longed to be a "sister" and why so many showed up for the banquet each winter.

People forget a lot—names, faces, ATM pin numbers—but they never forget how a woman like Cynthia Scout makes them feel. She was the sort of woman people told, unbidden, their innermost fears, desires, and shames. She held the group together, and so Ezra knew if he could get her talking, she could tell him most, if not all, of the group's secrets.

She headed toward the table but then veered back

out into the hallway.

"Excuse me." He stood and followed after Cynthia. He found her speaking with a caterer.

"You're missing your entire dinner," Ezra said. "Can I help with anything?"

She smiled graciously. "We wouldn't dream of it, Mr. James."

"Please, call me Ezra."

"But Mr. James is so becoming. It makes you sound like a character from a Victorian novel."

"Mr. James it is then."

"Our school is lucky to have someone with your background—what with everything going on."

He nodded. "These are trying times."

"I hear you're a Harvard man."

"Just for graduate school."

She laughed. "I believe that's what the kids call a humble brag. I went to Georgetown myself."

"Go Hoyas!" Ezra said.

Cynthia smiled and started walking again. Ezra walked with her.

"SJM ought to offer a forensics class, I've always thought," she said. "A friend of mine has a boy studying at Andover. They have an entire curriculum for future lawyers and students interested in forensic sciences. You could teach it. The one here, I mean."

She pushed the door open and re-entered the banquet. They walked from table to table, Cynthia greeting and thanking the patrons. Then Ezra found himself face-to-face with Ms. Jarno, the English teacher who supplied so much of his school business.

Jarno seemed to forget her friends and gave her full attention to Ezra. "At last, the very man I've been searching for."

Cynthia joined the head table, abandoning Ezra to his fate. He wondered what minor student-annoyance she felt required a full-blown investigation or perhaps a SWAT team.

"Is it possible," she asked, waving her arms around, "to pull DNA from a spitball?"

If Remy Mbombo hadn't stepped in through the double doors at that moment, he might have been stuck with Ms. Jarno all evening.

"Sorry," he said before she could continue. "I have urgent business to discuss with the pastor."

"The suicide?" she mouthed.

"Worse," he said.

He grabbed Remy by the arm and said in a serious tone, "Queen's pawn to D4."

"A queen's game?" the priest replied, surprised. "Very well. D4," he answered with his own queen's pawn.

Ezra responded with his C4 pawn.

"A gambit?" Remy asked. "You must be feeling brave."

Chapter Fifteen

Ezra and Remy found their seats at the head table. Finding the others deep in conversation and appetizers of softshell crab, Ezra leaned over and said, "Brooklyn's roommate thinks she was sleeping with Martin Durand."

"Since when?"

"October."

Remy didn't seem shocked by the news. Although, he rarely seemed shocked. "Is she sure the baby is Martin Durand's?" He pulled a succulent piece of crab out with his fork.

"She asked Brooklyn point blank, and Brooklyn didn't reply."

Remy swallowed the bite of crab. "And you heard this from the roommate?"

"Yesterday. Vargas and her partner spoke to the roommate, Autumn Elkhart. Vargas stopped by the banquet earlier to tell me."

"Autumn Elkhart." The priest seemed to contemplate the name. "This sounds like a game of *Arabic Telephone*. Do children play that in America?"

"Describe it."

The priest pointed to the far end of the long table where Evelyn and Jeanne sat. "Imagine I whisper something to someone down there, a sentence, and they whisper it back this way, one person at a time. At some point, a player mishears or intentionally changes a word, which has a ripple effect on other words and phrases, so that by the last person it is a completely different sentence."

"We have that game too, but we just call it *Telephone*."

"Then how do you distinguish it from a regular telephone?" Remy asked.

"No, we say *a game of telephone*."

"Ah." The priest laughed. "Of course."

"You seem unshaken by this news. Do you know something I don't? Has Martin perhaps spoken with you confidentially?"

"He is a young man; she is a young woman. They are both attractive strangers in an often uninviting environment. He is on the rebound, going through a divorce. It is feasible they could find each other."

"Is he your number one suspect?" Ezra asked.

"No."

"Then who?"

"Honestly?" Remy studied Ezra's face. "My number one suspect is you."

Ezra couldn't tell if Remy was joking or not.

Remy pointed at Ezra's plate. "Aren't you going to eat that?"

"I have a thing about shellfish."

"Allergic?"

"I don't like it." Ezra wondered if his pickiness made him seem like just another spoiled American in Remy's eyes.

"A free ticket to an overpriced banquet, and you do not eat anything on the menu. *Quel dommage*." He raised his glass and winked. "At least there is plenty of good wine."

As they both knew well Ezra didn't drink, Ezra continued. "The roommate, Autumn, also mentioned a break-in a few months ago."

"Did anything go missing?"

"A necklace. Brooklyn received it as a present in late October. It went missing on Thanksgiving weekend. A few days later it reappeared."

"Perhaps she just misplaced it."

"Autumn didn't think so. Brooklyn kept it in a case on top of her vanity."

"That reminds me, have you read Guy de Maupassant?"

"Who?"

"The book I lent you. It is a collection of short stories." Remy sighed. "What did Brooklyn's necklace look like?"

"Black pearls and white gold. Both women work during the day. Autumn came home first and found the front door wide open and the case empty."

A married couple who'd slowly migrated around the room, roaming from group to group, stopped at the head table to chat with Annette and Ellie. Ezra and Remy paused their conversation. Then the couple stopped to say a few obligatory words to Remy. Husband and wife were in their fifties, red faced and smiling broadly. They smelled like two bottles of champagne.

"Was anything else missing?" Remy asked once the couple had moved on.

Ezra shook his head. "Before Brooklyn filed a report, they found the door ajar again and the necklace back in the case."

"Let me see if I have this correct, someone breaks in to steal the necklace and then breaks back in to replace it?" Remy asked. "Peculiar."

"Most," Ezra agreed.

"You said the black pearls were a gift?"

"But Autumn didn't know from whom. Not at the time. Brooklyn never told her the name of her mystery man. She called him her prince. Then a week ago, Autumn found her sitting on the floor of the bathroom crying."

Remy shook his head.

Ezra said, "She had just taken a pregnancy test."

"But she didn't say it was Martin's," Remy said.

The evening progressed, and they spoke no more about Brooklyn Hannigan.

The auction came next. Cynthia Scout auctioned off a series of antiques for preposterously high amounts. Then Jeanne Sowers read several inoffensive scriptures, which only tangentially related to the evening's cause, "Women in Need."

Finally, one of the recipients from last year's fundraiser stood up at the podium and spoke about how the Little Sisters of Teresa helped her overcome a crippling addiction to methamphetamine and saved her from a life of dragging her two children from shelter to shelter.

"I'd run out of hope," she said through genuine tears. "Then these women gave me a fresh start."

"Now I feel guilty that I didn't pay for my ticket," Ezra said.

"I would not," Remy replied.

"Why is that?"

"Tickets ran two thousand dollars each."

Ezra took a sip of his water and swallowed hard. Though he was a two-time college graduate, he was still a scholarship kid at heart. Despite his impressive degrees, a stellar prosecution rate at the Bureau, and the international fame of his last case—at events such as tonight's deal with Sisters, he still felt like a small fish in a large pond.

"I think I'll check on that punch."

Ezra ambled about the room a bit before heading to the punch bowl. He took a sniff and then a sip, which stung his tonsils. He poured the glass back into the bowl. Not a complete teetotaler, Ezra ate food cooked in wine and took communion regularly, but with his brain chemistry, overindulgence spelled disaster.

Ellie Tien sidled up beside him and grabbed his arm. "I shouldn't be telling you this," she whispered, her words slightly slurred, her teal dress slightly askew.

"Aren't those the best things to tell?"

She considered this, looked around stealthily, and then said, "Brooklyn Hannigan was having an affair."

"With whom?"

"Oh, affair isn't the right word. I'm not sure there is a right word for something so wrong."

"Wrong how?"

She went tight-lipped. It was clear she wanted to tell him something but needed him to coax it out of her so it wouldn't be entirely her fault. In his experience, people craved mitigating circumstances. They needed someone to encourage them, to abet them—and the world was happy to oblige.

He offered her his most charming smile. "You can tell people I tricked it out of you." He filled a glass of punch and handed it to her. "Or tortured you."

This brought a smirk to her lips. She sipped the punch.

"Perhaps you could say I waterboarded you. Or worse, waterboarded one of your finer handbags. I'm sure you have one lying around somewhere that I could rough up."

She downed the rest of her punch in one gulp. "Don't even joke about that."

"It seems a small price to pay for justice."

Cynthia Scout appeared between them. "Do tell," she said like a fellow conspirator. "If Ellie is talking, it must be juicy."

The blood drained from Tien's face.

"It is," he replied. "Ellie here was just telling me about this new French instructor of yours, Monsieur Durand."

Ellie coughed. She seemed disoriented. Was she surprised Ezra guessed the affair was with Martin or was she not referring to Martin at all? Then he considered her discomfort at Cynthia's arrival. If the hot gossip concerned the French teacher, then Cynthia would be well aware of it. He thought of Cynthia and Evelyn's high-school-aged sons—Mason and Royce. He thought of their football aspirations. An unexpected pregnancy could throw a wrench into those plans. Whatever Ellie knew might not be known by Cynthia. After all, weren't we always the last to hear gossip about ourselves and our children?

"Mr. Durand is the talk of the town," Cynthia said, a note of disappointment in her voice. Perhaps she was hoping for better gossip. "With all the rumors floating around about his, well…" She trailed off, frowning at Ellie. "I just hope whoever is looking into the recent incident has a sit down with that man." Then she smiled brightly. "I'm so glad you could make it, Mr. James. Even if there's nothing here for you." She nodded at his water glass.

"I got plenty," he said. "I hear you have been mentoring Brooklyn Hannigan."

Cynthia smiled strangely. "I wouldn't call it that."

"But you did recommend her for employment at the school."

The strange smile disappeared. "I suppose I don't know what you mean."

"Catherine said you wrote a letter of recommendation but then withdrew it."

"Oh that." A look of distaste passed over her. "Brooklyn asked me to write her a letter. I didn't realize she meant a letter for SJM. When I heard she'd given it to Catherine, I withdrew it."

"So, Brooklyn's good enough for one of the public schools, but not SJM?" he asked.

"Your words, not mine."

"Were you aware of her pregnancy?"

Cynthia seemed to consider this information carefully and her response as well. "That's a nasty rumor to spread about an injured woman."

"It's not a rumor," Ezra said. "She's two-months pregnant."

Cynthia shrugged her shoulders. "I'll believe it when I see it."

Was Cynthia truly this incredulous or had she decided this was the best approach to take upon hearing a salacious fact she already knew?

The rest of the evening whiled away uneventfully. Remy threatened Ezra's king-side with a pawn assault during Cynthia Scout's final remarks, but Ezra successfully locked pawns with him. Then Remy advanced his light-square bishop and lined up his rook with Ezra's king. Before the closing prayer came, they decided to call it a draw.

Remy took the podium and addressed the gathering. He spoke to them about the recent events at the school, about Brooklyn Hannigan, who at that very moment lay unconscious across town. He then announced a vigil after the banquet. "For anyone interested, we will be praying the rosary, lighting candles, and offering our own personal prayers for her speedy recovery. Security Director James and I are headed there now to set up."

Ezra's jaw clenched involuntarily. Just when he thought the evening was nearing the end, the priest committed him to one more thing. Several eager parishioners offered to help as well, but Remy deflected them all. "We will have no trouble," he assured them, then led Ezra out the front doors.

"Thanks for the heads up," Ezra said outside the parish center.

Remy poked him with an elbow. "I'm sure you wanted an exit strategy. I have supplied one."

"What will people think if I'm not at the vigil?"

"I suppose I failed to consider that," Remy replied and quickly changed the subject. "Did you glean anything from your conversations with Mrs. Tien?"

"Not as much as I could've." Then Ezra explained, "Rumor of Brooklyn's affair is making the rounds through the parish. Ellie was on the verge of telling me who the affair was with when Cynthia interrupted her."

"*Tant pis.* But, as you say, it may be no more than

a rumor. I fear Ellie is like poor Mathilde, so desperate to belong to a world of gallantry that she will pick up and use anything she finds."

"Who's Mathilde?"

Remy threw up his hands. "Read the books that I give you!" He glanced at his scuffed shoes, then placed a hand on his white collar. "So are you coming then?"

"I guess I have to." Ezra stopped. "But I thought the banquet covered my penance."

"I fear you have more sinning to do before this all is done. We might as well get ahead of it."

****

The only thing wrong with Adrian Silva was his choice of restaurant. Everything else met or exceeded Lucia's expectations.

He rose from his seat when she entered, pulled out a chair for her, then complimented her on her dress—a plaid shirt dress of light tan with rich carmine that showed almost no skin other than her arms and legs. She'd settled on this modest dress in spite of her friend Trish's advice to show him the goods. Trish could set her up with every man in Chicago; that didn't mean Lucia had to parade herself off to each of them.

Then she saw Adrian, with his faded buzz cut, milk-chocolate skin, and strong pecs pressing against his tight-striped Oxford shirt and thought, *I could've shown a little skin...*

Adrian was the eldest of three children, he said. The only boy and the only one not born in America.

"Where are you from?" she asked.

"San Juan. I've been in Chicago since I was five."

"Puerto Rico?" she asked. "I'm sorry to break it to you, but that's America."

"Not to everyone."

She conceded the point.

"What about you?" he asked.

The waitress arrived, and Adrian ordered a bottle of wine. What variety? the waitress wanted to know. He deferred to Lucia, assuring her that dinner was on him. Lucia chose a middling rosé. The waitress suggested a slightly more expensive one and, when Lucia looked to Adrian, he nodded with a smile.

"So what do you do for a living?" she asked.

"I'm a drug dealer," he said, nonchalant.

Her mouth dropped open.

"I'm kidding." He laughed. "I'm a pharmaceutical rep. I do mostly heart medications. I could make more in the pain med field, but…"

"You don't want to sell your soul?"

"That and it's so competitive!"

Lucia laughed.

"You haven't mentioned me where you're from."

"Right here in Chicago."

He gave her an incredulous look. "Your accent."

"Okay, we left Chihuahua when I was in high school.

"Why?"

Her phone rang. How bad would it look if she answered? She slipped one hand into her purse to silence it. She could always tell the caller that her phone died. "Why did we leave Chihuahua?" she repeated the question.

The phone rang again.

"Is that Trish giving you an out?" he asked.

She looked at the number this time and immediately went to her feet. "I have to take this." She brought the phone to her ear and headed toward the restrooms. "This had better be good."

"Sorry to bother you, Detective. Officer Bradley here. We have a situation over at NorthShore hospital."

Until only recently, Bradley and Lucia had been colleagues. Now, it seemed, he was bringing her issues.

"Okay. Why are you calling me about it?"

"Someone pulled a gun on Brooklyn Hannigan, the coma girl."

"I know who she is."

"Someone said you were running lead on her case."

"Who? Who said I was lead detective?"

"The gunman. He says he knows you."

"Okay," she said impatiently.

"His name's Ezra James."

She didn't know what bothered her more, that Ezra pulled a gun on their victim, or that he did it in the middle of the only decent date she'd had in a year. "I'll be right there."

Lucia strolled back to the table, giving herself time to decide how to explain the situation to Adrian without him thinking she was bailing. The facts sounded preposterous—her pseudo-partner pulled a gun on the girl they were supposed to be protecting and needed her to come clear it up. The alternative was to come up with a more plausible but false excuse. One step from the table, she decided to just sidestep the whole excuse business and aim for sincerity.

"Look," she said, "I like you, and I'm really enjoying this."

He smiled.

"But my job is shit right now. Sorry, *demanding*. I probably shouldn't swear on a first date. If it was just business as usual, I'd deal with it later, but this is urgent."

He wasn't smiling anymore. "You have to go?"

"But I want to see you again."

"When?"

"Tomorrow," she said. "Tomorrow for lunch. It will be my treat."

The waitress arrived with the bottle of rosé and, before they could tell her not to, pulled out the cork.

"That too," Lucia said. "That's my treat."

She set two twenties on the table and left Blue Basil. From the steps of the restaurant, she could just make out Autumn Elkhart's car parked on a side street and, in the driver's seat, Autumn Elkhart. The girl ducked when Lucia's gaze met hers. Apparently, this artistic genius didn't realize a simple rule of perspective. If you can see someone, they can see you.

Chapter Sixteen

The only rosary Ezra ever owned was the one his mother-in-law gave him when he graduated from Quantico. The beads were wood and the chain sterling silver. Pope Paul VI himself blessed the St. Michael medal at the crux. She bought it during a tour of the Holy Land and claimed the wood was harvested from olive trees in Bethlehem. He didn't necessarily believe all these details, but he cherished the rosary, nonetheless. Even more since Julia had left.

Fr. Remy was standing in NorthShore's lobby when Ezra arrived. He led Ezra into the open elevator. As the doors closed, Remy chuckled.

"What?" Ezra asked.

"Do you know what I was just thinking? In France, they have a saying, *Coup de foudre*. People say this when someone falls in love right away."

"Love at first sight?"

The elevator ascended.

"Yes," Remy said, "but it does not mean that literally."

"What's it mean?"

"Struck by lightning."

"What do they say in Africa?"

"In Burkina Faso they say, *Être kaoté*. To be knocked-out."

Though they'd worked together since August, Ezra

still knew very little about Remy's life in Africa. Ezra assumed something had happened to bring him to America and that the priest was hesitant to share the details. Still, he pressed for information. "Burkina Faso, huh? So is that where you're from?"

Remy smirked. "I drove through there once."

"Before or after your stay at the Abbaye de Keur Moussa in Senegal?"

Remy looked surprised.

"I still have contacts in Air Force intelligence."

"And you waste your favors digging up dirt on an old priest?"

"Tell me, is Senegal where you were born?"

"I did know a wonderful priest who was born in Senegal. He told us one morning after lauds, that is morning prayer, about a man named Anansi from a village in West Africa. This Anansi didn't live in the village where this priest was born, nor in Dakar, which is where the abbey resides, as your contact probably told you."

"Who was this Anansi?"

"A trickster and a great storyteller. Anansi was incredibly wise but greedy for wisdom, so one day he set out on his eight legs to gather as much wisdom as he could into a giant pot."

"Wait, eight legs?"

"Yes, Anansi was a great spider."

"You could've just said you're not from Senegal."

"But where is the fun in that?"

The elevator doors opened, and Ezra and Fr. Remy stepped out into the ICU waiting room. Visitors took up all available chairs and couches. From the looks of things, housekeeping hadn't made their rounds recently.

The floor was streaked with water and crud from snow-slicked boots. A nurses' station sat at the dead center of the ICU, a long wall-less counter forming the center of a wheel from which the nurses could observe each hospital room. At the opposite end of the wheel, a broad-shouldered man in green scrubs strolled leisurely toward the stairwell. Ezra only caught the back of his head—dark brown hair, tan neck.

As they drew closer to Brooklyn Hannigan's room, Ezra spied a metal folding chair and a venti-sized coffee cup beside it. The officer guarding her room leaned his elbows on the circular counter at the nurses' station, talking to someone not visible to Ezra.

A clang, as though a bedpan hitting the floor, came from inside Brooklyn's room. Through the window, he saw that the bed was empty. Instinctively, he reached for the grip of his 9mm, or rather where it used to reside. Now in its place rested the bright yellow taser, courtesy of St. Joseph and Mary school. Being the director of security at a Catholic school came with many perks, but carrying a firearm was not one of them. Regardless, the taser would do just as well in a pinch.

Holding Fr. Remy back, Ezra inched into Brooklyn's room. The student-teacher lay sprawled on the linoleum floor, her IV pulled as taut as a kite string. In her simple white gown, she looked much younger than she ever did at the school. If he hadn't personally known her, he might've mistaken her for a child.

Ignoring Ezra's previous order to stay at the door, Remy moved close and leaned over Brooklyn's body. "She's still breathing. Go! Get someone!"

Ezra tore into the corridor and nearly bowled over the police officer who should have been guarding the door. "What're you doing!" the cop shouted.

"Your job, apparently."

The dark-haired guy dressed like a nurse was just opening the door to enter the stairwell. "Halt!" Ezra tried to shout, but the officer grabbed him from behind.

"Where do you think you're going?" the officer growled.

Ezra knocked his hand away and, in the scuffle, they both collapsed onto the floor slick with spilled coffee. The officer slid in one direction, Ezra the other. As Ezra's hip and knee collided with the floor, pain shot through his left side. From that powerless and uncomfortable position, he watched the stairwell door close shut—and needed to make a decision.

He dragged himself up from the floor and, when the officer grabbed for his ankle, he kicked the man square in the face. Ezra would pay for this, but he couldn't worry about it right now. He unholstered the taser and staggered, sore from the fall, around the circle of rooms until he reached the doorway. Ezra couldn't see into the stairwell from the hall. He would have to go in blind.

Since discovering Brooklyn on the floor of her hospital room, Ezra had run on a subconscious level. But now he felt the reality of his position. He was a private citizen carrying a taser, in pursuit of someone he'd only gotten a glimpse of. Prudence told him to return to the room, apologize to the cop he'd kicked, and await assistance. Didn't Proverbs say wisdom dwells with prudence? Then again, everyone since the Romans knew "Fortune favors the bold."

All at once, he shoved the stairwell door open and pointed his taser first down the stairwell and then up.

Cold air hit his face. His nostrils filled with the scent of blowing snow. He saw the exterior door a half flight above wedged open with a clipboard.

Ezra crept up the stairs and jerked the door open, his weapon trained on two figures taking shape before him. An ear-shattering scream made him almost fire the taser. Two startled Filipino orderlies stood stockstill, their cigarettes held high above their heads. Ezra lowered his weapon, yet still the one nearest the door screamed out, "Ahh!" high and loud like a terrified opera singer.

"It's okay, it's okay." He turned his weapon sideways, displaying its bright yellow handle. "Taser. Not a gun. Taser."

They stared at the yellow grip and barrel, cocking their heads to one side curiously.

Then he heard a click behind him and felt the round muzzle of a gun on the middle of his back. Depending on the caliber, the bullet would either burst through his chest or ricochet around the inside of his ribcage like a pinball.

"Drop it," said the gunman.

"Okay, but before I do, tell me why you did it," Ezra said.

The gunman considered this a moment. "I was protecting her."

"From what?"

"From you."

Ezra turned his head, perplexed to see not the male nurse in green scrubs but the police officer, the man's nose and mustache matted with blood. Ezra turned around more fully to explain himself and caught an elbow to the temple. It wasn't hard enough to knock him down, but it did convince him to place his taser on the concrete.

"I got the guy," the officer said into his two-way.

A term from Ezra's Air Force days came to mind. *FUBAR*.

****

Ezra showed the officer his badge, and the man cooled down some.

"Why didn't you just tell me?" he asked Ezra.

"You knocked me down before I had the chance," Ezra replied.

He examined Ezra's badge. "I'm still going to have to file a report."

"Fine," Ezra replied, embarrassed about the whole situation.

Reinforcements arrived within minutes. They took over the scene, grilled Ezra, and led him outside while they assessed the situation. It took Lucia Vargas twenty minutes to arrive. Once again, she looked as if she had somewhere better to be when she got the call. She wore a black leather jacket over a plaid dress and knee-high boots.

"What seems to be the trouble?" she asked the officer outside.

"This asshole here," he said, pointing a thumb at Ezra and trying to sound like a tough guy.

"I meant upstairs. I'll deal with this asshole." She flashed her badge at him. "Go get Officer Bradley."

The officer fixed his posture and straightened his hat. "Sorry, Detective."

Then he hustled off, returning a minute later with the officer she requested. Officer Bradley explained the situation to Vargas.

"Aren't you a sight for sore eyes," Ezra said.

"You're lucky I answered my phone. Otherwise, they probably would've called your ASAC."

He was sure they had anyway. "Were you on a hot date?"

"Maybe I'll go back to it."

"Fine, fine." But he couldn't help himself. "What's his name?"

She didn't respond.

"I almost got shot in the back following up a lead on your case. The least you could do is humor me."

She looked him up and down sarcastically. "Why? Are you interested?"

"I'm married, thank you," Ezra said, holding up his left hand and wiggling his ring finger.

"Didn't I read you were divorced?"

He forced a smile. "Separated. Not divorced."

They re-entered the hospital and took the stairs to the ICU. The bed sheets still lay on the floor. Where was Brooklyn? There were no shoe marks on the linoleum or any other obvious traces of their perp. He or she likely wore surgical gloves, just like half the employees in the building, and maybe even a surgical mask. Forensics would swab the place, but Ezra doubted they'd come up with anything usable.

Then Ezra noticed something he hadn't before. The rail on the right side of the bed was in the down position. Had Remy or someone else done this after the fact? The possibility that Brooklyn had simply fallen out of bed drifted through his mind.

Vargas walked over to the bed and pointed at the rail. "Was this down when you found her?"

Ezra smiled. "You know, I just don't remember."

Fr. Remy reappeared from the hall. "Brooklyn is stable, thanks be to God. The staff moved her to a room next door."

Over the next few hours, Lucia and Ezra interviewed every dark-haired male staff member at the hospital. Unfortunately, everyone at NorthShore—nurse, orderly, custodian—wore the same green outfits.

"It's hospital policy for staff to wear green scrubs," the charge nurse explained. "They can be obtained from dispensing machines found on every floor in the nurses' lounge or the showers. A fair number of male staff are working tonight."

"What's that mean," Ezra asked, "a fair number?"

The nurse shrugged. "A dozen at least, maybe more. Who knows?"

A review of the CCTV narrowed it down to one suspect, Tomas, an orderly from Argentina. He admitted to being on that floor at some point during his shift but not to being in Brooklyn's room. He had no motive and no connection to the school. Furthermore, he was working a double shift Thursday night, which ruled him out for the initial attack. He even remembered the EMTs bringing Brooklyn in.

"She kept screaming out."

"She was awake?" Ezra asked.

The charge nurse answered for him. "Brooklyn Hannigan lost consciousness immediately after they brought her in."

"Is that common?"

She shrugged. "Common is an unhelpful term. As for the scrubs, anybody can purchase them."

Ezra walked over to one of the scrub dispensers. It reminded him of a vending machine. "Could our perp have bought them here?"

"Employees have a code they punch in. Everyone's code is different."

"We'll need a record of everyone who received scrubs from these machines today and yesterday," Vargas told her.

Further examination of the security footage revealed that no one entered or exited Brooklyn's room in the hours leading up to Remy and Ezra's visit. At least not by way of the door. Tomas had entered the ICU, walked around the circle, possibly checking for spills or to see if the nurses needed him, and then exited into the stairwell just as Ezra and Remy arrived.

"Tomas didn't move her," Ezra said.

"Think someone climbed up the drainage pipe?" Vargas asked.

"Then back down again. Either that or our perp can fly." He rubbed his sore elbow. "I owe you one for coming so fast. How can I make it up to you?"

Lucia thought this over for a moment before responding. "Buy me a beer."

"I don't drink."

"Then don't buy yourself one."

Chapter Seventeen

Lucia arrived at Yeats Tavern, an Irish pub on the south side of Chicago, around midnight. The simple wood furnishings and strict code of conduct made it a favorite bar among Chicago PD. In Evanston, Lucia was the sole Latina detective, and one of only a few women in the entire department, but in Yeats, she frequently saw female police officers like her.

Well, maybe not frequently, but at least occasionally. The bartender wore a tight black T-shirt that hugged his bulging biceps and revealed the bottom of a black tattoo. From what she could see, it looked like the Marine Corps emblem. His shaggy red beard needed a trim, in Lucia's opinion.

She ordered a pint of Guinness, the only beer on the menu, and absentmindedly watched the television on the wall behind the bar. Every day at four-thirty, it played a popular game show that required contestants to give a response in the form of a question. After that, it went right to Fox News. At eleven p.m. this evening, however, the television aired an eerily appropriate program: "The Story of the CTC Killer."

"Everybody knew he was guilty," a bald man in a Bulls jersey said into the camera. The caption *Juror #7* appeared below his face. "That cop, I mean."

"Special Agent Ezra James?" the off-screen interviewer asked.

"Yeah, that James guy. The one who planted all that evidence. I lost a lot of respect for the Feds after they showed us everything he planted."

The screen cut to a black-and-white picture of Ezra at his desk in the Chicago field office of the FBI. Stacks of files loomed on either side of him, and he was frowning at the camera. His sharkskin suit was rumpled, and there were bags under his eyes.

The narrator continued, "But Agent James wasn't always an irredeemable monster."

Now a color picture of him in a University of Michigan tank top filled the screen. Beside him were three male friends. Lake Michigan filled the background. The narrator then told of Ezra's success at Michigan and his brief military career in the Air Force's Office of Special Investigations. Another photograph showed him in a Harvard sweatshirt. A girl ten years his junior was on his arm this time. Behind them snow-covered red brick buildings rose majestically.

"Oh, God." Ezra's voice sounded behind Lucia. "Is this a set-up?"

"Don't worry," she said without turning. "I'll have them change the channel."

"Don't bother. It will just draw attention." He pointed at the screen. "Did you hear what they said about me in the evening news yesterday?"

"No."

"Me neither." He smiled as if to dismiss the whole thing, but it seemed clear to Lucia that he had heard.

Lucia should've known that the Hannigan case would bring his name back into the news. "So how old were you when you became an agent?"

"Thirty-four."

"That seems a little young."

"Says the thirty-year-old detective," Ezra replied.

She aimed her beer mug at the screen, which now showed crime scene tape across the front door of a small white house overgrown with bushes and kudzu. "How'd you get on the case?" She had spent the little free time she'd had the last few days reading over Ezra's involvement with the CTC Killer. "I read that the murders were all on the coasts."

He waved over the bartender and ordered a cream soda.

"We don't got cream soda."

"What have you *got?*" Ezra asked the man.

"Guinness."

He ordered water.

The door to the bar swung open. Two couples in their thirties entered. They took up the rest of the counter and ordered drinks. From their rowdiness, Lucia guessed they'd been drinking all evening.

"Tell me about the Coast-to-Coast Killer," Lucia said, raising her voice to be heard over their rowdy neighbors.

"I got the wrong guy."

"I surmised as much," she replied. "Walk me through it."

His knee bounced twice before he could calm it. Lucia imagined he was trying to decide whether to lie, shut down, or leave entirely. Then he asked, "You know what the most damning thing about John Lewis Straugh was?"

She shook her head.

"His name," he said. "John Lewis Straugh just

sounds like a serial killer. If he had arranged his victims upright in the cornfields around his house, we could have called him The Straw Man or The Scarecrow Killer. The next most damning was his wife."

"I don't recall the wife."

"She was adamant for us to investigate him. Women only become that suspicious of their husbands when it involves infidelity or fear of impending death."

The more he spoke, the more he seemed to relax. "Did you read much about the case?"

"Not at the time."

"*The Tribune* came up with the name *The Coast-to-Coast Killer.* They credited him with four murders in four different locales."

One of the men beside Ezra knocked over his pint, and dark stout poured across the bar. The bittersweet scent filled the air, and Ezra pushed his stool back. The drink's owner leaned over to apologize. Ezra waved him off, but he clenched his jaws and had one fist balled up tight. He looked ready for a fight.

Is he an alcoholic? Lucia wondered. She'd met a number of recovered people in her line of work—and even more who ought to give it a try. In fact, the father of her best friend Trish was a "meeting maker," as he put it once. She thought of asking Ezra outright then thought better of it. "What locales?" she asked instead.

Ezra counted them off on his hands. "Atlanta, D.C., New York, and Charlotte, North Carolina. Charlotte was the outlier. When we analyzed flight itineraries, Charlotte turned out to be the location that suggested Straugh the loudest. Charlotte also made us wonder if our sights weren't too narrow."

"Us?" Lucia asked.

"The Bureau, I mean. If the killer was going up and down the coast, he could be stopping at countless sleepy coastal towns and minor ports. Unlike New York and D.C., it might take local PDs several months just to process the murder let alone connect the dots."

"So you thought he was the *East* Coast Killer?"

"The working theory for a few months was a man driving up and down the Atlantic coast with more murders to be connected. The doors baffled everyone, though."

"What about the doors?"

"There was no sign of forced entry, no signs of a struggle, no intercourse with the victims. These girls were beautiful, and they trusted the killer, let him into their home and didn't expect to be harmed. Possibly, he had a key. A one-night stand was another explanation, but surely someone would have seen him picking these girls up the night of the murder. Nothing came out of the initial interviews. It seemed these were long-term relationships. That's what the New York office decided."

The bartender came over and cleaned up the spill. When he finished, the couples beside Lucia and Ezra rose from their stools, paid, and left. The TV played on, digging deeper into Ezra's past indiscretions. She tried to ignore it and listen to the man himself.

"When did they pull in the Chicago office?"

Looking more at ease, Ezra laughed. "CTC sent a letter to the Charlotte Post, of all places."

"What's so funny about that?"

"It's their African American paper."

Lucia didn't get it.

"None of the victims were black. He was giving

national breaking news to a disinterested publication. It would be like if he sent it to Sports Illustrated."

"So did they publish the letter?"

"They had to! They contacted Charlotte PD first, of course. New York acquired the letter and distributed it across the country to the field offices. That's when I noticed the lowercase epsilons."

"The what?"

"Epsilons. Two of them. They're these curved Greek *E's*."

He wrote an "ε" on his napkin. It looked like a backwards 3 to her.

"I told my supervisor. Immediately, we started to make a list of seminarians, Greek immigrants, and Classics professors, anyone who would be likely to accidentally or intentionally slip in an epsilon instead of an *E*."

"So that was it?" she asked. "You spotted the epsilons?"

"Not just that. I think lots of people noticed that detail," he said, abashed. "There was more. One common thread among the victims was a mention by friends or relatives of a mysterious affair. Each victim was seeing a man who visited only sporadically. A mystery man. He was blond, middle-aged, fit, and obscenely rich."

"So then the West Coast?" she asked.

"Right, LA and Seattle. Same MO, same vague description of a traveling lover. I took a personal interest. I mentioned to our director my theory that the killer was flying from coast to coast, committing the murders as far from his home as possible. It was even possible he was from the Chicago area."

"You wanted CTC to be from Chicago."

Ezra smiled. "I took it upon myself to cross-reference flight itineraries, and I developed a list of possible suspects. Unfortunately, the murders by then were in seven different cities, all with multiple airports nearby. With a window of one week before or after the murder, this left us over three hundred names from forty different cities. Still, I took it up the line again."

"And they remembered about the epsilons and listened to you," Lucia said.

"Bingo. We shared the new theory with papers in our target cities across the Midwest. That's when we received the call from Stephanie Straugh, John's wife. She read the article in the *Tribune* and called the next day. She provided her husband's flight itineraries from the past two years—and there were hundreds of flights. Some for legitimate business trips. Others, a dozen or so, had nothing to do with business whatsoever."

"A story as old as time," Lucia said. She finished off her pint. "Mind if I order another?"

"Go for it."

She waved to the bartender and held up the empty glass. "How'd Straugh do on the Hare Checklist?"

"Ah yes, the Hare Checklist of Psychopathy. He barely raised a single red flag. Behavioral Science ran a number of tests, but they all came back normal. Egomaniac maybe but, considering that his IQ score came back through the roof, we expected a little excess in that department."

"How about the family, friends, and coworkers?"

"Everyone loved him—especially at work," Ezra continued. "The tech company he worked for, G. Carmen Industries, proved helpful. They cleared up which flights were business and which personal. The trips didn't all line up, but they were all within driving distance of the crime scenes. When a girl in Seattle was murdered, Straugh had stopped off in Portland, where he rented a car and put four-hundred miles on it. While he visited Miami, a girl in West Palm Beach was murdered."

"And so you found your man."

"Seemed like it," he said. "The Bureau adopted my theory. The killer was flying out of O'Hare, ping-ponging from coast to coast. He was The Coast-to-Coast Killer, and his name was John Lewis Straugh."

"But he wasn't," she said.

Ezra went quiet and contemplated his water. Lucia found the sight of a man drowning his troubles in H2O almost laughable, but the longer she looked, the sadder the situation became. "So then what?"

"The Straughs lived out in Roseland before the trial," he said, turning the glass of water between his fingers. "They owned a seven-bedroom Victorian on land large enough to hold a one-acre garden, a full-size basketball court, and an in-ground pool. You can see it from I-57. It's that big."

"I've seen it—or at least—I seen the neighborhood. All those mansions look alike."

"There was also an immaculate, green-all-year lawn with flower beds of different Illinois-native flowers. We tore up everything, brought in Bobcats and jackhammers and men with pickaxes and shovels. We dug up the garden and took the floorboards out of the house. The forensics team combed through every last inch of the property for murder weapons, body parts, or other souvenirs from his victims. They found no hard evidence or DNA in the initial sweep. We hoped if we dug around the house, we'd find something."

"Some kind of serial killer souvenir?" she asked.

He nodded.

The tavern doors blew open, and a gust of wind filled the room with cold air. A chill ran down Lucia's spine, caused either by the change in temperature or the thought of a killer's souvenirs. The bartender rushed over and shoved the doors until they latched shut.

Lucia pulled at her jacket. "Did you find any? Souvenirs, I mean."

"Just weird stuff. The house was chock-full of electronics projects, sculptures, a display of Chinese Shaolin knives, and the toothbrush collection, of course."

"What do you mean 'of course'?"

"You don't know about the toothbrushes? That's how we caught him." He became quiet again.

"Tell me."

"There were maybe a hundred. Every one he'd ever owned in a display case. On the witness stand, he said, 'They're just toothbrushes. They're funny, like, *look how much hard work went into keeping these pearly whites clean,'* and then he tapped one of his canines. His defense attorneys were out of ideas. It's never a good idea to put a killer on the stand, but they were desperate. The joke fell flat and no one, not even his attorneys, even smiled."

Lucia thought back to the most recent article she'd read. "Who is Cindy Dao? Her name came up in a couple articles."

"Long before the trial, we had the profile along with the support of the wife, but we didn't have eyewitnesses, so we leaked details to the press and found Cindy Dao, a young, beautiful marketing exec. She told us, without equivocation, that she was having an affair with Straugh for going on five years."

More patrons left the bar. Cold wind blew and the doors sprung open again, ricocheting against the wall. The bartender rushed over and shoved them into place, but the damage was done. The wind sucked the warmth out of the room, leaving Lucia chilled to the bone.

Ezra, on the other hand, seemed unaffected. He continued his story. "According to his mistress, Straugh would visit her whenever he came to San Francisco. Sometimes he stayed for a three-day weekend. Other times, he just dropped in for the night before catching an early flight the next morning. After every stay, he left flowers and chocolates, and a cleaning crew arrived to deep clean her entire apartment. He always paid them in cash and always anonymously."

"I read about that part," Lucia said. "As far as affairs ago, one who gives you chocolates, flowers, and cleans your apartment doesn't sound too bad."

"He was married," Ezra reminded her.

She smiled sarcastically. "Aren't they always?"

"Anyway, Straugh met Cindy Dao at a technology convention in San Francisco. He visited whenever he could talk his company into flying him out west. Even this affair, however, wasn't enough. On several occasions, he snuck out of Dao's apartment by the fire escape, returning just before sunrise."

As if called into being by their conversation, Cindy Dao now appeared on the screen.

"I couldn't believe it," Dao said from the screen. "My affair was having an affair!" she told the reporter

189

with an ironic smirk. She was even prettier than Lucia remembered. Sleek black hair, full lips, and mysterious hazel eyes. "I read the profile of the killer, how after he sliced them up and left these calling cards—diodes and transistors, an integrated circuit, some robotic wheels. I thought, *That's so something John would do!*" Her smile faded. "Then it stopped being a joke. Something came unglued inside me, and then I saw his name in the paper."

Ezra waved over the bartender. "Could you turn this off?"

The bartender crossed his big biceps. "We got cops in here."

Lucia couldn't tell if the bartender meant this as a general remark or if he recognized Ezra and meant it as a dig. Either way, she suggested they move to one of the booths out of hearing distance of the television. Ezra picked up their drinks and followed her.

Another distinct memory came to mind. "Was CTC the trial with all the crying women?" she asked.

Teary-eyed women confessing on the stand about how Straugh betrayed them became one of the main motifs of the trial, Ezra explained. The image of a woman crying on the stand became so iconic that every newspaper and magazine article had included at least one sketch of a woman hunched over, her makeup smudged with tears.

He continued, "Cindy Dao's testimony opened the floodgates. Soon, calls came in from St. Louis, Houston, Biloxi, Wichita, and Kalamazoo. They ranged from one-night stands to full-blown affairs. The more serious affairs knew his credit card number and how he liked his prime rib. They even knew which mission trip his kids took that summer. They all confirmed the same MO: flowers, chocolates, and a cleaning crew. Straugh left no trace."

"How'd that go over with his defense attorneys?"

"They switched tactics. They admitted to Straugh's affairs—though not with the murder victims—and recast Straugh not as an innocent church-goer but as a troubled sex-addict who, while deeply flawed, was not a killer. Not all the affair-cities lined up with murders. In fact, most didn't. But the die was cast. I don't think you could have bribed your way into a hung jury for all the money in the tech industry." Ezra sipped his water. "People hated Straugh that much."

Lucia nodded. The early articles she had read vilified Straugh and praised the Chicago FBI office. The latter ones focused almost entirely on making a villain of Ezra.

"It got much worse."

The bartender sauntered over to their booth and stood staring. "All right, love birds, we're closing up."

"We're not—what did you say?" Lucia asked him.

"We're closing."

"But it's hardly midnight," she said.

He pointed to the clock, which read two a.m., and then gestured around the empty bar.

"You heard him," she said to Ezra. "Pay the man."

Ezra dropped a twenty on the table.

"I'm going to be frank with you," she said. "Yesterday, I spoke with the lawyer, Mark Pierce. His wife had lunch with Brooklyn the day you found her."

"I know him. What did you think?"

"He's definitely not our guy. He said he was working until after the attack and then went to the gym.

Both alibis have eyewitnesses to corroborate them. Also, he didn't strike me as Brooklyn's type."

"Why do I feel like there's more?" he asked.

"Then he told me I shouldn't trust you."

Ezra broke eye contact with her and grabbed his coat off his seat. "Then don't."

"But I'd like to," she said.

"Do whatever you want. You're not my boss, and we're not courting."

"Courting?"

"It means *dating.*"

"I know what it means. I just didn't think anyone used it this century."

He put his coat on and walked out the door. Bracing cold air poured into the bar. She followed him outside. "If we're going to work together, I just want to know if you did what the papers said. It doesn't matter if you did. Everyone makes mistakes."

The second she said it, Lucia realized how it must have sounded. She meant to console not condemn.

"Do they?" he asked. "Do you plant evidence on innocent suspects?"

"No, of course not."

"Neither do I!" He climbed into his purple sedan and slammed the door.

"That's not what I meant," she said, but he was already pulling away.

Chapter Eighteen

Sunday

Sunday morning, Lucia did the utterly unexpected. She asked to attend church with her mother and sister. Her mother beamed in response; Areli, on the other hand, eyed her suspiciously.

"But I get to pick where we go," Lucia said.

"Okay," her mother agreed cautiously.

To Señora Vargas' great relief, Lucia chose St. Joseph and Mary which, though not their usual parish, was still Catholic.

Fr. Remy Mbombo wore a violet chasuble to indicate the season of Advent. Lucia surprised herself by remembering that each season had its own color. Although the significance of the color escaped her. Throughout the mass, Lucia shifted back and forth in her pew. The discomfort was worth it, if she could glean something useful from observing the families of SJM or from speaking with Fr. Remy again.

The Scouts, Flemings, Ainsleys, Martin Durand, and Benjamin Larson were all physically present, but they all appeared to be on the verge of sleep. Lucia Vargas, on the other hand, was wide awake. When the priest repeated again and again a line from the reading, "the poor have good news brought to them," she wondered what this could possibly mean. In what era did the poor ever receive good news? When the priest said, "Maybe the Church ought to pay taxes just like everyone else," her ears perked up again. When he concluded his homily with, "Christ did not come as a millionaire, but as a pauper," Lucia felt she was hearing not a suburban priest but a third-world revolutionary.

After the mass, Lucia introduced her family to Fr. Remy. "You are from Africa?" her mother asked.

He nodded. "I have lived in many places, but I was born there, yes."

"Your English is very good," she said.

"I take that as a great compliment coming from an American."

Usually Señora Vargas did not blush easily, but she did then. She took more pride in being an American than anyone Lucia knew.

"Perhaps we could all have lunch?" the priest suggested.

Taken off-guard, Lucia shifted from foot to foot. "I would, except—"

"Except she has a date!" Areli interrupted.

"I'm meeting a friend."

"A *boy*friend," her little sister added.

Lucia turned on her bigmouth sister. "How old are you, Areli?"

Then to her mother, she said, "*Puedes esperar en el carro? Tengo que hablar con el sacerdote.*"

The mother led her reluctant teenage daughter out of the chapel so Lucia could speak with Fr. Remy in private.

"Is this a faith question?" he asked hopefully.

"Ezra."

"Ah."

"I may have offended him last night."

"He is easily offended," Fr. Remy replied. "Did you ask him if he…" he started to ask but trailed off.

"Yes."

"Ezra's difficulty is that he believes good people do not do bad things."

"And he is a good person."

Fr. Remy nodded. "It is, perhaps, our greatest difference."

"What is?"

"This distinction. For a priest, 'All have sinned and fall short.' If Ezra is guilty of this accusation, then he is human like the rest of us."

"But the law is different," Lucia said.

"You say that because you are the law," the priest replied. "This is my point." He placed his hands behind his back and leaned back on his heels.

She wanted to ask if anyone had told the priest about their involvement in the case. Had anyone admitted to having an affair with Brooklyn or even to the attack itself? What had Ezra confessed to? Certainly if anyone knew the truth about the CTC case, besides Ezra, it was Fr. Remy. She let these thoughts build and then subside. Fr. Remy couldn't share about these confidences even if he wanted to.

"Whatever Ezra has or hasn't done," the priest continued, "he refuses to accept himself as he currently is. St. Paul writes, 'For no man hates his own flesh,' yet that is all Ezra knows how to do."

"He's not alone," she replied.

Fr. Remy agreed and then asked if Ezra mentioned Ellen Tiene. "She's Vietnamese, a member of the Sisters of Teresa."

"Doesn't ring a bell," Lucia said.

"She and Ezra spent a significant period of time together last night."

"At the banquet?" Lucia asked. "What did he find out?"

"Ms. Tiene believes she knows the identity of the father of Brooklyn's baby," he explained, "but didn't feel comfortable sharing, at least not last night."

"How reliable is she?"

"Somewhat less reliable than English teacher Jarno." He turned slightly to smile and wave at a passing parishioner. "Plus Tiene has far less direct information."

Lucia checked her watch. "I'd better get going."

"You don't want to be late." The priest smirked. "Would you like a nuptial blessing before you go?"

****

Lucia chose the restaurant this time. Le Bacon specialized in French Canadian cuisine, primarily breakfast and brunch, which was strikingly similar to American breakfast and brunch. The only real differences were the beret-clad wait staff, the French ambiance music, and the fact that each menu item came with optional *crème fouettée.*

After dropping her mother and sister off at their apartment, Lucia went straight to Le Bacon. Adrian already had a booth and was speaking with the waiter, a college student in a blue-and-white striped sweater, the kind you saw in French films from the '60s. Lucia believed they were called *marinières,* though she couldn't remember where she'd learned the term. Lucia ordered a *café au lait.*

"Sorry I'm late. Church ran long."

"Catholic?"

She sidestepped the question. "I'm investigating an attempted murder at the Catholic school, St. Joseph and Mary."

"God, that's terrible," he said.

She laughed.

"Why are you laughing?" Adrian asked.

"It's just refreshing. I usually talk about my work with other law enforcement."

"And they think violence is *not* terrible?"

No, she didn't mean that. Not exactly.

The waiter returned with their coffees and took their food order. Adrian ordered the most French-sounding thing on the menu, *crêpes Suzette* in orange sauce *avec bacon Canadien,* which he pronounced in a passable French accent, at least to Lucia's untrained ear. She ordered bacon and eggs. She didn't even try the dish's French name.

"What I meant to say is everyone knows these things are terrible, but no one says it. You almost have to detach yourself to deal with them day-in and day-out. I don't even try telling my family anymore."

"I get it," he said. "My job can be difficult to talk about as well. For instance, one of the heart medications I push causes spontaneous erections."

She spat her coffee back into the mug. "Is that true?"

"I can show you the literature."

Their food arrived and, through bites of bacon, they continued to become acquainted. Adrian attended an all-boys Catholic school in North Chicago, this while Lucia attended public school on the south side. As she finished up high school and her family relocated to Springfield, he matriculated to Loyola, graduating *summa cum laude* four years later. A question came to her then. Why was Adrian still single? She both wanted to ask and didn't dare. What would he think if she asked about his single status? Would he tell her about an ex-wife and a slew of children? It seemed too early for all that.

"Try this," he said, offering her a bite of crêpe on his fork.

She tried it, but confessed, "It's too rich for me."

"So what brought you to Evanston?" he asked.

"When it came time for my sister, Areli, to start thinking of college, my mother found a job at Northwestern. She works in their facilities department, and Areli's a senior at ETHS."

"Evanston High is a good school," he said.

"For a public school, you mean?"

"No, really, I had a lot of Loyola classmates from there."

"It's better than the school I went to," she admitted.

"Yet look at you now. You're certainly doing something more difficult and more noble than I am," he said. "And I went to some of the best schools in Chicago."

Lucia didn't know how to take the compliment. As a general rule, compliments caused her discomfort. They felt manipulative in some way.

Perhaps noticing her discomfort, Adrian changed subjects. "Is your sister going to apply to Northwestern then?"

"I think so. If she does, I'm certain she'll be accepted. That girl's a genius."

He smiled at her. "It must be genetic."

A fleck of *crème fouettée* remained on his upper lip. Even though she'd eaten an entire plate of bacon and eggs, she found herself suddenly very hungry. Could she kiss him? Over the table at brunch? Would that be weird? She leaned forward slightly but then behind Adrian, the doors opened and in walked Ezra James and an elderly woman, gray haired and slightly hunched. The two of them were in the middle of an argument. Lucia couldn't hear them, but Ezra sounded vexed.

Lucia and Ezra did an age-old dance then. Everyone who has seen an acquaintance in public knows it well. She looked away, and then he looked in her direction before looking away. Both knew they had been seen and knew they'd been seen seeing. Every second that ticked away thereafter, every moment the hostess didn't whisk Ezra James off to an out-of-sight table, added to the awkwardness. Finally, she waved in his direction. He, pretending to just notice her, waved back and mouthed "hi" but remained in his place by the hostess station. His elderly companion, however, shuffled toward Lucia, forcing him to follow along until they both stood beside the booth.

"I didn't see you there," he lied and forced a smile.

Was it better to fake politeness or to not even put in the effort? Lucia never knew. "I was hiding from you," she said with perhaps too much honesty. "This is Adrian Silva."

Adrian leaned halfway out of the booth to shake Ezra's hand.

"Have we interrupted a date?" Ezra asked.

"Yes," Lucia replied.

"I'm Ezra's mother." The woman put her hands on

her hips. "Although you'd think I didn't exist at all."

"Everyone is well aware of your presence," he said, lowering his voice.

"Are you one of Ezra's colleagues?" the mother asked.

Lucia assumed this meant a federal agent. "I'm a detective with Evanston PD. Your son is assisting us with an attempted murder."

"Oh," she said, a note of disappointment in her voice. She shuffled back to the hostess stand without another word to Lucia.

"I'll let you get back to it," Ezra said then.

"Can you come with me to ETHS tomorrow morning?" she asked him.

"The public school? Sure. Do you still need to verify that Martin Durand wrote Brooklyn a letter of recommendation?"

Brooklyn visited Martin the night of her attack. He told Ezra that Brooklyn stopped by for the recommendation letter and nothing else. "They could just fax it over, but I want to speak to the principal. If he personally spoke to Brooklyn or Martin, he may remember something helpful. The principal at Evanston may even be the last person to speak with Brooklyn before the attack."

"Besides the dinner date."

"He might even know more about that."

Ezra's mother called his name. The hostess was leading her to a table. A look of resignation passed over his face. "Fine," he said. "I'll meet you at the school."

He took a few steps but then turned back to her. "You'll never guess who followed me here this morning."

"Who?"

"Autumn Elkhart."

Lucia just shook her head.

"Who's Autumn Elkhart?" Adrian asked.

"Remember that girl I told you about, the one they found in the snow? Autumn's her roommate." Then she gestured toward Ezra. "And this man's the one who did the finding."

Ezra smiled awkwardly. Then his face turned all business again. "There's another problem: I think Autumn may be assisting in the investigation."

The two investigators then explained to the civilian, Adrian, how loved ones frequently became involved in their investigations.

"Became obstructions," were Ezra's words.

In the eyes of a father, a wife, or, in this case, a roommate, the police were dragging their feet. So Autumn had taken to following Lucia and Ezra around to discover who they suspected. Just as the investigators kept a persons-of-interest list, Autumn was likely building her own list.

"I'll take care of her," she said. "After we wrap up at the school, I'll pay our little private eye a visit."

Ezra agreed that Autumn wasn't time sensitive. Then he rejoined his mother across the restaurant and out of ear shot. Lucia learned nothing further about his argument with his mother, but she surmised its tenor from the way Mrs. James kept glowering suspiciously at various tables—an openly gay couple, an interracial family—and then whispering feverishly at Ezra. By the time Lucia and Adrian left the restaurant, Ezra had acquired a shade of red that could best be described as Embarrassed Rage.

Chapter Nineteen

Monday

One of the last people to see Brooklyn before her attack, Martin Durand claimed she came to his apartment for a letter of recommendation. Martin didn't know why SJM rescinded their job offer, but he did know Evanston Township High School needed a new choir teacher. He gave her the principal's email address and then, the day of the attack, she came to his apartment to get the letter. Or, at least, this is what he told Ezra, which is how Lucia came to learn of Brooklyn's job hunt. For all Lucia knew, Brooklyn and Martin's rendezvous had nothing to do with work but instead proved an illicit affair.

St. Joseph and Mary school paled in comparison to Evanston High. The red brick edifice always recalled a castle to Lucia's mind. Two battlements rose on either side of a glassed entryway and beyond the entryway, high above, waved an American flag. While most schools displayed their flag on a pole out front, ETHS hid theirs behind several layers of fortification as if guarding it.

Ezra arrived several minutes after her, and together they entered through the main doors. He held the door open a few seconds longer to let in a group of senior girls. Lucia knew they were seniors because she saw her sister Areli among them.

"Morning, *muchachas*," she said to them.

Her sister ignored her.

"Areli," she said more directly.

Areli ducked her head and kept walking with her friends. "Who was that?" one of the girls whispered as they moved down the hall and away from Lucia and Ezra. Lucia didn't understand teenagedom, nor had she ever.

The principal spotted them before his secretary buzzed them through the glass office door. He met them at the door and led them to his office. Ezra had to look up at a forty-five-degree angle to meet him eye-to-eye. Black, bald, and built like a truck, Principal Samuels was an imposing man, yet he smiled warmly at them.

Lucia spoke first. "Did you meet with Brooklyn Hannigan?"

"I did." He pulled a typed letter out of his printer and handed it to her. "She called about a week ago to see if we were hiring and then again on Thursday after school to see if we received this letter."

The top of Martin Durand's letter said "Principal Samuels" not "To Whom it May Concern" or even "ETHS Hiring Committee."

After the salutation, however, the letter lost its specificity. Martin Durand could've taken its content from a teacher-reference template. He described Brooklyn as punctual, adept, knowledgeable, and good with students. He failed to mention anything specific about her music or education background. He also neglected to reference any of the events she helped with at the school.

Lucia finished reading and looked up.

"It's boilerplate," Principal Samuels said.

"How did Brooklyn seem on the phone?" Lucia asked.

"Enthusiastic. They all do, though. In the job interview, every prospective teacher is Miss Honey. Then you go to see them the first day of class and they're Agatha Trunchbull."

"I'm sorry?" Ezra asked.

"Matilda," Lucia explained. "They're characters from the book *Matilda.*" She returned her attention to Principal Samuels. "So Brooklyn didn't sound depressed or nervous?"

"I'm no psychologist," Principal Samuels said, "but she sounded fine to me. When I read about her suicide attempt, it shocked me. Really it did."

Ezra took the letter and glanced over it. "What qualities do you look for in a teacher?"

"Punctuality, knowledge about the teaching arts and their individual subject, and respect for the students. You could be a genius, but if you don't come to work on time or you hate the students, you're not long for the profession."

Lucia thanked him and folded the letter in half. She doubted it would be important, but she'd add it to her case file.

****

Minutes later, Lucia and Ezra stood between their cars.

"I hate dead ends," she said.

"I love them," Ezra replied.

"Why in the world would you love a dead end?"

"Because, my dear Watson, 'Once you eliminate the impossible, whatever remains, no matter how improbable, must be the truth.' We're one step closer to the truth."

She opened her car door and climbed in. "If one of us is Watson—it's you."

"Yet I'm the one who knew the quote."

Lucia knew the quote, as well. She just didn't happen to say it just then. "I'm going to pay Autumn a visit and see what she's conniving at."

"Who knows, maybe she's found something convincing."

She gave Ezra a doubtful glance.

"I once worked a drug case in the Air Force," he said.

"That fell under OSI?"

"We didn't realize it was a drug case at first. A woman found her husband murdered in his car one morning. He came home late the night before and never made it inside. First Lieutenant Underhill was the guy's name. We checked doorbell cameras, interviewed neighbors, and interviewed his captain and others in the squadron. We couldn't figure it out."

He didn't say anything for a beat.

"Okay, so how'd you find out about the drugs?" she asked, still sitting in her car with the door open.

"The wife started stalking her dead husband's captain," Ezra said. "She couldn't sleep, couldn't eat, so she followed him around 24/7. Parked her car down the street from his house, followed him to work in the mornings, that sort of thing."

"Had she mentioned her suspicions before then?"

"She said he was an asshole, always overworking Lieutenant Underhill, but that could describe half the officers on base."

"What did she find?"

"About a week later, this captain left his house in the middle of the night. Didn't turn on a single house light, lest he wake the wife and kids, then drove off Scott Air Force base and across the state line into St. Louis. Wife Underhill followed him through every gang-ridden corner of East St. Louis, stopping here and there to make quick drug transactions, and then back to base. He drove to the house of another officer, Second Lieutenant Zubek, to drop off the case."

A bell sounded throughout the school grounds. Class change.

"What happened then?" Lucia asked.

"The wife turned the whole lot of them in, even her late husband. Called me up and gave me routes, addresses, times, and every officer and enlisted man involved in the late-night operation. We followed them around ourselves for a few weeks before we made our move. Eight men ended up in Leavenworth over that deal. Two more were fined and dishonorably discharged."

Lucia was surprised. "Why no prison time for them?"

"They said they were just following orders and hadn't asked questions about the packages they were handling."

She rapped the roof of her car with her knuckles. "They may have been telling the truth." She thought about it some more. "Didn't anyone question the captain leaving base in the middle of the night?"

"Sure, but they weren't about to report him. Furthermore, he oversaw the security gate logs, so whatever airman was on duty that night would've had to go over the captain's head and speak with the major. You and I both know that wouldn't have ended well."

"So the persistent wife saved the day?"

"That time."

They both lapsed into silence. Lucia recalled times an intervening civilian not only didn't save the day but actually brought about even greater tragedy.

"If you can, call me when you're done with Autumn," Ezra said.

"Will do."

****

Lucia dreaded visiting Brooklyn's roommate. Telling a civilian to back off was always difficult, especially one this close to the victim. She took the long way, stopping at Schlegl's Bakery for donuts and coffee first. She ordered a dozen chocolate ganache donuts, a dozen assorted cake donuts, and a black coffee. She ate a ganache, sipping coffee between each bite. She would save a second for after her conversation with Autumn, and then she'd take the rest back to the station.

Autumn's apartment complex consisted of three stories of mostly college students who put cheap Christmas lights in their windows, didn't decorate their doors, and left pizza boxes and other refuse in the hall beside their doormats.

When she knocked on Autumn's door, it lurched inward. She drew her service weapon slowly. Her .45 never felt heavy at the firing range, but in the actual line of duty, her weapon seemed to acquire mammoth heft. She clutched the grip tighter and pressed open the door with her shoulder.

The living room was empty. The rustic kitchen

table contained a single set of dishes, egg remnants on a plate, and a half inch of orange juice in a clear glass. Then, as Lucia turned a corner, the rest of the kitchen table came into view and with it the still body of Autumn Elkhart, face down on what appeared to be a leather-bound journal. A pool of blood had filled the open journal, spilled onto the table, and dribbled onto the white carpet.

Chapter Twenty

Ezra entered the side door of SJM school and ran straight into a German shepherd. He narrowly avoided kneeing Peppers, the drug canine, in the snout, which would've ended far worse for Ezra than the dog. He waved at Officer Higgins who, with Peppers, performed the school's quarterly drug sweep. Peppers did the lion's share of the sweeping, but Officer Higgins filed the paperwork and collected his check.

"Did you two find anything?" Ezra asked.

"Got a hit on some lockers," Higgins confirmed.

"What was it?"

"Don't know yet."

As far as Ezra knew, Principal Weeks had the combination to every locker on the school grounds, and consequently so did the K-9 officer. If they hadn't opened the locker immediately, there must be some other complication.

"What's the hold up?" Ezra asked.

"Padlock. Sister Dewberry's guarding it until I get back."

"Let's go then."

Higgins and Peppers led Ezra to the music wing. The capacious band room and the smaller choir room were connected by a small office packed with instruments and sheet music. By the far wall of the choir room, Sister Dewberry stood beside four ancient, turquoise lockers, one of which had a steel padlock that required a key.

"Huh," Ezra said. "I probably should've noticed that padlock before."

"It's new," Catherine Weeks said from behind him.

A bolt cutter balanced over her shoulder, Catherine pushed between the two men, secured the teeth of the tool onto the padlock's shackle, and severed it from the round staple. The locker's hasp popped free, and Catherine jerked on it until the door swung open. Inside the locker, a wristlet purse dangled from a metal hook.

Officer Higgins handed Peppers' leash to Ezra and put on a pair of bright purple gloves. He then laid a plastic sheet on the carpeted floor beside the locker. Now on his knees, Higgins carefully removed the wristlet from the hook, placed it in the middle of the plastic sheet, and unzipped it. Slowly, he removed a folded piece of notebook paper, a pregnancy test, and a gram-bag of marijuana. From its fluffy texture and the ample crystallization, Ezra guessed it was of high quality. Higgins turned the wristlet inside-out but discovered nothing further. He bagged the weed and pocketed it. Then he unfolded the notebook paper.

"Can I photograph that?" Ezra asked.

"Go right ahead."

The note was written in a graceful cursive script.

Ma Perle—

This morning as the sun rose through the golden-leafed trees and illuminated the first frost of autumn, I realized I have not been this happy, this truly fulfilled since, well, perhaps I've never been this happy. Yesterday in the music office was (how did you describe

Debussy?) celestial. I await you like a devotee of Dionysus awaiting the next full moon. I need nothing but you for my revelry—your lips my only wine, your hips my only ecstasy.

The note was left unsigned. At least the author had sense enough to not attach his name.

Officer Higgins pointed at the salutation. "What kind of name is *Ma Perle?* Is that, like, Mrs. Perle?"

Ezra replied, "It's a French term of endearment. It means *My Pearl."*

He immediately thought of the missing black pearl necklace that Autumn Elkhart had mentioned in her interview with Detective Vargas and her partner. They had yet to locate the necklace. The writer of this note was definitely the guy. He turned to Catherine. "Is Martin Durand in today?"

"He should be."

****

Shortly after Lucia made her discovery of the body, CSI arrived at Autumn Elkhart's apartment. They barricaded the door with crime scene tape and began collecting samples while Lucia and Gorecki interviewed every resident of the apartment complex. As is too often the case, no one saw Autumn or anyone else going into or coming out of the apartment the previous night or early that morning. Nor did anyone hear a gunshot. Worst of all, the superintendent explained that the cameras around the outside of the building were ornamental.

"We used to have a security service, but they kept raising their rates," he explained. "It was either cut that or cut the Wi-Fi."

"Tough decision," Lucia said sarcastically.

"Hey, the tenants pay us for the Wi-Fi," he replied. "No tenant has ever offered a dime for security cameras."

After knocking on every door in the building and speaking to nearly half the residents, Lucia and Gorecki were no closer to knowing who killed Autumn. Lucia suspected that Autumn had confronted the wrong person.

"I'm going to check the apartments across the street," Gorecki told her then. "Maybe their cameras caught something."

She doubted it. The building across the street was a quarter of a block down and mostly obscured by privacy trees. "I'll see what the CSI folks came up with."

A blonde evidence technician in a white Hazmat suit was waiting for Lucia when she turned the corner. "Are you the lead on this?"

She was about Lucia's height but fuller in the face and hips. Lucia recognized her but couldn't produce a name. "Guilty."

"You need to see this," the tech said.

She produced an SLR camera, turned the display toward Lucia, then scrolled through photographs. They showed Autumn Elkhart's head positioned atop the leather journal. The first picture showed a bullet hole at the back of Autumn's skull. She was killed execution style. The next showed another tech raising the head, a pool of blood rolling off the pages of the journal. The tech skipped ahead to show a bullet hole in the center of the journal as well. Whoever murdered Autumn shot her while she was reading the journal or while her face was forced down onto it.

As if reading Lucia's mind, the tech said, "We pulled the slug out of the wall opposite her body."

So Autumn had been sitting upright, reading when she was hit. "What caliber?"

"9mm. We also recovered the gun."

"Oh?"

"The gun, the case, the box of ammunition they used, and the registration information."

"Was it Autumn's gun?" Lucia asked.

"Home protection, maybe."

Lucia muttered, "This definitely isn't going in the NRA newsletter."

"There's more you should see."

She gave Lucia a face mask and shoe covers and led her into the crime scene. Autumn's body still lay motionless on the table, but the journal now sat in the center of a plastic drop cloth. The book was opened to the point of impact, its pages a smattering of sopping crimson and tacky russet brown. It looked like a painting, like something Autumn might've created.

The tech turned the pages right-to-left until she came to a legible one. The script looked ancient, long and angular like something from the middle ages. Lucia leaned closer but couldn't distinguish the words. French maybe? The tech turned back more pages until she arrived at the title page.

"Does this mean anything to you?" the tech asked.

"Everything."

Lucia didn't need to know the language to understand the title's import. *Le journal pédagogique de Martin Durand.*

"One more thing," the tech added. "Autumn was only wearing one earring." She held up a dangly gold-colored earring with a large topaz teardrop in the center.

"You'll tell me if you find the other one?"

The tech nodded.

Lucia's phone blared a sample of Latin music, a *cumbia* beat. It startled both of them. The caller ID read, "Ezra."

****

School policy dictated that all doors remain closed twenty-four hours a day per order of the fire marshal. That didn't stop Martin Durand from wedging his classroom door open each morning with a wooden door stop. Catherine Weeks had spoken to him about it. Jeb, the groundskeeper and janitor, had confiscated the door stops one after another. Even Ezra, who didn't particularly care, mentioned the legal liability to the French teacher one morning. Nevertheless, Durand left it wide open whenever he taught, allowing the mellifluous or cacophonous sounds of French recitation and discussion to spill from his room.

For this reason, Ezra heard Durand's lecture several yards before he made it to the classroom. As he and Catherine crept into the back of the room, Durand continued speaking, a yellow book held aloft. The cover featured an elephant on horseback, waving a giant, green flag.

"In book one," he said, "Babar's mother is *tué.* What's that mean?"

"Killed," several students answered at once.

"By?"

"*Un villain chasseur,*" a boy in the front row answered. He looked like the younger Ainsley brother.

"We would say a poacher," Durand translated. "Babar is forced to live in a strange city *plein de—*"

"Full of," came another chorus response.

"—French humans. In book two, *roi Babar*—"

"King Babar!"

"—and his queen, Celeste, honeymoon far from *la grande forêt* and run immediately into trouble. They're attacked by cannibals, lose their crowns, and are mistaken for ordinary elephants. Fernando captures them and forces them to perform in the circus. Who saves them?"

"*La vieille dame,*" answered the younger Ainsley again.

Durand nodded. "The old woman, *oui.*" He brandished the book again. "Now in book three, *que font les éléphants?*"

"They build their own city," a student in front answered. He recognized Fiona immediately from her curly blonde hair.

"*Et?*"

"And assign professions to everyone."

"*Oui! Les métiers.* But they are beset by what *problèmes? Répondez en Français.*"

Ainsley raised his hand. "*Par un serpent et un feu.*"

"A snake and a fire. *Très bien!*" To the whole class, he asked, "Do these elements remind us of anything else we've looked at?"

Fiona's hand alone rose into the air. He motioned for her to stand. She rose from her desk and, twirling a lock of curly blonde hair, nervously perhaps or flirtatiously, answered, "French colonialism."

"*Explique moi.*"

The hair twirling ceased. "The poacher represents France and the other European colonists. They arrive and take whatever they want, destroying the traditions they find, which is represented here by the mother."

"*Alors qui est Babar?*"

"Babar and the other elephants represent precolonial Africa, and the village is Western Civilization as it is imposed on them. Later, when Babar and Celeste are captured by Fernando and forced to work in the circus, that's slavery. Eventually, they construct Celesteville, which is their version of a colonial city."

"*Qui est le serpent?*"

"The snake," she said, then paused. "The snake and the fire, they both represent Satan. As the elephants leave life in their forest, their Eden, they face new evils introduced by a complex society."

"*Génial!*"

Fiona beamed. This was clearly her teacher's highest form of praise. Ezra also felt like commending this young woman's insight. He, too, had read these children's books in high school French class but hadn't gathered half as much from them. All he noticed was that everyone, regardless of their culture, loved dressing animals in human clothes.

"Tomorrow is the last day before finals," Durand said now, "so I have a special treat for everyone. I'll be reading aloud *Babar et le Père Noël,* the only book in the series to feature Santa Claus himself, and we'll be watching a cartoon adaptation *en Français.*"

The bell rang, but none of the students moved a muscle until their teacher dismissed them with an *"À demain!"*

Only then did they clear out. Contrary to Coach Larson's criticisms, Martin Durand didn't seem like an ineffective teacher at all.

Ezra waited for the room to clear out before addressing Durand. "I didn't know Babar was such a complex allegory."

The teacher began erasing his white board. "That's just one reading. I haven't looked at the literary criticism on Babar, if there is any, but I don't believe Jean de Brunhoff ever explicitly stated the comparison."

"I'm sure there's a biography out there. Probably in French."

He offered a weak shrug, as if to say, *Who's got the time?*

"We read *Le Petit Prince*," Ezra continued.

"We're doing that in the spring," Durand replied.

"And *La Peste*."

Another weak nod. "Do you still read any French literature?" he asked Ezra.

"Afraid not. I read some translations when Fr. Remy passes them along."

"He's a good source." Durand finished erasing the board, then asked, "So what's this visit all about?"

Ezra debated his options. If he confronted the French teacher about the note, he could just deny it. No names appeared on it. Plus they found it among Brooklyn's things, not Durand's. Ezra decided on a less direct approach. "Principal Weeks and I are dealing with another student issue."

Catherine nodded.

"Okay?"

"Could you tell us what the French word for 'pearl' is?"

He gave them both a curious look. "It's a cognate

217

with English. Why?"

"Can you spell it for us?"

Rather than awkwardly spelling it aloud, he uncapped a dry-erase marker and wrote it on the board. In crisp legible print, he wrote, PERLE. The author of the love letter had used cursive letters and not all-caps, but at least it showed the same spelling.

"Is it ever used as a term of endearment?" Ezra asked.

Now Durand wrote in a quick script, *ma perle.* "It's feminine," he explained, "so a lot of language learners prefer this to the masculine terms *mon cœur* or *mon amour* when referring to their girlfriends, wives, or what-have-you. To an English speaker, it feels wrong to masculinize their female lover."

A shadow of doubt passed over Ezra's conviction. Clearly Martin Durand, a native speaker, would have no problem using a masculine term.

Durand wrote all three terms on the board, all in cursive. The handwriting wasn't a match to the letter, but that didn't absolve him of Ezra's suspicions. For all Ezra knew, this was a show. A man who spoke two languages fluently could easily have mastered two forms of cursive writing, one for the classroom, writ large on a white board, and another for private messages.

"Is that everything?" Durand asked.

"Why? Are you eager to be rid of us?" Ezra asked in a mock-offended tone.

He looked to Catherine now. "This is my planning period, and there have been a number of interruptions as of late. I'm afraid I'm a bit behind on my grading."

Principal Weeks took Ezra's arm as if to lead him

away, but she didn't pull on it. "We'll let you prepare for tomorrow," she said. "Are you heading out early today?"

"No. Gemma has the kids during the week."

Ezra wasn't going to drop this so easily, and he felt Catherine would back him up. "If you were seeing Brooklyn Hannigan, we're going to find out."

Durand turned bright red in the face. From anger, fear, or embarrassment, Ezra didn't know. "I've already told you—" he began.

"I know you're hiding something," Ezra said, cutting him off. "Whatever it is, I'll find it. The trouble with intelligent criminals is they always discount the time factor. While you go on living your life, I'll be digging. Evanston PD will be digging, too. One shovel at a time, we'll uncover every last secret you have."

Now Catherine did tug, just barely. "That's enough, Mr. James. Thank you for your time, Monsieur Durand."

Two minutes later they sat in the main office discussing the events of the day with Officer Higgins and Catherine's secretary, Denise, who relished the excitement.

"We can have someone search his classroom," Higgins said. "You can't lie about evidence. If they were fooling around at the school, I'm sure something will turn up."

Catherine agreed.

"I'll call Detective Vargas," Ezra said, perhaps too eagerly.

Vargas picked up on the first ring.

"We found a note in Brooklyn's school locker," he told her. "I didn't even realize she had one." He felt like a dog bringing a pair of shoes to his owner and, while he knew it was below his station, the feeling lingered. What did he hope to achieve from this detective? Did he want to impress her, earn her professional admiration, or did it run deeper?

"If you're excited about a note," she said, "then what I have is going to blow your socks off."

"There's more," he continued. "The author called Brooklyn *ma perle*. It's a French term of endearment. I confronted Martin Durand about it and—"

"You did what? Is he with you?" she asked, sounding almost panicked. "Do you have Durand there in custody?"

"What?"

"Go get him! Keep him there. I'm on my way." She hung up.

Ezra looked up at Officer Higgins in a daze. "She said to hold Martin Durand."

"As in, *arrest him?*" the officer asked.

Ezra shrugged. "We can decide when we get there."

The two of them hustled back to Martin's classroom while Catherine checked the parking lot. By the time they got there, the room was locked and the light was off. Catherine entered through the exterior door at the end of the hall. "His car's gone."

****

By the time Detective Vargas arrived, two uniformed officers in tow, students lined the halls of Durand's classroom. "Why are all these kids here?" she asked.

"Homeroom just started," Ezra explained.

"Put them somewhere else." It was a command, not

a request.

"You heard the detective," he hollered, transferring his embarrassment into anger. "Everyone to the gym!"

The students began their collective shuffle in the direction of the gym.

All of them except Fiona Fleming who asked Vargas, "Do you need to get inside Monsieur Durand's room? Because Coach Larson can pick the lock." She gestured down the hall toward Benjamin Larson's classroom. "I've seen him do it on his own door."

"No, that's okay. Your principal is getting a key," Vargas said. She turned to Ezra. "We'll take it from here."

It took him a moment to realize the "we" did not include him.

Chapter Twenty-One

Lucia tried Martin's apartment in Rogers Park next. The building owner let her in, but the place was empty.

A half-hour later, Gorecki met her in front of the red-brick Tudor home of Martin's ex, Gemma. One day earlier, if someone had asked Lucia which partner she would prefer for the task, Ezra or Gorecki, she would've answered "Ezra" without hesitation.

After the events of this afternoon, however, Gorecki had risen in her estimation. A good old boy, a frat boy, sure, but at least Gorecki was one of the boys in blue. Police lived and died by a strict code, and she wondered if Ezra James, sore from his probation, still did. At the end of the day, if you didn't know a man's code, how could he be trusted?

The whole neighborhood, with its quaint homes, spacious lawns, and crack-free sidewalks, filled Lucia with real-estate envy. Then again, she hardly spent enough time at home to make owning a luxury home worthwhile.

Gemma answered the door but only opened it halfway. She wore her curly blonde hair short, reminding Lucia of a '90s "It Girl." Lucia didn't know what she'd expected. Maybe someone more butch-looking. The sound of children playing came from inside the house.

"My name is Detective Lucia Vargas, and I need to speak to your ex-husband."

"He stopped by a little while ago to say goodbye to the kids," Gemma replied. She seemed entirely unruffled.

"Where was he heading?"

"Don't know."

Gorecki stepped forward. "Do you have his phone on a tracker app or anything like that?"

"Why would I want to track him?"

"Do you mind texting Martin and asking him where he's heading?" he asked next.

"I do mind, actually. What's with the third degree?" Gemma asked. "Did Martin not pay a parking ticket or something? No, that's ridiculous—he'd never park somewhere illegally in the first place."

"I'm sorry to inform you of this, ma'am," Lucia said, "but your ex-husband is our lead suspect in an attempted murder."

"That's the stupidest thing I've ever heard," she said, more dismissive than defensive. "The man crosses himself when he kills a spider. Martin's an academic. What motive would he even have?"

"We believe he was sleeping with the victim," Lucia said.

A couple passed by on the sidewalk. Their white terrier resembled a child's stuffed animal. It stopped and peed on the snowy strip between the sidewalk and the road.

"Who?"

"Brooklyn Hannigan, the student-teacher."

Gemma scowled, red-faced. "This is absurd."

Gorecki offered an explanation. "Maybe they

bonded over broken hearts and started working on lesson plans together. One thing led to another, and the girl turned up pregnant."

"Pregnant?" She shook her head vehemently. "Impossible."

"Impossible? Are you saying your ex-husband is infertile or impotent?" Gorecki asked.

"No, it's just…Martin would never go for someone like her. She's not…his type."

"I'm sorry," Gorecki said, "but a girl like Brooklyn Hannigan is every man's type."

"You ought to get to know a person before you accuse him," Gemma said.

"We know all we need to know about your ex-husband," Gorecki assured her.

"Obviously not."

"You're pretty defensive for an ex-wife," Lucia added. "If Martin was such a one-of-a-kind man, then why leave him?"

"Look, I'm a lesbian. It doesn't mean I don't love Martin, and it doesn't mean I'm going to let you badmouth him just because you don't have your facts straight." She paused to let them consider this. "And another thing, if you're dumb enough to suspect a man like him, it's going to come back on you."

"What's going on here?" another woman asked, opening the door the rest of the way. The woman's fiery red hair reminded Lucia of Brooklyn's.

"Is this—" Lucia began but couldn't think of the proper term.

"This is my wife, Brandy," Gemma said.

Her name even sounded like the victim's. Brooklyn, Brandy, Brandy, Brooklyn. Maybe this was less about lust and ending a pregnancy and more about revenge. Martin Durand couldn't kill the woman who'd stolen his wife, so he did the next best thing, he seduced her doppelgänger.

Three possibilities floated through Lucia's mind: Martin was sleeping with his student Fiona, as Ezra had suggested, and Brooklyn found out about it; Martin was sleeping with Brooklyn, she got pregnant, and he threw her from the bell tower to cover it up; or Martin wanted to murder his ex-wife's new partner, Brandy, and transposed that anger onto Brooklyn instead. This last theory seemed like a stretch but, even without it, there was ample motive. Martin skipping town only heightened his guilt.

"A woman was murdered this morning," Lucia said. "Shot in the back of the head merely because she was involved in this case." She considered mentioning Martin's journal but then dismissed the idea. "If Martin is innocent, as you say, then that also means he's in grave danger. Whoever attacked Brooklyn and murdered her roommate may come for him next."

Gemma's demeanor softened. Brandy nudged her arm.

"He didn't say anything, but he does still have family up north," Gemma said finally.

"Michigan?"

"*Québec.*"

As they drove back to the station in Gorecki's car Lucia placed two calls. The first went to Homeland Security, giving them Martin's particulars in case he tried to cross over into Canada. HSO would put out a BOLO to every border patrol station along the north and south border.

The second call went to the CSI unit handling the evidence from Autumn Elkhart's crime scene. A male tech informed Lucia that Martin Durand's journal was being processed. They sent photographs of the journal entries to a French literature professor at the University of Chicago. "We expect a translation back by the end of the day," he said.

"Doesn't anyone in the building speak French?"

"One of vice secretaries is from Saint Martin, but she said the journal only starts in French. Then it gets weird. She didn't want to mistranslate it."

"Weird how?"

"The language specialist at University of Chicago says it's written in something called *Langue d'oïl?*" He struggled to pronounce the name of the language. "It's Old French or something. Also, the author used a special script from the middle ages."

"You mean we don't have anyone in-house who can translate *Langue d'oïl?*" She sighed. "I know we're short-staffed, but this is ridiculous," Lucia said. "That's a joke."

"Oh no, I got it," he said. "You should try out at Second City."

The tech sounded tired.

"When will we have the translation?" she asked next.

"Expect it later tonight," he said.

She hung up and brought Gorecki up to speed.

"I'll drop you at your place," he said.

"My car's at the precinct, and we still need to search Durand's classroom and apartment."

"We have officers watching both the school and his apartment complex. I can handle the rest."

"But I—"

"Need some rest," he interjected, "especially if you're going to be reading *Langue d'oïl* later tonight. I'll swing by as soon as we have a copy of Martin's journal."

He said this with finality, and a part of her was relieved that he did. Over the past few days, she'd worked the equivalent of an entire week, and sleep sounded sweeter than chocolate. This evening, Gorecki would handle the warrant and the search. Later tonight, Lucia would read Martin's journal. This division of labor seemed only fair.

****

"Rook to E5," Remy said after a moment. "What did Detective Vargas say exactly?"

"She said, 'We'll take it from here.' Then she started shouting orders to her officers."

"That could mean anything. She may have meant you did not need to worry about the details."

"Bishop takes the rook," Ezra replied. "I don't think so."

The after-school basketball game was louder than usual. Usually, hurt feelings were something he shared only in private, possibly not even then, but with the SJM girls clobbering Roycemore, fifty-eight to thirty, the crowd could not contain their excitement. Amid the noise, Ezra felt more emboldened to speak frankly without being heard.

"Queen takes the bishop. Check." Remy glanced from the court to Ezra. "Not mate."

"Not yet," Ezra replied with a frown.

"Have you spoken to Assistant Special-Agent-in-Charge Cromley about the case?"

ASAC Jeremiah Cromley oversaw day-to-day operations in the Chicago field office. During Ezra's work on the CTC case, he answered directly to the ASAC who coordinated efforts between the various offices—FBI and otherwise—during the investigation into John Lewis Straugh. During his probation he checked in once a week.

"No."

"I see. Do you believe he distrusts you?"

Ezra needed to change the subject. "Detective Vargas interviewed Martin's ex-wife this afternoon."

"I heard. Or rather, I heard about Martin."

"Do you still doubt his guilt?"

Instead of answering, Remy asked, "Can I tell you a story?"

Ezra nodded.

"My first post was at a church in what was then Zaire but is now the Democratic Republic of the Congo. The pastor, Fr. Khonde, took confessions only in a small wooden hut behind the yellow brick church. He used it as a separate office while I used an open area inside the church. I had but a flimsy desk and no walls. One afternoon, a woman entered the church and accosted me. She demanded repeatedly to see her son's baptismal record. I searched high and low but to no avail. As I did so, I asked her various questions about the boy and her urgency."

"Why could she possibly need a baptismal record?"

"There was a question of the boy's legitimacy, and she believed this record would resolve it. 'This is not a DNA test,' I told her. Nevertheless, she persisted. The record had the name of the boy's father in print. 'And it is signed by the priest,' she said."

"What did you do?" Ezra asked.

"I decided to ask the pastor directly. Without knocking, I stepped into Fr. Khonde's hut, thus interrupting the confession of a young girl of nineteen. He was embracing her and, as he pulled away, I noticed that her eyes were wet from crying. She grimaced when she saw me. Fr. Khonde said the prayer of absolution and sent the parishioner away. I noticed her kneel down to pluck her shawl from the floor. She wrapped it around her bare shoulders and left without making eye contact with me."

"What did the pastor say?"

"After she left, Fr. Khonde examined the latch of the door and said he usually locked it. Then he told me something important. He said, 'The seal of confession is a sacred thing. Unbreakable. Whatever you see or hear in the confessional must not leave it.' "

"Was he sleeping with that young woman?"

"No, but that's what I too thought."

"Why the secrecy then?"

"She was a spy. The city bordered the People's Republic of Congo, a Marxist state. She was an asset of the French government in Zaire. Fr. Khonde was assisting her. I say this now only because he and I discussed it often some years later and because both of them are now deceased."

"How did they die?"

"That is not important to the story. My point is things are not always as they appear." Remy linked his hands over his knee. "What physical evidence do you have on Martin Durand?"

"No physical evidence yet, but they're checking his

apartment. Plus he fled right after we questioned him. Lucia found Brooklyn's roommate in the morning, and Martin fled in the afternoon."

Remy examined his own black shoes. "All of us are guilty of something, Ezra."

"What could possibly be bad enough for him to run off like that, knowing it would make him seem culpable?"

"You are assuming his guilt."

"What do you mean?"

"You are assuming he knew Autumn had been murdered. For all you know, Martin fled an accusation of an affair, not an accusation of murder."

"Autumn believed the affair was with Martin," Ezra said. "Two days later, she was murdered, holding a copy of Martin's journal. What more do you need?"

"If Martin killed her, why leave behind his journal?"

"Maybe he panicked. It happens all the time."

Remy shook his head. "I don't buy it."

The game clock ran down to 0:00, and the gym erupted in applause and shouting. The team members waved to friends and families and, savoring the win, slowly exited through the double doors. As they filtered out, the boys' team came in. Ezra recognized most of their faces. Among them were Mason Scout, Royce Ainsley, and Daniel Toussaint.

Behind them, looking as haggard as an ISIS rebel after an interrogation, Coach Benjamin Larson staggered toward the bench. He took his seat and stared at a fixed point on the court a yard ahead of him. Larson presented a stark contrast to the raucous crowd. Then Ezra noticed another somber face. Cynthia Scout, a few sections over, was also staring off into space. Her gaze rested not on the court but in Larson's general direction. She appeared simultaneously dazed and transfixed. Then she caught sight of Ezra out of the corner of her eye and hurriedly began speaking to her husband beside her. She gestured and smiled with everything but her eyes.

"Mind if I sit with you?" a voice said behind Ezra. Before he could reply, English teacher Heather Jarno nestled up beside him. "I warned you about him," she said. "Martin, I mean."

"Did you? I thought you suspected Sarah Pierce's husband, Mr. Handsy."

"Months ago, when you first came. Remember? I'm the one who told you Martin used to be a stay-at-home-dad." She ran a bright red fingernail around the rim of her latte cup, then licked the foam from her finger. She really was an attractive woman, Ezra thought.

She offered him a sly look. "Which should've told you everything you need to know about the man."

Attractive when she wasn't talking, he amended, and pointed to the drink in her hand. "Did you bring that in?"

"No, silly. They have them at the concession stand now."

Even though Ezra himself attended SJM as a student, as an adult he'd encountered a daily show of extravagance and made himself adjust to it.

"Wasn't he a college instructor before working here?" he asked.

"He taught one class over the summer," she scoffed.

"Didn't he teach night classes before that?"

She waved her hand vaguely as if to acknowledge this could be true.

"What else have you heard about him?" he asked.

"What haven't I heard?"

"Tell me everything; spare no detail."

Ms. Jarno then settled in and related every single rumor she could recall. Everything she learned in the teacher's lounge, at dances and football games, and at parent-teacher conferences. According to Jarno, Martin Durand was sleeping with Brooklyn, obviously; but also with Mason Scout's mother, Cynthia; and Principal Weeks herself.

"How else could he land a job at such an elite school?" she asked rhetorically. "He also showers an inappropriate amount of attention on that Fiona girl."

Ezra perked up. "Oh, has anyone seen or heard anything substantial?"

She shook her head, a look of disappointment on her face. "Someone asked if I'd been out with him. I said, 'God no!' "

"Why so adamant?" Ezra asked.

"He's not my type. A man who'd let his wife work while he stayed home with the kids?"

"Involved fathers are the worst," he said dryly.

"Right? It's no wonder his wife ran off with another woman."

"So you think Martin turned his wife gay?"

She nodded.

"And if you dated him, you would, what, become a lesbian as well?"

"God no!" she said, seemingly offended at the rationale. "The whole thing just makes me sick. And sad." She patted Ezra's arm. "But enough about Martin. Tell me more about you."

Instead Ezra asked, "Beside Martin Durand, who else was Brooklyn sleeping with?"

"You think a girl like Brooklyn would be mixed up with more than one man?" the English teacher asked, again acting affronted.

"Let's say the affair wasn't another faculty member but one of the students."

"I already told you about Martin and Fiona Fleming, and I've personally seen him talking with a number of students after school."

He shook his head. "Not Durand, Brooklyn. Was she especially close or flirtatious with any of the students?"

Jarno went tight-lipped and glanced at Remy as if it were unseemly to discuss such things in the presence of a priest, never mind that she'd already been speaking about such matters for five minutes.

Remy gave her a reassuring smile. "Nothing you say will leave this bleacher."

The boys' game began. Royce Ainsley won the tip off and passed the ball back to Mason who drove down the court. Two players were wide open, but Mason pushed through triple coverage to make a layup that barely rolled into the hoop.

"I won't say anything either," Ezra added. "Unless what you say is admissible in a court of law, that is."

"Well, of course," Remy said.

Jarno shifted in her seat.

"Just tell us what you've heard," Ezra said.

She shot daggers at him. "Some of the students seem to think Brooklyn was. . .fooling around with a football player. It's ridiculous. It's just teenage boys being immature."

"Who specifically?" Ezra asked.

"I teach freshmen. If you believe them, they've all gotten to third base with her."

"A name," Ezra pressed.

"Mason Scout heads the list."

Mason was a reckless, disrespectful punk. His had mother pulled him out of school rather than have him speak with Vargas. Then, Cynthia swooped down on Ellie Tiene the moment she saw Ellie and Ezra speaking alone. Could it be Mason after all? As if taking a foot off the accelerator pedal, Ezra felt his conviction of Martin Durand's guilt lessen. Then he recalled the photographs of Martin's bloodied journal, and this entire train of thought derailed.

"Remind me," Remy interjected with a question for Jarno. "Did you and Martin ever date?"

"Never."

"What about Coach Larson?" Ezra asked next.

Jarno took a sip of her latte. A long sip. When she spoke, the words came out muffled. Then she glanced at her smart watch. "Shoot, I must go."

"In the first quarter?" Ezra asked.

She stood and hustled down the bleacher steps.

"That was suspiciously abrupt," Ezra said to Remy. Then he added, "King to B2."

"Knight to…"

"Yeah, yeah, checkmate in two" Ezra muttered. "Should I be worried about the English teacher?"

"I would not," Remy said and smirked. "Then again, I am not an eligible bachelor."

Chapter Twenty-Two

Lucia awoke feeling like a new woman. Was that a proper idiom? She could only remember ever hearing "a new man." She felt not only refreshed but completely content, a feeling she never had. Then Ezra James stirred on the pillow beside her, and she remembered why she felt so happy.

She couldn't tell if it was late evening or the middle of the night, but enough moonlight filtered in through the lattice blinds for her to make out the same expression of ease and contentment on his face. She wiggled an arm free from the covers and reached out her fingertips to brush the stubble on his cheek.

Then the bedroom door burst open.

Martin Durand raised something metal toward them. It was Autumn Elkhart's 9mm. How had he stolen it from evidence? How had he broken into her apartment? He aimed it directly at Lucia's chest. She buried her face in the covers. Bang-bang-bang!

Lucia awoke and discovered she'd sweated through her sheets. Her gaze shot to the open doorway. It was empty. She didn't have time to process the dream before the sound returned: Bang-bang-bang. Someone was knocking in the hallway.

"I hear you!" she hollered from her room.

The clock read quarter-to-midnight.

Once decent, she let Gorecki in, then brewed two

cups of Earl Grey tea. If Gorecki didn't want his tea, she'd drink it.

He told her about Martin's classroom first. If Martin and Brooklyn had done anything else at the school, he hadn't kept any traces. *He probably took everything with him when he fled,* Lucia thought.

His apartment proved more useful. They didn't find anything inside, but they pulled a trash bag out of the dumpster. Inside the bag, they found an old car battery, some 0-gauge wire, which was one of the thickest gauges, and finally, the *pièce de résistance,* Brooklyn's staff ID.

"And the necklace?" she asked.

"No such luck, but the contents of the bag are with forensics. There should be plenty of DNA."

"Every touch leaves a trace," Lucia quoted one of her college professors. "This still doesn't explain the lack of footprints in the belfry," she said, thinking out loud. "Also, why ditch it all in the dumpster right next to his apartment?"

"Maybe he dumped it on Thursday and couldn't risk going back for it?"

"Maybe." Lucia remained unconvinced. "It feels too neat."

"You're thinking someone is setting the French teacher up?"

Lucia nodded. Contrary to damning him, the evidence made her suspect Martin Durand less.

Once their tea finished steeping, Gorecki took his and sipped twice before asking about its caffeine content. When she told him it was caffeinated, he took another sip. Lucia supposed his wife Ash would have to deal with his tossing and turning. At least they didn't have babies waking them up throughout the night.

"Do you ever think of having kids?" she asked and immediately realized what a non sequitur this seemed. She hoped Gorecki wouldn't put together that she was just imaging Gorecki and his wife in their bed.

"Ashley can't."

No more needed to be said. Or, at least, neither of them wanted to say anything more.

Gorecki leaned over and pulled what looked like a report with its black plastic spine and translucent plastic cover. "Before you rule out Durand, you'd better read this." Through the cover, she read, "Teaching Journal of Martin Durand." Without another word, Gorecki packed up his things and left the apartment.

Alone again, Lucia finished her tea and got to work. The journal discussed several school functions the French teacher attended where he interacted with Brooklyn—several sports events and the Fall formal dance—his frustration over his divorce, the humiliation he felt at becoming a high school teacher after working at the college level, and then several run-ins he'd had with problem students at SJM.

Lucia couldn't help wondering why Martin Durand would leave such an incriminating piece of evidence at the crime scene. Even panic seemed a poor excuse.

Two columns ran down each page of the report. On the left side of the page was a transcription of the original writing in Old French; on the right side was the English translation. She glanced through the original but quickly moved over to the English. There were well over fifty entries, some short, some irrelevant to their investigation, and others that were ripe for analysis. When she came to a key selection, she highlighted it in its entirety. The highlighted passages read as follows:

September 1

I decided to work on my Old French once a day for my new "school" year's resolution, so here I am, three weeks into school and just now writing this down. I remember when the first day of September meant the first day of school. Now everything is so much earlier. Is that a sign I'm getting old? Thirty-three. The same age as Christ when they crucified him. By thirty-three, Jesus concluded his ministry and saved the whole world. I, on the other hand, haven't even started whatever great work I'm supposed to accomplish. If I even...never mind. Thirty-three, divorced, and a first-year teacher at a high school. A master's degree, work toward a Ph.D. in French Literature, and I'm teaching high school! Perhaps I shouldn't have started writing this journal. This is depressing me already.

Detentions—
Mason Scout
Warnings—
Fiona Fleming

September 2

No. Writing is good. I need to get everything out. I just told my students about how, in the middle ages, they placed leeches on the sick to suck out the "bad blood." These days, I'm in serious need of some emotional leeching. For my college classes, I planned lessons, lectured, and graded papers. Now there is so much more. At the college, if a student doesn't like a class, he stands up and leaves. Here the police literally bring kids back to school. Well, maybe not at St. Joseph and Mary, but they do still have to be here.

Day two, a student threw his shoulders back like he

was going to punch me. Mason Scout, a cocky football player. He kept falling out of his chair on purpose. So I asked him to wait in my office. I checked on him five minutes later, and he had dumped all the books off my shelves and laid them in a mound on my desk. All my bookmarks and notes littered the floor of my office. I asked him to put the books back on the shelves, which seemed like a reasonable request. Instead, he puffed out his chest, clenched his fists, and flared his nostrils at me. What could I do? I stood there, still as a stone, wondering if I could defend myself and then wondering how I would defend myself, and then the bell rang and the kids filed out of my classroom, Mason included. I almost didn't come back the next day. This interaction didn't scare me, per se. I just hadn't prepared myself for so much immediate conflict. I expected a private Catholic high school to be different from the public schools you read about in the papers, but I'm starting to wonder if SJM isn't worse.

I filed a discipline form a few days later, and Principal Weeks convinced Mason to drop French and enroll in Spanish instead. Apparently, Mason only started French freshman year because the teacher was someone's well-endowed, Swiss nanny. It is difficult to put myself back into the mind of a teenager, but I suppose I'll have to if I want to survive this place. Survive. That sounds so very melodramatic. Perhaps I'm thinking like them already.

September 29

I made a breakthrough today; although, as I'm reflecting on it now, it seems obvious. Joanie is three, but she still struggles with prepositions. "That's a J to Joanie" she'll say instead of "J for Joanie." My

students are doing the same thing with "à" and "de."
Growing up as I did, half in America, half in Québec, I
take a lot for granted. I constantly correct Joanie when
she says she "sawed a bunny" or "J is to Joanie" and
eventually she'll internalize these distinctions. Will my
students do the same thing? Will they internalize the
other things I try to pass along as well? Is that how we
pass on virtue, not through reason but through
repetition?

Or are they even listening? It's impossible to tell.

Lucia put down the journal and texted Gorecki.

—Did Homeland Security say anything?—

It was near one a.m., but he replied.

—Nothing yet. Customers and Border Patrol have
Martin's name, picture, license plate, passport, and
dog's maiden name.— A few seconds later, another text
came in. *—That last bit was a joke.—*

—Oh? I couldn't tell.—

Then she added, *—No hits?—*

—Not yet. Nothing from Highway Patrol either.
He's probably hiding out.—

She returned her attention to the journal.

October 3

I screamed at a kid today. Literally screamed at
him. All because he kept clicking his pen. I'm sure he
was doing it on purpose to annoy me, but still. I could
feel my blood pressure building, and then I released a
whole week's worth of frustration on him and him
alone. I even sent him to the office. For clicking a pen.
Tomorrow, I'll have to see him in the halls all day and,
by the time it gets to his class, we'll be starting at a
deficit.

Before I became a high school teacher, I always

thought, "Who would want to teach high school?" Now that I'm in the thick of it, I wonder, "Who even has what it takes?"

Maybe there's more than just frustration.

To be a Catholic man is to be a failure at the outset. What does it say in Proverbs? "The just man falls seven times a day"? That's how I feel. Even before Gemma left, lust, that devil, was my perpetual guest. Even with a holy outlet in marriage, I always wanted more. A battle raged inside me. Is that why Gemma left, could she not bear to see it tearing me up?

When Gemma left, she told me, "You're free! Free to do what you want!" But what sort of freedom is that? Doing whatever you want isn't freedom; it's slavery to your own impetuous nature, your own corrupt desires. Perhaps it's freedom for Gemma. Her desires have always been purer than mine. Although now I don't know. These days Gemma seems as eaten up by lust as I am. Our shared affliction does not go away. Like a weed, it regrows wherever it's plucked, unless you pull it out by the root. Even then, something remains. Something lingers like these girls linger in my classroom at the end of the day to ask for my help with reciting a passage or to show me pictures of their new puppy. If only there was a Roundup for the soul. If only the Church offered indulgences against future sin or against sinfulness itself instead of merely remitting past thoughts and deeds. Even with all I do—my sacred readings, my penances, and my prayer—I am still like Paul. I want to do what is good, but I do what is evil instead. I am a sinner, and I cannot not be.

The last entry was scratched through to indicate it had been blotted out but was nonetheless still legible.

October 6

Daniel Toussaint came to see me today after school. I don't know what the lines are in a high school, but I may have crossed them. No, I know I did...

A single line but a damning one. Lucia wished she had the original *Langue d'oïl* copy. She wanted to be sure Martin actually wrote "Daniel Toussaint" rather than the translator picking the name from an earlier post. Lucia contemplated sending another text to Gorecki, but not at three-seventeen a.m. It would have to wait until morning.

Then she remembered Ezra James, their pawn-shop scavenger hunt, and texted him instead.

"Martin Durand spoke with Daniel Toussaint on October 6th."

A few minutes passed. Obviously, he was asleep. Then her phone buzzed with a text.

—What about?—

She tapped out a response. *—I was hoping you could find out—*

Chapter Twenty-Three

Tuesday

After the initial attack, Lucia reviewed Brooklyn Hannigan's internet presence, especially her most frequently updated social media app, Finlox. Brooklyn did almost everything through Finlox. She posted photos and videos, messaged friends, wrote statuses throughout the day on her wall, and she even used Finlox as her phone provider. The company had everything Lucia could possibly need. Unfortunately, Lucia couldn't access the account, as its privacy settings were ratcheted all the way up. When she called the company's home office in Helsinki, she was forwarded to a pre-recorded message detailing their privacy policy.

"There must be some way to work around this," she told her captain, Jeremy Fitzpatrick, when he came in that morning.

"I'm afraid not. We've run into the very same problem with all the social media sites," Capt. Fitzpatrick said. "Privacy is what matters to these people—the only thing that matters."

"But she's in danger."

"Which just makes matters worse. If she were dead, we might have a shot but, as it is, we're asking to invade the privacy of a current customer."

This all took place three days *before* Autumn Elkhart's murder broadened their legal authority.

After her unhelpful chat with the captain, Lucia spent the rest of the morning making cold calls from Brooklyn's friends list, trying to find someone willing to allow her to view the victim's profile through theirs. It didn't take long. One of her coworkers at the clothing shop even handed over her login info so Lucia could do it from her work computer.

Brooklyn's wall didn't contain much in the way of lurid confessions. She referred several times to a mystery man, whom she always called My Prince, never by name. If this didn't suggest something secret and forbidden in itself, Lucia didn't know what would.

Several status updates on her home page referred to interactions with him at the school. Her Prince delivered flowers to the school office once, and he met her in the parking lot on a half dozen occasions, but someone not affiliated with the school could've easily done these things.

Lucia made a mental note to check the surveillance footage but, as the posts were months old, she doubted there would be any recordings that old. Next, she called the school secretary, Denise Stanton. The flowers were sitting out front when Denise arrived one morning. She didn't remember where they came from.

"They weren't from anywhere I recognized. Not Preston's or Millefiori," Denise said and paused to consider it. "They might have been grocery store flowers. They weren't even in a vase."

So not one of the wealthy fathers of SJM, Lucia thought. It was possible he was going out of his way to not be detected, but any self-respecting man of means would know how bad grocery store flowers left on the curb would look to Brooklyn. Lucia considered someone as sophisticated as Martin Durand, the bowtie wearing Francophile, leaving this sad attempt at romance in front of the school before hours, and the idea made her laugh out loud. Either Brooklyn's lover was not a man of means or taste, or he wasn't a man. A high-school-aged lover seemed more and more plausible to her.

She thanked Denise, hung up, and texted Brooklyn's friend.

—Is there any way to see old posts?—

—Just scroll down— the friend replied.

—Sorry, I mean posts that have been removed.—

—No, I don't think so.—

—Do you remember anything weird over the last few months?—

—I don't get on Finlox much, sorry.— the friend replied.

—Do you mind if I write something on Brooklyn's wall?—

—Go for it!—

Lucia wrote in all caps, "HELPING A FRIEND. IF YOU REMEMBER ANYTHING WEIRD OR OUT OF THE ORDINARY OR SEE SOMETHING MISSING FROM BROOKLYN'S PAGE, PLEASE TEXT ME" and she gave her personal cell number. She thought for a moment about adding a concerned emoji but just hit ENTER instead.

Then all she could do was wait.

That was Friday. Now it was Tuesday morning, and it looked like the gambit was going to pay off. Someone texted her first thing in the morning.

—Some little high schooler was writing a bunch of crap on Brooklyn's Finlox wall about a month ago.—

In addition to being able to post original status updates, Finlox users could post on each other's walls. This stream of messages showed the most recent posts first.

—Who's been posting?—

—Some Fiona chick.—

—Would you characterize it as harassment?—

—She posted a half dozen times, swearing at Brooklyn in all of them. Long posts.—

—Did Brooklyn block her?—

—Yes, but not before Fiona posted a photo of Brooklyn.—

—What kind?—

—You can guess.—

—A nude pic?—

—Yep. Maybe it was photoshopped, but it looked real to me.—

How would Fiona have gotten something like that? Lucia slid from her desk and over to Gorecki's. He didn't look up from his computer.

"Hey there, partner," she said in her friendliest tone.

"What do you want?" Gorecki asked, still staring at the screen.

"I have a lead on the Hannigan case," she said.

"Someone located Martin Durand?"

"No, there's another development from the school."

"The school located Martin Durand?"

"I'm saying—"

"I know what you're saying. More gossip." Finally,

he looked at her. "Until we have Durand in custody, I'm not interested."

She craned her head to peek at his screen. "What are you working on?"

"There was a break-in at Bryn Mawr," he said.

"The country club? Was anything stolen?"

"Worse. The perp scratched the club president's car when he jumped over the fence. Do you have any idea what I'll get if I figure out who it was?"

"A million dollars?"

"Don't be stupid. I'll—"

"Get into the country club?"

"—get into the, yeah."

"But this is a *real* case, and this could turn into something."

Gorecki gestured at their captain's office. "Take it up with him."

"I will."

First, though, she would see what she could get out of Fiona, and she would take someone who gave a crap.

He agreed to meet her before school at the Fleming residence in Lincoln Park, an affluent neighborhood of Chicago. SJM students had a morning off, Ezra explained, so teachers could attend a professional development workshop.

"Or we could speak with her at the school this afternoon," Ezra said over the phone.

"I'm beginning to cool on the school's involvement. Everyone seems to have some ulterior motive over there."

"You mean everyone but *me*," Ezra replied.

"Jury's still out on you," she said, half-joking.

And she really was only half-joking. She still

didn't know everything she wanted to know about the special agent. He told her a lot about the Straugh case over the last few days, but there was still a piece missing, a big piece, and it worried her.

The Fleming residence could only be described as a mansion. Lucia knew the families of SJM were well-off, but until she saw the size of the Flemings' red-brick home and its gated courtyard, she had no idea how well-off. Were their home located in Springfield, it would've cost millions. Lucia didn't want to know how much it cost here in Lincoln Park.

Fiona Fleming answered the door and scowled at Lucia. "Do you have a warrant?"

"Principal Weeks would like it if you spoke with us," Lucia said.

"That bitch isn't here. This is my house. She can't do anything here." She rolled her eyes and closed the door, but Ezra James stopped it with his foot.

"It's about Monsieur Durand," he said through the crack.

"I'm not telling you anything about Monsieur Durand."

Ezra kept the foot firmly wedged. "You don't have to. We found a copy of his journal, and it told us everything."

What could Ezra be referring to? Lucia wondered. She hadn't even given him a copy yet. *He's bluffing,* she concluded.

Fiona opened the door halfway. "What did it say?"

"You and I both know Durand is innocent, but he's going to allow himself to be put away for this."

"He's so noble," she whispered to the door.

"Noble, sure," Ezra said.

"What did he write, exactly?"

Fiona inched the door open a crack, and Lucia pressed.

"Let us come in, and we'll discuss it."

Fiona released her grip, and the door swung open freely.

Moments later they sat at the Fleming family dinner table. The table was an intricately carved block of mesquite in a wrought iron frame. It looked like it weighed as much as the rest of the house. On one side sat Lucia and Ezra and on the other sat Fiona and her mother, Annette.

"Can I get either of you something to drink?" Annette asked.

"We'll be quick," Lucia replied.

"Aside from Monsieur Durand, did Brooklyn show interest in anyone?" Ezra asked.

Fiona shrugged. "How should I know?"

"Actually, I will take a drink," Lucia said.

Annette exchanged a look with her daughter.

"I'm fine," Fiona said.

At that, her mother rose, hesitated a moment, and then disappeared through the doorway.

Lucia leaned toward Fiona. "Look, we know about your feelings for your teacher and about Brooklyn's feelings, too."

Fiona pursed her lips.

"We know you've been posting on Brooklyn's Finlox wall," Lucia said then. "Some hateful stuff. Some people might even consider one or two of your posts to be threats." Lucia placed her elbows on the table. "We also know about the photograph you posted."

Fiona tensed.

"Look," Lucia continued, "I don't think you're involved with the attack, but if I have to spend half the morning at the courthouse getting a warrant to bring you in for questioning, I might change my mind."

Ezra gave his best reassuring smile. "We all want the same thing, Fiona. I know it can be difficult talking about these things in front of a parent, so instead of saying *you* did something or heard something, maybe just put in someone else's name."

Fiona considered this. "Lizbeth. Instead of *me*, I'll say Lizbeth.

Annette returned with two cups of coffee. She set them on the table in front of the detectives.

"Was Ms. Hannigan hard on *Lizbeth?*"

"No, nothing like that. Brooklyn was a total pushover."

"So what was it, then? Jealousy?" Lucia asked.

Fiona fell silent again.

"Maybe Ms. Hannigan was getting close to a certain teacher?" Ezra asked. "Maybe she didn't like Mr. Durand. Maybe she preferred Mr. Larson."

Fiona shook her head. "Not a teacher," Fiona said.

"I think that's enough for today," Annette said, covering her daughter's hand in a sign of protective mothering.

"Mom, it's fine. Lizbeth was seeing Mason Scout over the summer."

Ezra jotted down in his green Moleskine a quick translation: *Fiona sleeping with Mason. Summer.* Lucia read it over his shoulder.

Annette looked at her daughter in surprise. "I didn't know that." She laughed. "Could you imagine if her mother only knew? That boy is nothing but trouble."

Fiona blushed. "Then I heard, well, Lizbeth heard that Mason found someone new."

"Who?" Lucia asked. Then she put the two different anecdotes together. "Brooklyn was seeing Mason? Who told Lizbeth?"

"Everyone knows. That's who took that picture."

"What picture?" Annette asked her daughter.

"Mason took credit for it?" Lucia asked.

Fiona shook her head.

"Then where did it begin?" Lucia asked. "Did anyone see them together?"

"A teacher."

Lucia tapped on the table. Why couldn't this girl just spit it out? Fiona, it seemed, wanted to torture her and Ezra. This felt like pulling teeth, though, pulling her teeth would be far more satisfying. "Which teacher? Monsieur Durand, Coach Larson, someone else?"

Fiona bore her gaze into the mesquite table.

Ezra changed subjects. "You're friends with Daniel Toussaint, yes?"

She nodded.

"What happened between Daniel and Mr. Durand October 6th?"

It was the same question that came to Lucia.

"I don't know." She clenched her fists on the table, her knuckles turning white. "You'll have to ask him."

Lucia knew what to ask next but also knew it was a long shot. "Do you remember either of them acting strangely around then?"

"Around the sixth of October? Oh yeah," she said, a mock-helpful tone entering her voice. "I remember

Daniel wore this red shirt with a dragon with a lightning bolt in its mouth, but he almost never wears red."

Lucia had to ask, "Sarcasm?"

"You think?" Fiona replied.

"We've answered your questions," Annette interjected. "I think it's time we conclude this. I still need to get Fiona to school for the afternoon." Annette stood from the table and took the coffee cups with her, placing herself between her daughter and the detectives.

"We have a few follow up questions," Lucia said.

"Have it your way," Annette said. "Just give us a moment." She ushered her daughter into the kitchen, presumably to discuss how to proceed.

"Let's give them a second," Ezra said.

Lucia shook her head. "Something feels off."

When she went to investigate, the kitchen was empty. The sound of a car starting in the driveway was the only indication of the mother-daughter getaway. By the time Lucia and Ezra made it outside, the Flemings' Mercedes was receding into the distance in the direction of SJM school.

"That was weird," Ezra said.

"We'll come back with a warrant."

"One problem."

"What's that?"

"Mason Scout has an iron-clad alibi. We have him on camera."

"Maybe," she said. "How fast of a runner is he?"

"You think he ran up and down three flights of stairs in under a minute?"

"Maybe he didn't have to."

"You think he had help?"

"One way or another."

"What's that supposed to mean?" Ezra asked.

"I'd like to visit with our tech guy. I have a theory I want to run by him."

"What are you thinking, Detective Vargas?"

"You don't have to keep calling me *Detective Vargas*. We're not in court."

"Okay, what are you thinking, Lucia?"

"Something shocking."

"I've been investigating homicides for a decade; I doubt there's much you could say to shock me."

"I think Mason shocked Brooklyn."

"Oh."

"Pendejo," she muttered playfully.

****

Henry Chen, Lucia's technology analyst, worked out of a basement lab. The overhead fluorescents flickered and buzzed. Not a single window let in light as the lab also served as a darkroom for developing film in the old days.

Chen confirmed right away that a wired bell could've shocked Brooklyn, but he admitted the scenario seemed unlikely.

"Why?" Ezra asked.

"The voltage," Chen said. "Even with a pure copper bell, which the one at SJM isn't, you'd need a terrific amount of voltage to carry through one ton of metal and reach your victim."

Lucia accepted this. The footprints in the snow almost ruled it out.

"What about something she wore? Like a pearl necklace?" Lucia asked.

"Sure," Chen told them. "You could wire a necklace to shock someone. Some dog trainers still use shock collars. With a little know-how, you could alter one to deliver a powerful shock." The three nodded in unison as they considered this. Then Chen added, "But I'd try to figure out who lured her up there."

Ezra shrugged. "She didn't tell anyone who she was meeting, didn't post on social media, and she didn't have her phone."

"Who doesn't have a phone?" Chen asked.

"She has a phone contract," Lucia clarified, we just can't find the actual phone. She didn't have anything on her, and the sweep of the car and apartment haven't turned up anything."

Ezra asked, "You think Mason ran out to get the phone?"

"The phone and whatever he used to shock her. He knocked out the power to the building and the cameras for two minutes, just long enough to gather the evidence he needed, and then he got back to his seat in plain view."

"It would have to be a serious piece of electronics to send her over the handrail," Chen said.

"Not if she was on the wrong side of it," she said.

"What would convince her to step over the handrail?" Chen wondered aloud.

"I can think of a few things," Ezra replied.

As soon as they were out of the building, Lucia said, "I'm hitting my head against the wall here."

Ezra checked his watch. "It's lunchtime. You're probably just hungry. There's an amazing Vietnamese place not far from here."

She turned in the direction of her car.

"No, let's walk," he said.

Chapter Twenty-Four

The decor of the Vietnamese restaurant was sparse. The tables were set close together, and the V-pop music filled their silences. The music reminded Ezra of 90s R&B but in Vietnamese. The requisite giant aquarium tank contained one oversized koi. The food, however, more than made up for these short-comings.

Lucia dunked her fresh spring roll into their shared peanut sauce. "So what happened?"

"That's what we're going to find out," Ezra replied. He seemed confused by her question.

"No. I mean why are you working at a school?"

"Oh! Oh." He remained silent a moment. "I'm on probation."

"Because of Straugh's acquittal?"

"Not exactly."

"Then what?"

"You want to know if I planted the evidence, I suppose?" he asked.

Lucia shook her head. "I just want to know why you're at SJM."

"Everyone remembers those women, the crying lovers, and they remember I was suspended after the acquittal. Nobody remembers the evidence I planted—and it's a wonder. We thought it would go down in the record books for the strangest piece of evidence ever submitted."

The waiter took their plates away, replacing them with entrees. Ezra took a big bite of his bún chả. He chewed slowly, deliberately, as if knowing she was growing more impatient with each bite.

"Okay, so what was it?" Lucia asked, on the verge of exasperation.

"To make the case a slam dunk, we tore down Straugh's character for the first half of the trial and then, when the jury was ready to hang him, we submitted one final piece of evidence for their consideration. The weeks leading up to the trial, we had a strong case. We knew we could get Straugh convicted, but the thing that sealed the deal we didn't find until two days before the trial began."

Ezra took another bite, took another pregnant pause.

Lucia sat up straight. She remembered. "The toothbrushes. I read about this."

He picked up his tea with a laugh. "I bet you did."

"Someone else found them, I thought."

"No one could've missed the display case. It covered most of the wall in his basement. Every toothbrush he'd ever owned. We found the victims' DNA on three toothbrushes stored behind the walls."

Lunch diners thinned out around them as they spoke. The V-Pop music continued, but soon it played just for them.

"I'd been conducting an interview in Ft. Lauderdale during the initial sweep of the house. When I came back, I kept thinking of that display case. My partner Dean Harris and I hit the house one more time when I got back. I asked the officer guarding the Straugh residence, 'What did we find behind the walls?' He checked his inventory and told me, 'Nothing.' Curious, I asked, 'Not even an old outlet box or a dead mouse?' He told me again, 'Nothing,' just like that.

"So Harris and I made our way to the house, down into the basement, and then stared at the seven foot by three foot discoloration on the wall where the eighty or so worn-out toothbrushes had been displayed. Forensics found nothing but Straugh's own DNA on those brushes. Then I noticed a slight indent in the drywall and a patch of fresh paint. A team had scoured every inch of the house, behind the walls and under the floors, but I made them come back that morning and search this one spot. They cut it open and, in no time at all, discovered three more toothbrushes in a plastic bag."

Lucia shifted uncomfortably in her seat.

"As I'm sure you know, forensics found DNA from three of our victims. The toothbrushes either belonged to them or Straugh had brushed their teeth after he'd killed them. The latter option sounded creepier, so that's what we suggested during the trial. The toothbrushes were a unique sort of trophy to keep but, as we had established earlier, Straugh was a unique sort of killer. Even for a serial killer, the guy was weird. I mean, who keeps eighty used toothbrushes?"

"You're not wrong."

Two teenagers in white aprons began bussing the tables around them. Soon the whole restaurant was cleared except their table.

"The DNA evidence wrapped everything up for us," Ezra continued. He seemed crestfallen. "They fit Straugh so well, how was I supposed to know they were planted? The crime scene was tampered with, evidence planted, and I set the wheels into motion. My partner's name also appeared on all the official evidence logs, but everyone knew it was my idea."

"That's pretty damning," Lucia said.

He nodded. "After the trial, Stephanie Straugh returned to her parents' home in Van Meter, Iowa. I made it out there a lot to visit the family and help them cope with the media storm that followed the trial. Straugh was the most hated man in America, and a lot of aggression spilled over onto his family. They egged the house, toilet-papered the trees, and bashed in the mailbox.

"Home calls weren't part of my duties, but I insisted on visiting them once a month to check in and assess the damage. My wife Julia hated that I kept driving out there."

"How did the sentencing trial end?"

"They voted for the death penalty almost without deliberation. The appeal process began. All standard operating procedure. Then a pair of photographs appeared online anonymously. One photo showed the Straugh basement wall during the initial investigation, the other moments before our forensics team cut open the drywall. The difference was obvious. The initial photos showed an ordinary, uniform wall. The latter photo showed a rough, off-color patch in the middle of the wall. After the initial examination of the house, someone clearly cut a hole in the drywall, placed new evidence inside, and then plastered over and repainted it. The date stamps showed both photographs were taken while Straugh was in a jail cell awaiting trial."

"And, as it often does," Lucia said, "the media went into a feeding frenzy."

"Oh, yes. Celebrities from Chicago, St. Louis, even New York spoke out against Straugh's sentencing. Money poured into the appeal, and the case was retried. Every piece of DNA evidence and every eyewitness account was reevaluated and much of it dismissed. Faked DNA evidence, it appears, is especially susceptible to re-examination."

"Who leaked the photos?"

Ezra shrugged. "Don't know."

"One of yours?"

"Maybe, but I don't think anyone did it out of spite," he said. "I have to imagine someone found it on a memory card after the trial."

"Couldn't they have just brought it to you?" she asked. "Publishing it anonymously feels malicious."

Ezra shook his head. "I don't know. Anyway, it didn't matter. Straugh's new team of lawyers uncovered a piece of circumstantial evidence in Straugh's favor—and that threw the whole thing out."

"What was it?"

"A video recording of him entering a hotel bar and hitting on at least a dozen women while he was supposed to be killing a young co-ed in her apartment twenty miles away. LAPD found the victim, Lydia Lawson, stabbed to death and a small white gearbox on her nightstand."

"He could've had help," Lucia said.

"With the planted evidence and the video, it was all too much. The defense claimed I planted the toothbrushes, then led my partner down to 'discover them,' " he said with air quotes. "*How did I gather the DNA? When did I plant the toothbrushes? Did I brush the teeth of the corpses or just pilfer their toothbrushes from evidence?* These were the questions Straugh's new defense attorneys asked me on the witness stand and the questions the reporters asked whenever they found me."

"You were famous," she said. "Every little boy's dream."

"It was awful. The reporters were relentless. They didn't even let up when Julia left and I stopped leaving the house. I went from a national hero to a national villain, from special agent James to Ezra the Pariah. Julia went from loving, supportive wife to ex-wife."

Lucia couldn't contain her indignation. "She left you because of the trial?"

"That's misleading."

Ezra paid the check, and they took their conversation back outside, he said, "Then there was the miscarriage."

Lucia nodded in remembrance.

"And my hospitalization."

This was news to her.

"That bit wasn't in the papers either, thankfully," he said.

"No. Was it on the job?"

"What?"

"Your injury."

"Sort of."

They walked in silence for a few houses before Lucia stopped. "Look, if we're going to be partners in this, you have to tell me these things."

"You're going to think less of me," Ezra said.

"Now how could I possibly think less of you?" She gave a slow shrug of one shoulder. "Especially since I already have such a low opinion."

"It was a seventy-two-hour psychiatric hold."

When she made no move to run for the hills, he finished the explanation. "My brain chemistry became imbalanced. I suppose it always has been. I've always had highs and lows, but all of the stress caused it to—" He searched for the word.

"You had a manic episode?"

He sighed, the toughest sigh in the world. "I imagined my partner was sleeping with my wife. I confronted them in broad daylight. I pulled my firearm on him."

"That's terrible. I'm sorry."

"My partner reacted quickly. He talked me down before anyone realized what was happening. People see a gun and they panic, but then they see that both men have badges and they dismiss it. I turned myself in. I knew enough to recognize I was on thin ice."

"So you lost it and threatened your last partner and now you expect me to, what, trust you?"

"You don't have to say anything else."

"I'm kidding! You're medicated and everything, right?"

Ezra nodded.

"And you take your meds?"

He nodded again.

"Then I'm sure you're saner than half the people out here," she said, gesturing at the busy store fronts.

"So what now?" he asked.

"You want to take another run at Daniel today?" She pointed to a parked sedan. "This is me. You're going back to school this afternoon, I assume?"

"I'll see what I can get out of Daniel, but I don't have high hopes."

She opened the door and slid inside. "We know a

lot more now. Use some of that," she said. "You still remember how to scare a suspect, right?" She shut the door before he could reply.

Ezra knocked on the window. After she rolled it down, he asked, "The journal?"

"Oh right." She picked her copy off the seat beside her and handed it to him. "You two have a lot in common, you know?"

"Who?"

"You and Martin Durand."

"How so? Wait, why are you smiling?"

"I just remembered a part from a poem. *How everything turns away/ Quite leisurely from the disaster.*"

"A poem?"

"It's about the fall of Icarus," she said, still smiling. "For him, it's a disaster, but the sun just keeps shining. You should read it."

"The journal or the poem?"

Lucia just nodded and rolled up her window. Ezra grew smaller and smaller in her rearview mirror as she drove away, but his perplexed expression remained clear as day.

Chapter Twenty-Five

Afternoon light suffused the sheer curtains in Ezra's tiny and little-used office. Empty bookcases filled the wall to the left of his desk, and the wide windows and curtains took up the wall directly in front of him. It was an office with a view, one might say, except the view was of the gas station across the street. With Daniel Toussaint sitting in the chair across from him, Ezra couldn't even see the station.

For the second time in a week, he found himself grilling the sixteen-year-old. For the second time, the taciturn teenager sat as silent as a stone.

After fifteen minutes of unanswered questions, Ezra decided to show his cards. "We know you took the golden chalice from the church." No reaction.

"Why did you need the money?"

Somehow less of a reaction.

"Why steal from Fr. Remy, of all people? The only priest to show you kindness and acceptance?"

Ezra was beginning to wonder if Daniel had fallen asleep with his eyes open.

"What happened October 6th? Martin Durand said something to you. What was it?"

Daniel opened his mouth as if to speak, but then yawned and closed it again.

Already, Ezra had given him far too much information. This was a piss-poor interrogation.

"We know you were sleeping with Fiona Fleming," Ezra bluffed.

The teen raised his eyebrows in surprise. At least he was paying attention.

After Ezra dismissed Daniel, he packed up for the day. Thirty minutes they'd sat there, and Daniel didn't say one word. Alas. He would put Remy on the task. Likely, Remy already knew why Daniel took the chalice, what he needed the money for—and possibly what Martin said to Daniel. The priest couldn't share any of it with Ezra, however, thanks to the seal of confession. Why bother keeping a priest for a companion if he couldn't tell you anything? Perhaps Ezra was a gossip after all.

The afternoon light had started to fade by the time Ezra arrived home. He mounted the steps to his red-brick bungalow. The top porch step wobbled beneath his feet. He meant to fix the step but hadn't found the time. He made a mental note to address it this weekend as he inserted the key into the deadbolt. Before engaging the lock, however, the doorknob turned easily and opened. Hand in mid-air, Ezra stopped. He always locked the front door when he left the house.

Two narrow, floor-to-ceiling windows of frosted glass on either side of the door allowed light to filter into the foyer. In front of each window stood small round tables, each with a painted-black lamp. This arrangement ensured that upon entering the house and flipping the light switch, Ezra was met with the warm glow of lamps rather than the harsh overhead lights. Everything thoughtful about the decor of the foyer, and indeed the house in general, came from Julia. Ezra's only contribution had been to place a snub-nosed revolver in a drawer by the light switch.

Instead of turning on the lamps as he usually did, he slowly slid the drawer open and removed the Smith & Wesson .38 Special from the drawer.

Expecting a burglar, he mentally cataloged every room of the house and its belongings and decided to start with the living room. The house wasn't pitch dark, the evening sky was still purple and red, but shadows filled every corner and behind each piece of furniture. He waited for his eyes to adjust to the dimness and then began clearing rooms one by one. The entertainment center, with its flat screen, speakers, and film collection, had apparently been passed over by the intruder. Likewise, the expensive kitchen gadgets still cluttered the kitchen. Even the change dish, which contained several five-dollar bills and a few handfuls of quarters, sat unmolested on the counter. He cleared half the house and saw no signs of anyone. Maybe he *had* left the door unlocked this morning.

He'd nearly given up on the idea of a real burglar—as opposed to an imaginary one—when the sound of metal on metal, as of a window screeching open, came from the study. More rapidly, he crept down the hall and pushed the door open with his shoulder.

Three things happened in quick succession. First, a burst of cold air poured into the hallway from the study. Second, the window jerked the rest of the way open. Third, a tall figure in a black hoodie leaped from inside the room onto the sill.

"Stop or I'll shoot!" Ezra shouted and aimed for the figure.

Without a second's hesitation, the figure hopped

out and hit the ground running.

Ezra turned on the ceiling light and found the typical break-in scene. All of the drawers in the room were open, their contents spilled onto the floor. Half the books were pulled off their shelves. Various documents lay in disheveled stacks. Instinctively, he touched his breast pocket, feeling for the Moleskine with its meticulous notes. Then Ezra tore through the hallway, booking it for the front door.

Even if he didn't catch the intruder, he might get a license plate. In seconds, he stood on the porch looking out at the neighborhood. There were no signs of the intruder, no footprints, nor any car tires squealing in the distance.

He raced down the steps, but the loose step was gone. He lost his footing and toppled, landing on hands and knees on the concrete path. Then something came from above, hard and fast.

When Ezra came to, his face burned with cold from the snowy ground and agony emanated from the back of his head. He touched the source of the excruciating pain and found a large welt. His fingertips came away covered with semi-dried blood. Beside him, cracked in half, lay a two-by-four. The would-be burglar had sprinted out here fast enough to pry up the loose step and wait. Two clean metal nails stuck out from the end.

At least they didn't use the side of the board with the nail, Ezra thought.

****

The bullpen was deserted when Ezra stopped by later that evening. He knocked on the metal desk of a woman in a knitted cat sweater. She didn't look up from her paperback novel. "Did EPD take a half day?"

She kept her face buried in the book. He gestured around the vacant desks. "Is there some emergency I'm unaware of?"

"Shh," she said.

"I'm here to see Detective Lucia Vargas about the Hannigan case."

"You're a rude one, aren't you?" She closed her book with a slap. "She thought he was dead this whole time, and now he's back."

"Martin Durand?"

"Who's Martin Durand? No, Flavius, the Roman centurion." She fanned the book's cover at him. There, an over-muscled model in costume armor embraced a woman dressed in even flimsier clothing. As she made eye contact with him, the secretary grimaced. "What happened to you?"

Ezra gestured vaguely at his bloody scalp. "Oh this? It's just a flesh wound." Already, he had a headache like a Sunday morning in a frat-house.

"More like a head wound," she said. "You'd better get yourself to NorthShore. This here is the police department."

Hopefully, she meant this sarcastically and was not about to call him an ambulance. "Can you leave Detective Vargas a message?"

Across the office, Lucia and her partner entered the bullpen. They marched toward the holding cells, pushing a handcuffed Martin Durand in front of them.

Martin's tie was loose and his shirt collar unbuttoned. Dark bags hung under his eyes. He hadn't changed clothes since Ezra spoke to him the day before. He hadn't slept either from the looks of it.

"We got him!" Gorecki shouted into the empty

bullpen. He grabbed Durand by the elbow and dragged him the rest of the way to the holding cells.

"Where was he?" Ezra asked Lucia.

"He turned himself in. Called from a rest stop across the Wisconsin border about an hour ago. Kenosha PD picked him up and escorted him down.

Ezra did the math in his head. It didn't add up. Only an hour ago, someone he thought was Martin Durand knocked him unconscious. If Martin was in Wisconsin, then who the hell broke into his house?

"Whoa what happened to your head?" she asked.

Ezra felt his scalp and then examined his bloody fingers. "I had a break-in. When I pursued the guy, he knocked me out cold with a two-by-four."

She examined the wound. "He really laid into you."

He considered his next statement carefully. "I think he wanted this." Ezra held out his green Moleskine. "All my notes about the case are in here."

She frowned. "Look, Martin Durand just turned himself in. Let's develop this lead first."

"But it doesn't make sense," he said, "Durand attacked Brooklyn, killed Autumn to cover his tracks, fled, and then—what—just turned himself in?"

"You know how it goes," she said.

She left him there, bleeding and alone, in the bullpen.

Chapter Twenty-Six

Wednesday

Judge Deering came through with the cell data warrants Wednesday morning. With the escalation in charges from attempted murder to first degree murder, and the likely suspect being formally charged, acquiring the data from Brooklyn's phone provider, Finlox, became relatively easy. Lucia still didn't have Brooklyn's actual phone, though. Neither a search of Hannigan's nor Durand's properties turned it up.

The GPS data gave them nothing new. Autumn's tracking app stopped at eight-fifteen when Brooklyn fell from the St. Peter bell tower. According to the GPS, the phone died within a minute of that fall. Either the electrical charge that seared Brooklyn's neck also short circuited the phone or, and this seemed more likely, someone took the phone and destroyed the SIM card. Lucia wondered what else they'd taken.

"Find anything?" Gorecki asked. He was chewing cinnamon gum, which she could smell clearly. The idea of chewing gum first thing in the morning made her stomach turn. He hadn't even finished his coffee yet.

"Nothing we didn't already know," she replied.

"What about Martin Durand's phone?"

"This guy's an anachronism," she said. It suddenly dawned on her that this word perfectly matched the

French teacher. He belonged to another time period, or several time periods, but all of them long ago.

"How do you mean?"

She wondered if Gorecki was racking his mind for the definition of *anachronism*.

"The clothes, the old French, and then this." She showed him a print-off of Martin's GPS. It listed a single data point over and over.

"I don't understand."

"He keeps his phone in a charging case on his kitchen counter," she said. Then she elaborated, "He treats it like a landline."

"He doesn't even take it to school?"

Lucia tossed the paper report across her desk. "This is worthless."

He winked. "Guess we'll just have to get a confession."

"Is the lawyer here yet?"

"I heard he asked for the ex-wife."

"No, it isn't her," Lucia said. "Someone else from her firm is coming. Durand requested her, but…" Lucia searched for the right words.

"She didn't think she could be dispassionate about the case?"

"That's the word." *Dispassionate* was the last word she'd use to describe Gemma in general. Although, to be fair, they'd only interacted once and then under considerable duress.

The captain's secretary, a middle-aged woman who knitted her own sweaters, shuffled over to Lucia's desk. "There's a lady here to speak with you." She pointed out a female attorney in a plum skirt suit. The attorney held her briefcase in front of her knees as if to extend the length of her skirt.

"Ready?" the attorney asked eagerly.

Too eagerly, Lucia thought.

****

The late model purple caddy in the Chicago field office lot told Ezra that Jeremiah Cromley was in. Middle fifties, salt-and-pepper hair, and a fixed smile, ASAC Cromley taught Ezra most of what he'd learned in his time as an agent, from investigative techniques and moving up the bureaucratic ladder to investing his money properly and ordering at tapas bars.

Like most men who grew up without a father, Ezra filled in the gaps where he could. Before Julia left him, they dined out regularly with Cromley and his wife, usually at the most expensive new restaurant in Chicago. The couples would laugh and drink and drop a few hundred bucks. Those evenings, like everything else he shared with Julia, were gone now.

Cromley's office resembled a sports bar more than a federal workspace. A signed photograph of Muhammad Ali hung behind his chair. Ali's signature was a solid cursive that looked almost Arabic. Opposite this was a similar framed photo of a prominent MMA fighter, also signed. Positioned as they were, the fighters looked as if they were about to face off. Many evenings out, conversation had turned to who would've won in their prime. Knowing nothing about either sport, Ezra always took the side of Ali out of blind loyalty. Cromley would then explain all the styles of fighting involved in MMA.

Now, as he sat across from Cromley, Ezra somehow doubted their conversation would develop along that well-trodden path.

"Has it been a week already?" Cromley asked.

Ezra nodded. "Time for my check in. Ah, the life of the suspended agent."

Cromley frowned. "No one suspended you, Ezra. This is just probation. You still have an assignment."

"Babysitting," Ezra said, "until I can prove myself worthy of my former post."

"Until you have recovered and can return to it," Cromley corrected him.

"That's just semantics," Ezra replied. "Every agent I've seen terminated began with a probation or a suspension."

Cromley replied, "I hate it when people say something's *just semantics.* Semantics is meaning. You act like a man who's never had a setback." Cromley smiled. "Half of my career has been setbacks."

"Were your setbacks posted on the front page of the Chicago *Tribune?"*

The ASAC smiled again. "You act like anyone still reads."

This last remark earned a chuckle from Ezra. Cromley was too agreeable to argue with for long.

"So how is the school?"

"A mess. I've been working with EPD on a case all week."

"So I read." He rummaged around his desk and produced a slick tabloid. "Disgraced Fed Ezra James Attacks Young Co-ed." Ezra groaned. Of course, the tabloids had picked up Ezra's involvement in the case. "I jest," Cromley said. "What are the names?"

"What names?"

"I assume you want me to do some digging. So what are the names you want me to look up?"

One condition of his probation was limited access to federal resources. "I'm not even sure what I'm looking for," Ezra said. "They've made an arrest, Martin Durand, but something doesn't feel right."

Cromley pointed to Ezra's bandaged head. "That?"

"Yes. Someone attacked me in my home while Durand was an hour away in Wisconsin."

"What did your Evanston friends say?"

"They think it must be a coincidence. They think it was a B&E. I asked them, 'Who breaks into a house, passes by the electronics, the petty cash jar, and tears apart the study instead?' They didn't have an answer for that."

"What was the intruder after?"

Ezra removed the myrtle green Moleskine from his breast pocket. "This, I think."

"Ah, the infamous dotted notebook."

"I think they wanted my notes."

"That would mean they've seen you use it," Cromley said, thinking aloud. "Do you think it's someone from the school?"

Ezra wrote down a list of names, which included Martin Durand, Mason Scout, Benjamin Larson, and Royce Ainsley. Immediately, Cromley pulled up all four names and scanned through them. "How well do you know this Lucas fellow?"

"Who?"

Cromley turned his monitor around for Ezra to read. He read slowly, deliberately, about everything Benjamin Larson had done before his name change. Benjamin Lucas graduated with honors from UNLV with a double major in physics and education. He then student-taught at a high school in southwest Vegas. From the photos, the school looked exactly like a prison. After that, Lucas took a position at a college prep academy with a facade half way between a suburban high school and a country club. There, he met Vanessa Maxwell, and his luck ran out.

Although of age and not one of his students directly, Vanessa was still a high schooler. Their dalliance became the talk of the school. By the time the principal discovered what was happening, her father had already reported it to local police, thus skipping right over the principal and school board and forcing the school's hand.

At the trial, the prosecutor argued that the county didn't want to see the first-year teacher hanged, but they also didn't want him teaching at another high school ever again.

Benjamin Lucas lost his teaching license, his reputation, and his name, though to be fair, he willingly parted with the last item. Two years later, Benjamin *Larson* applied for a teaching license in Illinois in order to teach science at a boy's juvenile detention center. The state of Illinois was more than willing to overlook his previous transgressions if he agreed to stay for five years. From there, Larson's career progressed little by little until Catherine Weeks hired him at SJM.

"Benjamin Lucas," Ezra said to himself. "Now I've got something to talk about tonight."

"What's tonight?"

"He runs a basketball clinic at the local rec center. I thought I would pay him a visit."

****

Durand's lawyer went into the interrogation room

first. On the short metal table lay crime scene photos of Autumn. Several showed the journal, bloodied and shot through. Durand and his lawyer conferred first before she motioned for Lucia and Gorecki to join them.

"Do you go by Mister or Monsieur Durand?" Lucia asked.

"Martin is fine."

Usually, Lucia liked to go into an interrogation with the dual weapons of knowledge and empathy. When she knew enough about the situation, she could guide the suspect in the right direction slowly, building rapport, even thanking him for his helpfulness. Then she would pivot. Only too late did she realize she should've conveyed these preferences to Gorecki ahead of time.

"All right, Martin," Gorecki cut in, "can you tell us why you murdered Autumn Elkhart or was it more of a spur-of-the-moment thing?"

Durand's brows raised fearfully. "I didn't kill her!"

His lawyer placed her manicured fingers on his shoulder as a way of reminding him not to say anything.

"Why did you attack Brooklyn?" Gorecki continued. "We know you saw her after school Thursday."

Great, Lucia thought. Her first question was going to be when he last saw her.

"Detective Gorecki," she said, "may I speak with you outside?"

"Okay?"

They stepped out of the interrogation room.

"What in the ever-loving world are you doing?" she asked.

"Are you not playing the good cop?"

"I was building rapport."

He threw up his hands. "Sorry, that's just how Benny and I did it." Gorecki worked with Benny McGowan for five years, Benny's last five years before retiring. Benny had a reputation for doing things old school. He often said he'd learned everything he needed to know in the 1970s. Lucia thought it unfortunate he'd chosen to stop learning once the '70s ended.

Durand wore a guarded expression when they reentered.

"Let's start over," Lucia said. "Martin, can you tell me the last time you saw Brooklyn Hannigan?"

He whispered something to his lawyer. The lawyer then spoke for him, "From five to five-thirty Thursday night."

"Was the visit social?"

He leaned over and whispered something to his lawyer. She responded, "No."

Lucia asked then, "Did Brooklyn mention her dinner plans?"

Again he leaned over to his lawyer, and again she responded, "No."

"Okay, when is the last time you saw Autumn Elkhart?"

"My client does not know Autumn, nor has he ever seen her," she replied. She then gestured at the forensic photographs between them. "Until he saw these photographs."

Gorecki slapped the table. "How did your journal end up at her house?"

The lawyer replied, "He doesn't know. He didn't even know it was missing."

"For an innocent man, he's certainly careful with his words," Gorecki told the lawyer, but his eyes were fixed on Durand.

"Martin," Lucia said more softly, "do you have an alibi for Thursday night after Brooklyn left your apartment?"

Silence.

"What about Saturday night? Or Sunday morning from four to six?"

He leaned over to his lawyer, spoke briefly. She replied, "On all of those occasions he was in his apartment either reading or grading papers."

"What was he reading?"

More hushed whispers.

"My client would prefer not to say."

This surprised even Lucia. She could empathize with a drug dealer in a bad situation or a person driven to murder by jealousy. She could talk to them like she understood their motivations. But what reason could Martin Durand possibly have for not revealing the book he was reading?

Gorecki chimed in unhelpfully. "We have access to all your books, buddy. We'll just check your nightstand or search for bookmarks."

Lucia thought of all the novels on her shelves with bookmarks a few chapters or halfway through, where she lost interest, or others that a helpful clerk stuck a bookmark into at random. Someday she would read all of these started, abandoned, and not-yet-gotten-to books.

"I don't think that's the point, Detective Gorecki," Lucia said. Then she fixed her gaze on Martin. "He's telling us he's done cooperating. He won't even tell us what book he was reading." She pointed at the lawyer. "Either that or *she* won't let him."

Just as she had hoped, the French teacher's brows crinkled. He bore the unmistakable expression of a teacher hearing a wrong answer. As a man, he didn't want to go to prison, but as a teacher, he couldn't abide someone misunderstanding him.

"If you're innocent," Lucia said, winding up, "then why flee when Ezra James confronted you?"

He whispered to the lawyer, but she said nothing. He whispered again with more force.

"I'm not telling them that," the attorney said.

"Why not?" Martin asked, just audibly.

"Oh, I don't know," the lawyer replied, loud enough for everyone to hear. "Maybe because it sounds bat-crap crazy?"

"Why did you leave?" Lucia asked him directly. "If you didn't attack these young women, we need to know why you left town."

"Because I needed to remove some books from my house," he said.

His lawyer threw up her hands.

"What for?" Gorecki asked, genuinely curious.

"To burn them."

These three words were the last Martin Durand would say to Lucia or her partner during his time at the Evanston Police Department.

Chapter Twenty-Seven

The young woman at the front desk of the Evanston Rec wore a Northwestern sweatshirt over black yoga wear. She looked, at least to Ezra, like a walking advertisement for the center's yoga class. "Can I help you?" she asked without looking up from the cell phone in her palm.

"Is Benjamin Larson in?"

"Coach Larson? Second set of basketball courts."

"Which is where?"

She gestured behind her with the phone.

"Is that headband knitted spandex?"

The girl nodded, still not taking her gaze off the screen.

"My wife has one just like it."

She looked at Ezra curiously.

He smiled. "It's my favorite of her many headbands."

She almost returned the smile but then frowned instead. "You can't have that here." She pointed with her phone at his belt holster, the yellow handle of the taser just visible beneath his suit jacket. Then she pointed at a no guns sign.

Ezra showed her his badge. "Coach Larson is a new hire, isn't he?"

"He's good, though. The kids like him, and they're improving a ton."

"He's been here a few weeks?"

She nodded.

"Are any of these kids from St. Joseph and Mary?"

She laughed.

"What's so funny?"

She just pointed again to the double doors down the hall.

When Ezra entered, he saw her point. There wasn't a new pair of sneakers in the whole gym. Some were covered in gray duct tape; others wore their holes proudly. The athletes walked in twos and threes around the edge of the gym. Larson jogged from clump to clump.

"Aren't *they* supposed to do the running?" Ezra asked.

"Ox, show Mr. James here your vest," Larson said.

A young man about a head taller than Ezra lifted up his shirt to reveal a weighted vest. Larson motioned for Ox to lower his shirt. "What've you been learning?"

"Enrique say I'm blocking my eye whenever I shoot."

"Is there an echo in here?" Larson asked rhetorically.

"I know, I know," the player said, "but he also say I been looking down when I dribble."

Larson punched Ezra's arm. "See! I hadn't even noticed that. You can't be everywhere at all times. These kids are perceptive. They can teach each other far more than I can."

As Larson jogged to the next group. Ezra tried to keep up.

"You're feeling better, I see," Ezra said.

"Forty-eight-hour bug," Larson replied without

hesitation. If this were a basketball game, one might say he pivoted with ease.

Ezra pivoted as well. "So Coach Lucas, I've been meaning to ask you about something."

At being referred to by his former name, the coach's eyes went wide.

"What did I say?" Ezra asked innocently. "Oh God, did I call you..." He face palmed comically. "I guess now the cat's out of the bag."

Larson/Lucas didn't respond. In fact, his body went rigid. "Have you told, what I mean to say is, Catherine, has she..."

"I haven't notified Principal Weeks. How old were you when it happened?"

The coach chewed on his lower lip and then began walking again as if the act of speaking required physical motion, like a car engine warming up before the heat would kick on. "That's just the thing, I was twenty-one. I entered college at seventeen. Vanessa was eighteen. She could've been a college freshman and I could've been a college senior."

"That's tough," he replied sympathetically. *Always sympathize.* "What happened then?"

Larson chuckled. "What always happens—everyone found out."

"How?" Ezra asked. Even though he already knew, he wanted to keep Larson talking.

"Kids talk among themselves, and then teachers catch on. Some teachers are parents themselves or personal friends with the parents. One of the science teachers told her father, and he came by my apartment one night. He confronted me, then bashed in the windows of my car."

"If you'd waited for her to graduate, he probably never would've found out."

The coach nodded. "But I didn't wait. The judge revoked my teaching license, forbade me from getting another one, and then sealed my records. I filed for a name change one day and left Nevada the next."

"Why the name change? If the case was dropped, I mean."

"Las Vegas Sun," he said simply.

Ezra was no stranger himself to the corrosive effect a newspaper could have on one's reputation. Every major city paper in the country had mentioned his involvement in the CTC case.

Coach Larson jogged to the next pair, made observations, asked questions, then moved on. They jogged from group to group like this, working harder than Ezra's high school coach ever had.

"Martin Durand," Ezra said during a long stretch between players. "Say he was to come off our list of suspects."

Larson slowed to a walk. "But he's still in custody?"

Ezra nodded.

"He seems a bit limp-wristed for something like this," the coach admitted.

"And say a student went on our list," Ezra said.

Larson pulled Ezra to the side of the gym, out of earshot of his players.

"There is someone on the basketball team. His family is royalty at SJM. I'm not sure if you've spoken to him yet or not."

Ezra sensed Larson was waiting for him to guess. Ezra resisted.

"Mason Scout," Larson finally said.

"God, you think?"

Ezra pretended to have a light bulb moment. He came up with a plausible lie on the spot: "That makes sense. I didn't want to say anything, but the family did approach me about keeping his name out of the papers." He felt a twinge of conscience lying outright, but the gravity of the situation called for it. "I shouldn't be talking about this." Ezra went tight-lipped.

"What did the family want?" the coach asked. "I might be able to help."

Ezra pretended to think this over. "I suppose I'm not bound by law."

"Out with it."

"The family lawyer approached me earlier today. He said he wanted to assist with the investigation."

Another lie, but it had the desired effect. Larson's jaw clenched, and his eyes darted back and forth.

Ezra continued, "He wanted to assist financially. He offered me ten grand for my efforts."

Larson looked baffled but then smiled and said, "Well, there you go. It sounds like the Scouts have something to hide."

He shrugged. "I suppose it could just be about recruiting, not wanting to sully their son's name. Still, Evanston PD is bringing the whole family in for questioning."

"If they keep questioning people at that school, they'll soon discover everyone is guilty of something," Larson said.

They started walking toward the next group.

Larson seemed more at ease now. Either he was getting used to Ezra's presence, or the suggestion of investigating Mason made him feel safe. Whatever it was, Larson got a strange smile on his face and leaned over to tell Ezra a joke. "They executed a serial killer today in Taiwan. He had the second most murders in the country. Before his execution, they asked if he had any last requests. Know what he said?"

Ezra shook his head, a smile forming on his lips.

"One more."

"You're a sick man, Coach."

"Hey, you're the one who laughed, Mr. FBI. I just related the information." He stopped walking. "Can I ask you something impertinent?"

"Sure."

"What was it like tracking down a serial killer?"

Ezra used to get asked this often. During the trial, the Chicago field office received calls daily from national and international journalists. Due to his significant role in the investigation, Ezra was allowed to provide answers.

"It's just like with any other killer or terrorist or drug dealer. You put aside the nature of the crime and follow the evidence."

"But CTC must've been a little different. There was no motive, and the killer didn't fit any of the standard psychological profiles. With such randomness, such carefulness, it must have been a challenge."

"Every system has a flaw. Most would-be serial killers get caught after murder one and no one ever hears about them. Even more killers fail to overcome their first victim. I don't know how many people I helped put away who would've become much worse over time. You mentioned randomness, and that's also right. Some of the biggest serial killers of all time were almost caught early on but were saved by blind luck."

"But not the Coast-to-Coast Killer," Larson said, his eyes bright. "You must have felt you were up against a worthy opponent."

"It's not chess," Ezra said. "All told, he murdered ten women in cold blood. Mutilated their bodies and then left little pieces of electronics to ensure he got the credit. If anything, he's only my worthy opponent in egotism."

Larson frowned. "So you don't feel outsmarted?"

"It takes far more intelligence to catch a serial killer than to be one," Ezra said. "Didn't your teachers make you read *In Cold Blood?* The Clutter murderers were uneducated, career criminals who bumbled through every step. Yet it took one of the most brilliant Kansas lawmen of all time to track them down."

Larson moved to the center of the gym. He clapped twice, and his players sat cross-legged on the hard court. "I trust that's everything?" Larson asked Ezra.

The rumor concerned Mason Scout, but it originated from Fiona Fleming who heard it from an unnamed teacher. If Larson was steering Ezra toward Mason now, perhaps he was Fiona's unnamed source.

"Sure thing. Want me to pass along what I can from the Fleming family interview?"

Larson's lip quivered. "You mean the Scout family."

"Of course. My mistake."

****

The second he returned to his car, Ezra called Lucia with the news.

"So?" she asked, dismissive.

"So, I think we need to bring in the families, both

the Flemings and the Scouts. We need to shake them down and poke holes in the rumor Benjamin Larson has been peddling."

"I don't know," Lucia replied.

How could she be so stubborn? "We need to strike while the iron's hot!"

"We? Because it sounds like you're saying I need to do all this."

"This is the right call," he said.

"Maybe it is, maybe it isn't. Look, Ezra," she said. "I have a captain to report to, and he says this is done for now."

"But it's not!"

"I can't make all the calls myself," she said. "We have our primary suspect in custody, and we're working that angle. If it turns out to be wrong, we'll open things up again."

"Benjamin Larson isn't his real name. It's Lucas. He had to leave Nevada for—"

"We know all about Ben Lucas."

Feeling betrayed, he whined, "I see how it is."

"Ezra—" she began but he hung up.

Chapter Twenty-Eight

Thursday

Ezra spent the better part of Thursday organizing his office. This was a major feat considering he had almost nothing in his office. One week had passed since Brooklyn's attack; in that time, he'd been brought into the case long enough to remember what real police work was like, then summarily pushed aside.

His office didn't need organizing, but he preferred to stay busy rather than confront the possibility that the Hannigan case was concluded—or at least his part of it. While working alongside Lucia Vargas, he momentarily forgot his probation and irrelevance to the world. Now the truth presented itself again, and he didn't care for it.

Furthermore, he lacked her certainty over Martin's guilt. Had the false conviction of John Lewis Straugh rendered him incapable of certainty? Would he spend the rest of his life second guessing his instincts? If that were the case, it was probably best he stayed far away from real police work of any kind.

No. The welt on the back of his head was to blame. The intruder suggested there was more to the situation. By twelve-thirty, after the office had been organized, cleaned, and rearranged to the last inch of its life, a knock came at Ezra's door.

There, in his khakis, white oxford shirt, and blue plaid tie, stood Daniel Toussaint. He was tall and beginning to fill out, so much so that when he didn't wear the school uniform, Ezra sometimes, momentarily, mistook him for a member of the staff.

"Mr. James?" he asked, an eyebrow raised.

"Mr. Toussaint." Ezra liked calling students by their last names when they came to see him. Coming in voluntarily seemed like an adult thing to do. "What can I do for you?"

"I can sit?"

They both sat, and Ezra waited for Daniel to speak. Instead, the teenager pointed out a University of Michigan pennant pinned to the wall.

"Ann Arbor," he said.

"Yep," Ezra replied.

"I watched them in the finals."

Ezra remembered the game well. "2018," he said. "We lost to Villanova. Ugly game." He shook off the memory. "Why'd you come in today?"

"Monsieur Durand." The teenager paused. Though he had the height of a man, he still had the shyness of a child.

"You've heard about the arrest, I assume?"

He studied the carpet. "I talk…talked to Fr. Remy."

Ezra took a shot. "Is this about the chalice?"

Daniel looked down at the floor, ashamed, and shook his head.

"Then what?"

Daniel scanned the hall, searching for eavesdroppers. Then he rose and shut Ezra's door gently, as though he were sneaking in after curfew and didn't want anyone to hear him. He returned to his seat, met Ezra's gaze, but then broke it immediately. Ezra was rapidly becoming impatient with Daniel's reluctance.

"I understand you don't wish to speak ill of your teacher and also that you don't want to incriminate yourself. These are natural instincts." Ezra let this sink in before continuing. "But a man's life is at stake. A man with young children." The fact that Daniel had lost his own father at a young age didn't slip Ezra's mind. "So whatever you have to say, say it."

"In Haiti, there is a saying about *the masisi. Mettre des roches sur nos épaules.* It means they put rocks on their shoulders."

"Okay?"

"It is a way to say they act *different* to how they really are."

"What are the—" Ezra began to ask but stopped himself. Daniel didn't want to say it, and Ezra didn't want to force him to say it. A line from Martin's journal came to him then, *Our shared affliction.* "Thank you, Mr. Toussaint. You have done a brave thing."

Daniel left the same way he entered, cautiously and checking the hall for eavesdroppers.

****

The holding cell for the Evanston PD was divided into three compartments, each set off by solid concrete walls. The same sickly tan paint covered the brick walls and the inside of the cells. Ezra imagined the paint had a name like "sandstone" or "desert heat" and that someone picked it out specifically so this area didn't have the hopeless feeling produced by white and gray paint. It didn't help, though. You could paint a holding cell any color you liked; it was still a holding cell.

When Ezra arrived, Martin Durand was lying on his bed, reading a thin paperback novel. Ezra asked what it was. The French teacher held it up for inspection. The cover read *L'Etranger* by Albert Camus.

"Isn't that a bit on the nose?" Ezra asked.

Durand shrugged.

"You weren't sleeping with Brooklyn Hannigan," Ezra said.

"No?"

"Not Fiona Fleming—nor any of the women of SJM."

The teacher kept his face in his book.

"In fact, none of these women could've seduced you," Ezra said. "As much as they may have wanted to, it's hard for a young woman to seduce a gay man."

"I'm sorry, Mr. James, but you have your facts wrong."

"Let's be frank with each other for a change."

Ezra recounted the story as best as he could, how Durand left college to do mission work in Africa and to break off a same-sex relationship. In Africa, he realized the priesthood was the solution to his problem. Then he returned to Chicago and met Gemma, a beautiful, intelligent woman who also struggled with desires she couldn't reconcile with her faith. She had tried celibacy, but every time she tried, she failed. They both wanted kids and to remain a part of their respective families and the Church. They were both Catholic, intelligent, attractive, and kind. Their offspring would be gifts to the world. Marriage was a viable solution for their "shared affliction." However, it stopped working for Gemma. "You're free now," she told her husband when she left. She found her freedom in Brandy and now

Martin was free to find his. Only he wasn't. He couldn't let himself be who he knew he was.

"Did Gemma tell you all of this?" Martin asked. "Because she can have quite an imagination."

"No, she wouldn't out you like that. I put it together myself," Ezra said.

"It's quite a story."

"Tell me it isn't true."

Martin sat up in bed. "If you tell anyone else, I'll deny it."

"How were you able to keep up the ruse for so long?" Ezra asked.

"What ruse? Gemma and I love each other. We entered into a covenant with God, which we both intended to keep. We brought children into the world and are raising them in the faith. By the Church's standards, our 'ruse' is better than ninety percent of marriages."

"It *was*, you mean. You and Gemma are divorced, or have you forgotten?"

"Only in the eyes of the law."

"Gemma left. She isn't coming back."

"Is that what you believe about your own wife, Mr. James?"

"I'm beginning to."

A small beetle appeared from an open drain in the back of Martin's cell. It scuttled around in one direction, then another, before finally returning to the drain and disappearing. The cell was too bleak even for a beetle.

"Let's say you're right," Martin conceded. "What would the Church have me do? Live a cloistered life? No spouse, no children, like someone with a terminal illness, whiling away the rest of my days in quarantine?"

"At least come clean about this with your lawyer, or let me tell one of the detectives on the case."

"And ruin my reputation?" he scoffed. "If the school finds out, they won't renew my contract."

"This is your ticket out of here." Ezra punched the bar of the holding cell for emphasis. "Don't you see that?"

"All I see is a man fighting a jail cell when he should be out there solving this case. You put me in here. You can get me out."

He leaned back on the bed and reopened his book.

"Before I go, tell me one more thing. What was the line you crossed?"

"Excuse me?"

"In your journal, you said you crossed a line. This led us to believe you had begun the affair with Brooklyn—or perhaps Fiona. Now I'm wondering if it had to do with the Haitian athlete."

"I'm afraid I can't say, Mr. James."

"It might hold the key to solving this."

"It won't."

He shut his book, then closed his eyes.

How had Ezra found himself here again? He'd falsely accused another man who would serve prison time. This man might have his life ruined because of Ezra, because of his bungling of the case. If he didn't solve this now, he would never forgive himself.

He left the holding area and went directly to Lucia's desk.

She looked up from her computer. "What's up?"

"You got the wrong guy in there."

"I know, I know, Benjamin Lucas—"

"It's not that."

"Then what?"

"I can't say," Ezra replied.

"Why not?"

"I'm sorry, I really can't."

She frowned. "Then I can't help. Bring us something more substantial, and we'll go from there."

"I'd like to bring Mason Scout in."

Lucia glanced back at her captain's office and shook her head. "As I said earlier, I don't make the calls." She held up a thick stack of papers. "This is all for Durand. The prosecutor needs to start building a case."

"But I'm telling you, you have the wrong guy."

She gave him a strained smile. "Bring us something, okay?" Then she returned her gaze to her computer screen.

****

"Under no circumstances are you to speak with Mason Scout about this again." Principal Catherine Weeks shut the door of her office as if to place her seal on the edict.

"Is the family threatening you?" Ezra asked.

She replied with a haughty laugh. It was not convincing.

"This is a murder investigation," he continued. "And I just told you Martin Durand is innocent."

"You've been wrong before," she said and averted her gaze.

"Catherine."

"It's done. The police will handle it from here." She smiled, also unconvincingly. "Now we can go back to what we're good at—helping young people learn."

Catherine opened the door. The gesture had a feeling of finality.

Ezra wasn't so easily diverted, however. He stalked down to Ms. Jarno's room, unsure what he meant to ask Mason.

Each teacher, in addition to having six classes and a planning period, also ran a homeroom. Catherine, knowing Ms. Jarno was one of the strictest teachers at SJM, placed Mason in her homeroom freshman year, and he'd never left it.

There being no reason at this point to be evasive, Ezra found Mason and placed his hands firmly on the desk. He lowered his face into Mason's. "Where were you Tuesday night?"

Mason stared at him, teeth clenched.

"Someone broke into my house. Was it you?" Ezra withdrew the dotted, green notebook from his breast pocket. "Were you looking for this?"

The grimace turned into a forced smile. "I believe they call this harassment."

"Don't get smug with me."

"Okay, mall cop. How about this, I was living my best life." He held an imaginary joint up to his lips and closed his eyes in a Rastafarian pose.

What happened next surprised them both. Ezra grabbed Mason by the collar of his Oxford shirt and lifted him from the desk. Though a state-champion, Mason was still only a high schooler, tall but light. English teacher Jarno dropped the black dry erase marker she was using to update her board. The marker rolled across the carpeted floor and stopped at the hardwood wainscoting.

All the cockiness drained from Mason's face, replaced with disbelieving fear.

"You may think this is all a joke, but someone's going to prison for a long time, and it isn't going to be Monsieur Durand."

Ms. Jarno regained her composure and walked swiftly into the hall, her heels clicking

"Fiona told us everything," he whispered into Mason's ear.

"Told you what?" Mason's voice came out thin.

"About you and Brooklyn."

His eyes turned from fearful to pleading. "There's no me and Brooklyn."

Ezra and Lucia had heard about the affair from Fiona Fleming, but she didn't know it first-hand. She heard it from an unidentified teacher who heard it from who-knows-where. The chain of communication was beginning to feel like a game of Arabic Telephone as Remy put it. Did someone start the rumor to throw Ezra off the scent? Was it Coach Larson?

"Then whose baby is it?" Ezra asked.

Mason's jaw fell open as if to respond, but before he could speak, Catherine appeared in the doorway. "Mr. James," she said sternly.

Ezra released Mason's collar, straightened his shirt, and followed Catherine to her office.

Once there, she didn't waste time speaking. She merely held out a hand, palm up. Ezra, in turn, unclipped his name tag and placed it in her hand. She cleared her throat and nodded at the yellow taser clipped to his belt. He removed it, holster and all, and shoved it into her hand.

"So that's the end then?" There was no note of

disappointment in his voice, just inevitability.

"We can discuss it on Monday," she said. "That is, if the Scouts haven't decided to press charges by then."

Her message rang loud and clear. *Leave this alone if you want to have any hope of staying at SJM and the FBI.* The trouble was he didn't know if he wanted to stay.

Chapter Twenty-Nine

Concrete walls and floors invited more cold into the holding cells than anywhere else in the building. Whenever Lucia visited prisoners there, she recalled her own destitute childhood in Mexico and thought, *At least I was warm.* The stinging cold always made her pity the prisoners just a little, regardless of their crimes. For this reason, above all, she avoided going there—unless absolutely necessary.

Martin Durand, lying supine on his bed, appeared less pitiable than she'd expected. He wasn't sick with drink or drugs, which helped. She rapped on the bars, and his head popped up.

"I hear you had a visitor."

He nodded noncommittally.

"Left here pretty convinced of your innocence."

He laid his head back and shut his eyes again.

"You must've told him something colossal."

Martin remained perfectly still.

What could Ezra have possibly found out? And how? And, more important, why couldn't he tell her? "Do you know who Brooklyn was seeing?"

He shook his head.

"Or who attacked her?"

Another head shake.

What if Martin was telling the truth? Without a viable alternative, there was nothing she could do. "For an innocent man, you sure aren't trying to get free." Then she thought of something clever to say. "If I speak, I am condemned, if I stay silent, I am damned."

Martin looked up with a bolt. Apparently, he too had read Victor Hugo.

"A cop who can read—you must be shocked," Lucia said. "So you're just going to sit in here and make us do all the heavy lifting? If it's not you, then there's a killer on loose in Evanston."

Martin shrugged as if to say, *Then what are you doing wasting your time with me?*

She was wasting her time, wasn't she?

****

Fr. Remy's chess board sat on his desk when Ezra entered the office. It was his wooden board—mahogany and African blackwood, the pieces black and white marble—all of it locally sourced in Senegal. Dakar was Remy's final post before coming to Chicago, but he refused to talk about any of the posts before Dakar, at least with him.

Ezra nodded at the board. "Did Catherine tell you about what happened?"

"What happened?" the priest asked innocently.

He couldn't tell if Remy was playing dumb or if he honestly didn't know. Remy palmed a white and a black pawn and mixed them behind his back before extending two closed fists to him. Ezra chose the left. Remy's hand opened to reveal a black pawn.

Ezra sat. "I'm being let go."

Remy opened the game with his king-side pawn. "I doubt that."

Ezra replied with the Sicilian Defense. "She took my nametag."

"Not your nametag!" Remy cried in mock horror. Then he made the game a closed Sicilian with his queen's knight. "What does she want you to do?"

Ezra should've known Remy would guess the situation. It was the very situation he kept finding himself in lately. Someone with more power would give him a directive, and Ezra would respond with stubborn refusal. Cromley wanted him to take his psychological condition seriously; Julia wanted him to sign the divorce papers; and now Catherine...

"She wants me to back off and leave Mason Scout alone," he explained. "Leave all of them alone, really." He answered with his own queen-side knight. "Go ahead. Tell me I'm being stubborn."

Remy advanced a pawn. "Why would I tell you that?"

"That's what you usually say."

"Usually you are being stubborn."

Ezra expanded his queen side. "But not now?"

Remy raised his dark-square bishop and held it in his hand. He pointed it at Ezra. "What is more important to you, this job of yours," he asked and placed the bishop on the board, "or justice?"

The answer was perfectly clear. By the middle game, Ezra was up a bishop and a pawn and had the center secured. Then he forced a trade. He gave up his queen-side rook for Remy's queen. The priest resigned after that.

****

Ezra thought about the situation forward and backward on the drive over to Evanston PD and decided that justice took precedence. Justice superseded his job at the school, his chances of being reinstated at the Bureau, and even Martin Durand's confidence. He only hoped Lucia would feel the same way. He was waiting beside her desk when she returned from the holding cells.

"To what do I owe the pleasure?" she asked.

"Martin Durand is gay," he said without preamble. "I don't have proof. There's no documentation or anything, I mean. But it's a fact."

"I believe you."

He wrinkled his brows in surprise. "You mean you'll just take my word for it?"

"I didn't mistrust you," she said and placed a hand on her desk. "I just needed to know your reasoning."

"The necklace, the one that went missing weeks before Brooklyn was attacked. Have you found it?"

She consulted her notes. "Black pearl and silver or white gold. No."

He stood abruptly. "I think I know where it is."

"Where?"

"I'll explain on the way."

When he walked right back out of the bullpen and down the stairs, Vargas grabbed her jacket and raced after him. "Wait, where are we going?"

****

Lucia had never seen Ezra so certain. He spent the entire drive drumming his fingers on the steering wheel and humming what sounded to her like a grunge rock song. He still hadn't told her where they were going.

While they drove, Lucia reread the Autumn Elkhart interview. Brooklyn's necklace had disappeared for several days following a break-in at their apartment. Then the necklace reappeared, in plain sight, nestled in its case. After Brooklyn's attack, however, it disappeared again. As they sat outside Heinz Pawn and Loan once again, Lucia wondered what the necklace could possibly have to do with the chalice they tracked down earlier.

"Where would you go if you needed a necklace fixed?" he asked.

"I don't know? A jewelry shop?"

"A jewelry shop in the mall or a repair shop that specializes in fixing necklaces?"

"Probably the latter," Lucia said. "Why?"

"But what if you'd stolen the necklace? What if you'd stolen it and broken it but couldn't get it back together, at least not so the owner wouldn't notice. Where would you go then?"

Lucia looked up at the bright yellow sign. It didn't *say* repairs.

****

"Officers," Heinz said as they walked in. "Always good to see repeat customers. Have you returned for that .38?" he asked Lucia.

"We'd like to see your repair records from the past four weeks," Ezra said.

"Is this becoming a habit?"

"We have a young teacher in a coma," Lucia said.

"And another young woman who's been murdered," Ezra added. "Shot execution style."

"I read about that in the papers." Heinz considered their proposition a moment more. "I don't keep records of my repair jobs."

Ezra elbowed Lucia. If you wanted an illegal repair, this was definitely the place to go.

"But I do remember my work well. What are you looking for?"

"A black pearl necklace," Lucia said.

"I had one a few weeks ago." Heinz checked his wall calendar, turning back to November. He gave the date the necklace was brought in. "I remember because it was the Monday after Thanksgiving."

The repair date fit with the time frame of the break-in at Brooklyn's apartment.

"A man and wife came in. Husband said he'd already tried to fix it and botched the job." Heinz narrowed his eyes. "But there was something funny about the whole deal."

Lucia started taking notes. "How so?"

"They were like two actors playing a husband and wife. The way they interacted, it was too affectionate. He should've been frustrated that she broke the necklace in the first place, and she should've been mad that he tried to fix it himself first. The way they talked about it felt wooden. There was no history there."

"What else?"

"He had a gold wedding ring that was perfectly shiny, no scratches, no smudges, like he never wore it. Also, the band was a size too big. It kept slipping over his knuckle."

"You can always call the authorities when you see something suspicious," Ezra said.

Heinz sighed, and his shoulders slumped forward. "If I called about every shifty customer, I'd be on the phone all day long."

"Can you describe them?" Lucia asked.

"He was about six foot or a little taller. Both of them were middle-aged."

"Were they a good match?" Ezra asked.

Heinz nodded.

"Was he balding by chance?" Lucia asked.

Another nod and he offered, "What was left of it was blond."

She shared a look with Ezra. The description matched Benjamin Larson. She got the impression Heinz was willing to tell them anything—so long as they asked the right questions.

Ezra showed the pawnbroker a picture of Larson. Heinz confirmed it was indeed the basketball coach who brought in the necklace.

"Would you swear to it under oath?" she asked.

"I mean, it certainly looks like him."

"How about the woman?" Lucia pressed.

"Brunette, not bad on the eyes. Tight little—" he started but then gave Lucia an apologetic frown. "She had a real Jackie O. vibe, big sunglasses and a colorful scarf covering her head and neck. She almost looked, you know, she almost looked like a woman in a film noir. A woman hiding her identity."

There were plenty of good-looking brunettes at SJM, from the teaching staff to the mothers. Or it could've been a woman Benjamin Larson was seeing. Even if they brought back a catalogue, Heinz would likely conflate some of them. She pulled a picture of Cynthia Scout up on her phone and extended it.

"Is this her?"

Heinz rocked his head back and forth, uncertain. "Have you got any other pictures?"

"I'm not her talent agent," Lucia replied.

"What sort of alteration did you make to the necklace?" Ezra asked.

"It had a floral clasp. The husband said the clasp cracked, so he welded it back together. All he wanted from me was to smooth out the job he'd done and reattach everything."

"Do you have the dimensions of the necklace?"

"Right here." He handed Lucia a piece of paper with different sizes jotted down.

"Mind if I keep this?"

"Not at all."

She pointed to a security camera. "Does that work?"

"It does," Heinz said, "but I don't keep footage longer than a week. Storage is limited, you know. I have it mostly for break-ins."

The three glanced at the useless camera. "I do have this though," he said and ducked under the counter. He riffled through a box of papers and then pulled the whole box onto the glass counter. It overflowed with credit card receipts.

"They paid credit?" Lucia asked hopefully.

"No, but I make all my repair customers sign a blank slip. Sort of a cover my ass situation."

Lucia and Ezra craned their heads to make out the signature. It was cursive and hurried but the name was clear as day—Mason Scout.

They thanked Heinz and left.

"Why in the world would Benjamin Larson sign Mason's name?" Ezra asked once they were at his car.

Lucia ignored the more difficult question for the moment. "Brooklyn wasn't wearing those pearls when we found her."

"That's only a problem if we can't find the necklace somewhere else."

The sun ducked behind the buildings around them. Sunlight slanted in between the high rises as they drove back to the station.

"Have your people found any DNA at the Elkhart crime scene?" he asked.

"Nada."

"Any hope in sight?"

"At this point, it's just you and me," she said. "Does Mason Scout have a part-time job?"

"Works in Daddy's car dealership."

"Take me there."

Chapter Thirty

Henry Scout, Mason's father, owned twelve dealerships and counting. Six were located in Illinois and six across the lake in Michigan. He oversaw all of these personally, but Mason preferred European Prestige in North Chicago. He'd even convinced his dad to give him a job there. Compared to Henry Scout's mega dealerships, all of which were located on interstates, Prestige was tiny. The dealership had just a few showrooms and a small selection of cars out front—but what a selection it was. Given the choice, Ezra would've made the same decision as Mason. Those big highway lots may have paid the bills, but those cars and trucks were nothing compared to these.

"That's his Porsche," Ezra said when they pulled up. He parked and got out to investigate. The red cherry coupe gave Ezra an immediate case of car envy. He felt like a boy at a racetrack. "It's a beauty."

"The kid probably doesn't even know what he has here," Lucia said and ran a finger along the roof.

"And what, you do?"

"My uncle's a mechanic back in St. Louis."

"You never told me that," he said. "I feel like I don't know anything about you."

"It's not my fault you only want to talk about yourself." She peered into the tinted windows. "We may have something here."

He came around to her side and had a look. A small hand-rolled cigarette or joint lay on the floor of the passenger side. Through the tinted windows, they couldn't tell which.

"Probable cause?" she asked.

"Don't see why not," he said. "Let's try to get more, though, just to be safe."

Walking into Prestige was like walking back into the sixties. Old posters and pamphlets, prominently displayed, gave the showroom a vintage feel. A black and white poster of a Ferrari 166 S covered one wall and a yellow Lamborghini Countach another. From the ceiling hung a hand-stitched Alfa Romeo flag, from the '70s Ezra guessed. Stand-alone racks displayed pamphlets for new roadsters, coupes, and convertibles. A classic, ivory Porsche 356 took up most of the adjoining room. He assumed the roadster was for display-only.

The wood floors of the dealership were painted black. Ezra knew this trick. You could pull up floorboards, sand them, refinish them, and nail them back in place, but you couldn't do it indefinitely. At some point, you had to fill the holes and paint the boards black. In fact, the entire dealership, from the walls and ceilings to the radiator and outer brick, felt done-and-redone to the last inch of its life.

"For a mechanic, you're suspiciously clean," Ezra told Mason.

The teenager pointed at his name tag, which read, "Sales."

"That makes more sense," he said. "I suppose you can tell me every color these models come in, though."

"And where to put the blinker fluid," Lucia added.

"What is this?" Mason asked. "Dumb cop and dumber cop?"

Ezra placed a hand on the counter. "We know you were seeing Brooklyn before her attack."

He considered this. "I wasn't." Then his face acquired his trademark smug smile. "But what if I was? You have nothing on me. Or have you forgotten I was on camera when she fell?"

"How about Monday morning, say around three a.m.?" Lucia asked.

"What happened Monday morning?"

"Somebody shot Autumn Elkhart in the back of the head."

"Oh, right." He laughed. "I was at home. We have surveillance cameras and everything."

"Always with the sound alibi," Lucia said.

Ezra nodded. "That's how it is with clever criminals. They think they can somehow outsmart the scientific method."

Mason laughed.

"What's so funny?" Ezra asked.

"I'm just imagining you getting fired. You thought coming to Joseph and Mary was playing in the minors. At the rate you're going, I'll be visiting your kiosk in the mall soon."

Ezra felt like punching this arrogant kid in the mouth, but he caught sight of Lucia out of the corner of his eye and calmed down. She was looking out the window at the Porsche, and somehow he knew she had a play in mind.

"It's a shame, don't you think, Ezra?" she asked, still looking out the window.

Ezra unclenched his jaw. "What is?"

"That such a fine piece of machinery is wasted on a salesman."

"Hey," Mason said, "I know just as much about cars as anyone in here."

"A hundred bucks says my friend here can beat you in a quarter mile." She indicated Ezra. Was she really suggesting a drag race? Was this part of her plan?

"What do you drive?" he asked.

"That." Ezra cleared his throat and pointed at his sedan.

"4.6 L twin-cam V8, I'm guessing?" Mason asked.

"Yep," Ezra said, trying to sound confident. He was officially out of his depth.

Mason laughed. "There's no way."

"Why not?" Lucia asked.

"Are you kidding?"

"Explain it to me like I'm a spoiled white boy who had his Porsche handed to him."

"Your friend here has a solid engine, sure, but it only gives him three hundred horsepower. My six-cylinder puts out almost four hundred."

"So you read the specs," she said.

"No, I've lived the specs. My coupe can go zero to sixty in four seconds. He'll be lucky to get there in seven seconds. By nine seconds, I'm already done."

"Sounds like you're a good racer," Ezra said.

Lucia laughed. "Well, you would be too if you had a widow maker like that just handed to you," she said. "I bet he's never done a thing to that car himself."

"I've done plenty," Mason said. "I change the oil and rotate the tires."

She laughed again. "My *abuela* rotates her own tires."

Mason looked puzzled.

"*Abuela* is her grandma," Ezra explained.

The twerp wasn't done. "Last month, I swapped out the changeover valves."

She shook her head. "That doesn't make your car faster. What have you done that the manufacturer didn't already put in there for you, Mace?"

Without a second thought, Mason announced, "I installed my own nitrous. Show me a novice who can do that." He was smiling broadly at them, but then the smile vanished.

"You hear that, Detective Vargas?" Ezra asked. "The kid put nitrous in his street car."

"I did hear that, Special Agent James. You think a judge would issue a warrant to search it?"

"Just on those grounds alone? I think the judge would have his little deathtrap impounded on the spot. You never know what other dangerous modifications he's made."

"Does that take a long time? Impounding?" she asked as if she didn't know.

He nodded. "Expensive, too."

"But they're careful with the cars down at the impound, right?" she asked.

"Oh sure. They get paid seven, eight bucks an hour, just like a valet at a restaurant."

"No tips, though, to make sure they don't scratch the paint," she pointed out.

"Oh, I didn't know he was worried about scratches."

"What do you guys want?" Mason finally asked.

"Just a peek inside your ride," Lucia replied.

"Fine."

Mason was right, of course. Even if the cigarette turned out to be a joint, it wouldn't prove anything about his involvement with Brooklyn. What they needed were the black pearls. If Lucia's hunch was correct, the necklace would be their smoking gun, and finding it in Mason's car or house or the garbage behind his house would be as good as catching him in the act. If this joint could get them a search warrant for the rest of the Scout properties, it would be worth it.

The interior was pristine. The black leather shone, the carpet lay uniformly in one direction, and the metallic sparkled. The joint was the one outlier. Lucia picked it up, using an inside-out baggie as a glove, and sniffed it.

"Tobacco," she said sadly.

"I'm eighteen," Mason said.

What wealthy eighteen-year-old rolled his own cigarettes?

Ezra checked under the seats. No necklace. In fact, there was nothing at all. Then he started fiddling with the controls on the side of the driver's seat.

"What are you doing?" Lucia asked.

"I'm trying to look behind this seat."

She stepped between him and the car and folded the seat forward.

"There's a backseat!" he exclaimed.

"Don't get excited. You don't want to sit back there," she said. Then she added under her breath, "Or do anything else back there."

Ezra was beginning to realize more and more that Lucia's past was far more interesting than his. "There's nothing," he said. "I can't even find a receipt. He must have cleaned everything out this morning."

"Everything except that cigarette," she said.

Neither of them said how strange this was, but Ezra could tell they were both thinking it. Why leave a loose cigarette out in the open and take everything else? Most smokers kept them in their jacket or hid them away in a glove compartment—and rarely did they roll their own.

"Trunk next," Lucia said. She took the key fob out of her pocket and pressed a button. Ezra walked toward the back.

"Hopeless," she said. "The trunk's in the front."

"Oh, like a slug bug."

"I'm going to pretend you never said that."

They circled around the front, Lucia moving along the driver's side, Ezra along the passenger's side. When they met in the middle, their eyes were drawn simultaneously to the dead center of the trunk.

Everything that had been in the car before Mason cleaned it was crammed into this tiny space, including his sweat-stained athletic clothes, a yellowed gym bag with the SJM saint logo embroidered along the side, empty energy drink cans, beef jerky wrappers, and various other junk food wrappers and receipts. Here were all the things Mason wanted to hide about himself, presenting instead a clean, wealthy, and cultured facade. He could pretend he was a full-fledged man all he wanted, but here was the proof of his adolescence.

Then in the middle of the open gym bag, like a cherry atop a heaping sundae, sat the *coup de grâce*. There lay a topaz teardrop earring, the golden metal tinged a solid maroon with dried blood. Autumn's missing earring.

"What is that?" Mason managed to ask a split second before Lucia had him up against the brick wall of the dealership, his hands cuffed behind his back.

"I need back-up," she said into her radio.

****

Gorecki, arrived five minutes later followed by two uniformed officers. "This had better be good, Vargas. You know this kid's dad is friends with the chief."

She just pointed at the open trunk.

Gorecki meandered over. He saw the earring, stained with blood, and stared for a solid minute before coming back dazed. "Sorry I doubted you." Then he shouted at the two officers, "Get forensics out here! And don't either of you dim-nuts touch it."

"We've collected evidence before," one of them insisted.

"This is a homicide, not a traffic violation. Set up a perimeter and wait for the professionals. We'll take the kid in."

Lucia read Mason his rights and put him in the backseat of Gorecki's car.

"Guess I'll meet you back at the station," Ezra said.

"I'll call you," she replied. "We need to question him, contact the parents, and see what forensics says about the earring, make sure the blood is Autumn's. It's all official business."

"As in, none of mine?" he asked.

She frowned.

"What about Larson?" he asked.

"We're working on a warrant. In the meantime, we'll press on the Scout kid and see where it goes from there," she said.

Gorecki came over and slapped Ezra on the back. "This finally came together," he said. "Although it looks like we didn't need your help after all."

Ezra wanted to point out that they were only here because of the leads he had followed, but he feared the logic would've been lost on the detective.

"Don't frown. You'll get your name in the paper too," Gorecki added.

"My name in the paper? Just what I've always wanted," Ezra replied.

Chapter Thirty-One

For the rest of Ezra's life, he would wonder what would've happened if, before setting out, he'd told Lucia Vargas his plan to follow up with Larson himself—alone.

The college student-receptionist at Evanston Rec was decked out in yoga wear again. This time she wore Harvard rather than Northwestern. Ezra wondered if she was planning to transfer. Then he considered that she actually might be a high schooler weighing her options. Or she could've just liked collegiate apparel. He decided to not mention it.

"I'm the guy from the other day…" She didn't seem to recognize him. He decided to use this to his advantage and pose as a concerned parent rather than law enforcement. "Sunday night's scrimmage," he said and pointed at the schedule behind her. "Coach Larson missed it."

It was a guess. Autumn was murdered late that night or early the next morning, and if Larson was involved, he may have missed the scrimmage. A murder like Autumn's would've taken planning and a little covert surveillance.

She looked down at her computer and clicked through a few screens. "That's correct."

"I know it's correct," he said, his tone switching from friendly to indignant. In Ezra's experience it was always best to take an indignant position when lying. "I want to know why he wasn't here."

"Scrimmages are more for the kids and the parents. An official was present, though," she said. "The fees you pay are for the—"

"I didn't say anything about the fees," Ezra continued. "Why wasn't he here?"

"That's confidential."

"I'll need to speak with your supervisor then."

She bit her lower lip.

Ezra already had all the information he needed. His hopes of getting even more, however, were dashed by the arrival of Coach Larson himself.

"I guess you can ask him yourself," she said, her self-assurance returning.

"Special Agent," Larson said, clasping his shoulder.

There were two plays here. Ezra could respond with clever banter or he could cut to the chase. "We know you weren't here the night Autumn was murdered."

Larson smiled woodenly. "I had the stomach flu. You knew that."

"That isn't everything."

"Mason Scout. I know."

This caught Ezra off guard.

"I can explain everything, but not here. You never know who is listening." The coach looked around the lobby suspiciously. "There's a Mexican restaurant across the street. Meet me there."

A man entered, and Larson ducked behind the counter. The man was in his forties, wore a sweat suit, and toted a blue gym bag. Ezra had never seen him before. After he passed, Larson whispered, "Let's go."

They strode outside: Ezra walked toward his car.

"No," Larson said. He seemed legitimately unnerved.

"I have to grab something from the trunk," Ezra said. His 9 mm. After handing over his taser to Principal Weeks, he'd completely forgotten to strap on his sidearm. He hoped it wouldn't prove to be a fatal oversight.

"Now or never." Larson was trembling. "I'll tell you everything, but it has to be *right now*."

Ezra considered his position a moment. Worst case scenario, he could restrain Larson the old fashioned way. They crossed the street. Several minutes later, they were seated inside the restaurant, surrounded by blaring trumpets and strumming guitars.

"So," Ezra prompted.

"Excuse me, *señorita*," Larson called to the waitress. "Could we get a large queso?" Then to Ezra he asked, "Do you like spice? Even if you don't, you'll like this."

"Mr. Larson," Ezra started again, but the waitress returned immediately. She took their drink orders, then left. "The quarterback is involved. We know this already," he continued.

"Then why hasn't he been arrested?" Larson asked.

Lucia was, at that moment, interrogating Mason while a team searched the Scout residence. There was also a search warrant issued for Larson's apartment.

"Making this easy on us," Ezra said. "It will go a long way."

"During my murder trial, you mean?" Larson laughed bitterly.

317

The waitress returned, placing a soda in front of Ezra and a margarita in front of Larson who drained the drink in short order and asked for a second.

"We see a lot of two-man jobs," Ezra said. "Robberies especially. It takes at least two people to rob a bank—as I'm sure you know. Thing is, whoever confesses first always gets the better deal."

"It was a two-man job," Larson confessed. "But you have the wrong two."

****

They were taking Mason Scout back to the interrogation rooms when she came in. Every time Lucia had seen her, she was the perfect picture of composure, preened and adorned in every outward insignia of wealth. Now she looked bedraggled. Bags hung below both eyes, stray brown hairs stuck up like hay from a bail, and her mouth gaped utterly expressionless.

Lucia intercepted her. "Cynthia Scout?"

She was shaking and struggling to breath. "Where? Where? Where?"

Lucia grabbed a chair and instructed her to sit and place her head between her knees. She ran a hand up and down the woman's spine as she breathed in and out, each breath gradually longer and fuller, until Cynthia had calmed. "My partner has your son in the back for questioning."

Cynthia nodded numbly.

"He's eighteen," Lucia said. The implication was clear. The mother couldn't intervene. "But you can provide him with a lawyer."

"He doesn't need one," Cynthia said. "But I do."

"You?"

She nodded repeatedly and began sobbing into her hands. Then her head shot up, and her eyes became crazed. "Do you have him?"

"I just told you we—"

"Not my son. Benjamin Larson."

Lucia motioned to several uniformed officers. They unclipped their sidearm holsters and drew their handcuffs. Cynthia latched onto Lucia's forearms, fingernails digging into her skin. "He knows about you! He knows everything!"

"Knows about what?" Lucia asked. The information was more important than the pain.

"Your addresses, your schedules, your—"

"My schedules? You're not making sense. Are you saying I'm in danger?"

"Not you."

All at once it dawned on her. Her mother and sister had schedules as well.

She told the officers to hold off taking Cynthia from her chair. "Mrs. Scout, is my family in danger?"

"Oh God," the woman wailed. "He already has her. I know it."

Heart hammering in her chest, Lucia demanded, "Has *who*?"

"Your sister."

Lucia tried calling Areli, but it went straight to voicemail. She dialed again and got the same. She called her mother next.

"You cannot call me," her mother said. "I am at work."

"Have you seen Areli today?"

"No, why?"

"You have to find her. Someone from my work, a

person we're investigating, he may be tracking her."

"*Ay Dios mio!*" her mother yelled into the phone and then spoke exclusively in Spanish, so quickly that even Lucia couldn't understand her. Once she wound down, she said, "I'll meet you at the apartment."

She left with two patrol cars, lights and sirens blaring the entire way to the apartment. When they got there, the door was kicked in, Areli's room was trashed—a broken lamp, torn sheets, and a cracked window—but there was no sign of her sister.

In her heart, Lucia knew the truth. Areli had been kidnapped.

****

"You're going to tell me Martin Durand is behind this?" Ezra asked over the table.

Larson shook his head. "The mother. She's the one who found out about the pregnancy. She made sure Mason was in the view of a camera the night Brooklyn was attacked and was tucked away at home when the roommate was shot."

"How do you know all this?"

The second margarita arrived. Larson let it sit there. "Mason told me. About the pregnancy, I mean. I gleaned the rest myself."

Larson was lying, obviously, but maybe if he believed his story was strong enough to tell Evanston PD, he'd implicate himself just enough in the process.

"Excuse me." Ezra left the table, walked to the bathroom, and called Lucia. No answer.

He texted her, —*Larson is willing to talk. Already turning on Mason. Come or send someone ASAP.*— Then he texted the name of the restaurant.

After he returned to the table, Larson picked up

where they left off. "I ordered you the Mexican tacos. It seems kind of redundant but whatever." He was at ease again. Ezra noted the half empty margarita, his second. Perhaps it was the alcohol, or perhaps Larson had learned of Mason's arrest and knew it was all over for him, now, too. Perhaps this was the calm of acceptance.

"Cheers!" Larson clinked Ezra's glass, drank again, and motioned to the waitress. "Sure you don't want something stronger?"

Ezra sipped his soda. "I'm on the job."

"SJM is a tough place. There's the money and the status. That would be enough," Larson said. "Then you have the families. Half of them intermarried. Brooklyn never had a chance in their world."

"No."

"I feel sorry for the students who get left out."

"Ones like Daniel?" Ezra asked.

"Those scholarship kids never quite fit in at these prep schools. They don't have the clothes, the cars, or the attitude. How can you teach someone to act wealthy?"

Ezra nodded.

"You must have experienced that in your own time there," Larson said. "Poor boy from the South Side." He said this in a thick, cartoonish accent.

Ezra didn't react.

"Never quite accepted, not even at Michigan. Sure, it's a state school, but you were in classes alongside all those doctor's sons with their beamers and loft apartments. Meanwhile, you were eating microwaved noodles in your dorm room, poring over psychology texts, dreaming of the day you'd be important enough to track down a killer."

Was this high school coach psychoanalyzing him?

"You even had an abusive father—or was it an alkie mother?"

To correct him at this point—disclosing his dad had died or his mother was tormented by untreated bipolar disorder, not alcoholism, for most of his upbringing—would be to confirm everything else he'd said so far.

"I don't know what you've heard," Ezra said.

"It's what I've read. After your trial. That trial was the first time anyone at SJM even took notice of you. Harvard? We send a few students every year. The FBI? Even the public schools have agents and agents. But catching a world-famous serial killer? You must have finally felt accepted."

"Does this little fantasy of yours have a point?"

"You're interested in my motives, my whereabouts, trying to figure out why I'd want to murder that girl. Maybe someone should be investigating you. That's all I'm saying. You have the right mix of frustrated rage, thirst for attention, and mental unbalance. Maybe I should make some calls, you know, as a concerned private citizen."

"It's a free country."

This disarmed Larson for a moment, but then he smiled anew. He swirled the margarita glass two, three times, and then drained it. He looked less and less like the all-American coach and more like an eccentric millionaire.

The food arrived, and as promised, it was spicy. Ezra took two bites of his asada taco and had to stop. "What's in this?"

"Diced jalapeños."

His sinuses felt like someone had cleaned them out with a bottle brush. He drained the rest of his soda.

"Who were you calling when you hit the head?" Larson asked. "That little police friend of yours? Vargas, was it?"

"What's it to you?"

"Lucia Vargas, originally of Chihuahua, Mexico, now lives on Sherman Avenue," Larson announced with a degree of pride in his voice. "Father's deceased, violently, but I'm sure you know all about that. Mother's alive but with cancer. Little sister is just about the only family Lucia has left. Such a tragic story. It would be a shame if something happened to Areli."

"Threatening the family of a police officer is a—"

"Felony," Larson interjected. "Just another thing you'll have to add to my list of offenses. You can add it to the supposed murder."

"We know you broke into Brooklyn's apartment and stole a necklace."

He smiled again. "I did nothing of the sort."

"Or at least broke in to put it back. We also know you altered the necklace to deliver an electric shock. We have the testimony of the man who did the repairs. He positively identified you." He paused to let this sink in. "What did you say to Brooklyn? What convinced her to step over the guard rail?"

"Me?" Larson asked disinterestedly.

Then his eyes widened at something or someone behind him. As Ezra turned to look, Larson dashed from the table, sprinting toward the back exit. Ezra sprinted after him, out the door, and into the alleyway where Larson stood, a revolver trained at Ezra's chest.

Adrenaline surged in his stomach. As he reached

for his sidearm, he remembered he'd left it in the car.

"You can scream if you'd like," Larson said. "Really. I'd like nothing more than to hear you call for help a second before I blast you."

"You really think you're some kind of badass."

Ezra felt his heart in his throat and heard the slight tremor in his voice but hoped Larson wouldn't notice either. "Did you kill Autumn yourself, or did Mason do all the heavy lifting there, too?"

Larson pointed the gun down the alley. "Walk."

They walked in single file. Every time Ezra slowed to look into a doorway, Larson shoved the barrel of the revolver between his shoulder blades.

A few blocks in, Ezra's left leg gave out and he staggered. The adrenaline that had pumped through his veins seemed to shift to his gut, turning it inside out like a backpack during a drug search. A sense of vertigo overtook him. He felt like a boy on a roller coaster twisting left, right, and then plunging two hundred feet. He was going to be sick. Was this sending him into another manic episode?

"Doing all right there, Mr. James?"

"Shut up."

"I hope you're not losing your hold on reality. Again."

Ezra placed his hands on his knees to steady himself.

"I don't just read the newspapers, you know. The Internet can prove very interesting if you have the right access."

"You run the robotics class," Ezra said with difficulty, "which means you must know a lot about computers."

Larson sighed, bored. "You're ahead of schedule." He glanced at his watch. "In more ways than one. Perhaps I overdid the dosage."

"What are you talking about?" *Oh, God. He's poisoned me.* "What have you done, Larson?"

"It wasn't poison," Larson replied.

Ezra looked up in alarm.

"You don't even know when you're talking out loud, do you?" He laughed. "Don't worry. It's nothing one of these undergrads wouldn't pay good money for. Though, as I said, I may have overdone it. What's your usual dosage of LSD?"

Ezra's eyes widened as he remembered the more upsetting parts of his previous break from reality. He recalled the frenetic bursts of energy, the delusional thoughts that led from one rabbit hole to the next until everything in the universe seemed connected and meaningful, and above all he remembered the sense of self-importance that rose to God-like levels.

In the mental hospital, he described some of his experiences to a fellow patient and the man replied, "That's some all-natural acid right there. Don't need to pay nobody for your trips, man."

Would LSD match up with his most recent manic episode? Would it wax for a few hours and then wane, ebbing back into plain reality, or would it launch him into another episode, worse than the last? The thought seized him and made his blood run cold.

"Take solace in the fact that you're not losing your mind for real," Larson said. "Although, I'm sure they'll just lock you up anyway."

"You'll never get away with this!" Ezra shouted at the top of his lungs.

325

"If you get there early enough, you might just save Vargas the Younger."

Ezra hardly even registered these words. His entire attention remained focused on not falling through the concrete. When he looked up again, Larson had vanished.

"Call the police," Ezra whispered to the brick wall beside him. He crawled along it, fingers grasping the gap between bricks like a mountain climber finding his grip along a cliff face.

Soon, he found himself standing in a doorway, composure returned. He stepped through the door, entering a college bar, and walked right up to a young woman behind the bar. "I need—" he started to say but could not produce the words.

The bartender turned a crooked eye on him. Then her body receded from him, fingers and lips curling away like a tide. He felt instantly as helpless as a toddler in a foreign country. With two college degrees and years of criminal investigative experience, Ezra stumbled onto the street, unable to remember why he'd come back outside.

His cell phone rang. "Lucia Vargas" the screen read. He stared at it for a long time, staring desperately because he couldn't remember how to answer a phone.

Somewhere deep inside his consciousness, the rational portion of his mind looked on with one single thought. *I am so screwed.*

Chapter Thirty-Two

Lucia's next stop was the Mexican restaurant where Ezra was having dinner with Benjamin Larson. In her haste to find her sister, she'd left her cell phone in her car. Therefore, she missed Ezra's call and her opportunity to warn him. By the time she saw his text and called him back, his phone, like Areli's, went straight to voicemail. Lucia's thoughts automatically went to worst case scenarios.

She, accompanied by two uniforms, approached the front of the restaurant while Gorecki and two more officers entered through the rear. Captain Fitzpatrick assured her two more black and whites were en route, but she hadn't seen them yet, and she wasn't going to wait.

"Police!" she announced as they stepped inside.

Every diner in the place looked up, some surprised, some curious, some genuinely fearful. Then they all turned to the back of the restaurant as Gorecki and the other officers burst in.

There was no sign of Ezra or Larson. She lowered her weapon and instructed the rest of the EPD officers to lower theirs as well.

The host, a college student, had both hands raised high.

"You're fine," Lucia told him, fishing for a photograph of Ben Larson. "Have you seen this man?"

Hands still in the air, he nodded.

"When?" she asked.

He nodded toward the back door. "He ran out the back ten minutes ago. Another guy chased him."

"Did anyone go to check it out?" she asked, then added, "Put your hands down."

He lowered them slowly. "We didn't want any trouble."

So Ezra and Larson had seemed like trouble. She wondered if they had fought.

"Did you see anything back there?" she asked Gorecki, gesturing toward the alley.

"Nothing," he said.

"Guess we're canvassing then."

Lucia drew her side arm again. As she did, the host's arms shot straight into the air.

****

For several seconds or minutes, or possibly still only in his head and not aloud at all, special agent and former director of security—though in actuality he was only suspended from the latter job currently while on working probation from the former—Ezra James spoke into his cell phone without realizing he had pressed not the green "answer" box but the red "decline" box—although really, they weren't boxes but rectangles—and the more he contemplated it, the more tangential and expansive his train of thought seemed to grow.

Still held against his ear, the phone rang like a great bomb exploding on the surface of the sea. He felt the currents rippling through him, beginning at his ear drum and riding the blood stream across the rest of his body. He needed the noise to be far from him. Without a second thought, he chucked the phone violently, and it shattered against the exterior brick wall of the bar he'd just left. *That,* he thought instantly, *was an overreaction.* He remembered Larson's words, his mention of Areli and Lucia's home address and, yes, the bell tower.

Did he actually say "bell tower" or did he just imply it? Or did I infer it? What did I imply? I need to call Lucia! Lovely Lucia!

Ezra looked around for his phone and spied it on the ground, here the screen, there the guts, farther still along the concrete the camera, which had come dislodged. *I can tape it,* he thought. *Tape it!* The thought made him laugh aloud and then laugh louder. *Alouder and alouder!* he thought and peeled manically until everyone on the street stood still, staring at him.

A police officer turned toward him and crossed the road. Instinctively, Ezra wanted to flee. It was a strange impulse, one he didn't recognize. Intellectually, he knew he'd been drugged, yet he still felt in the wrong, still felt like a criminal.

Have I always felt like this? Not a criminal but culpable. Then the memory of drawing his weapon on his former partner flashed through his mind. He was a criminal, just one with a badge. He thought of Julia, whom he refused to release. *Ezra James, hostage taker,* he thought.

The officer came at him with hands slightly raised, talking calmly, though Ezra couldn't hear or couldn't understand what he was saying.

"Special Agent James?"

Ezra gave the officer a feral nod. *At least I think I am.* Had he thought that or said it aloud?

The officer began talking into his radio, "I found

him. I don't know what the hell's the matter with him, though." A muffled voice spoke on the other end. The officer continued, "He was shouting nonsense. He says he thinks he's Mr. James." He listened a second longer. "Now he's eating his tie."

Ezra, finding the tie was indeed in his mouth, spat it out.

****

The officer wasn't lying about Ezra. By the time Lucia arrived, he was all bat and no belfry. He jittered and muttered so much that she pictured his mind as a Jackson Pollock, the one she saw at The Art Institute in high school. Ezra was making no sense. He kept uttering a dinging sound and psychoanalyzing himself.

As she led him to her car, he exclaimed, "That's why zebras make me feel uneasy! Ding!"

She placed him in the back seat and locked the doors. From the description, she thought he might've been drunk; perhaps he tried to get the coach to open up and had a few too many drinks in the process. Now that she saw him, she thought only of Ezra's mental condition. Had something triggered another episode? Was this what his episodes looked like? It seemed far more extreme than the break with reality he'd told her about. If Lucia had to guess, Ezra was under the effects of a hallucinogen or a club drug, but why?

"Can you handle that guy?" he asked her.

"I'll be fine," Lucia said with more confidence than she felt.

"Be careful. That guy makes Miedzianowski look good."

"What?" she asked.

"I'm saying he's a crooked cop. He planted

evidence and turned on his partner. You can't trust a guy like that."

"I've got it."

"I'm just saying."

"You don't know what you're saying." She pointed at his single chevron insignia. "Fall in line. Now, go brief Detective Gorecki."

She slid into the driver's seat and locked eyes with Ezra in the rearview mirror. "Did you take anything?"

"Ding!"

"Did Larson slip you something?"

"Ding dong!"

"What was it? Do you even know?"

He nodded vehemently, as if trying to knock the information loose. Then he started singing, *"Ding dang dong. Ding dang dong. Sonnez les matines! Ding dang dong. Ding dang dong."*

Lucia recognized the melody. Of course!

She engaged her radio. "We need a SWAT team ASAP." She gave the address. "Suspect is a middle-aged, white male, armed, possibly with a young female hostage. Hostage is Latina, eighteen, Areli Vargas. He could be anywhere, but give special attention to the school's bell tower."

****

They arrived at the school promptly and parked across the street. They'd beaten SWAT there but hopefully not by long. Lucia stepped out and circled the car to open Ezra's door.

Throughout the five-minute drive, he'd unbuckled and re-buckled himself four times, choosing a new seat each time, until he finally ended up as far from Lucia as possible. As she circled the car, he climbed into the passenger seat and locked the doors.

Lucia jerked the handle, but it just snapped back. "What are you doing?"

"How do I know you're not working for Larson?"

"That's absurd," she said.

"Or you could be working for Evanston PD!"

"Well, I *am* working for Evanston PD."

"You know everything about me," he said, "but I don't know anything about you."

From her pocket, she pressed the unlock button on her key fob. Ezra was too quick, though. By the time she pulled the handle, the door was locked again.

"Come on, Ezra. We don't have time for this."

"How do I know you aren't in cahoots with Catherine?"

"We're all on the same side." She pointed through the glass at the radio. "I need to call the SWAT team."

Lucia tried the key fob again with the same poor results. "Larson has Areli. He has my sister!" she shouted at the glass. "We need to go, Ezra!"

"Prove it."

"Prove what?"

"Prove I can trust you. Tell me something." His eye jittered back and forth as though searching for the answer to a riddle. "Tell me why you left Mexico."

"I'm not talking to you about that—not here, not now."

She tried the key-fob a third time. This time the door unlatched but didn't move. Ezra had a vise grip on the inside handle, and he was even stronger than she'd expected. It latched again and locked.

Lucia stomped off, but before she made it to the school grounds, she changed her mind and returned to the car. "He was killed," she said through gritted teeth.

"What was that?" Ezra asked.

"My father was killed."

"Why?"

"Look, I told you what happened. Now, let's go."

He turned his back to her.

"Fine! My father worked for bad men who did bad things—and it affected him."

"These men killed your father?"

Lucia shook her head. "Worse. They made him just like them. My mother—"

"—killed him?"

She nodded.

Ezra opened the car door and explained himself. "Larson drugged me, it seems," he said in a Sherlock Holmes-esque accent. He stroked his chin. "He placed a draught of lysergic acid upon mine beverage."

"Oh boy," she said. "Maybe you should stay in the car. I'm going to sort this out."

Lucia reached inside and pulled her radio receiver. "SWAT, this is Detective Vargas. Do you read?"

"We're en route, Detective," a woman's voice came over the line.

"What's your ETA?"

The SWAT van came careening around the corner. Lucia waved and gestured toward the curb. Six SWAT members poured out of the back, adjusting their black body armor and helmets. All of them toted assault rifles with the exception of the last member out of the van. She had a Remington 700 slung over her shoulder and a tripod and scope in her hands. The SWAT sniper walked directly to Lucia.

"Detective Vargas?"

Lucia nodded.

"Where's this bell tower of yours?"

"I'll take you."

When she looked back at her car, illuminated now by a streetlight and the thinnest sliver of a moon, she didn't see Ezra. Either he had slunk down onto the floor of the car, which wouldn't surprise her, or he was out here somewhere. She scanned the empty street, the school grounds, and the few buildings between them and the bell tower, but she didn't see anyone.

****

By some great miracle of miracles, Ezra found himself standing before the side door of the upper school. When he'd first set out, he immediately confronted a dozen insurmountable problems. First and foremost, he kept forgetting where he was going. Stepping out of Lucia's car, he saw the road unfurl in two opposite directions. Then there was the sidewalk leading toward and around and through the school grounds like a concrete labyrinth. The coordination of muscles and joints required to walk upright also proved problematic.

Twice, he found himself shuffling along on hands and feet over the ice and snow until his fingers burst with pain from the cold. Buildings lurched in and out of shadows, existing and then disappearing, as the sun set for good; gnarled trees reached their leafless claws toward him; dissociative thoughts turned him left and right, as did crippling surges of anxiety; and finally bona fide visual distortions of varying severity made his passage through space-time at times impossible. He recalled his harshest tests at Quantico and wanted to laugh at their relative simplicity.

At last, Ezra arrived at a familiar path, a short stretch of sidewalk that led straight to a staff entrance into the upper school. Before he set the first step onto it, however, Zeno's first paradox of motion broke upon his mind like a fresh egg. Of all the times he could've recalled with perfect clarity his college education, this was perhaps the worst.

Eight perfect squares of concrete lay between him and his goal, but before he reached the eighth square, Ezra would need to reach the fourth, the halfway point. Before he reached the fourth, he'd need to reach the second. Before the second, the first, and so forth. His mind divided the distance by halves until he was subdividing the single square in front of him—1, 1/2, 1/4, 1/8, 1/16, 1/32, 1/64, etc. He couldn't move.

Was this a metaphor for his entire life? Unsure how the endgame would play out, he couldn't make the first move. Lucia's words echoed in his mind.

"*He has my sister!*"

Ezra shut his eyes and willed himself forward until he nearly toppled over the concrete steps leading to the building. Now he just needed to locate his office—and remember where Larson's classroom was. There was no way the coach was holed up in the bell tower. Maybe Areli was, but Larson would be somewhere else. How many times had Remy sacrificed a bishop to checkmate with a knight across the board? He meant to find Larson, and he was going to be armed this time.

****

"Areli! Are you up there?" Lucia shouted up into the bell tower. She felt like she was going to be sick right here.

Five SWAT members lined up beside the entrance

to the stairwell. The sixth had positioned her tripod on the auditorium roof with her sniper rifle.

"Areli! If you can hear me, speak up!" she hollered louder.

This time, Lucia heard a shuffling in reply. Then someone spoke as if through a gag. There was no logical way for her to recognize the voice, but she knew it was Areli. She just knew it. Her heart raced, and her body moved instinctively toward the stairwell, but two arms grabbed her and held her back.

"What are you doing?" asked the burly SWAT member holding her. His voice was deep and gravelly like a cowboy's. She wondered if it was his natural voice or an affectation.

"I'm getting my sister," she said, her words steady though her body shook in tiny tremors from her neck down to the soles of her feet.

"That's a negative," the cowboy replied. "We're waiting for the go ahead."

"From whom?"

He nodded in the direction of the auditorium. "Samson, up there. She's got the best line of sight."

For a cowboy, he certainly knew how to follow orders.

"So how can we speed things up?" she asked.

He looked around at the decorative pathway lights and the exterior lights hanging off the chapel and surrounding buildings, all of which were dark even as the last remnants of sunlight slipped beneath the horizon. "We think someone cut the power," he said. "Samson has a spotlight up there, but a little extra light certainly couldn't hurt."

Lucia needed this to be done and her sister to be

safe. Her left knee began shaking uncontrollably, turning from tiny tremors to spasms. She placed a palm to steady it and, as she bent down, her shirt stuck to her sides, slick with sweat.

"Night vision?" she asked, once she'd recovered.

"If we go in there guns drawn—"

Somebody might accidentally get shot, she thought.

"You're right," she said. "It's better to see what's going on first." She pointed out the auditorium. "The breaker box is in there, but the building's locked."

"Martinez," the cowboy whispered.

Another man joined them.

"What's up?"

"We may have some doors for you to open."

Martinez unzipped a pocket on his pant leg and removed a black, jangling pouch. Lock-pick set.

Martinez let them into the auditorium easily. Then the cowboy clicked on his flashlight and followed behind Lucia down a corridor to the utility room. When they found it, she jerked the metal doors open. Every breaker was turned off.

The cowboy engaged his radio. "Samson, we found the problem. Over."

"I read you. Are you ready for me? Over."

"Thirty seconds on my mark," he said. He turned to Lucia. "You think this will do it?"

She nodded and placed two clammy hands onto the switches, ready to bring this negotiation into the light. Before the cowboy could set his mark, however, three gunshots rang out—bang! bang! bang! They sounded close but not in the direction of the bell tower.

Chapter Thirty-Three

Ezra hadn't locked his door when he left that afternoon, and neither had Catherine or the cleaners, because it swung right open when he pulled. Catherine had taken his bright yellow taser, but he had a stun gun in his desk drawer. The smaller stun gun didn't project, but if he got close enough, it would deliver one hell of a jolt. He found the stun gun and made his way back to the hallway. At the other end, he saw the faintest glimmer of light. It was too faint to be a hall light or even a classroom light. Ezra guessed it came from a flashlight or something equally small and localized. Stun gun in hand, he crept toward it.

The spring after his father died, Ezra was haunted by a dog. Hegewisch wasn't a bad neighborhood—working class Chicago—but at the end of their alley lived Demon, a red-brindle pitbull. Its eyes were red, too, but unlike its rusty coat, they were bright as blood. Someone trained that dog to be vicious, his father told him, and so each day after school he would walk along the opposite side of the alley. The pitbull would growl and paw at the underside of the weak wooden fence separating them. Each day it dug a little deeper into the wood and the grassless dirt on the pitbull's side. Ezra, five years old and forty pounds sopping wet, would've been quick work for Demon. Most afternoons, he clamped his eyes shut and darted through the alley, picturing the pitbull bursting forth through the wooden slats and Ezra's father having to tear down the alley to save him. Then his father died, and all he pictured was the pitbull, bearing down on him and taking chunks of flesh from him.

As he moved through the darkened hallway now, Ezra remembered Demon, heard its sharp nails clicking against the hardwood floor behind him, and he was powerless to turn to face it. In fact, he found himself once again incapable of forward motion, though this time stalled by fear rather than logic. His skin felt both too hot and ice-cold, and a drop of sweat rolled down his spine, sending shivers all the way to his tailbone.

Ezra continued down the hall, passing the office windows, bedecked in lifeless Christmas lights and green garlands. Obviously, there was no dog. Demon died years ago, but the sensation of being followed persisted. Perhaps, it wasn't the dog of his childhood, but Larson. Larson, revolver held outstretched, comfortably stalking the man he drugged and intended to murder.

The hair rose up on the back of Ezra's neck, and he could almost feel the muzzle of the revolver, cold metal brushing tense skin. He pressed the trigger of his stun gun and a bulb like a penlight illuminated a short distance ahead of him. Surely this would be the moment for Larson to fire, but nothing happened. He turned the stun gun's light on the hall behind him, and there was only darkness and empty space.

How in the world was Ezra supposed to sneak up on anyone in his condition? Still, he had to. He turned the corner and saw the lights were indeed coming from Coach Larson's classroom. One wall of the laboratory was a long window. Students and faculty passing by the lab could look in on the experiments or watch Larson work out long equations on the whiteboard. What Ezra saw now was a man working by the light of a battery-powered lantern. He frantically stuffed a suitcase with expensive looking scientific equipment, gold communion ware, and silver and gold jewelry—rings and necklaces lent to the school by SJM families.

Ezra recalled the electrical experiments Larson was running. He had asked Remy and school families to donate these items in order to test the conductivity of different metals. Once he knew the jig was up, Larson must've remembered all this gold and silver sitting in his classroom. He couldn't resist coming back for anything he could pawn. Above all, a man on the run needed cash.

He kicked the door open, extended the stun gun, and shouted, "Freeze!" Then he remembered the stun gun didn't project. He might as well have been pointing a stapler.

Larson wheeled around clumsily, knocking his bag off the counter as he reached for his revolver. As he twisted toward Ezra, his leg caught the arm strap of his bag and he tripped sideways, but not before getting off three shots. Bang! Bang! Bang!

Both men hit the ground hard.

****

Lucia didn't wait for the cowboy's mark. The second she heard gunshots, she flipped the breakers on, three and four at a time. Almost immediately, Samson's voice came over the radio. "I have eyes on the hostage. Teenage Latina, five feet and change, freckled skin, bound in an upright position, gagged. There appears to be something around her neck. Black pearls, maybe."

"Any sign of the suspect?" the cowboy asked.

"Not from my angle."

Lucia missed almost all of this exchange. At the words "teenage Latina," she broke into a dead sprint out of the utility room, out of the auditorium, and across the school grounds to the bell tower. Had any of the SWAT team tried to stop her, she would've laid them out right there, but none did. She climbed the stairs two by two and had eyes on Areli within the minute. Her sister was bound to a wooden support beam, and she was alone.

Lucia removed the necklace first. The metal clasp was singed from its previous use, but she worried it could still be operational. Once the necklace was off, she threw it onto the snowy floor and went to work on the zip ties binding Areli's wrists. Her pocketknife sliced through them. Once removed, they revealed long cuts in Areli's wrists and forearms where she had apparently struggled to break free. Good for her.

Areli removed her gag herself. "Luciana!" she shouted through tears. "I thought, I thought, I thought he was going to—"

She didn't have to say what she feared Larson might do. Few abductions of young women ended so happily. "From the way your room looked," Lucia said, "I'd say you gave him a run for his money."

"I got him in the knee with half a scissor," she said. "And I think one of my fingernails broke off in his eye." She raised her right hand. The index finger was shorter than the others.

"That's my sister."

After hugging her tight for several moments, Lucia led her sister down the narrow stairway. Areli limped slightly, favoring her right leg as she went. At the base of the stairwell, the cowboy took Areli's free arm, and together the two cops led her to a waiting ambulance.

"We have teams of twos checking the other buildings," he said once Areli was loaded into the ambulance. "They're still not sure where the shots came from, though."

Another shot rang out.

"The upper school!" Lucia said.

"Where?" he asked.

In response, she darted in that direction. He trotted after her, talking rapidly into the radio.

****

The first shot went wide of Ezra, shattering the glass window that ran along the wall of Larson's classroom. So did the second. The third shot hit him dead center in the left bicep, shattering something inside. As Ezra lay in the cold hallway, he knew he had only seconds to formulate a plan. The stun gun still rested in his right hand, but the element of surprise was gone. Or was it?

Emergency lights clicked on, turning the pitch-black school into a dimly lit disaster area. Bits of glass lay all around him, and his left arm leaked blood into a pool beneath him. The blood loss made him both nauseated and uncomfortably cold. Without thinking, Ezra grabbed his left arm by the wrist and pulled it slowly, excruciatingly, until the bullet wound rested beside his head. He grasped the stun gun again in his right hand, let his head fall limply, and closed his eyes. Larson would think he'd hit Ezra in the head rather than the arm.

Eyes closed, he listened to Larson as he continued

342

to pack up. The zippers of a bag opened and then moments later closed again. With unsteady footfalls, he moved toward the hall, toward Ezra, and then stopped. Ezra held his breath. He let it out, slowly—so slowly, like a man underwater—knowing he could not inhale again.

"Christ," Larson said. "Lucky me. I didn't even aim."

He kicked Ezra's side, jostling the bloody and shattered arm, but not dislodging it from his face. The pain would've made him vomit if he were free to do so. Larson would lean over soon, would lower an ear to check Ezra's breathing and place a hand on his neck to check for a pulse, but Ezra would be ready. Larson took a hesitant step forward. Then he unzipped the bag. Ezra could hear something metal scrape against the zipper.

Was Larson just going to finish him off? Larson's boot scraped against Ezra's toe and, with that sudden point of contact, Ezra hooked the heel of the boot and kicked with everything he had left.

Larson toppled backward, and the revolver sailed down the hall, cartwheeling and then spinning out of sight. Ezra scrambled toward it, searching for the gun in the shadows along the side of the hallway. In the corner where two corridors met, he saw the glint of metal. That's where the revolver had landed. He reached down for it, but an incredible force slammed him into the lockers, head first. His brow caught a thin metal latch and gashed his forehead above the right eye in the process. One-eyed and one-armed now, he wheeled on Larson and, in a sudden drug-induced savagery—wild and feeling no pain—he began punching his attacker like one of Cromley's MMA fighters.

They were on the ground again, Larson pinning Ezra on his good arm. Then, seeing the obvious advantage, the coach shoved a thumb into the bullet wound on Ezra's arm. New parades of agony stomped through his nervous system. Larson then reached to the back of his belt and pulled out a black hunting knife, the blade not much longer than four inches, but pointed and sharp. He turned the blade toward Ezra's neck.

"Like a dog!" Ezra yelled.

"What?"

Ezra twisted his hip enough to pull his right hand out, stun gun and all, and raise it. Larson knocked the implement away easily and lowered the knife. The two men grappled then, Larson pressing down with both arms and his entire body weight while Ezra held him off just barely with a single working arm. But he couldn't hold out forever. He felt a sudden release of pressure and knew it was the end. His eyes rolled back and he—finally—lost consciousness.

****

The corridor leading to the science wing was dark and silent. Lucia didn't know for certain if this was where Larson would go, but she knew it's where Ezra would check first.

As she and half the SWAT team drew closer, they saw the flashlights of a second team entering from the south, and then they saw Ezra and Larson. They were grappling in the corner where two hallways met.

"Hands up!" Lucia shouted. Neither man seemed to hear. "Freeze, Larson!"

The men continued to struggle. She ran to them, grabbed the coach by both shoulders, and flung him against the opposite lockers. Three SWAT members descended on him immediately. They knocked his knife aside and cuffed the bastard.

Ezra was a bloody mess. She saw at least one bullet wound and what looked like shards of glass embedded the length of both forearms. Blood covered his face and neck. Lucia leaned down and could just make out labored breathing. She tore her shirt off and wiped at his neck. The veins were intact. She wiped away more and realized his neck was unscathed.

"We need that ambulance over here, stat!" she yelled at the cowboy. "Tell them to park at the entrance."

She tore her shirt into three strips and applied a tourniquet to his upper arm first. Then she wrapped his forehead where the brow was bleeding. She used the final strip as a makeshift sling for the injured arm. Then she and the cowboy carried him outside to a waiting ambulance.

"Is he going to live?" she asked the EMT. It was the same stout blond fellow from the night of Brooklyn's attack one week earlier.

"I never make a promise I can't keep," he said. "But I've seen worse."

They drove off, lights twirling and sirens blaring.

Samson approached Lucia. The sniper lowered her rifle; took off her helmet to reveal long brown hair.

"Is that why they call you Samson?" Lucia asked.

"Seven locks of long dark hair and stronger than a lion," she said with a smile. "Trudy," she said and extended her hand.

They shook.

"That was brave of you back there," she told Lucia. "And stupid."

"The hostage was my sister."

"That makes a lot more sense." She gestured toward Larson who was handcuffed and sitting on the icy ground. "You want a go at the bastard?"

She shook her head. "I want him to know, without a doubt, that the people who put him away are better than him—in every possible way."

"You're a better woman than I."

"I'm sure you'd surprise yourself." Then she thought of Ezra. "Anyway, I have a friend to visit in the ICU."

"He'll probably be in surgery awhile."

"It's all right. I have the whole night off."

Chapter Thirty-Four

Tuesday

Ezra spent the next few days in a comfortable haze. Upon his arrival to the ER, the surgeon pumped him full of a powerful anti-anxiety medication because he kept trying to dart from the hospital bed. The surgeon also administered a local anesthetic while they assessed his injuries, which were extensive. They included an entrance and exit wound in the upper arm, a shattered humerus and a hairline fracture on the opposite ulna, a two-inch forehead laceration, two broken ribs, minor lacerations throughout, some embedded with glass, others not, and extensive muscle and bone bruising. They put him under and took him directly to surgery.

"Most men would've tapped out after the gunshot," the surgeon later told Lucia.

"The man had a job to do," she replied.

"His toxicology helps explain it as well," the surgeon replied. "Agent James was high as a kite, as the kids say. Although, *kite* may be an understatement."

When Ezra awoke from surgery, he found himself in the grips of a drug-induced manic episode. After he asked to know what she was giving him, the white-haired nurse said, "Chlorpromazine." He slipped back into a comfortable sleep.

By the time he regained consciousness, it was

Christmas Eve. He awoke not to some gruesome scene or mental panic but to the sound of carolers singing "Silent Night" to the occupant of the room next door. His mother sat in a chair near his bed.

Lucia and Remy stood on the opposite side.

"He's awake," Lucia said to the others.

He smiled. "Have you come to finish me off?"

His mother huffed from her chair. "Don't say such a terrible thing."

A smiling Remy took a step toward the bed. "You gave us quite a scare. I wasn't at the school for any of the excitement, but Lucia gave me the highlights."

Ezra sat up with some effort. "Did you get to your sister in time?"

Lucia placed a hand over the cast on his forearm. "We did. And thanks to you, we arrested Larson."

"It was his child," he said.

She nodded.

"He convinced the mother it was Mason's to get her involved."

"Did Larson tell you?"

"No."

Ezra's mother rose and placed a territorial hand on his other forearm. "Job well done, honey. Now you can leave that piddling security job, return to your regular duties, and get Julia back." She stared at Lucia's hand, then said more pointedly to Ezra, "Your *wife* Julia. You remember her, right?"

"That reminds me," he said as if missing her subtext, "I need you to bring some paperwork to me."

"What paperwork?" she asked, suspicious now.

"Julia sent me divorce papers last week."

"I'll shred them myself and save you the hassle."

"The hell you will. She wants me to sign them, and so that's what I'm going to do."

His mother turned on Remy now. "And you support this?"

The priest nodded. "These matters are complicated. Dragging this out is not doing your son any good."

Then she said to no one in particular, "Well, I guess whatever Ezra wants! The Church be damned." To Remy, she added, "You ought to be ashamed."

"You're being rude, Mother." Ezra closed his eyes again.

"Rude? You speak to your mother like that when you don't have anyone else in the world to look after you?" she asked rhetorically. "I ought to leave you here, let you celebrate Christmas in an empty hospital room."

It was time for Ezra to beg forgiveness, to pretend he'd never dare upset her on purpose. Instead, he replied, "That would be fine. If you don't want to be here, I won't keep you." He opened his eyes and looked into hers. "But if you decide to stay, I won't have you disrespecting them—or me."

She got a fighting look on her face but then turned away and sat in the chair by the window where she could look outside at the gently falling snow without losing too much face.

He'd spent his whole life navigating the narrow road of his mother's approval. Most of that time, however, he'd driven down its cold shoulder. Not even Julia had been good enough for the ideal Ezra of her mind, at least not until Julia left him. Then Julia became one of the many should-have-beens of her should-have-been son.

"Ah!" Lucia said and perked up. "Here's someone I'd like you to meet."

A Latina woman fifteen years or so Ezra's senior entered the room hesitantly, looking to Lucia for confirmation.

"You must be Señora Vargas," he said.

Señora Vargas took his hand and held it to her face. Then she kissed the hand. Her words came out measured and rehearsed. "I owe you a great debt for saving my daughter. I can never repay you this."

He nodded at Lucia. "You should be thanking your daughter. I was in no shape to save anyone, but your Lucia was brilliant."

Señora Vargas pointed at his chest emphatically. "But you, you caught him. You do a noble job *every day*. Thank you."

"I'm just—" he started.

"The schools need men like you, men to protect everybody, men to show these boys how to be."

Lucia nodded. "They need role models."

Señora Vargas thanked him, kissed his hand, and left.

Perhaps the Vargas women were right. He wasn't tracking down serial killers but working for a school was work worth doing. He thought of Catherine Weeks and decided to call her first thing in the morning. He would wish her a Merry Christmas and discuss his return to the school for the spring semester. He would do the job in earnest, no chip on his shoulder, no pity party. He would commit his entire self to the job.

Remy cleared his throat. "What Señora Vargas said reminds me, I spoke to Catherine Weeks yesterday."

"And?"

"With all the excitement at the school this semester, she decided to reach out to EPD about getting a new resource officer. EPD obliged." He paused. "She's not renewing your contract."

Of course not. As soon as Ezra realized he wanted something, it vanished. *Is that what happened with Julia?* he wondered. He wasn't sure he wanted to know the answer.

Epilogue

"Then what happened?"

Dr. Palacios sat uncharacteristically at the edge of his seat. He'd never been so engaged in what Ezra had to say.

"Larson lawyered up, as we expected. The trial is set for February. It shouldn't be a long one, or a difficult one for the prosecutor to win."

"And the mother?"

"Cynthia Scout confessed and, in exchange for her testimony against Larson, she should get a lenient sentence."

"How lenient?"

"Five years," Ezra said. "She claims she only knew about the first attack."

"The student-teacher?"

He nodded.

"How is she?"

"Brooklyn came out of her coma the day after we caught Larson. Some think—" he paused. "Well, it's just gossip."

"That's okay."

"They think she was faking her coma, that she didn't want anyone to find out about her and Larson. The affair, the baby, none of it would go over well. So when we found her on the floor in the ICU, she might have been trying to escape."

"She heard you coming and threw herself on the ground?"

Ezra nodded.

"Wild stuff," Palacios said. "And your wife Julia? How are things on that front?"

"I signed the divorce papers and faxed them from the hospital. The ball is in her court now."

"Some things in life are inescapable," Palacios said sympathetically. It was the first sympathy he'd ever offered Ezra. "Has your supervisor reached out about your probation?" He sifted through a file on his desk. "Cromley? I imagine he's impressed."

"He came to visit me in the hospital and said I could return to work once I was discharged."

"So you are back to work then?"

Ezra glanced at the photograph of Palacios' brother, deep in thought in front of the Angel Falls waterfall. The brother looked as unsure about the future as Ezra felt.

Palacios pointed at Ezra's cast with the bottom of his pen. "Perhaps when that comes off, you'll be ready."

"Perhaps," he agreed.

The two men sat in silence for a time. Then Palacios broke the silence. "Is that all then?"

"I think so. Why?"

Palacios looked surprised. "This is usually the point where you tell me about some minor symptom—itchy eyes, swollen tongue—and ask me to remove one of your medications."

"Nothing like that," Ezra said.

"That's good." Palacios nodded. "I believe you are making real progress."

"Why is that?"

"You have finally accepted your condition."

"Is that such a great step?"

"A man cannot win a fight by running from it," the psychiatrist said. "You have been through a great ordeal, but if it has helped you face everything and begin to recover, then it is worth the price of admission." He filled out Ezra's prescriptions and passed them across the desk. "Some people never get that far."

Ezra thought of Larson, who fled Nevada just to run into the same problem in Illinois, only worse this time. He thought of Martin Durand, who was no longer in a jail cell but was still in chains. He thought of his mother and her resentments and prejudices, which only soured with time. Then a vision appeared to him, a picture of the whole of Chicago hurrying to offices, to the L, to appointments they simply couldn't reschedule or miss, all of them in urgent flight from fears they only vaguely understood.

The vision faded, and Ezra saw now only Dr. Palacios and the small paper slips. He reached out an open hand and took them.

A word about the author...

Steven earned his undergraduate and graduate degrees in English from Kansas State University. He started his writing career as a lowly student worker for the prestigious literary journal The Southern Review. (If you received a formal rejection letter from the mid-2000s, he probably sealed the envelope.) He has published fiction, poetry, and nonfiction in various newspapers, magazines, and journals since that time.

He lives in Southwest Kansas with his wife and three children.

http://www.stevenjkolbe.com

CPSIA information can be obtained
at www.ICGtesting.com
Printed in the USA
BVHW072257020921
615900BV00012B/601